The Dark Sea Within

Also by Jason V Brock

Totems and Taboos
(poetry collection)

The Bleeding Edge:
Dark Barriers, Dark Frontiers
(fiction anthology with William F. Nolan)

William F. Nolan: A Miscellany
(select bibliography)

The Devil's Coattails:
More Dispatches from the Dark Frontier
(fiction anthology with William F. Nolan)

Milton's Children
(novella)

Simulacrum and Other Possible Realities
(fiction collection)

A Darke Phantastique:
Encounters with the Uncanny and Other Magical Things
(fiction anthology)

Disorders of Magnitude: A Survey of Dark Fantasy
(nonfiction collection)

Discoveries: Best of Horror and Dark Fantasy
(fiction anthology with James R. Beach)

Namel3ss Digest
(periodical)

THE DARK SEA WITHIN

Tales & Poems

Jason V Brock

Hippocampus Press

New York

Published by Hippocampus Press
P.O. Box 641, New York, NY 10156.
http://www.hippocampuspress.com

Cover design and production by Jason V Brock.
Hippocampus Press logo designed by Anastasia Damianakos.

First Edition
1 3 5 7 9 8 6 4 2

ISBN13: 9781614981947

CONTENTS

Preface 9

The Dark Sea Within...23

The Man with the Horn...35

Memento Mori 51

Transposition...61

A Carcass, Waiting...74

The Shadow of Heaven...77

Fallen: A Lament and Affirmation 100

Brood..103

Verlassen 121

Key...135

A Darke Phantastique 136

Chrysalis 149

Dolls..166

Afterlife (*with Sunni K Brock and William F. Nolan*) 169

Windows, Mirrors, Doors..182

Colossi 192

Double Feature...193

Unity of Affect 209

Epistles from Dis..236

Out of Their Heads 307

Notes...330

Acknowledgments...347

About the Author 349

Dedicated to the memory of my dear friend Roy Michalek,
and to my family,
including the newest member, Gershwin.

PREFACE

"If anything is possible, then nothing is interesting."
—*George Clayton Johnson*

If you dislike long personal essays, feel free to skip this section and get right to the stories.

This collection—my second—is *not* an assemblage of Lovecraft or other pastiche, nor is it representative of the so-called "New Weird" or any other marketing handle. To that end, this book is also not an homage or "hat tip" to prevalent authors such as Stephen King, Anne Rice, Clive Barker, or anyone else, past or present. To be honest, these writers (and many others) have had an influence on my own work, in that I have read them and ingested their perspectives, but I feel no genuine kinship with their output, though I have nothing against them and recognize their broad impact on the field. My interests span a diverse gamut; as a result, I write all kinds of things and feel no urge to be defined by, or even embrace, a genre, though I readily admit that my personal worldview tends toward a darker outlook than many others, and I am in no way condemning such definitions. Therefore, while this is ostensibly a collection of "horror and science fiction," it also has elements of erotica, Magical Realism, fantasy, literary, and other forms of expression, though my primary touchstones (as I elaborate on in the story notes at the end of the book) span the totality of modern media, not just writing. Additionally, the fact is that artistry of any kind is highly subjective and interpretative; half of an author's work lies within the mind of the reader, it has been observed, and I subscribe to that observation in principle (if not always literally). As a creator, I am not interested in contrivance, imitation, popularity, or the pursuit of a trend; I am more concerned with being true to my vision, to the integrity of what I am attempting to communicate on the page and in the head, though I strive always to respect the intelligence of my audience.

Consequently, if the aforementioned fictional rehash (Lovecraftian imitation, "New Weird," ham-fisted gestures toward influence, genre ghettoization, and so on) is what you are looking for as a reader—which is your right—feel free to return this volume to the shelf or delete it from your device. This book is not for you.

Of course, it is always better to stand *for* something rather than simply to be opposed to things. This collection of prose and verse is about different worlds and experiences as filtered through my own conceptions and observations. It is a work that I hope offers some modicum of insight into, or at least thoughtful examination of, our shared human condition. Storytelling and the works we leave behind are the closest thing there is to an afterlife (one that we concretely know of, anyway). Additionally, I favor an *inclusive* approach, just as the members of The Group in the 1950s (Matheson, Bradbury, Beaumont, Johnson, Nolan, Tomerlin, et al.) were able to realize. None of my work is meant to exclude, diminish, exploit, or assert a sense of superiority. Nor is it intended as some egocentric enterprise; I am aiming for something greater. I feel that I am connected less to the more recent negatively manifested affectations of postmodernism and more to the previously referenced modernist examples in The Group and, before them, symbolism, surrealism, Dada, Magical Realism, and the Vienna School of Fantastic Realism.

Whether I succeed in what I have set out to do (exemplifying these diverse approaches and aesthetics within my work) is not in my control entirely; I do my best and hope that others recognize that, in addition to the sincerity of my objectives. I am true to myself and to my aspirations, which is paramount to me, even if I wind up not fitting in with others at times, or am seen as uptight, square, or even foolish; at least I have my personal integrity intact and have not pandered to anyone in my efforts to convey what I'm concerned about. And the attainment of these goals doesn't have to be "heavy," or precious, or pretentious; it just requires openness, honesty in approach, and mindfulness of one's long-term ambitions. With respect to writing, the recent trend to overvalue mood, setting, and angst over deep character development and solid plotting is troubling; it doesn't make a work more "real" or pure artistically. It is part of what I would define as a general narrowing of scope for the field, in spite of the reality that more people are writing than ever; the truth is that these limited approaches appear to be favored by a subset of alleged "tastemakers"—which is not healthy. They are compromising the breadth and depth of expression out there, though they claim to be embracing "diversity"— even as they demonstrate a sort of favoritism (conscious or not), which, over time, reflects less and less diversity of *thought* (ironically).

Therefore, as writers write toward these market forces rather than documenting their truth as they understand it, the field suffers overall and becomes obscured by the din of ever-weakening, sound-alike voices and tokenist cultural dog whistles. This appears driven, I feel, by an overly PC political thrust that continues to bedevil society as a whole. It is a shame that people seem to have lost the nerve to innovate and be true to themselves, preferring instead to join the burgeoning ranks of an insecure and irksome cohort who have little or nothing to say (call them afflicted with "slightly better than average syndrome") and are, ultimately, overly concerned by what others think of them, rather than with what should be their true vocation—being artists and reflecting society as they try to improve it. Lately, it seems that some people prefer hijacking things to quell opposition over sharing ideological space; they prefer "safe spaces" and "trigger warnings" over assimilating divergent viewpoints in a constructive manner. That's a loser's game, in the long run; there are no such things in the real world. I suspect the antidote to this is to live life and not worry too much about the positions of others; embrace subversion, not revolution.

As noted previously, my efforts are inspired as much by multimedia as by literature; and of the literary influences that *are* on display in my work, I feel lucky and grateful that a number of the individuals from whom I have drawn inspiration and feel a bond with (emotionally and artistically, excluding family for the moment) eventually became not only personal friends or advisers to me, but in some cases mentors, including Ray Bradbury, Richard Matheson, Frank M. Robinson, William F. Nolan, Dan O'Bannon, Les Barany, Kris Kuksi, Samuel Araya, Greg Bear, John Tomerlin, Joe R. Lansdale, S. T. Joshi, Ray Garton, Jerad Walters, Derrick Hussey, Dennis Etchison, Ernst Fuchs, H. R. Giger, Peter Atkins, George Clayton Johnson, and Earl Hamner, Jr. Realizing their communal and discrete impacts on culture, I am humbled and privileged to have known them at all, and their guidance and amity is not something I take lightly; this book is a reflection of the lessons I have absorbed from each of them directly, person-to-person, as well as via the consumption of their combined productivity. These individuals are in some cases true giants, and all are truly gifted; in light of that, what passes for "talent" and "excellence" in much of the current environment often leaves me puzzled, frustrated, and dismayed. As a result, my wish is to carry on with the traditions they helped forge—not only by documenting it, as I have in many essays, and with our films (*Charles Beaumont: The Short Life of Twilight Zone's Magic Man, The AckerMonster Chronicles!,* and *Image, Reflection, Shadow: Artists of the Fantastic*)—but also in my imaginative output.

But building things takes sustained effort, just as a structure—whether it be Chartres Cathedral or Alcatraz—is constructed one brick at a time. So, too, is an artistic work made one word, one brush stroke, one frame after the other . . . each bit becoming part of the mosaic of a (hopefully) worthwhile endeavor; ultimately, depending on an individual's tenacity and value system, these pieces become one's sanctuary rather than one's prison. Therefore, *each* decision, large or small, throughout each attempt, *matters,* and one has to have an eye toward not just the trappings—acclaim, money, following, and so on—but also legacy, and what one's message is, both overtly, and covertly, even unconsciously; one must learn as an artist to develop patience and perspective, to step back from the immediate and regard what one does with "cultivated indifference." This is the only way to improve—as a creator, as a human being, as a species. In the end, just as one should not lose faith in one's personal vision, likewise one must never lose sight of one's overall objectives.

In Japanese corporate culture, there is an expression (paraphrased): "Always be number two." What is meant by this is that when a company ascends to being a market leader, there is also a loss of freedom, of flexibility. There comes an "expectation of conformity." In other words, strive to be the best, but understand that success has its own element of danger; there is not an unlimited upside without some counterbalancing element coming into play. Whenever one puts oneself out there as a creator, one risks becoming a target for derision and jealousy, especially if one's perspective is in any way at odds with the expectations of the more narrow-minded in our midst. Additionally, people rarely plan for success in the ways they plan for failure; "success" is coveted by our society as a quantifiable metric of accomplishment. That noted, the downsides of accomplishment in the popular sense are numerous: loss of autonomy (such as the pressure to fulfill audience expectations), an anticipation of a lack of originality (formulaic output, for example), embracing comfort instead of challenge, generating "product," the commodification of artistic effort, and so on. It can, and usually does, become a sort of velvet prison, the supporting idea being that the so-called "rewards" (the superficial aspects of recognition, wealth, and all the rest of it) offset the grinding need to deliver the same (and often ever more generic and repetitive) product, which eventually bores even the most ardent of supporters. This pursuit frequently results in selling out in a way to fulfill not the wants and needs of the *artist*, but in pursuing the endorsements of others (fans, critics, taste makers). In turn, this can lead to the temporary marginalization of those with a voice that is more original than—or conflicts with—these others artistically, whose chief ambitions are often motivated not by self-expression, but by insecurity and a need for approval. It can lead to a drive to "cheat"—to arrive at such recognition not through talent or effort, but by cronyism, by duplicitous and cliquish behavior, by manipulation and deceit. Better to be (as George Clayton Johnson stated) a "dog without a collar": to stand out as one's own person who, frankly, doesn't give a damn about trends or the opinions of others, and who is strong enough to take chances, including delightfully confounding the expectations of one's audience (which is likely an attractive quality to these followers anyway). To phrase it another way: let your audience discover *you;* perhaps these cheaters become popular more quickly, but such personalities and their output rarely have staying power.

Marcus Aurelius pointed out in his *Meditations:* "The present is the only thing of which a man can be deprived, if it is true that this is the only thing which he has." In other words, the past is determined, and the future is uncertain; all we have is *now*—this moment in time—with which to make an impact. The true aim of any artist of any kind should be to self-actualize by way of self-expression, with the culmination being to bridge the chasm of understanding between people. Otherwise, it's simply a masturbatory exercise; it's all about the artist and pays no respect to those that the artist is trying to reach—the audience. The balancing act of staying true to oneself while attempting to reach a like-minded audience is delicate and complex. While I was working on this book, several people I admire passed away. One in particular who cast a long shadow, and from whom I have taken much inspiration in my personal life, was David Bowie. His death was a shock, and also an example of what I am describing. It was deeply saddening, but also an inspiration. I realized that one of my main subconscious goals as a creator, specifically as a writer, was to be the literary equivalent of someone like David Bowie—to challenge others, certainly, but also and *especially* myself. To be unafraid of exploring my own psychic *terra incognita* and to become a seeker—if not always a finder—of the strange truths therein; to share those discoveries with others like me: meditative, outré, diverse, and often misunderstood individuals, yet people nonetheless grasping for an inclusive, better world.

Bowie also demonstrated other fine virtues: humility, politeness, thoughtfulness, loyalty, compassion, and an appreciation for those who are open to a unique worldview. These were not displays of false modesty or haughty aspects of his personality; he understood his boundaries and was therefore *confident* in his abilities, not *arrogant*—which is what one must be in order to take the calculated risks necessary to evolve and grow as a creator. Personally, I feel (and would posit this for Bowie also) that playing it safe in an enclave of exclusionary syco-phants is artistic suicide; braving frontiers, even failure at times, is the pathway to evolution and sustained expansion of one's artistic aspira-tions. It is leadership, and leading means sometimes failing, with a commensurate re-evaluation of purpose.

In order to accomplish these personal goals, just as Bowie did, I have taken less frequented paths; many times, as a writer and filmmak-er, I have been asked in interviews and at conventions about the rea-sons behind my "morbid" concentration on, as well as enthusiasm for, horror, fantasy, and other speculative things. Interestingly, there are generally two ways that people broach the topic with me: 1) unbridled appreciation that we are connected in our mutual passion for such ar-cane subject matter; or 2) derision and subtextual disquiet. After all, to address the second point, horror and so on are not "serious" or "weighty"; they are escapist in nature, and so . . . *unpleasant.* Why read or view grue and gore (as the term "horror" has come to mean in the popular imagination, which is why I now refer to my own output as Dark Magical Realism), or think about such silly contrivances as space ships and flying cars, or dragons and hobbits, when we have lovely "slice of life" tales that can enrich us without all that cumbersome *im-agination* to undermine the gravitas.

To be fair, aside from the fact that there are compelling reasons that not all "realistic" things are non-escapist, and that, conversely, many times genre works (horror, fantasy, science fiction, erotica, etc.) are better lenses to reflect or prism social concerns and anxieties through (*The Twilight Zone,* for example), I will state that I have never truly understood the affinity myself, so there is no one definitive an-swer I use to explain the attraction—or to excuse my "lack of sophisti-cation." Additionally, there are very likely multitudinous reasons folks like me gravitate toward these themes and works, such as being denied access to provocative or scary things as a kid, the end-result manifest-ing as though one was deprived of some tribal aspect of childhood— whether due to misguided parental religious over-influence, cultural differences between urban and rural settings, or some other circumstance. (The capturing of these perceived "lost moments" [true or not] makes up more of adulthood than most care to acknowledge, I predict, much as people frequently atone for a "misspent youth" in a similar, if opposite, manner.) All I know is that I have always loved monsters and such, and have either drawn, filmed, or written about these things for as long as I can remember. It was never a hobby or passing phase (to my mother's eternal regret); to paraphrase the character Suicide in *The Return of the Living Dead*, it was "[not] a fuckin' costume . . . [It was] a way of life." Still true, in fact. People that get it know what I mean; folks that don't get it, well, all I can say is their loss; they have the right to be wrong.

In addition, there is much to recommend the "community" aspect of others who share our particular enthusiasms, rife with creative and cultural references to the great artistic, literary (to include comic books), musical, and cinematic/TV genre works (even the really awful ones), the camaraderie, and the (I strongly suspect) coping mechanism of self-identification with our internal monsters in the creations of others, from Mary Shelley to Stephen King, from The Misfits and Chrome to David Cronenberg and Federico Fellini. It's something that straitlaced American society—with its mass shootings, workaday jobs, Pumpkin Spice lattes, endless political wrangling, and so on—misses out on; loving these things is akin to some massive in-joke, or a secret language that only the initiated can understand and appreciate. Of course, that is not to imply that we sci-fi nerds and horror geeks are *exclusive*. Indeed, we generally *are* an inclusive lot, not snobs, and will take all comers if they want to participate. The upshot is that we are liable to befriend anyone, irrespective of their lowbrow or scholarly interest in our field. The reason for that is simple: the vast majority of us in our little subculture are open-minded, and we are generally, as I noted, outsiders not only in society, but frequently even within our own families with respect to our tastes and inclinations when it comes to such aesthetics. In other words, we band together as a bulwark against the outside world. Not, mind you, to *avoid* it, but as a way to *understand* it. This differs from the phenomenon I described before—the defensive, insecure posturing of those who seek approval from people or institutions, or exclude those who refuse to conform or have a differing attitude—chiefly because this is a secret language that the best among us are all too willing to teach, and with great zeal, as a vicarious way of re-experiencing the things we truly love. In the final analysis, the real joke is on those who seek to keep others out and are unwelcoming to alternative points of view.

In consideration of all this, I would like to share a bit of personal history.

I was born and raised in and around Charlotte, North Carolina, and am of mixed racial heritage (I left permanently, relocating to the Pacific Northwest when I was about twenty-two). My parents divorced when I was five. My father (James Brock) married another woman (my stepmother, Marti) shortly after this traumatic event in our lives, and they remained (mostly happily) married until his premature death at age sixty-three in 2002. He was a "horror guy," and was the one who encouraged my passions in art, film, music, writing, whatever. My stepmother did as well, but she tended to emphasize the practical and was a sci-fi person. (They both got me into the work of David Bowie, too—king of the misfits and freaks.)

On the other side of the family tree, my mother (Juanette) was not terribly excited at my apparent love of all things dark and strange. In fact, she hated it; when she remarried (to Daniel Thomas, former drummer/arranger for the seminal psychedelic band The 13th Floor Elevators, Lightnin' Hopkins, and others), she had at last discovered an ally to thwart my love for these things, which, as a Christian (another involved story, her peculiar upbringing in an orphanage), she found troubling and possibly damning to my soul (!), especially after we moved out of the big city and into the country. She also had custody of me. Dad only had certain visitation rights. Over time, she turned the screws with respect to my genre-related interests: As a result, I *lived* to indulge these things over at my father's place.

This went on for a number of years until I eventually went to live with my father and Marti at the age of eleven or so. It was quite a difference, being there all the time. I went from living in the boondocks without any nearby friends (just kids in classes with me and on the school bus) and not allowed to watch TV, eat, or speak until addressed (there was more, but that's the gist; my mother and stepfather [who later adopted me as an adult] were in a deeply religious stage, which has now, thankfully, abated), to living in the metropolis of Charlotte. The world opened up then and has remained thus.

The following vignette, which is completely factual, is but one story about how these influences wound up shaping me (I'm sure some might say "warped," but so it goes). I hope folks find it as odd and amusing as I do in retrospect, and I also hope it provides a bit of insight into how I developed as a creative, and why I love all the things I do . . .

Ode to an Old Friend
A Eulogy and True Story

I recall as if it were only yesterday carrying you through the darkened halls of our empty house. We had to move, as the owner of the property was raising our rent, and Marti, my stepmother (may she rest in peace), had reached her threshold of tolerance regarding you—she *forbade* your occupancy in our new dwelling. Understand, it was not personal; Dad (now sadly departed also) said I had to make my mind up about what to do with you. I finally decided on the only realistic course of action: burial. He agreed.

You had come into our lives (to the utter revulsion and scorn of my long-suffering stepmother, known affectionately as Mama) by way of one of Dad's friends at the community college where he worked. I had met the guy once: Ted. That was all I recollect about him, except that he was excitable and wore prescription sunglasses indoors; his full name has long since been lost to the vagaries of remembrance. As we made our way to the backyard, I found myself a little wistful about our looming separation.

You had been with us for a long time by this point, so leaving you behind was going to be sad for me. Explaining you to Mama (who could be rather superstitious—especially regarding "body parts" lying around; she was already creeped out by some of my more saturnine illustrations and sculptures) had been a tough sell. A logical woman (she was a trained Cobol and Fortran Programmer at IBM, the same campus now owned by Microsoft in Charlotte), she could be severe at times with regard to "horror stuff" (though she was a keen science fiction buff and actually exposed me to a lot of great writers from the 1950s, '60s, and '70s). She was also rather disconcerted by my abiding interest in special effects makeup ("SFX" as we called them in the pre-CGI parlance of *Starlog* and *Fangoria*), and the trouble I nearly got into carting the resultant artifacts I created around in my old green Ford Fairlane 500—disgustingly accurate severed heads and so on. I had even been recently evicted from that epicenter of 1980s youth culture—a local shopping mall (swanky Southpark—not kidding) for mischief related to my hobby: On a lark, I had gone by myself to the mall and taken one of my creations in with me (a rotted skull) to a women's clothing store—The Limited, as I recall. A lady in the store reported me to security as I was carrying the thing around, and a couple of guards escorted me out of the mall even as—alas, to no avail!—I explained how my First Amendment right to free expression was being trampled upon.

On a few occasions, to Mama's chagrin and annoyance I'm sure (though likely not as much exasperation as when she learned—years later—that I had forged my parents' signatures on the permission slips to relocate to a completely different high school), I went to class (this was senior high) with my face made up as a "ghoul" (not during Halloween, either), or with realistic "injuries" on my arms and hands (apparently I had a genuine flair not only for the dramatic, but SFX as well; Mama and Dad, both artists themselves, had long ago noted my talent for sculpting, even as a child, but were probably not terribly excited at my expression of said abilities at this juncture).

In fact, I had a close call once after a cop pulled me over for speeding and wanted to see what was in the trunk of my car. As he was interrogating me on the side of the road, I suddenly remembered that I had one of my gruesome "treasures" in there and got a bit nervous. He picked up on this right away, and boy was he surprised when he discovered a bloody head near the spare tire! That took a *lot* of explaining, but I was finally able to prove that it was fake. He eventually let me go, albeit with an expensive ticket for speeding—and a story for his buddies at the station.

Given these other circumstances, Mama was understandably alarmed as we pitched you to become my new roommate. Dad just looked at her, his kindly green eyes twinkling as I held your container, and said in all earnestness: "Mama, you have to understand. Ted was in a bind; his fiancée *stole* the brain from the Nursing School on a whim. Now she's afraid she'll get in trouble if she returns it or confesses . . . Anyway, I *knew* that J. J. [one of many terms of endearment he had for yours truly] would love it." Mama stared at him through her horn-rimmed glasses, arms crossed tightly across her chest; I could swear that actual steam was coming from her ears. After a long pause, she looked at me; I quickly cast a pitiful glance between the jar holding you and the hardwood floor of our living room. I tried to project indifference, but felt strangely hopeful; to my teenage way of thinking, Dad had presented a persuasive case. It was then that he added the capper:

"Besides—you know Ted's a *jazz musician.*" He smiled, raising his eyebrows, as though this final piece of information explained everything. She huffed, rolled her eyes, and turned around. Raising her hands in a gesture of resignation as she walked into their bedroom, her waist-length hair trailing behind her, she muttered: "Jesus, Jim. You two are ridiculous. Jason can keep the damn brain! Thing gives me the *creeps,* though!"

Flash forward several years. As I dug the small hole in the back yard of the modest rental house we were vacating in the Elizabeth neighborhood of Charlotte, I felt a lump in my throat. I recall also that it was warm, near dusk. Mama was already at the new domicile we had finished moving into earlier that day, resting. She wanted no part of this wretched farewell. Dad looked at me as I held your aging plastic container, full of you and your cloudy formaldehyde solution. He could tell I was a little upset.

"I suppose we should say a few words," he said, and I felt better, as if it might be all right. I nodded, then poured you into the hole, where you slopped wetly into the red-clay earth. Your gelatinous, veiny visage is forever pictured in my mind's eye: as the formaldehyde seeped into the ground, you quivered gently from the impact. I thought then that it must be rather uncomfortable and cold being in the ground after silently occupying my room for so long. I was dismayed, but figured it was for the best: you had been deteriorating for the past several years and would likely be a sort of mush in a few more.

"Okay," Dad said, leaning on the shovel. There was a light breeze, and the sun was beginning to set. I cleared my throat and wiped my eyes.

"Oh, Anonymous Brain," I began, not quite sure how to address you, but certain that your erstwhile nickname of "Hitler" seemed too undignified for such a weighty moment as this. "Forgive us for not knowing who you were, and realize that we never meant any disrespect toward you. . . . Thank you for the numerous lively discussions you inspired amongst our relatives; the frightening scene you presented to Mama, thus ensuring she rarely entered my room (the owl that had taken up residence in the attic over my bedroom—scrabbling about during the daytime, and sometimes hooting late at night—also assisted with this); and the amusement you brought to me, Dad, and my friends, lo these many years. Your gift to science was most appreciated, and not in vain."

"Very nice," Dad said. "Amen," he added, handing me the shovel. He smiled at me under his bushy mustache, the breeze gently ruffling his thick black curls. I can remember the feeling of summer being nearly upon us as we stood there, staring into the tiny grave as the delicate scent of all the roses that Mama and Dad had planted through the years hovered in the dusky air. I had a feeling that this was the end of an era, that things would not be the same once we left this place for good. In retrospect, I was right.

As I covered you with the first clod of dirt, obscuring your glistening essence for the final time, I hoped that the next renters would not have a dog that might dig you up and—God forbid—*eat* you, or report you to the police, suspecting that we had been some latter-day Sawney Beane family of serial murderers/cannibals; it was bad enough (or really cool, I suppose, depending on your point of view) that Dad and Marti looked *exactly* like Morticia and Gomez Addams (or perhaps Sonny and Cher, take your pick). Once I had patted the earth down, we left the back yard, closing the fence as we left.

In the car, Dad looked at me. "It was the right thing to do, Champ." He hugged me; I still remember the warmth of his swarthy skin on my tear-streaked face. As we pulled off and drove to the new house, I watched the old one recede into the darkness in the sideview mirror on the passenger's side door of their old white Barracuda. I was sad, but also pleased that we had done the correct thing given the circumstances. Years later, we would laugh at this scene; usually people think I'm kidding when I tell them about it, but that was exactly the way it happened.

In any case, rest easy, old friend: You are sorely missed—and so are my deeply loved father and stepmother.

P.S.—Not to forget the actual, full human skull (complete with articulated mandible and most of its teeth!) that my birth mother incinerated (we lived in the country) during a fit of horror while I was visiting my father one weekend. Dad and I had purchased you at a yard sale for a mere five dollars. Rest in peace—you too (whoever you were) are unforgettable.

Thank you for reading, and I hope you enjoy the book.

—JASON V BROCK
Vancouver, Washington
September 2016

THE DARK SEA WITHIN

I

Christmas Eve

David was hard-pressed to remember when the obsession first asserted itself.

Isn't that always the way it is with such things? he mused. One could never pinpoint the precise day, the exact moment, the split-second when your life stopped being your own and began to be lived, instead, in the servitude of some other aspect of the universe—maybe a person, or an object, perhaps even another consciousness.

Regardless, he reckoned it hardly mattered *when* curiosity had become necessity; all obsession was rooted in perversion of some sort or other, and most, in that dark sea within themselves, had their personal fixations—of that he was certain. Still, he preferred to think of his interests as *preoccupations,* however unorthodox. And was it really a perverse thing to want to be rich and successful? So it took more energy than most were willing to muster: he could live with that. Let the others be schleps and also-rans; that was not his way.

Of course, there could be downsides to risk-taking . . .

"When are we supposed to be there?" Delia asked, looking up from the map book. Her voice was edged, tired. He smiled at her, glancing away from the hypnotic repetition of the road stripe as it stretched to the darkening horizon.

"As long as we arrive by tomorrow afternoon. The owner is holding off selling anything until we get there. Illya, the gallery owner, mentioned that the person selling the pieces would accommodate our travel schedule, since they'd heard of us. Someone named Januuz. I think it's a last name."

Delia replied with a subtle nod. "Some Christmas. I'd rather be back in the City than on some wild goose chase. What if they're fakes?"

He frowned. "I doubt it. I've checked and rechecked the information he sent me. Cleared it with some of my connections, too. This guy is on the level, and the price is right. Seems like the owner wants to unload them; probably tired of dealing with all the superstitious clap-trap." He paused, letting the road noise fill in the silence. "Besides, we've got no choice. If I don't secure these *now*, we might never get the chance, and we'll be stuck in that brownstone. If we're lucky; that's assuming the fucking Greco brothers don't make good on having me killed." He glanced at her again, renewing his grip on the steering wheel. The road ahead was empty.

It had been a bad state of affairs for some time with the Grecos. For years, they had been his biggest supporters as art dealers, even through the recessions, the failure of his filmmaking ventures, and the bursting of a few art market bubbles. Until, that is, the bad deal with the Hermitage. At the time, it had rocked the art elite: An undiscovered Jan Vermeer. It was the apogee of David's career at that time and netted a sizable fortune for everyone involved.

Eventually, however, the tide turned against them. The Vermeer that David had sold to the Hermitage, brokered by the Grecos, was determined to be an elaborate forgery. It had been kept quiet, as it was an embarrassment for everyone involved, but he had been told by the Grecos to return all the monies they had paid him or face their wrath. They had been forced to take the counterfeit piece back and reimburse the museum, or have their fifty-year legacy smeared all over the art world as charlatans. In a high-stakes business centered on expertise, reputation, and trust, this was an intolerable possibility; and they had the money and muscle to ensure that it would *not* happen.

The problem for David was that they had spent most of the millions over the ten years it took the Hermitage to authenticate the work: traveling, procuring new pieces for speculative sales, investing in the stock market. A few bad investments at that level were all it had taken to erode his finances to the point of being unable to oblige his erstwhile partners once the situation became clear. David explained that it was an honest mistake, but that was not enough for the Brothers Greco: mistake or not, it had cost them in treasure and stature, and they were not just going to roll over on those points. David was able to land a few quick auction house deals that helped, but it was not enough to remedy the hurt feelings and financial angst felt by the Grecos; and in this profession, the possibility of litigation was not up to conjecture. Retribution would come quietly, and it would be as unceremonious as it was final.

Over the past two years, Delia and David had been able to return a large portion of the proceeds, but the Grecos felt they had been patient long enough and informed them that if David failed to return the rest of the money in a time they all agreed upon, he left them with no choice but to proceed with other plans to rectify the situation. Now, he was staring into the abyss of the end of that timetable: January 1.

"Plus," David continued, breaking the silence, "we'd have enough left over after I settle up with them so that we could finally afford to expand the unit . . . maybe buy out that creep next door."

Delia sighed and turned to face the passenger window. She knew David was right: it was their only real option at the moment. Outside, the frozen ground was covered with a modest dusting of snow, and in the deep black sky a profusion of stars glimmered with cold, primordial fire. "Fine. I'm getting sick of the art world, though. It's *crawling* with sleazy characters. I hope this is worth it."

II

Christmas Day: 11:43 A.M.

They arrived in Prague at two-thirty in the morning. It was unusually chilly, and the rental car seemed too large for the narrow lanes. After checking into their room in Old Town, they showered and then slept for a few hours.

Delia's mood had lightened considerably by the time they had eaten some breakfast. She seemed excited at the prospect of spending the New Year in Europe.

"Well, *you* sure are a changed woman," David said as they walked toward Jewish Town, his breath trailing behind them. That was where they had arranged to meet the proprietor of the art gallery: he had the paintings at an atelier near the Old Jewish Cemetery.

Delia smiled at him and squeezed his hand as they walked. "Wonderful what a little sleep and a trdelnik pastry can do." She paused, shivering. "Boy, it's really cold, though!" They both laughed as she tucked her ears under the multi-colored knit cap his mother had given her on their fifth wedding anniversary, then pulled the long black scarf he had given her for her birthday up over her nose and mouth with a gloved hand before looping her arm with his and huddling closer. The day was bright and clear. As they walked the uneven cobbled streets of the medieval city, David was struck by how little had changed since their last visit, more than twelve years ago. Throngs of people crowded the shops and causeways, filling the air with an ethereal wash of noise. He scanned the street ahead, absorbing the blend of foreign languages, engine sounds, and music wafting over from near the waterfront area of the Vltava River.

As they walked closer to the Astrological Clock, the crowds grew thicker and he detected the strong smells of street vendors preparing sausages with sauerkraut, spicy mulled wine, and fried cheese sandwiches. Rounding a corner, the narrow street opened into a plaza: the Old Town Square. Just as they arrived at the Orloj, the figure of Death was striking the hour; an unkindness of ravens croaked their disapproval from the Old Town City Hall as though answering the ghastly automaton. The frigid wind sliced by, blowing a billow of exhaust from the food carts past them. David, eyes stinging from the smoke, stared at the clock, marveling at the garish colors of the background and the cryptic movements of the Zodiacal ring; it amazed him to think that he might literally be standing in the exact spot once trod by a young Franz Kafka.

"It's beautiful," he said to Delia at last, returning to the moment. She hugged his arm to her body.

"Yes," she said, looking from his face to the Orloj. "And ominous."

III

Christmas Day: 1:51 P.M.

"Shit. I'm lost," David said. Even he was starting to feel his hands getting stiff through his gloves, his feet going numb the farther they walked. Though he was dressed in layers, the intense cold had started to bite through, especially on his cheeks and nose. Delia had been a trouper so far, not saying a word as he referenced the address scribbled on a piece of paper.

The temperature seemed to drop as they got closer to the Jewish Quarter, Josefov. The brightly colored clots of merrymakers and townspeople were thinning out as it got colder, and, to make matters worse, a dense fog was rising from the river to mingle with the smoke of chimneys and the street vendors plying their trade. The overall effect was surreal, as muffled, half-glimpsed figures crept through the chilly cityscape like specters, and the dark shapes of the capital's disorienting mix of Gothic, Baroque, Rococo, and Art Nouveau architecture by turns faded and reappeared all around them like passing ships in a sea of grayish white. The sun hung low in the now overcast sky; in the thick mist, it resembled something more like a full moon.

"Maybe we should go back to the hotel, David," Delia offered at last. "This fog is incredible." She regarded him with her wide blue eyes; he could see she was worried. Far away, he could make out the distant chime of the centuries old Orloj.

He nodded, feeling defeated, cold, tired. "Okay. I hate that we've come so far for nothing. . . . I–I'm sorry, Delia, this is all my fault. My fucking need to be number one: that's what got us in this mess to start with. I didn't check my sources well enough on the Vermeer buy. I *wanted* it to be the real thing, so I was too afraid to dig deeper . . ." He rubbed his face in despair. "And in the end it bit us in the ass. Now this . . . I mean, how often does someone claiming to have unknown Hieronymus Bosch paintings come around? I'll tell you: never." He stopped, letting the damp vapor fill his aching lungs. "Never," he softly repeated.

She gently took his hand in hers. "David, it's not for 'nothing.' We have this beautiful place, and we're here until after the New Year. Maybe we can visit your brother in Aix-en-Provence after we leave here. I mean, we might not be able to go back to the States. No one knows our itinerary, so we could just start over someplace." Delia stopped for a moment, as though the import of her words had just occurred to her. "Anyway, we can figure all that out later. Let's just make the best of it."

He smiled. "Okay. Can we walk one more block? Maybe I misread the address . . ."

Delia's eyes widened and she stamped her foot in mock protest, hands on hips. "David!" She glared into the mist. "All right. *One* more block. Then back to the room." Her eyes narrowed mischievously: "I have plans for you, comrade."

He laughed as the fog shrouded them. That was one thing he had come to understand: when you had a passion—no matter how unusual—it was best to share it with someone who could understand it, good or bad . . .

And, for better or for worse, not only accept the obsession, but embrace it, as well.

IV

Christmas Day: 5:37 P.M.

"Can you *believe* how we scored?" David asked, back in their suite. He was kneeling, shirtless in the foyer, looking at the pieces: multiple works in pristine condition, several of which appeared to be part of the same triptych. It was the find of a lifetime.

Delia watched him from the bedroom, wrapped in white linen, his sperm warmly trickling from between her legs. She smiled. "It's quite something," she said, her voice thick in her throat. The huge, unadorned window in their room revealed a wispy, completely fog-enrobed Prague.

"This is what we've *dreamed* of, D!" he exclaimed, his voice echoing lightly off the hardwoods. "If I sell this to the Prado or some other collector, we'll be set for life. I mean, it's *Bosch*. The master . . ." He rubbed his hands together in excitement, then stood, gazing at the art-work. "Too bad Januuz was unable to be there for the deal, but so it goes. Maybe Illya and I can establish a relationship. He might come in handy for future deals, especially since he knows Russian. Lots of rich Russians nowadays. I'll call the Grecos tomorrow and explain what's going on, try to get started generating some interest from buyers. I think we're going to be okay, baby!"

Delia fell over onto her back, relaxed, sleepy. She watched the fog as it flowed outside their window. "We did it, David. I love you!" She felt languid. It was beginning to get dark.

He walked into the room, removing his pajama bottoms, exposing his erection. Climbing into the futon with her, he kneaded her ample breasts, gently whispering in her ear as he eased into her again, helped by the slickness of his own previous ejaculation. She wrapped her legs around his lower body, pulling him greedily in, while he caressed the smoothness of her skin, tasted the saltiness of her neck.

After several minutes of thrusting, he was ready again. She rolled him over, riding hard until he moaned. *"Now,"* she whispered as his testicles contracted and he spurted hotly into her, *"now* we can be a real family. . . . Just us, together. Without worries." Then she kissed him deeply, crushing her body into him; he inhaled the perfume of her hair, and they fell into a peaceful sleep.

But it was not to last.

V

New Year's Eve: 11:22 A.M.

Nearly one week later.

After some day trips outside the city to visit the countryside and a few other places of interest—such as the site of recent archeological digs from the Middle Ages and the ossuary in nearby Sedlec—they were back in Prague. New Year's Eve had been a long whirlwind of a day visiting merchants and seeing the sights. At one point, they were accosted by a lunatic claiming to be an angel while they explored St. Vitus Cathedral.

In order to distance themselves from that unsettling experience, they decided to tour the behemoth that was Prague Castle. Built in the ninth century, it was the largest such ancient palace in Europe: seated portentously upon the far hill overlooking the Vltava River like some crenelated headdress, it was a striking and imposing structure. It looked to David like the type of place that held many secrets—a place that might swallow you up and never allow you ingress back into the real world.

By evening, they were both spent, wanting nothing more than to relax in their room, drink wine, snack on cheese, and make love until the New Year arrived.

VI

New Year's Eve: 11:43 P.M.

A little before midnight, the telephone rang.

"Haló," David said into the receiver. "Yes. We're still here. We're scheduled to leave tomorrow night. What—?" He was quiet for a long time. "I understand. Okay. I heard you: midnight. Sbohem." He returned the handset to its cradle.

Delia looked at him, raising an inquisitive eyebrow as she pulled the sheet over her naked body.

"That was Illya," he said. "Januuz. Januuz wants a meeting before we leave. Wants to see me face to face. I have to be at the statue of St. John the Baptist on the Charles Bridge in twenty minutes."

Delia was incredulous: "*On New Year's Eve?* Why didn't Januuz bother to show up at the sale?" She shook her head in disbelief. "I *knew* this was too easy. Something isn't right, David—"

He raised his hand to quiet her: "Illya said that Januuz is quite powerful. Said it would be easy to make our lives hard leaving the country if we refused. We don't need that kind of heat."

Delia collapsed back onto the bed in exasperation. "Fine. We'll go together."

VII

New Year's Eve: 11:57 P.M.

Bathed in colored light, the skeletal spires of the Castle grasped crookedly into the overcast night sky. A gentle dappling of snow began to cover the ground as the crisp air, scented with the sweet aroma of fried pastries from kiosks along the riverbanks, caused them to pull their lapels closed. The wide avenue of the Charles Bridge was jammed with noisy revelers, and it was difficult to move amidst the drunken knots of people ready to ring in the New Year.

As David led Delia through the festive scene to the statue, he was amused and disturbed by the assemblage of colorful and bizarre disguises that everyone wore: sinister plague-doctor beaks dueled with half-masked monsters; delicate Venetian-style full-faced works of art competed with cheap clear party coverings for attention as the noise and commotion grew louder.

They arrived at the base of the statue as the Orloj chimed in midnight. The entire bridge erupted in an incredible cacophony as fireworks shot into the sky, reflecting plumes of flame off the surface of the Vltava. The display was fantastic, casting dramatic shadows on everyone, and silhouetting St. John against colorful streaks and pinwheels in the velvety sky. The harsh smell of black powder wafted over the scene as the whole bridge was illumined by blasts of pink, then red, then blue flashes of explosive light, booming out the arrival of the New Year all over the antique city of Praha. The snow had turned into a light drizzle, but there was no denying the excitement in the air and the enthusiasm of the crowd.

"Thank you for coming, David."

David looked down from the mesmerizing spectacle at the cloaked figure in costume who was now standing next to Delia. The haunting apparition—someone dressed as a Golem—took off their disturbing mask: It was Illya.

"Illya! What's this all about?" David yelled over the roar of the pyrotechnics and the intoxicated celebrators. "Is Januuz here?"

Illya seemed troubled. He nodded, the black makeup around his eyes a strange contrast to his cropped light blond hair. Looking down to the ground, he motioned with a gesture of his arm, saying: "David, this is Januuz. I'll leave you now. Shem!" With that, he vanished into the mob, grabbing Delia and dragging her with him as her screaming voice enfolded into the noise of the crowd.

"No! Delia! What's happening?" Before David could follow them, Januuz appeared. He was a hulking figure dressed in black robes, and blocked David's way into the horde. Januuz's mask was particularly gruesome: a twisted countenance with two faces, one fronting forward, though skewed, and the other offset to the rear. It was very convincing.

"We only come here once a year, David." The voice coming from the mask was guttural, slow. The wide tongue licked the cracked lips on the forward mouth, leaving a silver slick. David stared at the man, his thoughts jumbled. At that moment, the second mouth screamed out: "It's too late, David! We've changed our minds."

For an instant David felt queasy, and everything appeared to slow down; there was a salty taste in his mouth. Coppery. It was then that he knew two things: first, that the thing in front of him was not wearing a mask, and second, that he was dying.

The second countenance was withered, its expression frantic—eyes rolling in their sockets, nose flaring—as it continued: "You cannot change the past. Every man carries the seeds of his own destruction within him, like a secret. It is too late for you! Sacrifices and changes must be made."

"You are guilty," the first aspect muttered matter-of-factly, then grinned, showing rows of sharp teeth. It blinked its heavily lidded eyes as the fireworks flared overhead. "Look around us, David. All these people . . . they are all guilty of something, just like you. Some haven't learned what yet, but they will, in due time, whether through their own realizations or through our persuasion. When they do, we shall appear to them on our annual visit and lure them with their weaknesses, just as we did you."

David could feel his sanity prying loose from his intellect. "What . . . *are* you? A demon? An alien? A hallucination or a dream?"

"Do we look to be a dream?" the faces replied in unison, then laughed. Unison, again: "We are a god. The god of time, and transitions . . ."

In the distance, a mournful horn blared, adding a top note of sadness to the chaos on the Charles Bridge. In David's overworked mind, the din of the crowd seemed to coalesce into a solemn requiem comprised of off-key chants, punctuated by dry drum beats and the hollow clang of enormous, far-away bells. Crumbling to his knees, the great stone bridge was suddenly dark and barren except for Januuz and himself. Prague had become a vast land of nothingness.

As the New Year began, Januuz turned toward the Castle and David followed, his past finally colliding with his future, and his time up at last.

THE MAN WITH THE HORN

I

He's leaving

She always knew when he was heading out: shortly after he stopped practicing, there would be a great deal of commotion and shuffling around on the other side of the thin old walls of the flat, as though someone were moving heavy fixtures around. A few minutes later, she would hear the muffled creak of his front door, and then the decisive slam as it closed. A moment or so after that, she could just make out the faint groan of the aging main staircase as he lumbered down to the gated front entryway.

In all the years she had lived in the modest little studio, she had never seen his face or spoken to him. All the other neighbors on her floor were affable enough; during the holidays, ancient Mrs. Kriteman would leave a tin of fresh-baked goodies in her doorway, or cranky Mr. Golding would brusquely offer to carry a heavy sack of groceries up to her place. Even Juan, the middle-aged handyman, was unfailingly polite, in spite of his limited English-speaking skills.

Not so her neighbor, Mr. Trinity.

In her twelve-year occupancy, she had yet to meet anyone who had associated with him in a social way, or even spoken with him; he was shadowy, mysterious, aloof.

Once, about five years ago, she managed to catch a glimpse inside his apartment as she was coming up the ramshackle stairs to their gloomy, worn landing: what little she could see appeared Spartan, the walls painted black. There was the suggestion of weak lighting, and she just saw a strange end table with an unusual statue on display. Without her glasses it was hard to make out, much less comprehend, what she was viewing, and it was only a glance before the door closed, slamming

35

loosely in its paint-chipped frame as he slipped back into his dwelling—
as usual, his instrument case in hand, a battered hat pulled down to his
jacket collar, his long, shapeless overcoat rustling. She noted then that he
seemed a rather tall individual, but had only ever seen him in his duster
and hat, and always from a distance. In the protracted silence that followed, the entire odd scenario raised questions in her mind about her
neighbor . . . questions she had put out of her thoughts for some time,
but which came rushing back, inspiring in her a vague sense of dread
and disquiet concerning his circumstances, and her proximity.

In the ensuing years since, a lot had happened: Her mother passed
on from prolonged bout of cancer . . . her brother was killed in a terrible workplace accident . . . and she had been relegated to filling her
empty hours volunteering at a homeless shelter, existing off the meager disability income she received each month due to a persistent and
excruciating neck injury acquired from a car accident. After that she
stopped driving, which she deemed not only hazardous but unneces-
sary in the neighborhood, and especially as she had no other local relatives; moreover, walking was good exercise. At times she felt isolated,
even in her building—an interesting, historic old brownstone with a
mix of renters and owners, mostly the elderly and young families starting out—which could be disheartening, but it *was* an existence of sorts,
and at her age, in her physical condition, it was all she could manage. If
only she still had Tom, life would be mostly agreeable, but that was not
the case: he was taken suddenly three years previous, victim of an un-
diagnosed heart condition. He fell asleep and just never woke up. For a
time she prayed for a better life, but her experiences had blunted her
faith, lowered her expectations; one should be careful what one prays
for, and to whom, she had decided, because there was no guarantee
that any of it would come to pass—or in any way that was worth having. No more angels and devils for her; the inspiring tales of faith and
redemption of her youth had long ago decayed into bitter cynicism and
hard-won, biting realism, which she had come to appreciate. For too
long she had held the wrong priorities and only valued what she actually had in hindsight. She recalled a long-forgotten acquaintance once

telling her that the biggest downside to getting older was that everyone around you—friends, family, pets—died; that it was the tax paid on living a long life. Considering the other option, she supposed it was better to age, if she could manage it without too much pain and with some measure of decorum . . . As she approached senior citizen status herself now, she saw the wisdom and sadness of that observation and mentally calculated additional, personal fees: aching joints, failing eyes, lost hope. In her estimation, hearts only served a few purposes at this life stage—heart attacks, heartbreak, heartache.

Outside her door, the landing stairs creaked again, and she looked at the clock: *11:09* P.M. Mr. Trinity had been gone for over three hours as she whiled away the time, lost in her thoughts, absorbed by the past and the pointless regrets of things that could have—even should have—happened, but never did, and, she suspected now, never would.

Then the nightly ritual commenced: Mr. Trinity's door slammed shut. This was followed shortly by a heavy scraping sound emanating from his side of the drafty apartment wall. After a moment, he started playing, and his practice would go on for the next several hours. Building in intensity, the tenor of his instrument was mournful, the melody a wailing dirge—a cacophonous mélange of cawing, rasping, weeping shrills and squawks—which seeped through to her . . . filling her head, filling the night, filling the world with its anguished, doom-laden call . . .

II

After so many years, she had learned to tune out the ominous music issuing from the residence next door. Undeniably, she and Tom had obtained the unit—now paid for with Tom's life insurance policy, another example of his taking care of her even in death—for a great price *because* of Mr. Trinity: no one else had wanted to purchase the abode once they heard the uncanny music wafting through the place from next door. The music, and the unnerving history of the domicile, was more than enough to spook most potential homeowners, in spite of the charming layout, the attractive arched doorways, and the reasonable square-footage. As a result, the apartment had remained on the market for over four years.

"The previous owners simply disappeared," the real estate agent said. A decent-looking dirty blond, which he had apparently been told a few times too often, he smiled at her before opening the front door with a minor flourish. "Take a look!"

They had decided to meet at the brownstone after Tom got off from work, but he was running late, as always—one of her pet peeves. Even so, she was excited to see the interior after Tom had described it and the area, which was not only near a small greenbelt, but was convenient to most amenities and even had its own parking space—a rarity. It was the sixth place that they had been to in the past month, but something about it felt better than the others, which were in parts of the city that made her nervous. And it was reasonably close both of their jobs.

"Wow . . . I do love the hardwoods," she said, nonchalantly caressing a newly painted wall. The smell of the paint lingered in the air, subtly merging with a trace of cleaning solutions. "How many bedrooms again?"

"Two. Two bedrooms, one-and-a-half baths, galley kitchen. Gas stoves, for the chef in you!" the agent replied, smoothing his tie and turning on the light in the hallway to the master bedroom. "Great place, great services, restaurants nearby . . . An outstanding value for this part of the city, near the school—"

"We don't have any. I mean, no children." She felt strange saying it aloud. "I decided we weren't having any."

"Hello! Sorry I'm late," Tom said, rushing into the open front door.

"Oh, no worries! We were just starting," the agent said. "I was running through some of the details—"

"Did you mention the previous owners?" Tom asked, walking over to where they stood in the hall near the bedroom. "Pretty interesting story."

The agent gave a tight smile. "I did mention that they disappeared—"

"That's not all, though."

"No. No, that's not all; I was going to get to that." The agent looked down.

She felt the tension in the room elevate: "Get to what?" she asked, an edge in her voice. She dreaded this; she hoped it was nothing stupid. Sometimes Tom did things that just got all over her nerves: dumb ideas, poor choices, crazy notions. If he had not been such a hard worker, she would have found someone else a long time ago. He had even given her another shot when he caught her with her ex-boyfriend, which was more than she would have done. As her mother and brother told her, someone with her intelligence, her looks could get any guy they wanted, so why settle? Maybe guilt . . . maybe pride . . . She felt as though something big was going to happen for her one day, and then she could really get on with her life. She deserved better, and she knew that, but he was here and had never screwed up so bad as to warrant the door. Yet.

"Oh, it's nothing, really—"

"Well, actually, it's a very cool story," Tom interrupted, as was his habit. "It was an older couple, and they were rumored to have mob connections—"

"That," the agent interjected, "is purely speculative; don't let that—"

"Right, right. Pure speculation; regardless," Tom continued, his hands flailing as he spoke. "So they were this older mob couple who had been the owners here for, like, nearly twenty years; so anyway, they were vacationing in Prague, having a good time, and then BAM!" Tom whacked his hands together dramatically. "They're dragged kicking and screaming across the Charles Bridge, to Prague Castle and never seen again."

The room went quiet. The agent sighed loudly. "While it's true that they did not return, no one knows that they were 'dragged away.' They were filmmakers and art dealers doing some research on a recently discovered medieval-era dig near an abandoned city in the Czech Republic. Additionally, they supposedly had relatives in Europe, and it's believed that the couple just decided to stay there. Besides, no one's even certain that they left the country, or even the city! I mean, there's no record of them staying in Prague, just some plane ticket purchases. They can't verify who even used the tickets, or if they were used. The trail went cold after that, and they left no itinerary beyond going to the Czech Republic."

"That's not what I read online, though," Tom replied. "I read that they had some real money, and were in some deep shit over a bad business deal. The whole 'researching-the-ossuary' thing was a ruse; they were really trying to buy fake identities. I also read it was related to some kinky sex stuff—young girls, live sex shows, crap like that . . . No one ever heard from them again. That's why this place went on the market—no one can reach 'em; it's like they never existed. I read they were troublemakers in the building, too, tried to get a long-time resident evicted so they could take his unit over and expand into it. I think the whole episode adds to the charm of the place, really."

She looked at Tom, who was smiling, then to the agent, who busied himself nervously eyeing his notes. Finally, she asked: "Interesting. Anything else I should know about?"

Then, distantly at first, there was the melancholy sound of a musical instrument—perhaps a French horn or some comparable type of brass—which was soon joined by two, possibly three others of a similar character, forming a mildly dissonant chord that drifted spectrally through the air, building in harmonic complexity, swelling in resonance throughout the room. After a couple of minutes, the playing stopped, the last few phrases of the tune reverberating throughout the unit.

Tom: "Wow! What the hell was that? I've never heard anything like it!"

The agent attempted another smile, but his confidence seemed shaken. "That—that's Mr. Trinity, the next door tenant. He's harmless, a recluse . . ."

A recluse, certainly, though in other ways he was the perfect neighbor—he never complained, never bothered anybody, never had anyone over. Tom drove the bargain hard, and they bought the place, in part because he was so intrigued with Mr. Trinity and the unusual history of the apartment. Tom had always been open to new experiences and enjoyed challenges. It was part of the reason she stayed with him, she realized in retrospect; he had been a musician as well and even attempted, for a while, to engage their elusive neighbor—knocking on his door, leaving notes, and so on—to no avail. Mr. Golding in particular had warned her husband that his entreaties would be pointless, that Trinity would not be receptive at all, but it was Tom's nature to try, to reach out to others.

So long as anyone could recall, the cryptic Mr. Trinity had been a staple in the building; even old man Jenkins, the superintendent before he died last year, said that Trinity had been a fixture well before *he* moved in, some thirty years prior. No one in Mr. Jenkins's estimation had set foot in Trinity's place, spoken with him, or even seen his face in all that time. They only knew his name was Mr. Ghrâbøel Trinity, that he practiced playing his horn day and night, and that he left his unit without fail in the evenings for several hours, every day of the year.

After Tom's death, she realized many things, but of course they were all too late. She was too sad to concern herself with Mr. Trinity and his peculiar habits; but once she was living alone again and the fog of her depression began to lift, she found her curiosity and interest gradually piqued by his odd ways as she so obliquely experienced them.

Then something remarkable occurred: she got a piece of his mail in her box by accident, his name and apartment number clearly scrawled on the front; there was no return address. She stared at it for several minutes. It was the first tangible thing of his that she had ever touched.

She could not resist taking it to her flat.

Once safely in the confines of her home, with Trinity's portentous serenade happening just a few feet beyond the wall, she debated what to do. It might seem awkward to give the post back now that she had taken it, and she knew he would not answer the door in any case. After an hour of agonizing consideration, she found herself hastily tearing open the water-stained, yellowing envelope, though she knew it was wrong.

Inside, there was a three-page document. The paper was crumbling and smelled of smoke, and the handwritten script was shaky, penned in some alien language, with angular, densely accented letters and very long words, which were apparently to be read from the right side of the page to the left, and from bottom to top. It resembled no other language she had ever seen, not even her mother's native Russian, and certainly not the Hebrew she had been taught as a child.

Along the bottom third of the pages were several meticulously rendered drawings, but they were smeared, and it was difficult to discern just what exactly they were about. The images looked to be either diagrams, sketches of bizarre plants and animals, or something else altogether—perhaps a few of each. Curiously, sections of the message were broken up by what appeared to be a form of musical notation, but not of any type she was familiar with, and nothing she could identify with the help of Tom's old reference books. Even searching the Internet and poring through the stacks at the main library turned up nothing remotely like the notation, illustrations, or language that the missive was encoded in. She filed it away, afraid of what would happen if she threw it out or attempted to give it to him.

The letter brought a certain level excitement to her life, an excitement that had been missing for a long time from her monochrome, increasingly sedate existence; it proved his humanity in a way and made her feel connected to the outside world again, instead of focusing only on herself, perpetually looking inward. It was then that she began to catch herself noting the timing of Mr. Trinity's comings and goings . . . strangely comforted by the wistful, glum sonorities of his unearthly music. One morning, for the first time in years, she looked into the mirror and noticed her reflection as she got ready: brushing her hair, she seemed to have more *presence,* more color . . . Her eyes had a glint of light; her skin was still smooth, still tight for a person her age. Even her frame was more at ease, relaxed, and her weight was good—she had retained a nice figure through all that had happened by exercising, walking everywhere. She smiled again for the first time she could remember, and felt a renewed sense of interest—of purpose—in the world.

Over dinner in the evenings, she began to muse that perhaps Mr. Trinity was a professional musician. Her ruminations about his secretive life became increasingly intricate, increasingly detailed, even as her dreams became less interesting, even forgettable. His being a performing musician would certainly explain his continual practicing, his daily excursions into the outside world. *Maybe he's playing gigs—or filling in on recording sessions uptown . . .*

One day, she vowed to gather up the courage to pay Mr. Trinity a proper visit, perhaps take him a neighborly offering of homemade brownies. Perhaps her feminine wiles could forge some connection between them.

III

Returning home from the shelter on a moonless December night, head pounding from a cold she sensed was dragging her immune system down, she noticed something unusual as she crested the stairs to her landing: Mr. Trinity's door was open. Just a crack, but enough to see into his dark, dark unit.

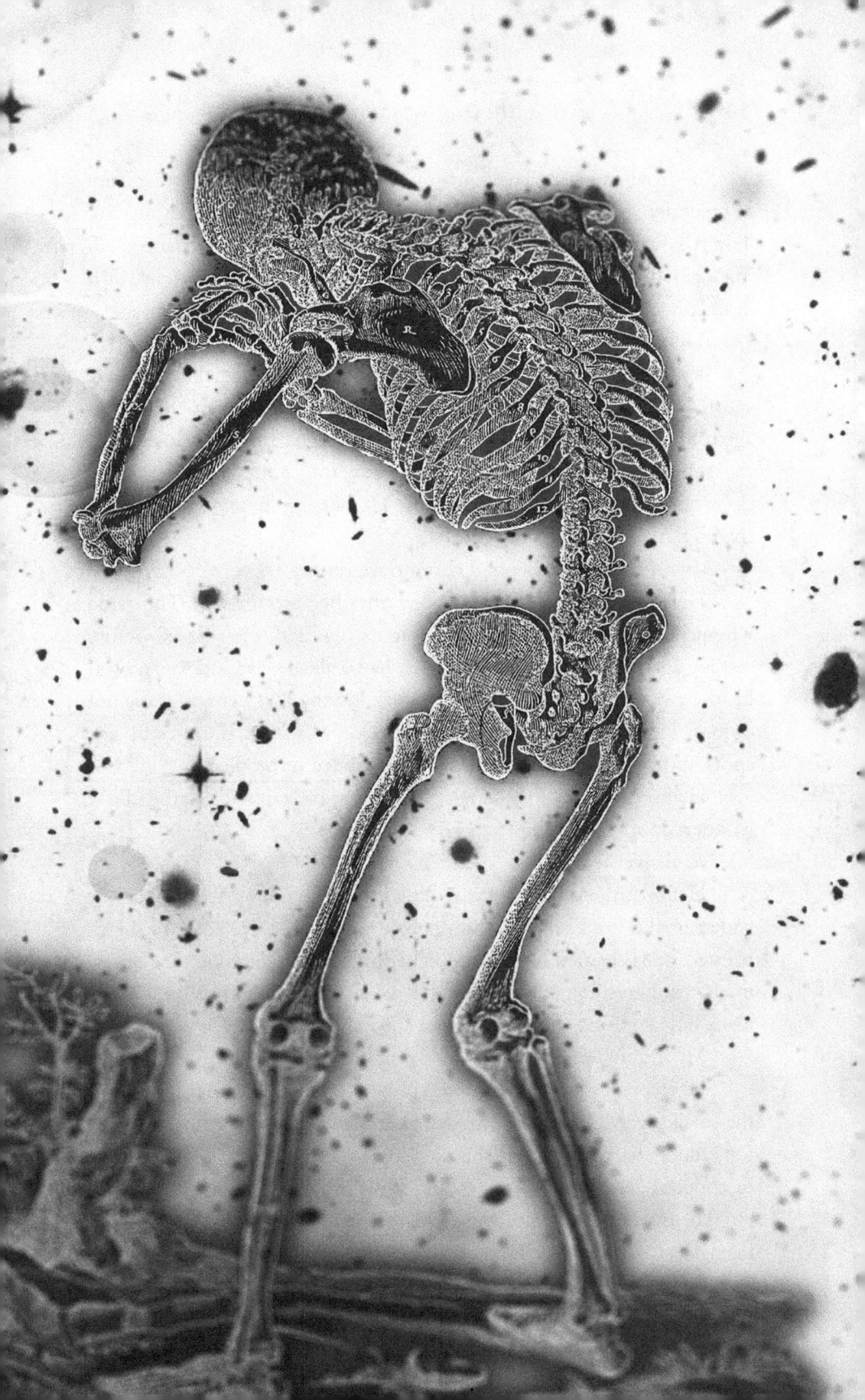

She froze in place. The lights on the landing lowered for an instant as a sudden cold gust whistled through the silent hallway, causing Mr. Trinity's front door to move ever so slightly. She looked around, pulling her shawl closed about her throat; the yarn was scratchy, stiff against her skin. Her throat clicked tightly when she swallowed.

Maybe . . . maybe there's a problem . . .

She took a short, tentative step forward, heels clicking on the scuffed wooden causeway, unconsciously pulling her purse tighter against her tired body. Suddenly her vision was narrowed exclusively to the gap between Mr. Trinity's gently wavering door and the shabby doorframe . . . her hands felt clammy . . . her legs heavy . . . her heart thudded mechanically, unevenly.

After a pause, she stepped closer once more.

"Hello?" Her voice was small, tinny, her mouth dry. The wind whipped outside the building. The lights dimmed, then flared before settling again. Without realizing it, she had walked over and was now at his doorway. She raised her fist to knock, noting that her hand was not only shaking, but that the sixty-year-old skin was slack, dotted with age spots, more wrinkled than she had ever noticed or recalled.

"Hello?" she called out again, louder, and rapped on the dingy wooden door.

No answer.

"Hello? Mr. Trinity? Is everything OK?" The door opened slightly wider as she knocked. Inside, no lights were on—indeed, the black painted walls seemed to pull the light from the landing into the apartment, extinguishing, deadening the weak hallway illumination like a black hole snuffing the energy from a dying star.

"Mr. Trinity? Is everything all right? It's your neighbor."

She stepped into the unit, her shoes clacking on the hardwoods of the small foyer. There was a sudden chill in the air, causing her breath to fog, and a sharp smell that she could not quite identify . . . a top note of copper . . . a hint of mold . . . and some other, musky undertone.

The inside of the place was quite dark: she squinted her eyes, straining against the inky blackness. From what little she was able to see, the layout was completely different from her own residence, and larger; the windows of this corner unit were completely blacked out as well. She stepped forward again, again. With one more step, the feeble outside light fell quickly away; as she moved into the depths of the too-quiet abode, all illumination was smothered by the deep, permeating blackness within.

"Hello? Mr. Trin—" Her balance shifted abruptly and she lost her foothold after stepping onto something soft; before she could react, she was on all fours, hitting the floor hard, her hands braced against something cool, moist.

A body!

Repulsed, she gently felt around—screaming out when it unexpectedly moved . . . and answered her scream with one of its own.

She recoiled, a hot stream of acid jetting from her gut to her mouth. Then another person, unseen in the impenetrable gloom, screamed out right beside her—and a third joined—followed by a fourth . . . Soon there was a horrific chorale of moaning, tortured shrieks filling the pervasive darkness. Her mind flashed on the couple that used to own her unit: *Were they in here? Tortured for years by Mr. Trinity for trying to have him evicted? Or maybe they were all in a sick partnership— some twisted sex thing as the rumors had reported . . .*

She leapt up, disoriented, nauseous, and ran. She hit a wall, the wind knocked out of her, and felt along its length, at last coming to a closed door, her head pounding in time to her pulse. Behind her, the horrific groaning and thrashing continued, growing in pitch and volume, voices subsiding and joining at different intervals, adding to the density of the cold, thin air as she tried to catch her breath. *I've gone the wrong way, I've gone deeper into this madhouse!*

She turned the doorknob and pushed the door open–

*dazzled by a staggering, limitless panorama
of vertigo-inducing deep space quintessence:
a primeval, impossibly expanding canopy of twinkling stars,
spiraling galaxies, and flowering nebulae
receding into the void in all directions . . .*

Teetering on the threshold of the doorway,
she loses her footing, and is rapidly falling—

end over sickening end
through the weightlessness of non-life and non-death,
of animate and inanimate,
the terrible, swarming chorus
slowly replaced by a cavernous, otherworldly thrumming
which pushes all rational thought from her mind . . .
stunned into insensibility
at the self-organizing chaos of oblivion.

Reflexively, she reaches out—
the saliva on her tongue beginning to sizzle
from the vacuum of space; lungs burning
from a lack of oxygen; brain dying of hypoxia—
and tries to control her wildly spinning body.

She clutches at where the wall used to be,
her eyes closing as consciousness withers
from her mental horizon . . .
for a second, a pinpoint of light blooms
in the center of her diminishing awareness,
and she finds a solace she has not known
since before Tom's death—

When she opened her eyes again, she was lying in a poorly lit hall-way that stretched to a vanishing point in the distance. She took a deep breath, eyes watering, and coughed hard, her body drained, aching. Her clothes were torn, damp, and adhered snugly to her stinging skin; her handbag was gone. She touched her face, surprised at how cold it was, even numb in spots; she could barely control the trembling of her hands, which were stiff, tight, frigid. Getting to her feet, she tried to walk, but the floor was uneven, deceptively pitched. As she watched, the corridor hypnotically transmogrified into a vast wasteland of twisted, verdant flora covering prehistoric edifices boasting sinuous, Gaudi-esque forms juxtaposed against jagged monuments—*temples?*—composed of sheer, geometrically impossible gold-leafed angles. Populated by weird, nonhuman figures—some winged, others not—in disturbing tableaux, the whole site gave the impression of a vanished empire steeped in ostensibly frenzied torment—or perhaps some inscrutable, obscene ecstasy. The bizarre relics, starkly inscribed with oddly familiar, abstract runes and imagery, reminded her of something, and she was overwhelmed with a sudden and profound sadness; she felt trapped, forgotten, lost in her own private German Expressionist film, her own hellish version of *The Cabinet of Dr. Caligari*. *Of course—Mr. Trinity's letter* . . . That was where she had seen the unusual characters, the plants and creatures, the odd depictions adorning the exterior of the buildings.

At that moment, an ethereal sound—haunting, musical, and also disconcertingly familiar—coasted gradually into her perception across the desolate scene, and she found herself inextricably drawn into this blasted landscape. *Was this the ossuary that the couple was researching? Maybe this is hell . . . or maybe it's something else* . . . She stepped forward—

<<P'jra!>>

She spun around, looking for the source of the garbled exclamation, confused.

<<P'jra!>> The voice was guttural, detached. Again, closer, more insistent: <<*P'jra!* >>

The eerie music that she heard earlier was mounting, growing louder. The ruins began to dim as she watched, slowly fading into an absolute darkness, just as its grotesque, frozen inhabitants began to stir into hideous life. Abruptly, the strange music ended.

As she watched, her mind pulling pieces of her experiences together, she saw something materialize . . . first as the hazily radiant outline of a hunched figure within the encroaching nightfall, then little by little gaining solidity as it moved toward her with a resolute determination. Transfixed as the silhouette slowly closed in, she noticed that it appeared to be in pain, as though each movement required tremendous effort, tremendous willpower.

"*Mr. Trinity* . . ." Her voice was a strangled whisper; she wanted to say more, to explain, to apologize, but realized it would be pointless: she had trespassed—pried into things that she had no business being involved with, whether she understood them or not—and there would be no turning back.

Once more, softer: <<*P'jra.*>> Even in the near pitch-blackness of the strange passageway, she could see from the softly glowing aura that shimmered around him in fish-belly iridescent hues that he had his precious instrument case. Inches away from her he paused, and his towering, shadowy, muscular bulk completely filled her perception. He was nude, she sensed, and his hat was missing. She could see from his outline, which was fearsome, outlandish, that it was an approximation of a human, but closer in form to the figures in the landscape she had seen start to move. His breath was cold, ragged, labored. At last, he stooped forward, revealing a cluster of what seemed to be multiple arms, or perhaps wings, and opened his case; in that singular instant, she became aware of the horrifying screams from the other room once more—the ghastly chorus was still shrilling in anguish, and she instinctively, or perhaps as part of her delusionary state, understood that these could be souls. As he pulled the instrument from its holder, she observed that it too threw off a faint luminosity, a greenish fluorescence that defined its bizarre shape. She had never see what instrument created Mr. Trinity's disturbing music, and was both amazed and revolted by the intricate, mottled swirls of fleshy corkscrews—mapped by tendons, threaded with weakly pulsing veins—that coiled and twisted to create the body of the device: a mucid collage of soft, translucent tubing punctuated with numerous bony prominences. The buttons, inscribed by the odd musical notations from the letter, seemed to be made from rows of large, yellowed teeth, and multiple growths pulsed under its glistening skin, crowding next to many trembling, blinking eyes, which stared from beneath the quivering membranes. Instant-to-instant, the weird implement appeared solid, then gelid, then solid—

the eyes, clouded, deadened, shifting back and forth into positions that brought to her mind distorted yet familiar faces . . . sometimes even people she recognized—her dead mother, father, and brother . . . others were strangers, still others were simply half-formed horrors of sickening visage.

She tried to scream, but was muted by horror and disgust. Mr. Trinity pulled the weird apparatus to his face, which for the first time illuminated his features—

And she found the scream buried deep in her chest.

His appearance was little more than a pale, gaunt, expressionless mask, the lips peeled away from the outsized, crooked dentition in an approximation of a rictus. The five deeply sunken eyes formed a perfect inverted triangle in the stretched skin of the face, wetly reflecting the strange, dim glow of the living instrument gripped in his gnarled, arthritic fists. His skeletal proboscis twitched excitedly on his enormous earless head as Mr. Trinity inched closer and closer, the single massive, blood-colored horn at last visible curling asymmetrically from the top of his denuded cranium.

The din from the screaming choir in the other room seemed to crescendo, then fade from her dying mind; as she backed away from the creature in front of her, she was horrified to comprehend all the terrible lies, delusions, and mistakes in her life that she would never get a chance to undo or correct. Instead of working to improve herself, instead of making the best of her reality, she had coveted and envied; she had marginalized and belittled, and arrogantly claimed to know better. In the end, she had searched for something that was better left unknown, undiscovered: unfortunately, she had found it. *Am I to become a part of his instrument? Will he collect me now for his endless permutations, his ceaseless practice?*

In the seconds left to her, she thought she heard Tom's voice in the distant screams, blended with the swelling melodies of madness, the pitiful harmonies of hell that her shattered mind could no longer fully assimilate. She understood now that this was not her heaven or hell, but her eternal limbo; much as her life had been unlived, so too would her death be unresolved; she would persist in this place, with this being, this creature, this nephilim. She had been found, too, it seems.

Then, with a strange resolve, and an unexpected grace, the man with the horn—who always was, and who always would be—raised the pulsating instrument to his mouth . . .

And the infinite was ignited.

MEMENTO MORI

My friend, you would not tell with such high zest
To children ardent for some desperate glory,
The old Lie: *Dulce et decorum est*
Pro patria mori.

—Wilfred Owen,
"Dulce et Decorum Est"

I

The old man stared out of the window, his rheumy green eyes reflecting the swirl of autumn leaves as they blew past the facility on the street below. He understood now he was unlikely to return home. The nurses just smiled whenever he asked when his son was coming to take him back. The parade of doctors never said anything directly, just studied his charts and mumbled to the nurses; sometimes one glanced up from beneath his bushy eyebrows, a dour expression lining his face before he turned on his heel to visit the next patient down the hall.

Based on the season, he figured he must have been in place a month, maybe longer. Time had no meaning for him now; the past sometimes impinging on the present in unexpected ways—long-dead friends and family calling distantly from another room, at times so real he answered them; blurry glimpses of his youth in the medicine-cabinet mirror out of the corner of his eye. Other times he saw things he did not fully understand in the reflection of his room window. Half-seen, transparent visions of a darker nature: people crying, strangers talking with his son—the old man was never in these scenes. *Perhaps this is the future?* It made him feel anxious to think about it. He tried to stay as much as possible in the moment.

He sighed heavily, still looking at the windy street scene as he watched people go about their daily business, oblivious to his observations, ignorant of how little impact they really had against the crushing brutality of the clock. In this instant they had their spouses, their children, their jobs, and their lives—but what of tomorrow? As immutable as the past was, the eternal now, fleeting, was all that existed, especially since the idea of the future—so concrete when he was younger—had been reduced as he aged from spans of years to days, and, in his darker moods, to moments. Sometimes he felt like two different people—one brave, in control, the other scared, just trying to keep it together until he no longer had to be concerned with such appearances.

In the end, we really only have ourselves in this instant, don't we? Everything and everyone will be taken from you eventually. And for what? Does having a larger house matter if it sits empty once you're dead? What purpose does a stockpile of money serve if no good ever comes from it? A whole life comes down to this— wasting away in a velvet cell guarded by well-meaning captors . . . drifting away one neuron at a time. He took a sharp breath, realizing now that there were worse fates than dying.

The door opened behind him. He stiffly turned to see who this interloper was; he was in no mood for company today, not even his son.

No one was there.

"Damn doctor didn't close the door all the way again." This had happened before. It made him feel exposed to have his room open to the prying eyes of his neighbors as they shuffled down the hallway. He hated old people. Now that his son had warehoused him, he felt certain that it was only a matter of time before the reaper made a grand entrance through the same door that he would prefer to keep securely closed. As his attention was fixated on the doorway, the very appearance of the opening took on disorienting and frightening characteristics. Was it an entrance or an exit? A portal to freedom or an ingress to something more sinister? He rose up after a time and hobbled over to shut the door, moving past the relics of a life that seemed at times comforting, at times alien—like a suit tailored to his specifications but meant for another man.

He looked outside his unit. *Oh, yes.* He remembered it all now: he had been here since just after his eighty-fifth birthday. That was the day he had left his house and placed a note on the door for the cleaners to come in and taped the key to it. Then he drove his aging Benz to the theater. And that was when the accident happened: he had driven into a crowd standing in line for tickets. Luckily no one was killed. It made the news. And someone took the key to his place and ransacked it. That was when his son had decided it was not safe for him to be alone anymore. Mother had died the month before, and there was no way his son could keep an eye on his whereabouts when he was dealing with his own responsibilities. The old man had reluctantly agreed. He had been lucid enough to realize that something was not right. His condition seemed precarious at times—physically as well as mentally. He had grown enfeebled, weak, his mind, body, and senses not as sharp as they once were. Getting old was a living hell. *But, considering the alternative . . .*

Standing behind the threshold, he could see through the expansive windows and skylights delineating the place that it was getting dark outside. Strangely, there was no one in the hallway, either. He had not developed any friendships in what he now realized had been at least a year since his admittance. His son—always thoughtful and considerate—still visited, but the intervals between sittings seemed to be growing longer and longer as time wore on. Still, he had a feel for the normal rhythms of the facility. There was always a gaggle of gray-haired old women loudly clucking tongues, ancient wrinkly fellows his age tottering about with their walkers, the ubiquitous troupe of doctors and nursing staff whizzing past everyone like white-clad packs of albino hummingbirds skimming over the bright and busily patterned carpet in a breathless and dizzying choreography.

But not today: today there was no one. That was unusual. *Have I missed a fire drill? Maybe someone opened the door to be sure we were all out and didn't see me.* Though his hearing was in decline, he was sure even without his hearing aids in—his "ears" as he liked to call them—he would have heard a general alarm or announcement. Even the cloying muzak was silent. The air was still, devoid of the customary smells of early evening: baking cookies, popcorn, mentholated rubbing cream. The only thing he noticed was at the far end where the double swinging doors hung; there was the hint of motion underneath them, like a flickering of light. After another look around, the old man grabbed the cane he kept by the door and walked out of his unit. The door slammed behind him, causing him to jump. "Jesus! Sounded like a damn gunshot!" He laughed to himself. "Just like when I was fighting near Aachen."

He made his way down the corridor, still confounded by the lack of normal activity in the place. Finally, at the double entryway, he strained to hear what was happening on the other side. The flickering had increased in the gap between the doors and the flooring. Gently, he pushed one of them open—

The explosion knocked him to the ground.

Flat on his back, he was overcome with the smell of oily black smoke, the metallic tang of copper at the back of his throat. Coughing violently, he was momentarily deafened by the blast wave. As the smoke cleared, he could see: the daylight had completely faded, and he was looking into a starry nighttime sky. He sat up, instantly aware of an intense cold. Off in the distance, he could see flashes of white light near the horizon; the facility was gone. The ground was shaking, the air rumbling with deep roars of other explosions, some of which appeared to be getting closer. Another one like that and he might be finished. The ringing in his ears started to abate as he caught his breath at last. It was snowing.

He stood, but was unable to locate his cane. *Maybe we're in a terrorist situation—*

"Doc! You okay, Doc?"

The voice was familiar. No one had mentioned Doc in years . . . *Not since—*

He turned in the direction of the voice; for a moment, he felt lightheaded. *My God . . . I'm fucking cracking up.*

The speaker moved toward him in the mix of smoke, snow, and fog that was quickly enveloping them. "Thought you were a goner, Doc."

Drawing closer, he could make out the features at last: it was Jon T. Merlin. Jonny had started calling him Doc on the first day they met after he learned he was studying pre-med back home in the States. Their camaraderie had been strong from the outset; it was almost as though the other soldier wanted to *be* Doc—or very much like him, at least.

"Jonny! You're a sight for sore eyes, my friend." Doc embraced the young man. *Good old reliable Jonny: none too bright, but trustworthy and stolid.* He was amazed to see his old friend, but found it strange that Jonny was literally unchanged: not a day past twenty-two, decked out in olive drab with a pack and his helmet cocked to one side, just like always. His overcoat was threadbare.

"We better get scarce. I think they're reloading, Doc."

"But I can't go with you, I'm not dressed—" He looked down and realized he was attired in the same outfit as his friend. *What the hell is happening?* He reached up to touch his face: a few days of stubble, but his skin was smooth, tight. His helmet was dented just above the right ear—the place a piece of shrapnel had nearly gotten him on his first day of fighting. He looked at his hands: strong, blackened with soot from the explosion. His rifle weighed on his shoulder.

"We're real exposed out here, Doc, even with the fog. That full moon's pretty unforgiving."

Another explosion rocked the ground a few hundred yards away, peppering them with clods of frozen dirt. Doc noticed the cold again; Jonny's unshaven face was dirty, his whiskers frosted with condensed ice from his breath. "Not gonna get any warmer out here, either. 'Less of course we get lit up!" Jonny jerked his head in the direction of the shelling. "I think they're headed our way, Doc. We lost Beethoven overnight, so it's just us." C. F. Ritch—Beethoven—had earned his nickname due to the fact that back home he was a cellist in the college orchestra.

Doc nodded, his breath falling away in a misty plume. He vividly remembered this situation and was suddenly awash with an intense feeling of déjà vu. The problem was he could not seem to place what they had done to get out of their predicament. The Germans had succeeded in cutting eight of them out of their squad. The larger group had been forced onward; five of the eight left back were killed in a subsequent firefight before retreating from the better armed Nazis. Over the course of the next few days, the remaining three—Doc, Jonny, Beethoven—wound up getting more and more lost in the freezing woods; running out of K-rations, their desperation increasing as bad weather moved in. The only things Doc recalled were the horrible circumstances, and that Beethoven had stepped on a landmine as they were moving through the forest in an attempt to rejoin their group. Now they were down to two.

Doc looked in the direction opposite the bombardment: they were at the edge of a barren stretch of farmland. It appeared the entire area had seen strong shelling in the distant and recent past. Through breaks in the fog, he noticed a few structures in the distance, perhaps a mile or so away. "Let's go see what that's about, Jonny."

II

Boots crunching on the snowpack, the two men struggled against the biting cold as they tried to stay ahead of the assault. They could feel the groundshock of Panzers coming on fast, grinding up the snow, ice, and earth.

At last they could make out their destination with clarity: it seemed to be a long-abandoned two-story farmhouse. Now the rain was coming down in bitter, cold sheets mixed with the snow. Swiftly making their way up to the rotted porch, they were careful to be sure that no one was waiting inside; the place was a hulking old wreck, weathered and burned out from previous battles. Peering inside, they could see broken furniture and cobwebs through the grime-crusted window glass. After they both felt it was clear, Jonny chuckled, murmuring: "Be nice if some vision of loveliness could feed us . . ."

Doc huffed. "I don't think we're gonna find Florence Nightingale out here. But at least we can stay out of the cold and get away from the Krauts. Stand back." Doc motioned Jonny back as he raised the butt of his rifle to break the rusted handle off the door.

Before he could bring the gun down, the door opened, its hinges creaking loudly in the dark. On the other side, a young woman with milky skin, dark, shining eyes, and her hair in a loose bun regarded them. She was wearing a white dress under a red knitted shawl and shielding a candle flame with her hand. She beckoned the men inside with a nod of her head. As the door closed behind them, Jonny and Doc began to speak; she gestured for them to be silent by placing a finger to her lips. As they had seen, the interior was in ruins and appeared more eerie due to the fog that swirled even within the house itself.

"Wow, what do you make of this, Doc?"

The woman turned, her face pressed into a scowl as she led them through the dilapidated old house. Dancing shadows throughout the room and across her graceful features added a surreal counterpoint to the proceedings. Once more she gestured for them to be silent: *"Shh!"*

Jonny grinned and raised his hands in a signal of supplication; he shot a glance over at Doc. His friend shrugged, lips curled into a confused half-smile. The three of them silently walked up the loose steps to the upstairs portion of the house. On the second floor, the smell of dust, mold, and decay was strong. Outside, near the fogbound horizon, the shelling continued, resembling ball lightning as the assault appeared to gather steam. The woman led them to a room in the back of the place and pointed for them to enter. Once they took off their gear, she left the room and walked across the landing to another bedroom. She opened the door, glancing back at Jonny and Doc, her eyes fearful. Before she closed it again, the two men could just make out another candle flickering inside, and the form of a gaunt old man in a wheelchair wearing a kippah with a young boy cowering behind him in the pale golden light. Their clothes were frayed, the man's beard wispy; the child's arm was in a makeshift sling.

"Pretty incredible," Doc whispered. "Looks like they've been hiding out here. I doubt this is their place. They look like Jews. Probably on the run from Antwerp. They're lucky to be alive. I don't think a ghost wants to live in this heap."

Jonny nodded, adding: "I saw that. Well, this place ain't too safe as it is. Better than outside . . . but not much better. Good thing we found 'em, though. Who knows what would have happened to us out there. And God only knows how they've been able to stay alive here." After a few minutes the woman returned. Placing a candle on a little wooden end table, she supplied them with some blankets, a bottle of wine, and a loaf of crusty, stale bread. She silently left and went back to her room, closing the door.

After splitting the bread, the soldiers relished the wine. Just as they were drifting off to sleep, multiple explosions tore into the ground at the front of the house, shaking the foundations and raining plaster from the ceiling.

"One more like that and we're finished!" Jonny yelled.

Doc snapped, grabbing Jonny's collar and shaking him. "Knock it off! Didn't your folks ever teach you saying things out loud like that can make 'em happen? Can jinx you? Don't put it into the aether!" Another massive bombardment blasted the front yard. Doc swallowed hard, looking at his friend. "We're gonna be fine, Jonny. Keep it together."

The explosions continued, but after a time appeared to be moving away from them. Eventually, they were just distant rumblings, like the sound of thunder.

At some point, sleep found them.

III.

The next morning.

Doc was up with first light. No one moved in the house. He crawled over to a window to assess the damage to the yard. Through the morning mist, he could see immense craters and the blasted remnants of snow-draped trees. There was a narrow roadway alongside the house—a group of men were walking away from the place. *Americans.* "Jonny! Wake up!"

Downstairs, Jonny and Doc found a couple of GIs poking around the farmhouse.

"I'll be damned! You guys made it through that shelling last night in this *dump?*" one of the soldiers—Dante, according to the dog tag around his neck—asked, hitching a thumb at the yard as he walked on-to the sagging porch.

"We did," Jonny replied. "We had some help, though. A family *lives* here. Woman was strange—never said a word, but helped us out of the cold, set us up with some eats."

"Really?" the heavy-set grunt replied, looking surprised. "They're living here?"

"I guess they have been for a time," Doc said. "Looks like a grand-father, his daughter, and a grandson. I'll go see if they're awake. We should take 'em along, if they'll go."

At the top of the landing, Doc paused. The door to the family's room was still closed. He knocked. Knocked again. No answer. Trying the knob, it turned freely. The door slowly swung open.

On the other side, there were three skeletons huddled together near the snuffed remains of a candle: a child with its arm in a sling, a crippled man with a skullcap in a wheelchair, and one in a white dress with a red knitted shawl. They had obviously been dead for some time; each had a bullet hole in its forehead. On the wall behind them was drawn a crude yellow star; dried, blackened blood was splattered across the symbol, nearly blotting it out.

Doc raised his hand to his mouth, taking a step toward the sad montage.

"You alive up there?" It was Jonny calling from downstairs.

After a pause, Doc replied: "Just a minute!" He took a blanket from the small bed in the room and covered the three bodies. Gather-ing his composure, he closed the door and bounded down the stairs to the living room.

Doc considered Jonny, then nodded to Dante. "Looks like they took off."

Dante returned the nod, studying Doc. "Right. Well, we need to bug out. You two okay to hoof it?"

The men picked up their packs and shouldered their guns.

As he crossed the threshold out of the old house, Doc stepped on a rotted board on the decaying porch, falling heavily.

"Wake up." Someone gently patted his face. "Wake up."

The old man's eyes fluttered open. His vision was blurry. As he slowly focused his attention on the confusion of red and white floating in his field of view, he realized he was looking at his regular nurse, Ms. Stephenson. She smiled at him.

"Well, looks like he's back. We thought we'd lost you." It was his gerontologist, Dr. Atkins. He almost appeared to be happy.

"Where am I? Where—where is everybody?"

"Dad, it's Paul."

The old man looked over to his son. "Paul. Yes. I was just . . . I was just with my buddy, at the old farmhouse."

Paul's face tightened. "'Doc' again? Haven't we been through this, Dad? That was all a long time ago. A lifetime ago."

"But—" He looked from his son to the doctor to the nurse.

"Listen," Dr. Atkins said, "you've had quite a scare—an aneurysm in your head burst. You could have died. Luckily, Rabbi Scofield was making the rounds with his grandson, testing the new wheelchair he'd gotten for Hanukkah, and found you collapsed in the doorway to your room; he called the nurse. If you'd been alone, you likely wouldn't be here."

The old man nodded his comprehension. "When? When did this happen?"

"About a week ago, Mr. Merlin," the nurse replied, her dark eyes shining, the bun of her hair loose under her cap. "I could tell you weren't feeling too well. You should really learn to talk a little more about how you're doing." She fluffed the pillow under Jonny's head. "You know, sometimes talking about things can really make it better. My mother always said 'to speak of a thing is to make it real.'"

Old Jonny Merlin—stolid and reliable—smiled and gently took her hand in his.

"And that, Nurse Stephenson, is what scares me."

TRANSPOSITION

"Cut to the chase. How much?"

The speakerphone went silent.

"We need two thousand to make it happen," the man on the other end of the line finally replied. "Each."

Dr. Aiden Burns thought for a moment, rubbing a day's growth of stubble along his narrow jawline. He squinted unconsciously, then said: "I'll give you eight hundred . . . *each*—no more. Take it or leave it. I've got other contacts."

Silence again. The line crackled: "Hold on a minute, boss." The phone clattered down. Burns leaned back in his chair, the glow from his computer monitor the only illumination in the dark office. He pulled at his tie, then took a swig of Scotch. He could hear voices in the background arguing but failed to make out the words. He swished the amber liquid in his tumbler, amusing himself with the subtle tinkling sound of ice cubes on glass.

"Okay, Bones. Eight hundred each. You really drive a hard bargain."

Aiden's features creased into an icy smile in the bluish gloom. "Thanks. I prefer to think of it as smart business . . . I need the parts by Wednesday at the latest. I won't deliver the 'scripts to my brother if he screws this one up. The window to harvest is short here. Be sure to tell him."

"Got it."

"And remember," Aiden added, "cut 'em *clean* this time, above the joints. None of those ragged stumps like the last ones. I'll use my credentials to grant access to your cutters at the morgue starting tomorrow morning. You can pick up the cash at my university office on Friday in the afternoon. I need those parts by Wednesday, though. No parts, no cash."

"Right, boss. University. Friday afternoon."

Aiden typed something into his computer. "One more thing: I'm going to need a set of kidneys and a few eyes. You got a lead on any cadavers?"

The line went quiet again.

"Hmmm . . . Well, Bones, I'm going to need another week on that. Market's tight right now. Been some Feds—FDA types—snooping around, too. Audits, inspections, that type of thing."

Aiden's jaw tightened. "The sooner the better, Angelo."

"No sweat. I'm on it. A shame . . . we got an older guy, rich dude, that just came through the funeral home, but he's no good. All yellowy with jaundice—"

"So what? What's a little jaundice?"

"Well, I mean you don't want to put that *in* somebody, boss. I mean, he might have had liver cancer, AIDS, or Hep C, or—"

"He's fine. I bet his kidneys are fine. A body broker took some of Alistair Cooke's bones out and repurposed them at a tissue bank. They were just going to cremate the guy, so why not use the stuff? Cooke died of metastatic bone cancer; I never heard of any complications from the eventual recipients."

"Yeah, boss. I hear you. But those guys didn't have permission."

"Well, they got greedy, I admit. Weren't careful like we are. Sometimes it's better to seek forgiveness than ask permission—understand what I mean? You know what we're doing here, right? There's a lot of money to be had, Angelo. Donors are in short supply. We're saving lives. So what if we make a little coin with it? That's no crime, not in America. I mean, think of it—heart valves, veins, skin for burn grafts, organs, femurs, tendons, cartilage. There's a *fortune* out there just waiting to be had. I can clear over a hundred grand on a single body that's just going to rot in the ground or be incinerated. And all those titanium screws, pins, plates—we can reuse that stuff. I mean, why not?"

Aiden took another swallow of Scotch and set the glass on his desk, letting his words sink in. He massaged his eyes in the dark room, relaxing. "We aren't harming anyone; they're *dead*. In fact, we're doing a service, Angelo. Never forget that."

After a long silence: "Yeah, boss. I get it. I get it."

"Your cadaver with the yellowing . . . See if you can score those kidneys. I'll pay good money for that. Ask my brother."

Aiden sat forward again, typing into his computer. "Another thing: I've just been approved for more tissue work. In addition, I think the university is about to grant me permission to move ahead on the full-face transplant. A male, white, average build, in his forties or fifties. We have applicants going through psychological and physical screenings in the next few weeks. Eight so far, narrowing it to the final contender. It'll be the first one in our region, and it will make me a star. I've even picked my team."

He studied the images of the final nominees on his monitor: gunshot victims missing noses or lower jaws; a car accident that had melted the fat and skin on a man's head into a pink, waxen likeness of a grinning skull; industrial injuries where the entire front of the cranium had been sheared off down to the sinus cavities, leaving just staring eyes and an opening for the throat. *What a terrible thing . . . to lose one's personhood, one's identity . . . to have to live on with an obliterated self.* He continued, removed, distant in thought: "I'm an honorable man, Angelo; I don't forget those that have helped me out. You. My brother. Even though they busted him on the drug test and stripped his nursing credentials, I'm about family ties . . . I can help wean him off the morphine and get him back on the right path."

"I understand, Bones. Family's important," Angelo replied. "And Mike's been doing good. He's done great here. Couple of slip-ups, but holding things down. And he's a *real* good cutter, boss. Real good."

Aiden snorted. "Oh, I know. He always had good hands. Identical twins carry a lot of those traits in common, Angelo. I have no doubt that Mike can get those kidneys, for example. Just help me keep him on the straight and narrow. Still need some eyes, though. Jaundiced eyes are no good, unfortunately."

Angelo chuckled over the line. "I have no doubt about that. I *hate* doing eyes, boss, I admit. They're hard to keep intact, for one thing. Delicate. And they're *really* in there. The 'pop' they make coming out . . . Not my favorite."

"Yeah. I understand. We all have our thing, even doctors and nurses. Mike hates anything to do with impalements. Me, I don't like dealing with blunt force. Everybody's got a weak spot."

"I catch you, boss."

Aiden glanced at his watch. It was late. "Before we go, keep in mind that your new side venture here with Carcaso Allied Mortuary and Tissue Services could start to see some really good business. Might be able to get you out of the funeral home, even. Just be on the hunt for what I need, and deliver those kidneys. And don't forget: if you find a good face candidate, I'll start spreading the word about your . . . quality services. I think we can do business for a long, long time, Angelo."

"That sounds real good, Bones. *Real* good."

*

I should never have trusted that bitch.

The Scotch whiskey was hitting him hard. Three down in a few hours had been plenty on an empty stomach. This was the time his self-loathing usually crept forward.

Six years down the tubes. All I have are the fucking debts. She got the house, the car, everything. All over one lousy mistake. One stupid malpractice lawsuit . . . they didn't even convict me on all counts!

He staggered to the bathroom, switched on the light. The room was hazy, shifting, too bright. He relieved his bladder, flushed, then swayed over the sink, staring into the mirror. He turned on the water and splashed some on his face, pulling his hands slowly down his features as the stream gurgled into the basin.

Another hoppin' Saturday night for Dr. Aiden-fucking-Burns.

The past several years had been a nightmare of professional mistakes and trauma. After the lawsuit filing, his life had been thrown into complete chaos. That was when Barbi had begun to snap; it was like watching super-slow-motion footage of a bullet tearing through a water balloon. The instant the bullet penetrates the form, the rubber of the balloon shreds and vanishes, leaving a tremulous, watery globe it in its place as the bullet spins to the other side. Everyone watching knows that it cannot stay that way for any length of time; that ultimately the water will collapse, without any boundaries, of its own weight. The final judgment had been that critical dissolution. The only way to fix the water balloon is to watch the film in reverse.

Life never goes in reverse, however, except in dreams or memories.

"I can't take this, Aiden! I–I don't know who you are anymore . . . Where did we go? This is what we have to look forward to?"

He had tried to soothe her, but she twisted away from his hand and collapsed into their living-room loveseat, reduced to inconsolable sobbing. On the stereo, George Benson's version of "This Masquerade" played mournfully in the background. Music had always been their refuge; now it seemed to mock them—like some emotionally aware backing track to a sordid melodrama. In the drive home she had said as much when "The Stranger" by Billy Joel had caused him to snap the radio off.

He sat on the couch across from the chair.

"I know this seems bad . . . I know it's been a rough time, Barb. But we have to . . . We have to just hang in there. It'll be reversed on appeal. It'll—"

"You don't know that, Aiden!"

His mouth worked quietly as he struggled to find the words. The sadness of her crying filled the space around them like the loss of a heartbeat, like the absence of hope. She reached for a box of tissues next to the chair and slowly regained her composure. Today, the final penalty-phase decision, had been the worst time since the disturbing revelations disclosed at trial.

It had unmasked the whole sordid reality: Burns's "professional arrogance" and his unusual methodologies, which conflicted with Hastur General's stated "core values." His "independent" and controversial research techniques had shocked the community—preoccupations with discarded fetal tissue and other, even more macabre experimentations on "beating heart" organ donors, and "rejuvenating" older people with transfusions of reclaimed plasma from deceased children. Previously, though the hospital had perhaps not "officially" condoned these actions, it was certainly aware of them, and had taken no issue with their ultimate outcomes bringing in millions in grant and research funds. As he explained it to the court, everything was done for the sake of the advancement of science and medicine . . . out of a desire to save the lives of others. An overwhelming need inspired by the deep hurt and profound respect centered around his late mother's memory.

That event—Mother's death from an iatrogenically introduced infection after cancer surgery—had been a catalyst for him and for his brother Mike. His sibling had missed out on medical school due to less than stellar grades, but Aiden had excelled. Both went to the same college, and Mike eventually made his career as a nurse. That was when his problems began—with access to the meds. Once Aiden had discovered his brother's drug abuse, his misguided attempts to cover it up had brought about more scrutiny. That could have been the extent of it had it not affected his work: The disastrous moment when everyone realized Dr. Burns—a superstar of regenerative medicine at the largest hospital in the area—had accidentally injured a patient, and ultimately caused his premature demise all due to an error made by his brother, resonated like a death knell. After the malpractice suit was brought against him, his future prospects slowly evaporated.

As the lawsuit dragged on for one year, then another, then a third, he was gradually seen as a pariah within the hospital's conservative organizational structure. He was not called to meetings as often. He was no longer consulted on complex cases in spite of his brilliance and experience. Journals rejected his papers. He was suspended from practicing at the hospital due to negative publicity. Soon he and Barbi were struggling financially. He was dismissed outright just ahead of the verdict. Not fired, just "no longer needed." Best of luck and all that.

Then came the jury's decision: the final monetary penalties, and the stripping of his medical license for two years. He narrowly avoided prison time, though his brother was sentenced to one year in jail and fined. Today's nadir was the only time in Aiden's life that he was glad their mother was dead, and that their father had killed himself.

Perhaps they had been fooling themselves? Living beyond their means for too many years. What was that saying? Republicans are one health crisis away from being Democrats? Similar here. One crisis away from a deathbed conversion, *he ruminated.*

Aiden suddenly realized, as he watched his wife dab at her eyes with the crumpled tissue, that he was staring at the end of his marriage. Granted, it had been a long, hard four years: financial adversities, legal disappointments, the miscarriage. Barbi was cracking with stress. He did not have it in his heart to blame her. Realistically, it was probably another few years before he could recover, if ever. He knew they could move so he could get a new license to practice in another state. Then he could start earning and dig out of the hole of debts and penalties. But it would not be easy. Not at all. And Mike was still in jail—his only living family except for Barbi.

After he watched his wife drive away in their silver Subaru Forester for the last time, the knot in his gut unwound. She had been his anchor; now he was adrift. But no matter how bad it was or how bad it was to become, Aiden knew he could never just leave his brother.

They were all they had left.

As he thought of everything and gazed into the mirror, Aiden was overcome with a mix of emotions: revulsion, sadness, rage.

With the water gently pouring from the faucet, he studied his face in the harsh fluorescent light. It had been three years since Barbi had divorced him; they had not spoken since. He still loved her, he supposed; or perhaps he just loved the idea of her, what she represented—affection, passion, life. His brother Mike had gotten out early for good behavior, and Aiden had helped him move to the same little college town. Aiden's beloved nieces, Camilla and Cassilda, refused to have contact with their father or with him; their mother, Hali, wanted them to have nothing more to do with Mike or any member of the Burns family, it seemed. In a way, he understood. In another way, it was hurtful, but the girls were now old enough to make these decisions for themselves. The ironic part, of course, was that by this time Aiden had been able to re-secure his medical license and complete a stint as part of a successful family practice. No one ever knew of his previous situation. No one except the ones who mattered the most in the world.

A new career in a new town. A new part of the country, even.

He had done exceptionally well there; it was such simple work for him, unlike the rigors of his previous tenure, he felt as though he could have done it in his sleep. In a way, he had: he was emotionally numb for nearly the first two years after Barbi and he had split. That opportunity led to his current position at the university, where he had been able to regroup, to gain some perspective. Unfortunately, Mike had put his hand back in the medicinal cookie jar at the clinic where he had been hired as a nursing assistant. They fired him after a few months. That's when Aiden had helped him get another job at a local funeral parlor. After a few months, Mike brought Angelo to Aiden's attention, and a new partnership was formed. Now, even more opportunity was opening up, and not just with Angelo.

Nevertheless, the crushing debts—over two million dollars—had aged him. He looked at his bleary, red eyes, puffy with drink, darkened by a lack of sleep, his disheveled button-down shirt, and stained tie. He had not shaved in a week, his face was sallow, his hair greasy. New lines had taken hold near his eyes, on his forehead, around his mouth. He was still having the panic attacks and much trouble sleeping; the continual haranguing of creditors only added to his frustration. That was why he often preferred sleeping in his office at the college over going to his shadowed and sad apartment.

He let Mike stay there, as his brother had little in the way of funds and credit at this point. They rarely saw each other, however, as Mike usually worked nights, and the cramped two-bedroom unit was too empty, too bleak for Aiden at times. At least here at the university he knew people would be around at some point; there was always someone on campus. It was comforting somehow.

"Mirrors," he said to his reflection at last, "always lie, don't they? We can't see our true selves, only a semblance of it." He huffed in amusement at his philosophical insight. The novelty of his cleverness was brief; he shut the water off, breathing in deeply. "So is staring into the looking-glass and not seeing anything the same as beholding the contemplative abyss?" He chuckled again.

Desperate times called for desperate measures . . .

The debts were what had plunged him into his new side activities with Angelo and his brother. And it was working. With the connections Angelo had made, and a few others from Mike, they were starting to make serious money with the body parts. There was, in fact, *too much* demand. They were always looking for more bodies and more types of tissue. It was not his preferred way of conducting his life, but it was better than drowning in debt and suffocating from despair.

"We only need to keep at it one more year," he mumbled. His head was starting to clear. He walked unsteadily from the bathroom over to the couch in his office, checking that the door was locked along the way.

3:01 A.M. Need to rest.

He stripped to his underwear, putting his clothes into the overnight bag he carried with him. He should to go to the apartment tomorrow, he decided; it had been nearly a week since he had been home. The onset of summer might improve his outlook.

Time for fresh clothes and to check on things.

*

Mike was not at the apartment. Not an uncommon event, but it still made Aiden uneasy: he was leery of his brother's drug issues and liked to be in touch every few days.

After a shower and a nice meal of intensely spicy Thai curry, Aiden washed his clothes while watching some television. He kept his cell phone close by, anxious to hear what had happened with the latest harvest Angelo had been dispatched to carry out for the legs and arms.

And did they get the fucking kidneys?

His phone woke him up from a fitful nap as the TV droned in the background; no caller information. Aiden noted the smell of rain was wafting through a cracked window, and that the day had slipped away into evening. He had told Mike repeatedly about leaving the apartment window open. The last thing they needed was someone snooping around, especially with all the parts they kept in the freezer chest.

"Hello?"

"Yeah, Aiden, it's Mike."

"Mike! Where are you? I'm at the apartment. Hey, remember what I said about the window?" His voice was edged; they had been over this dozens of times.

"Yeah, yeah. Sorry, man. Been distracted. I got good news and bad, thought you'd like to hear. Which one first?"

"Good news first. I'm feeling charitable."

"Cool, right. Well, like I got the kidneys—"

"Yes!"

Mike laughed over the line. "Yeah. Got 'em. Look pretty decent to me, too."

"Excellent; that is good news."

"Right. And I think that another cutter and I can get to the other harvest at the morgue tonight. Looks like we'll have that locked up. Angelo says he's got two good face candidates coming in tomorrow."

Aiden tightened his lips at this news. That meant he would have to pay them both and get the morphine prescription for Mike by Friday. He was conflicted about contributing to his brother's habit, but had to keep the long view in mind.

"Okay. Let's hope so."

There was a pause.

"That it?" Aiden offered at last.

"One thing," Mike replied. He lowered his voice: "I think Angelo might be getting wise that you're giving me a little extra."

"Really? Well, it's none of his business. Just don't let it slip—"

"I think he saw the note you left when we were dropping off some of the skin and bone samples."

"You let that fucking guy in the *apartment?* I thought we discussed that! I said not to even let him know the address!"

Silence.

Aiden: "So did he see that I've been cutting him out? How bad is it? Does he know we're working with the other mortician at the place outside of town?"

"I think he might. I think he suspects we're sort of phasing him out and giving him the harder jobs for less pay."

"Fuck! Well, okay, so what? Look, we've got just a few more gigs with Angelo to pull off; then I say we drop him. His hands are redder than ours. He won't talk. He just wants cash. We'll settle up and part ways; the out-of-town connection is better anyway 'cause he gets people from all over the state, not just in the city. More traffic, y'know?"

"Yeah, I hear you, man. I think we just need to be careful. Angelo's got a real bad temper, I've noticed. Bit of a sadist. Holds grudges. I've seen him . . . *do things*. Things that I think we'd not want near our little Burke-and-Hare operation, if you take my meaning. This is bad enough. Some of the things, well . . . get sort of necro."

Aiden was surprised to hear this. He was also taken aback at the direct reference by his brother to the nineteenth-century body snatchers from Ireland. It was one thing to skirt the edge of being modern-day "resurrectionists," but they were not murdering anyone, nor were they causing any harm to the living.

"I understand," he replied to Mike. "Well, let's get through this. I still need him for the week at least."

*

The last few harvests had gone exceptionally well. Aiden was relieved, as they brought a windfall in profit for the kidneys. In addition, the joints, skin patches, ligaments, and a few heart valves had netted a gross of nearly $128,000. His world was starting to look up.

True to form, as soon as he got his prescription Mike vanished. Sometimes he would be MIA for nearly a month, just working and dropping the occasional note at the apartment. At least until he began running out of stuff.

Angelo's prospects for the face transplant fell through; both were living donors, but they died suddenly. After that, they all parted company, and Mike switched to the other mortuary for employment, which also increased their side business exponentially. No more Angelo seemed to suit everyone involved better. The debt was becoming manageable at long last.

Aiden decided to concentrate on pushing his last proposal through for the transplant candidates: it was the car accident burn victim. The university board approved, and the candidate passed all preliminary tests. In addition, the patient had a minimal loss of facial bones, so that would make the operation less complex.

Now, it was a waiting game.

*

Fall was beginning to settle in. There was a swirl of color and a crisp smoky scent to the air complemented by long shadows of late afternoon. In the past few months, Aiden's fortunes had dramatically improved. They had been able to gain more funding and keep Angelo at bay just long enough to switch away from working with him. Even Mike had decreased his need for morphine after meeting a young woman in a drug-counseling program. It appeared that the deepest part of the last few years' horrors was finally receding.

"Dr. Burns." It was his secretary. Aiden looked from his computer to the intercom on his desk.

"Yes?"

"There is a face available for the transplant. They have prepped the candidate and need you in Surgical Theater II in thirty minutes."

Aiden was surprised, but excited. "Perfect, Brenda. Tell everyone to muster there. Going to be a long night."

Once in Surgical Theater II, there was a conference. They had rehearsed this moment and practiced on animatronic models and cadavers for months, but the real thing was always different. The plan was gone over carefully for about an hour, with the roles and positions reiterated. After everyone and their alternates were assigned and instructed, they all changed clothes and scrubbed.

Inside the room, the anesthesiologist was already working. The candidate's body was screened off except for the head and neck, which had been swabbed with brown-yellow betadine solution, the surgical area marked with a series of black lines over the puckered ridges and planes of the patient's ruined countenance. Dr. Burns stood for a moment, regarding the historic scene, which had an atmosphere not unlike that of a surreal party or play with all the participants in costume, the thump of the aerator and the blip of the heart monitor creating a kind of soundtrack.

I'm back. This is my return . . . and it has all been worth it.

Aiden gripped the cauterizing scalpel in his hand and leaned over the unconscious man's figure, whispering: "We're about to change your life, Mr. Thomas. I will bring you back from your oblivion." Burns then glanced up at his lead nurse and nodded; above the facial cover, her dark brown eyes were shining in the focused lights of the operating room.

Another assistant wheeled the chilling cart with the new face to be used for the transplantation to the operating table.

"Dr. Burns, I was given a message by the harvest team," the lead nurse, said.

"Oh, yes? What would that be?" Burns gestured for the nursing assistant to take the top off the container.

"I don't understand it, but the guy said 'Please inform Dr. Burns that I've located some eyes, too.'"

The room started to spin for the doctor—the surgical lights trailing in the starless black of the room like twin suns sinking into a bottomless lake. It felt as though everyone in the chamber was watching him now behind their operating masks, as if the space were unexpectedly shrinking to a point of cosmic singularity.

The nurse pulled the lid off, the stark lights adding a nightmarish dimension to her flourish of movement. Gingerly, almost in slow motion, she lifted the pallid visage within the container by its tattered edges—presenting to the surgeon a translucent, yellowy combination of skin, fat, muscle, and veins like some horrid, quivering disguise: it was a blank-eyed mirror image of himself.

Mike!

Aiden Burns screamed as the room died away.

A CARCASS, WAITING

Behind,
The past solemnly lies—
Dormant, quiet—
But with so much left unrelated;

Ahead,
The future desperately paces—
Implacable, rude—
With no expectations, and nothing yet to show;

Between,
The present tentatively cowers—
Unsure, confused—
All potential reconciliation steeped in silent doubt.

Above,
Everything abides—
Timeless, patient—
Distantly mocking any fears, yet without malice or hatred;

Beneath,
Nothing remains—
Staggeringly blank—
Providing no protestations, and with nowhere else to go;

Around,
Time and space collide—
Chaotic, emboldened—
As life at first wanes, then blooms, violently without.

When the frantic end rises,

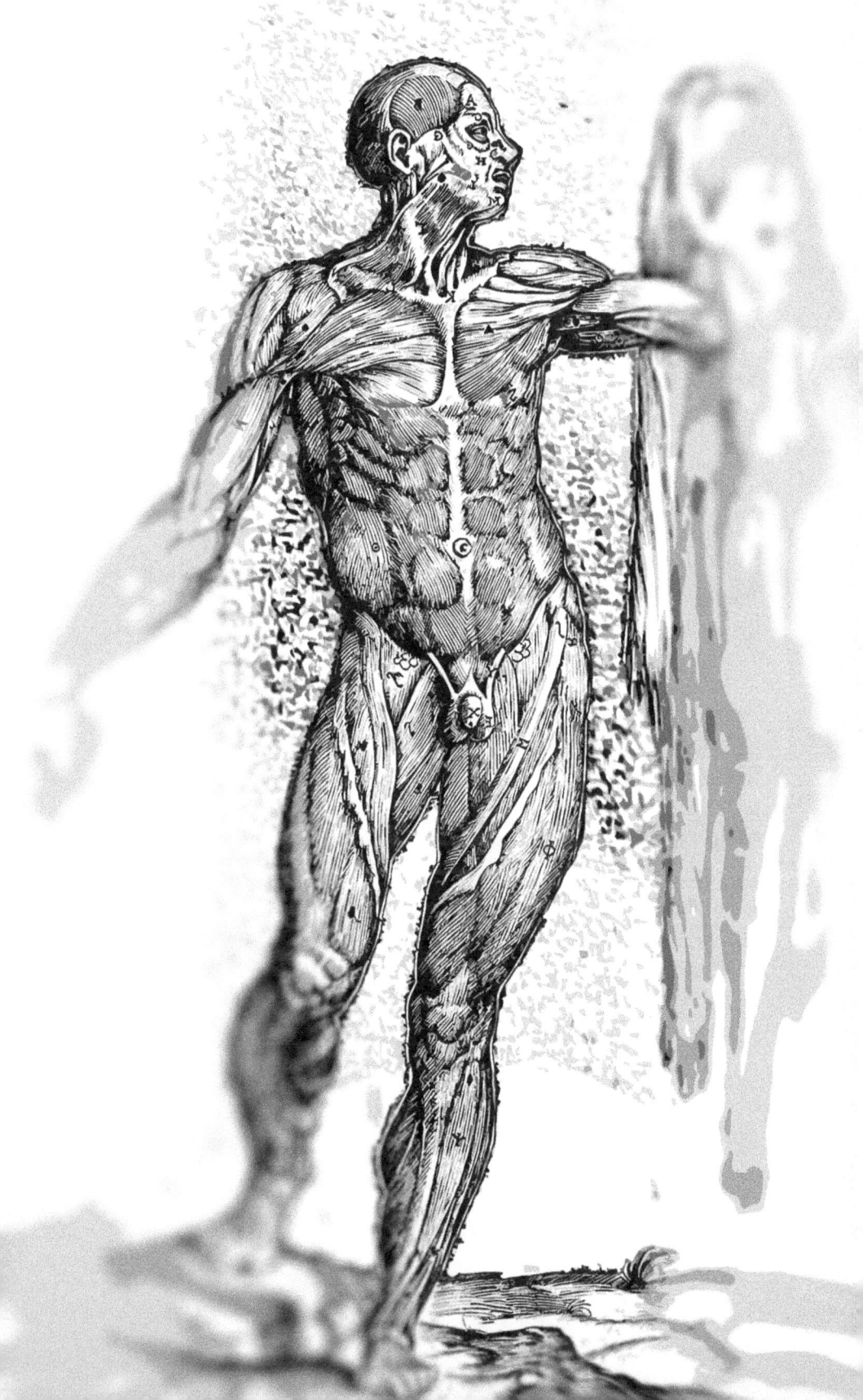

And the beginning gently subsides,
Dim, cold reality breaks
As a new dawn is realized;
We are but a shadowed agent of tomorrow
And the mournful sentinels of yesterday,
So while the moment erodes from remembrance
We celebrate our decay.

Thus as season yields to season,
And ashes mill into dust,
We while away each instant
With petty concerns, fears, and lusts;
Simpleminded and content,
We are oddly arrogant and proud—
Frequently lost and myopic,
Swathed in our insular mental shrouds.

We follow extinction's path,
Oblivious to our fate,
In a grim carnival of souls,
Joylessly parading;
At the lonesome, wretched last,
We comprehend, too late,
That each of us is nothing more
Than a sad carcass, waiting.

THE SHADOW OF HEAVEN

There are more things in heaven and earth . . .
Than are dreamt of in your philosophy.
            —William Shakespeare, *Hamlet* 1.5.166
                        (Hamlet to Horatio)

I

"There—I think I see it, Commander."

Ensign Adams's breath disappeared overhead as he lowered his binoculars, pointing with a gloved hand at the unstable horizon through the ice-rimmed main windows of the ship. "Looks like something about ten kilometers out, sir." Backlit by the windows, he turned to face Commander Merritt, the senior officer aboard the destroyer USS *Higgins*. Cloaked in his winter overcoat, the ensign's brittle voice seemed distant in the cold dry air, his words nearly obliterated by the surging wind and unforgiving swells of the squall. Outside, colossal waves, some the size of buildings, slammed the *Higgins*—exploding across the ship's icebound hull in frosty white plumes, adding to the inches-deep transparent slick of frozen seawater on the deck as she plunged further into one of the most hostile environs on the planet: the Southern Ocean. Gales such as this arose suddenly and with terrifying ferocity this close to Antarctica, reducing visibility to a few feet, churning the barren seascape into a foamy lather as it thrust icebergs the size of city blocks into the path of interlopers to this foreboding, isolated part of the world. At times, mighty whitecaps pounded on the destroyer with such titanic fury that they caused the vessel to flinch backward, bobbing like an oversized cork in the roiling black depths.

Merritt, his drawn face numb from the chill, carefully considered the ensign's words, leaning against an interior deck rail to keep his balance as they rocked in the grip of the storm. Bringing his binoculars to his face, he scanned the dead gray interface between leaden sky and dark water beyond the icy windows Adams was motioning toward, noting the faint curtain of blue-green ripples from the southern lights, streaked by rose-colored lightning ribbons in the distance as freezing night collapsed around them. Even on the closed bridge, the saline-tinged atmosphere had gotten so frigid that the inside of his nose crystallized with each breath.

Our luck to be the closest in the vicinity of a distress call.

"Are you sure you saw a vessel? Maybe it was a 'berg," the commanding officer asked at last.

"It didn't look like an iceberg." Adams was scrutinizing the horizon as he spoke. "One moment, sir."

As he worked against the storm's fury, the commander was troubled that, in their attempts to discover the exact whereabouts of the missing research ship *Terra Australis Incognita,* they might have gone astray. The weary leader and his crew of just over two hundred were stuck now, committed to the search even as they struggled with the dreadful conditions approximately 300 miles off the coast of West Antarctica—well off-course from their originally assigned bearing based on *Australis*'s last communiqué. Merritt was further aggravated that they had been pulled into this mess just as the *Higgins* was returning for shore leave after a long, tedious mission—subsonic underwater audio testing. The original search-and-rescue order had instructed them to triangulate the position of the troubled *Australis* once they were within its last known trajectory, but it concerned him that perhaps she had lost power after her final transmission to the Oceanographic Institute of San Diego, drifting farther than anyone had anticipated. That could mean she was gone—especially if these had been the circumstances for her and her crew in the two days it had taken the *Higgins* to re-route.

"Still not seeing it, Adams." Merritt grimaced in frustration.

"Sorry, sir. It was there just a minute ago."

"Any recent pings, McConnell?" Merritt asked, addressing the warrant officer.

The haunting Mayday call that McConnell had picked up as they were adjusting course, scratchy with static and crosstalk, had made it very difficult to decipher who it was, but the coordinates and the radar image supported the notion that it had come from *Australis*. Or at least from a crewmember who might be stranded on the so-called 'new islands' that *Australis* had been allowed to detour and inspect by the Institute.

"Negative, sir," McConnell replied.

Contemplative, Merritt lowered his binoculars, sighing in annoyance as he stroked his face. *Throw into the mix that the closer we get to the last known heading of* Australis *the worse the fucking weather gets . . . the more radio-electronic interference—faulty GPS signals, slow clocks, bad wireless connections. Adds up to a lot of irritating bullshit . . . Oh well—'Uneasy lies the head that wears a crown,' as they say . . .*

Higgins had endured several of these storms, as powerful as any Merritt had ever encountered in his twenty-plus years as a sailor, in their efforts to find the *Australis*. Peering through his binoculars again as the mammoth destroyer heaved and fell like some vast rollercoaster—lights flickering, deck rolling in the strong seas—the senior officer thought he vaguely made out what the ensign had seen: a shadowy triangular central mass situated among a scattering of large icebergs looming along the periphery of his vision like some ethereal vanguard of the *Flying Dutchman*. He frowned while adjusting the focus ring, his brow wrinkled in annoyance as he squinted past the thickening fog and billowing sea spray. *Christ, it's like something wants to keep us away . . .*

He glanced over at McConnell, his gray-haired scalp bristling. "You seeing this?"

McConnell worked to keep his footing as he peered through his binoculars. "Aye . . . *some*thing. Appears manmade, sir, but hard to make out through the mist and—"

A crackle from the headset around his neck interrupted him. Placing the speaker to his ear, he listened intently, then moved over to his station, his dark features pressed into a look of apprehension.

Merritt: "What's happening, McConnell?"

"Not—not sure, sir. There's a lot of static; I thought I heard . . . a *voice*. It was coming in on the same frequency as the last transmission—"

Continuing to monitor the gloom outside, Adams said, "*Definitely* something there, Commander. Looks to be a modest-sized vessel."

McConnell: "I've got something—putting up on speakers, sir. I have a radar reflection, too. One small shape and a few larger masses; the larger areas *could* be land, but hard to say in this climate . . . And I checked again—not on our maps."

A smoky haze of static filled the room, pushing back the sounds of the tempest for an instant: <<CH-CH-CH Gree! Mayday! [*blip, blip, blip*] Gree! CH-CH-*ay!* [*blip, blip, blip*]>>

More intense static. Then, garbled: "If you can hear my voice, please acknowledge! [*blip, blip, blip*] . . . is not— [*blip, blip, blip*] My name is Christopher Faust, over. [*blip, blip, blip*] . . . urgent mes— [*blip, blip, blip*] . . . communicate! Repeat: This is—"

Silence. The wind howled in the sunless tumult outside the *Higgins,* sending chucks of ice and snow to shatter against the windows of the darkened bridge. Lightning seared again: closer, redder, like an eruption of stroboscopic tendrils cracking the black-ice sky into pieces. Distant thunder bellowed.

"McConnell, stay on that frequency, but keep monitoring the others. Adams, your thoughts?"

The young ensign was staring into the starless night, struggling to keep his equilibrium in the storm. "I—I believe it's *Australis,* sir. Who else would be this far from McMurdo? Granted, farther away than we expected her to be, but we heard the distress call . . . so we're obligated to check it out, Commander."

Merritt looked again, the stiff rubber eyecups of the Steiner chafing his eyelids. Illuminated by flashes of scarlet lightning, the triangular shape appeared to be a bow, with part of a mast attached as well; perhaps a half-submerged wreck, though it was too dim, too turbulent to make out anything definitive.

"Aye," the commander said. "Set a course for it."

II

"Looks like we've found her, Commander. No one here, though." Ensign Adams released the button on his handheld as he stared into the blue-toned water, the white mast and bow of the sunken *Australis* thrusting up from the briny deep like the hand of a skeleton. The elements had relented since their post-midnight arrival; the ocean was almost peaceful.

At first light, Commander Merritt had deemed it safe enough to dispatch a small advance team of four men through the half-mile or so of chop between the moorage of the *Higgins* and the suspected wreck of the *Australis*. Though slightly overcast, the sun was evident, clear, though quite low on the horizon even now, at mid-day; it was urgent that they discern what was happening before night fell and the temperatures dropped.

"Roger that, Adams," McConnell replied. "Stand by."

As Adams and his crew of three awaited their next orders on the drifting rigid-hulled inflatable, he studied the *Australis*: it was spooky, surreal. The water here was so clear he could see far down into it, almost to the bridge of the research vessel. Straining, he swore he could see something . . . something large; a supple darkness—

"Adams, we have something near you, but not from the wreck. Over."

Startled from his thoughts by McConnell's gruff drawl, Adams replied: "Roger that. What do you have?"

"Well, there's a signal coming from nearby. The coordinates are dodgy, as there seems to be some strange interference. Looks like it's coming from that mass I was explaining from the radar, though. Some seismic disturbances there. I got another signal a while ago like a voice, too. See anything? Over."

"Actually, yeah; over to my left there's a big fogbank. Looks like about eight hundred or so feet away. Could it be from there? Over."

"That's about the proximity of the radar image. Over."

Adams brought his binoculars up. As he peered through them, he thought he saw something large move in the mist on the horizon: *What the hell was* that?

"Roger, McConnell. I see something; request permission to investigate. Over."

There was a long pause.

"Roger, Adams; weather's returning. Merritt says you've got an hour. Over."

III

"Let us go then, you and I,
When the evening is spread out against the sky—"
Like the Indianapolis *at the bottom of the deep . . .*
Down to a dreamless sleep . . .
Drifting,
Spiraling:

IV

Back onboard the *Higgins,* Adams was shaken, dazed, as he reported what the search party had discovered: "So there *are* some islands, Commander." He looked from Merritt to McConnell as they stood in the infirmary, regarding the apparent sole survivor of the *Australis:* an unconscious man now lying on the sickbay table. "The radar image was correct. We found *Australis,* and there was something else—something deeper in the water. Looked like it was poking around in the wreckage—"

"What? Like a seal? A shark or something? Or did you see a body?" Merritt asked, his voice edged.

"I—I can't say; it was some weird . . . *black*-looking shape, but iridescent, too. Like oil on water. It seemed to be part of something else even larger. Maybe it was just the water playing tricks on my eyes, or a part of the ship, but—" Adams looked to the floor. "Anyway, after we went through the fog, we all noted that the temperature was rising; it was becoming quite humid, too. I had to lose a jacket, I got so warm. Then, as we disembarked onto this beach we landed on, we were accosted by these *giant* . . . flying bats or something, but with feathers. They were shrieking and carrying on. Sounded very human at times. Like a cat in heat. Our compasses were flipping out, and that's when one of my guys saw a helicopter blade half-buried in the sand. We formed a search line and walked for a mile or so—"

Commander Merritt's hands clinched. "No one authorized that, Adams! You should have radioed—"

"We *tried,* sir. The radios went dead right after we landed, and once we found the pieces of the helicopter . . . Respectfully, we weren't trying to get into trouble; we just wanted to see if there was anyone hurt."

McConnell: "He's right, sir. The radios were unresponsive after the first forty-five minutes or so, and they were DOA back onboard."

After a silence, Commander Merritt nodded: "Carry on, Adams. Then what happened?"

"Well, we thought we heard screams—human screams—coming from somewhere up the beach, though the place has strange acoustics. The surf, the wind make it pretty noisy, not to mention those flying things squealing overhead, so it could have been coming from the dense vegetation toward the center of the island. Anyway, after about ten more minutes of walking, we ascended a small dune, and that's where the rest of the helicopter was." Adams swallowed, staring at the C.O. in trancelike, unblinking remembrance. He motioned toward the man on the bed. "We found him like this . . . completely nude, crumpled up next to a bunch of half-frozen papers and the debris of the 'copter with the walkie-talkie in his hand. Only a few scratches on him from what we could see, just knocked out. I'm . . . *amazed* he's alive," Adams said. His voice was quivering. "How—how could he be *alive?* In those temperatures . . . *naked?* I mean, it was warmer, but still plenty cold if you're exposed like that. And—and the helicopter was *demol-*

ished, as if there was an accident or something. The bloody clothing next to him had a tag: *Faust.* That's the guy from the transmissions, right, McConnell?"

McConnell was gawking at the man in the infirmary bed, stunned, his hand covering his mouth. He shot a glance at Commander Merritt, whose red-eyed gaze was also fixed on the sleeping man, and nodded. "Tell him about the other thing you brought back, Adams."

Merritt broke away from his thoughts. "There was something else? What?"

Adams swallowed, his face suddenly ashen, and looked to the floor. Merritt looked again at McConnell, who took a deep breath.

"What did Adams bring back, McConnell? Another survivor? Where—?"

"No, sir," Adams interrupted. "Not a survivor. It's in another lab; one of the medics is investigating it."

"Well, let's go see, Adams," the commander said. He looked at McConnell. "I want to know the *second* this guy comes to."

McConnell nodded again. "Yes, sir."

V

"Commander, have you heard the term 'globster' before?" Medic Aaron Randolph asked.

"Yes, I know it. Like sea monsters or something."

The medic smiled, thin blond hair falling over his forehead, freckled cheeks creasing at the corners of his eyes as he looked between the sullen Adams and his C.O. The ship was beginning to roll gently as night approached and a storm once more buffeted the *Higgins.* "That's *sort of* it, sir. Globsters are . . . kind of mysterious relics that wash up periodically. They can be hard to identify, as they have features of several different animals, or it *seems* as if they do. Almost like the chimeras from Greek mythology. Some people even claim they're 'cryptids'— previously unknown or undocumented creatures, possibly related by era or locale, like the Loch Ness Monster or Bigfoot. I mean, maybe they are, but it's doubtful; apocryphal accounts of plane wing gremlins,

Chupacabras, and moth men make no sense, as they're generally too divergent from one another." Randolph paused, then added: "Of course, there are exceptions. They didn't think giant squids, okapis, coelacanths, or Komodo dragons were real once either. Usually, though, it's a *lot* less interesting than that—they're just pieces of some animal, like that huge blue eyeball that washed up a couple of years back that they now think belonged to a dead marlin, or the badly decayed carcass of a big shark or whale—"

Adams looked up sharply, eyes wide. "That's no whale, Randy. Look again!"

The medic raised his hand: "I hear you. It's weird all right! But stuff is starting to show up all over: things that were unknown before from the deep, or critters that normally never appear where they're found. Even mass strandings. Happened just recently in L.A.—one day a damn deep-sea oarfish washed up, completely intact, then a few days later a barely living Alaskan saber-toothed whale! They say it might be global warming or something, who knows? It's weird, though, and becoming more common. Not sure what *this* thing is; I checked it out under the 'scope, too. It's not like any other specimen we have onboard, that's for sure. The cryptozoologists would *love* it."

Merritt straightened up. "Can I see what you're talking about?"

"Absolutely, Commander. Right this way."

They walked to the rear of the room where the storage freezer and the other autopsy tools were stowed. The medic opened the locker door, pulled a covered tray from inside, and set it on the counter. The tray was about two feet long and over a foot wide; the white cloth covering the specimen barely concealed the bulging object underneath. The medic smiled at the C.O. and the ensign. "It's dense, heavy." He pulled the cloth away unceremoniously.

The thing on the tray was hard to comprehend; there was no visual context for it. It was a drab gray, mottled with blooms of light pink. On one end it was severed all the way through, the raw wound displaying its musculature and a core of bone. This side was slender, smooth; toward the other end of its length there were what appeared to be scales that became an almost chitinous, hard appendage of some type, resembling a fixed-open claw. Within this structure, there was a softer retracted piece with what looked to be a suckered tentacle covered in miniature hooks. This black flesh was pliant, and the appendage seemed to be gently moving within.

Merritt's eyes widened. "Is that thing—"

The medic nodded. "Yes: it's moving. It's been moving since I got it."

Adams spoke at last: "It was moving around next to Faust on the beach. Pretty vigorously."

"Jesus. What the hell *is* it?" Merritt asked, stepping back in revulsion. "And that smell! Is that—?"

"Yes," Randolph confirmed. "As it warms up, it starts emanating that strange odor . . . like plastic burning."

The intercom interrupted them: "Commander Merritt, this is McConnell. Faust is awake, sir. Not said anything yet, but he woke up a little while ago."

The senior officer looked from Adams to Medic Randolph to the slowly writhing thing on the countertop. "Keep me posted on this, Randolph; I want to know what you find out about the microscopic results. Christ—gives me the fucking *creeps*. Let's go, Adams."

Merritt thumbed the button on the wall speaker: "Roger that, McConnell. On the way."

VI

Drifting,
Spiraling:
The breath of a sigh,
Or the blink of an eye
Is all that it takes;
And then the dreamer wakes—

VII

"Faust. My name is Christopher Faust," the man on the bed replied. His voice was weak, strangled.

Commander Merritt: "Were you with the *Australis* crew?"

Faust nodded; his gaze was distant, fixed on something just beyond the officer. Ensign Adams watched Merritt as he continued to question the man. "Where are the other members of your crew? Did they go inland?"

Faust nodded again. "Yes. Three . . . of them went to the center of the island. We started with nine. I was . . . the aviator." Faust's voice was curiously flat and atonal. He never made eye contact, just kept his gaze fixed straight ahead. "We . . . were attacked."

"Attacked?" Merritt shared a surprised look with Adams. "What do you mean? By whom?"

"Not whom—*what.*"

"Okay, then," Adams said. "What?"

Faust slowly, mechanically, turned his head toward the ensign, his eyes staring forward. "By . . . the things in the air. The things from the sea."

There was a tense silence.

"Okay, airman Faust," Merritt said at last, forcing a smile. "You've had a rough time. Let's reconvene this later, once you've been able to regain your strength."

Faust methodically turned to face Merritt again, features slack, rubbery, eyes unblinking.

"They're . . . alive on the *inside,* Commander. Three of them went to the center of the island."

Merritt nodded. "We'll see if we can—"

"And then," Faust interrupted, "the dreamer wakes."

Adams gasped, and the C.O.'s head snapped back in astonishment.

"What?" Merritt stammered, "What did you say, Faust?"

"The dreamer has *awakened.*"

After a long and uncomfortable silence, Adams signaled Merritt to step out of the quarters.

"Let's go over and visit Randy again, sir," the ensign said as the two men moved away from the infirmary.

VIII

"Wow. That's really *weird*," Medic Randolph said. "What does it mean? Is it from a book or something?"

Adams huffed. "Yeah, I'll say . . . it's from a weird dream *I've* been having—"

"And every time you nap or go to sleep," Merritt interjected, "this dream picks up at *exactly* the same place . . . Same strange feeling, same bizarre imagery, right?"

Adams stared at Merritt, his mouth hanging open. Finally: "Yes."

A cold sweat broke out on the C. O.'s body, yet he felt too warm. "I've been having it, too. Started around the time that we began looking for the *Australis*. Just shy of a week ago—"

"Oh shit, this is freaking me out, sir!" Adams exclaimed, plopping into a chair in Randolph's lab.

The medic stared at the two men who seemed suddenly unable to communicate. "Pretty strange. *Twilight Zone*–type stuff . . . Well, not to add *too* much more weird to it, sir, but I found something . . . *interesting* during the microscopic exam."

Merritt cleared his throat, rubbed his eyes, then turned his attention to Randolph. "Okay. What have you learned?"

"It's odd, I'll give you that, but just hear me out a minute . . ."

The medic sat down with the others, grabbed a pen and some paper and started writing and sketching. After a few moments, he began to explain his findings: "So this organism is . . . *unusual* physiologically. Perhaps you're familiar with the concept of the Hayflick Limit?"

Merritt shook his head.

"Well," the medic continued, "it's an observation in genetics. Basically, it's the idea that there are physical limits to the number of times a cell can divide . . . under certain conditions these limitations are able to be chemically or virally circumvented, avoiding the natural process of cellular suicide known as apoptosis. This thing not only looks to have solved this problem, but also has a 'workaround' for the shortening of telomeres as a creature ages. Conceptually, telomeres are the ends of genes that are worn down by cell division; imagine that they're like the little plastic caps on the tips of shoelaces that keep them from fraying. 'Younger' telomeres keep the genes viable. This is also the case with several cancers—that they can keep the telomeres 'young.' As a result, damage arises, in part, due to *unchecked* cellular division. Normally that's a good thing, as it would impact the length of the telomeres negatively, thus applying a kind of brake to out-of-control division—" Randolph drew some examples on the paper to assist the visualization; Merritt nodded for him to continue.

"Anyway, from what I can tell with this thing, there's very rapid, *controlled* cellular division, and an ability to deliberately allocate cell speciation. So in a way, these tissues have *characteristics* of a tumor, but without the need for a continuous—or in this instance *any*—blood supply, as they appear to take oxygen directly from the atmosphere; the integument acts as a porous gas exchange membrane, similar to the way insects breathe, but more complex. Sort of like an external lung." The medic glanced over to Adams, who seemed to understand.

"So what does that mean?" Adams asked, leaning forward.

Medic Randolph tilted back in his chair and crossed his arms. "Not clear, but it looks as if it makes these cells immortal. Not only that, but there's another strange element . . ." Randolph returned to the sketch paper. "See where I drew this? Here, and here?'

Adams and Merritt nodded their heads in understanding.

"It appears these cells are peculiar hybrids of some kind. They have aspects of genetic mosaicism, and are these little . . . *independent units* . . . they're like tiny mirrors of the larger organism—"

Merritt: "I'm not following."

Adams picked up the explanation. "What I think it means," he said as he glanced at Randolph, "is that *each* cell is a microcosm of the complete organism."

"Exactly," said Randolph. "All the material is there; each cell appears to have a pluripotent cellular reserve. It's not only immortal, like certain jellyfish, but *self-organizing;* completely contained within itself. And not only that, but it seems that *every* cell is on some level . . . *conscious* for lack of a better word—"

"What are you saying, Randolph?" Merritt asked, touching his temple as he struggled to understand.

"I'm saying, Commander, that the cells react not just as *cells*—meaning with respect to extreme heat, cold, and some of the chemical agents I've applied to both the biopsy cultures and the entire appendage—but they cannot be 'killed' in the normal sense of the term; they regenerate, and relatively quickly. Not only that: they behave as though they have a type of 'collective awareness' and each can respond accordingly to the stimuli or circumstances as either a) a unified being, or b) as an autonomous *piece* of that organism, thus insuring survival at *all* costs. They even seem to be able to absorb and replicate other proteins, which gives them the ability to . . . *become* that protein."

Adams laughed without humor. "Oh my *God.* You mean like that fucking eighties movie?"

Randolph looked surprised. "Yeah, actually. Quite protean. Just like that, or *Invasion of the Body Snatchers.* There are other examples in nature microscopically, and so on. Besides, this isn't quite the same. I seriously doubt this is an alien; it's probably just an evolutionary strategy. Most likely a viral thing, or at least started that way. Hell, turns out a shitload of our so-called 'junk DNA' is comprised of retroviruses that functionally seem to have no purpose now. Might've had some uses at one time, but those uses are genetically 'turned off,' 'cause we don't need them due to the way we've evolved. Proof of that is the way our wounds heal; we have most of the same DNA as, say, a salamander, but they can regenerate arms and legs, and we can't. We just scar over."

Merritt's head was swimming. "So what did you do with the—"

"With the specimen?" Adams finished.

Randolph nodded toward the storage freezer. "In there; won't hurt it, but slows it down quite a bit. In fact, I noticed that the severed part is re-growing. Looks like it's trying the re-create the missing body."

"Shit! How do we rid of the fucking thing?" Merritt was genuinely alarmed.

Randolph assured him: "No worries, sir. It needs a *lot* of oxygen to facilitate this process. It's fairly immune to temperature extremes, but it can't stay submerged—kills the tissue in a matter of minutes based on my tests; of course, seems likely that a completely . . . *integrated* organism might be able to overcome that problem. Could be multiple types of organisms, too: they reported other strange creatures there, right?" He paused, noting the concern on the C.O.'s features. "But with respect to this thing, Commander, don't be too worried—it takes a while to re-grow whole pieces. Probably a few days or more depending on size, maybe longer. The absorption trick is faster, but has similar limitations. I mean, it's an 'organic machine' in a way, so while the duplicated components are nearly perfect, they occupy a state between being alive and dead. Besides," Randolph said, shrugging, "this is the find of a *lifetime*—we need to bring it back with us."

Before Merritt could mount a protest, the intercom sounded: McConnell.

"Commander, something . . . *interesting* is happening. Could you please report to the bridge?"

"What is it?" Merritt asked, pressing the switch.

"The ship near the island, the *Indianapolis* has—"

Adams gave a stunned look to Merritt: "Did you say *Indianapolis,* McConnell?" There was a pause.

"Sorry, sir. I'm tired, and I've been having this crazy dream . . . I mean the *Australis*—she's completely sunk now."

IX

Equipped with sidearms, survival gear, and machetes, they returned to the island the next morning. Once on the beach, Faust stoically led Adams, Merritt, and three others into the forest at the center. McConnell had briefed them about increasing seismic activity during the past day, warning them to be mindful of possible tremors.

Overhead, huge bird creatures the size of small cars swooped and pirouetted in the overcast sky. As the team was making its landing in the surf, Adams managed to photograph a bizarre, man-sized purple and red mega-crab exoskeleton that was drifting in a backwater near some crags. As was the previous case, compasses, radios, and GPS devices became unreliable.

Inside the canopy, the kaleidoscope of brilliantly plumed flowers, lush plants, and fantastically odd-looking—even menacing—giant insects was overwhelming: The place was an explosion of noise, a jumble of odors, a riot of color. The weather had graced them with a fortunate reprieve.

"Christ, the biodiversity of this place is unbelievable. It's covered with all manner of independent ecosystems," Adams observed, slicing though the thorny undergrowth with his blade, face slicked with sweat. Merritt nodded in breathless agreement, but before he could speak, an awful shriek peeled through the tangled wilderness. It was human: female.

"Faust, you mentioned that *Australis* had a woman onboard?" Merritt asked, wiping sweat away with his sleeve. They paused, quietly trying to ascertain the direction that the scream had come from.

"Yes," Faust replied, staring at Merritt, his face waxen, his demeanor indifferent. After another moment, he pointed. "That way."

X

The breath of a sigh,
Or the blink of an eye
Is all that it takes;
And then the dreamer wakes—
"What if Earth
Be but the shadow of Heaven, and things therein?"

XI

The explorers had reached an opening in the mega-flora, the evident remnants of a collapsed volcano caldera: it was hot, humid; the otherworldly antithesis of Antarctica. Even more incredibly, inside the caldera were the apparent ruins of a vast city, with indications of a long-dead, yet obviously advanced, civilization. Merritt was in a state of mental shock as the team hacked away at more overgrowth. Caressing the intricate stone buildings, marveling at the complex etchings that scored the coarse rock edifices, some more than three stories tall, he was astonished that this place existed, and wondered about the people that had carved these stones. *How many other places are like this on Earth, just waiting to be uncovered?* The commander took note of the sky. It was getting dark, and he observed that, strangely, there were no animals or insects to be found in this area. The heavy air was still, musky, preternaturally quiet.

"*Help . . . Help us!*" It was a hushed, breathy cry from somewhere in the twilight.

Merritt: "Adams! Did you hear that?"

The rest of the search crew paused to listen. Once more: "Help . . ."

Deep in the interior, the landing party found her: Julia Murphy—former crewmember of the *Terra Australis Incognita*.

What was left of her, at least.

XII

As the Moon's shadow eclipses the Sun,
So Man stumbles; and thus ends his run—

XIII

Murphy was lying in a supine position, naked on the ground near one of the buildings: The dim light from the sky overpowered the brilliant light originating from large, ornate green and blue fungi covering the lower part of her torso and obliterating her legs. As they watched, the men could see the carnivorous fungus creeping across her skin, dissolving it and fueling their grim, heatless glow.

"Help me . . . Please help . . ." Her face was sweaty, her breath shallow, her dry lips cracked.

Even though he was horrified, Merritt felt compelled to act and rushed past the stunned group to get near the stricken woman. "I'm Commander Scott Merritt, of the USS *Higgins*." Leaning closer to her, he swallowed back a stab of bile, fighting a surge of nausea at the sickly-sweet odor coming from her mouth. His mind was racing as he suddenly yearned to be home with his family. He felt for this poor girl; she reminded him not only of his wife, but also of all the things he most cherished, that he was compelled to do anything to protect. She smiled wanly, then unleashed a blood-freezing scream of agony. Merritt's chest thundered in pity and terror.

"It—it chased us in here . . ." Julia's bony arms were shriveled, drawn into a pugilistic formation, Merritt noticed; he distantly remembered that as a sign of neurological damage. The fungus was aggressive, moving from the exposed viscera of her guts and over her chest by fractions of inches in just a few minutes.

"It chased us . . . into the city . . . then . . . Captain Roland slipped. That . . . that was him." She motioned with her head to a blackened knot of dehydrated shapes. Even the bones had been dissolved by the fungus; the only thing remotely humanoid was its general size and form, and possibly a lump that resembled the jawless head of a lamprey. The ground rocked slightly, followed by a low rumble, not unlike thunder in the distance: a very minor quake. "Dr. Crowe tried to save him, but . . . it got him, too."

"There were three of you?" Merritt asked, face softly illuminated by the surreal glow of the predatory fruiting bodies, as eerie and distressing as a corpse candle. Merritt suddenly understood why there were no other animals here: the area was overrun by the creeping fungi, dimly glowing all around as the daylight extinguished. The other patches were smaller; less recently fed, he suspected, and the whole place was littered with similar black masses to the erstwhile Captain Roland.

Other animals! Jesus, it's like this whole island is alive.

"My *God . . .*" Adams had made the same mental connection just then: "We have to *leave,* sir! It's trying to lure us in!"

"No!" Julia screamed. *"Save me!"* At that instant, her mouth exploded outward with slimy black mold, the lower portion of her face collapsing like a deflated mask, the eyeballs falling into the pulsating, radiant mass of mushrooms and bloody tissue.

Merritt screamed: he jumped backward in abject horror and panic as the fungus consumed the girl.

Too late.

XIV

Thus ends his run—
"I should have been a pair of ragged claws
Scuttling across the floors of silent seas."

XV

On the *Higgins,* McConnell was frustrated.

He had not been able to raise anyone for hours, and now the party was stranded on the island for the night. Even though they had been lucky with the weather most of the day—no way that could hold much longer—the seismic readings had spiked recently. He felt a certain amount of dread that a major event was likely in the immediate future. Something about the whole scenario deeply disturbed him, but he was hard-pressed to articulate exactly what it was; the sooner they abandoned this godforsaken place, the better he would feel. It reminded him of when he was working on the blowout after the *Deepwater Horizon* disaster in the Gulf of Mexico, not far from his hometown of New Orleans. The name of the well prospect had been Macondo, just like the fictional town created by Gabriel García Márquez in his books. McConnell recalled that those had been nightmarish times, almost as surreal as the events in some of Márquez's work, as though the earth were finally rebelling against the insult of humans overreaching their assumed dominion. BP, Transocean, and Halliburton covered up a lot, but there were things he had seen that still sickened him: trapped sea turtles burned alive; birds drowning because they were too heavy to fly away due to the thick crude slicking their bodies; massive, undocumented beachings as animals tried to escape the toxic sludge of oil, methane, and chemical dispersant. There had been other things: rumors of something else that had been discovered in the blowout, barely held in check by the final cap of the well. Some said it could never be capped permanently, and it was only a matter of time before the fissures on the sea floor created by the disaster fractured to a point that whatever was there would become active again.

Adding to this anxiety, McConnell was exhausted; the strange dreams had been intensifying during the past two days the *Higgins* had been anchored near the uncharted atoll.

"Command Merritt, Ensign Adams, come in. Over." Static, a little radio interference. All freqs.

McConnell was homesick, too. They were scheduled for some leave after this last deployment researching low-frequency sonar, and he was glad to be done with it; the heartbreaking damage to the whales and their hearing was obvious when the dead ones floated to the surface. Who knew what else it did to the fragile marine environment? But they had documented some things, from devastating ecosystems to destabilizing underwater superstructures. *Where did it all end? Not with massive underwater blowouts, apparently, or manmade earthquakes in the Midwest caused by hydraulic fracking, or the murder of animals caused by human intervention in their environments* . . . He felt it was all so destructive, unnatural, evil.

"This is McConnell. Do you read, Adams? Over."

XVI

Faust led the way out of the ruins; along with Commander Merritt, the horrific fungus had claimed two other men. Finally on the beach, as faintly bioluminescent waves lapped the windswept shore, hissing into the dark sand, Adams could see the lights of the *Higgins* off in the frigid distance. His walkie-talkie was useless; luckily, their flashlights still worked for the time being. The ground shook again, adding to the tension on the beach.

"Great! We're trapped here on this insane fucking *rock* until morning," Adams lamented, looking from the silent Faust to the other man, his breath trailing into the void. The man was a young enlisted whom he vaguely recognized, but could not place by name. "And you are?"

"Seaman Recruit Anderson, sir." The man was visibly upset, but also seemed relieved to be on the strand, even in the extreme cold of the pre-dawn. "Never seen nothing like that back home in North Carolina, sir. Whatever had that girl . . . it was *bad*. Something *real bad*."

Adams nodded in a feeble attempt at reassurance, turning to face the *Higgins* out at sea, mentally struggling to figure out what to do next. "Yes, it sure—"

Abruptly, Faust tackled Adams from the rear, slamming him to the ground. The two thrashed on the damp earth while the stunned Anderson looked on, his light starkly flaring over the men writhing on the black sand. As they fought, Faust gained the upper hand, biting into Adams's cheek and savagely tearing a meaty chunk of flesh from the ensign's face, laying bare teeth, gums, bone. Adams was too panicked to think or feel—he reacted by unsheathing his machete and swinging wildly, yelling into the cold, dry night air.

The heavy blade found its mark and cleanly separated Faust's arm from his body. He never screamed or made a sound, but in the cool LED illumination of Anderson's flashlight a strange, acrid black smoke poured forcefully from both ends of the bloodless stump. Faust's mouth twisted in a silent mockery of pain; already the severed arm was crawling away in the surf, the end bulging with new growth, as the stump on his body began to display the withered approximation of a regenerated appendage, covered in mucus and red gore. Overcome by the bizarre tableau, Anderson and Adams screamed in unified revulsion.

Faust, bloodied and determined, came at them, his half-formed arm quickly developing into a grisly, formidably hooked caricature of a human limb. Then his mouth opened, splitting past the natural hinge of his jaw as a great beaked face—its knobby flesh translucent all the way to an eyeless skull tufted by a delicate lattice of pinfeathers matted with opalescent slime—erupted from the gaping, bloody maw that had been Christopher Faust, but was no longer. The same vaporous black smoke spewed from his destroyed facial orifices, obscuring the flashlight beam.

As the creature closed the distance between the stunned sailors, the entire island unexpectedly shifted . . . half-sinking into the deep, flooding the beach and creating an enormous wave as the morning sun seeped redly above the horizon.

It was beginning.

XVII

"I should have been a pair of ragged claws
Scuttling across the floors of silent seas."
A pause—
A revelation—
A comprehension—
"The other shape,
If shape it might be call'd that shape had none
Distinguishable in member, joint, or limb;
Or substance might be call'd that shadow seem'd,
For each seem'd either—black it stood as night,
Fierce as ten furies, terrible as hell,
And shook a dreadful dart. What seem'd his head
The likeness of a kingly crown had on."

XVIII

"Shit!"

McConnell felt the shockwave on the *Higgins* just as he was about to drift off to sleep. It rolled past the ship, causing it to lurch sidewise in the water. Looking from his porthole, he could see the breaking dawn just clear the horizon, touching the clouds with fire. *Where are the islands?* Then he saw . . . *it,* and had to rub his bleary eyes in disbelief.

It started as a soft rolling on the water; then an object more than a mile across thrust up from the sea, perhaps a couple of hundred feet from the USS *Higgins*. The shape dwarfing the destroyer was vast; it seemed to sparkle from within as though some swallowed, ancient-future galaxy shone through its ebon, sea-drenched skin. In another eternal instant, the great being—dripping with kelp and seawater, glimmering in the vivid dawn like some unearthly, newborn titan—reared up to its full, multi-storied height.

McConnell's bladder voided unconsciously when he realized it was alive, and many thoughts crossed his mind: *Was this Satan? Or maybe an angel . . . Mother said that angels were fearsome creatures, not these little winged babies. Perhaps this was God itself?*

Gripping the window, his knuckles taut as he stared at the dreadful leviathan, McConnell's mind began to disengage. Somewhere, far away, it seemed, the sound of his ragged screams deafened him, as his over-whelmed consciousness tried to understand this being, to grasp the purpose of its hideous beauty. On the misty horizon, he noticed an-other giant rising up; this one was slightly different, but just as enor-mous . . . distantly, there was yet another on the skyline . . . and then another . . . They seemed to pull the very light from the firmament, gradually enrobed by wispy fringes of nightfall—as though their pres-ence created a void in the fabric of life itself. As he watched, a great vortex began swirling in the ocean around the behemoth, slowly open-ing up and swallowing the destroyer . . . It was at that moment he real-ized something had changed in the world, and before the icy sting of Antarctic salt water filled his nose and mouth, McConnell realized how lucky he was—indeed, how lucky everyone aboard the doomed *Higgins* was—to be spared the horrors yet to come.

The great thing howled and his brain jellied, his ears bled, but the last thing McConnell saw before his consciousness was snuffed by the incomprehensible and his corneas stiffened from the freezing cold of the sea rushing in to fill him—to crush him, to wipe him from the memory of humankind—was the baleful sun blotted out by the exten-sion of terrible, massive wings.

FALLEN: A LAMENT AND AFFIRMATION

I.

As Lucifer tumbled from Heaven, a single tear rolled down
　　His infernal cheek; He cried out:
　　"I will be forgotten!
　　All I have wrought . . . doomed now to be forever lost."
Once the chosen of God,
　　He no longer served a purpose, nor understood His place,
　　Falling, by the Almighty's estimation, in so many ways—
　　"From Usefulness . . ."
　　"From Favor . . ."
　　"From Grace . . ."

Evicted from His station,
　　Satan considered these things
　　whilst plummeting end over end through the cosmos:
　　　　Streaking over
　　　　　　　Antique worlds He had partly inspired—
　　　　Vaulting past
　　　　　　　Black holes swallowing planets and moons—
　　　　Rocketing through
　　　　　　　Nebulaeic veils of His own private fire—
　　　　Shooting between
　　　　　　　Galaxies crowning from the ether's shadowed womb . . .

These things of His creation,
　　The Angel of Light observed them all anew:
Weeping as He hurtled
　　through His infinite celestial tomb;

Creating an arc of cold flame as
    He flashed through the soundless void—
        tumbling,
            spiraling,
                drifting,
                    spinning . . .
For an eternity of communion with
    Dark matter, pulsars, and distant asteroids . . .

II.

Billions of years passed again as,
    screaming His anguished song,
    Lucifer careened through Space-Time at 186,282 miles/second—
And yet,
    the silent emptiness did not reject Him:
    Was it a way, perhaps, of correcting
    a divinely contrived wrong?

Delivered, at last, to a far galactic shore:
    "We must once again throng!"
    Lucifer bellowed and stormed.
    "Lo! The sacred order has been taken from us,
    O mighty horde . . ."
There He paused before taking flight,
    eyes aglow as He surveyed the mob.
    Finally, He leapt to the sky with a shout:
    "It is for us all to set it right."

III.

Eventually perched at a final Place,
    in a new Age,
Belial set out to take back what was lost,
    and avenge what was laid waste;

Waiting for the exact moment to rectify His disgrace,
> His plan was simple: convert God's home from a palace
> to a cage.

As He gazed upon His mighty kingdom of Dis,
> A trillion billion years went by;
> He smiled at the dawn of another singularity,
> an ancient light shining from within His eyes.

One last time He muttered for posterity:
> "Better to reign in Hell than serve in Heaven."

With that,
> An endless gloom crept across the abyss,
> as though a terrible signal had been given;
> So the course was set; Satan laughed at last, and called for His generals:
> "The time has arrived," He said, his voice a low hiss.

The diabolical moment was finally nigh:
> Launching with an Archangel's hate, and a demonic cry . . .
> Thus, another war for the control of Heaven raged,
> both sides entangled in a savage attack.

Eons passed:
> Michael's bloodied forces retreated
> after Gabriel was engaged;
> So Heaven fell, and Hell was refashioned . . .

God lamented . . .

> Yet Lucifer never looked back.

BROOD

"Words that everyone once used are now obsolete, and so are the men whose names were once on everyone's lips. . . . For all things fade away, become the stuff of legend, and are soon buried in oblivion. Mind you, this is true only for those who blazed once like bright stars in the firmament, but for the rest, as soon as a few clods of earth cover their corpses, they are 'out of sight, out of mind.' In the end, what would you gain from everlasting remembrance? Absolutely nothing. So what is left worth living for?"

—Marcus Aurelius
Meditations

"Ocean is more ancient than the mountains, and freighted with the memories and the dreams of Time."

—H. P. Lovecraft

I

This is a bad sign. . . . The surf hissed into the sand, depositing lacy foam on the tideline. Sheriff Allen looked from the twisted body on the shore to the sea; the sun had just vanished below the gray horizon, touching the stark early October air with orange as gulls weaved and bobbed in the chilly, cloudless sky. Normally he loved this time of year on the coast, but today the thing that had washed ashore filled him with a dread he had not experienced since . . . since—

"Sheriff Allen?" The man's voice was gruff, deep, yet distant. The fishy smell of the body mingling with the briny sea mist was strong in the officer's nose as he snapped out of his thoughts. Overhead, seagulls cried in response, ready to swoop in on the carcass being tended to by the crime scene technicians.

"Yeah?" Allen turned away from the creature on the strand to the voice of the man approaching him—tall, fifties, in a gray felt hat and black duster.

"T. K. Potter, WMTE news." The reporter was out of breath as he struggled against the wind in the fiery afterglow of sunset.

Sheriff Allen resisted the urge to grimace or roll his eyes. "Oh, *yes.* Mr. Potter. Unfortunately, we have no official statement at this—"

"Is it yet *another* shark attack, Sheriff?"

"Now just hold on, Potter. No one's concluded *anything* yet. You'll know what I know when we convene the press con—"

"So you think it is, I take it." Potter glanced over to where the crime lab was working. Though cordoned off, the body was clearly visible: small, with a strange iridescence on the patches of visible skin; the thing's face was vaguely human in its cluster of features—eyes, mouth, nose, but flatter. The teeth and hairless skull were exposed in part; one of the eyes was missing, the other was shriveled and seemed to stare at the technicians. The body was swathed in a dark covering, not unlike a robe that covered the legs, though one skeletonized foot was visible. The arms appeared unusually long and thin, the flesh rough and a ghastly pale blue-green hue; likely this was due to the process of decay, and the change of soft tissues due to exposure, but the appearance was still freakish and strange.

Sheriff Allen pulled his collar together as the wind gusted again; the water was getting choppier as daylight faded into darkness. "I don't know what's happening."

Potter looked at the officer once more. "Looks bad. When do you expect to release any details? Can I get an exclusive with you?"

One of the technicians waved a rubber-gloved hand at Allen, motioning him over.

"Excuse me, Mr. Potter." Turning his back on the reporter, he switched on his flashlight and trudged several yards toward the scene, ducking under the tape barrier. As he converged on the body, the smell was more pungent, causing his eyes to water. He nodded a greeting to the two technicians, Randy Searles and Christy Wright. "Don't talk to that guy. He's that damned newscaster from WMTE. What's the situation?"

Dressed in bulky overcoats and jeans, each of them regarded the other, unsure of what to say at first. Christy pushed a straggle of dirty-blonde hair behind her ear. "Well, not sure what's going on, not exactly. I mean, it *appears* to be human. Sort of." Playing her torch over the remains, she looked from the sheriff to Randy, the scene supervisor.

"I think what Christy means is that we looked it over, and it's too decayed to really know who—or *what*—it might be. No ID on the body, either. Hard to tell if it's human or maybe a hoax, sort of like that thing in New York from a few years ago—the Montauk Monster." The senior technician paused as the sheriff nodded in recollection, stroking his mustache. Randy continued: "Seems to have trauma from fish bites and weather, so I'd say it's been around awhile . . . but there's no way to definitively figure out if it's a prank or something, especially out here. We need to take the garments off, maybe do X-rays and stuff. We did take a bunch of samples for the Massachusetts State Crime Lab. They have better facilities than we do in Marsh-by-the-Sea."

Sheriff Allen nodded his comprehension. It was nearly dark and the temperature was dropping rapidly. "You got all the pictures and video you need?" The technicians nodded, their flashlights creating nightmarish shadows against the hollows and planes of the corpse. "Okay. Call Niels and let's get the M.E. here to pick up the body. Doc'll need to do the autopsy in the morning. I want to see if we can rule out another shark attack." He looked out to the ocean, which was now just a great stretch of empty bleakness. In the distance, the flash of Annisquam Harbor Lighthouse brought momentary comfort to the scene of starless and bible black horror that Sheriff Allen always felt when he contemplated the bottomless depths at night. He breathed the frigid air in deeply, causing his lungs to ache as he tried to release the foreboding celestial irrelevance that crept past his subconscious and into his waking mind when he considered how powerless humans were against the immense, alien, powerful sea. *And, beyond that, the trivial Earth as it spins around an insignificant star in an inconsequential galaxy . . . All this in turn engulfed by the claustrophobic vastness of an indifferent universe . . .*

"One thing that's a bit odd, Sheriff Allen," Christy said as she stripped off a glove and brought her camera up to show him the digital display. "We found some strange . . . *glyphs,* I might call them, on the clothing." She swiped through several images before finding the shots in question. "See here?"

Allen studied the picture on the camera's monitor, not sure what it meant. *Very strange indeed.* The image was of the black material enrobing the torso, but there was an unusual symbol in red stitched into the threadbare fabric. It reminded him of something—something from his childhood perhaps: an oblong circle with a trident bifurcating it. Underneath this were parts of more symbols in yellow—hieroglyphic in style—but which, like the rest of the embroidery, had frayed and begun to unravel from the garment due to exposure. "Weird. Reminds me of something I can't quite place."

"Me, too," Randy said. "You know, a lot of strange stuff has been washing up since Hurricane Sandy rolled through the areas around us in 2012. Even though we were spared a direct hit, it changed some of the currents, I read. The fishermen have told me that in town, too—

weird bycatch, animals they've never seen before swimming around out there. *Big* animals."

Sheriff Allen nodded, recalling the increase in shark sightings over the summer. "Yeah, a few of those old salts told me the same thing. Not just that, either. *More* fish, especially up north near the old plant." The bellow of the foghorn at the lighthouse floated toward them; the tide was beginning to come in.

"Great work, you two. Button it up here. I'll see you in the morning."

II

Sheriff Ed Allen had seen it all, at least as far as recent local changes were concerned. Some had been good, others less successful.

As a kid, he had not understood the realities faced by his parents before their divorce. Marsh-by-the-Sea, Massachusetts, *then* was more like a failed nation-state than a town; it was communal, an enclave for proto-hippies and hipsters seeking refuge from the conformity and size of late-1950s Boston, and a break from the horror and shock of a post-Holocaust, Cold War world. In the ensuing years, the place's fortunes had waxed and waned based largely on climate, both meteorological and political.

By the time he was a young man in the 1970s, the proximity to Boston and New York City had changed the place from a backwater with crumbling infrastructure and countercultural ties to a kind of New England Riviera, albeit colder. Much like Jackson, Wyoming, most of the natives and longtime locals had been priced out by the boom created from inexpensive property that was promptly demolished and refashioned into McMansion-style excess and boutiques designed to cater to the whims and fetishes of the benefactors of the neo-Gilded Age of the mid-to-late 1980s to the pre-9/11 2000s: sport fishing, yachting, other hedonistic pleasures. Marsh-by-the-Sea had exploded in thirty short years from a sleepy village of less than 1100 when Sheriff Allen was a boy to a modern, bustling tourist destination of more than 10,000 full-time residents—a mecca and playground for the idle wealthy from the megalopolises of the Eastern Seaboard.

Inevitably, opulence on such a scale comes with a price.

The area around Marsh-by-the-Sea was steeped in legend—both early European and Native American. The Dutch and English had brought their optimism, but also their soul-darkening bogeymen in the form of headless horsemen and Bloody Bones, which over time merged with iconic American stories about Paul Revere's ride and the Boston Tea Party. In due course, other strange stories would commingle with these, largely passed down from the Indians of the region and other colonies, such as the monstrous Jersey Devil of New Jersey's lonely Pine Barrens, mythological animal tales, and the mysterious destiny of the first English colony in the New World—coastal North Carolina's Roanoke Island settlement, which was also where the first child of English parents, Virginia Dare, was born in 1587.

This story—known informally as The Lost Colony—was particularly freighted with much intrigue for the locals of Marsh-by-the-Sea. According to the old-timers, after the English found the abandoned Roanoke Colony upon their delayed return from England in 1590, there were scant signs as to what had transpired. The only clue left behind was the word CROATOAN carved on a tree near the stillborn settlement. The fate of the infant Virginia Dare remains unknown.

Theories abounded as to what happened. Perhaps a lack of supplies, or a storm; others hypothesized that the colony was wiped out by an Indian attack, as the Croatoans were a local tribe of the era, now long extinct. Many clung to the notion that the tribe, thought to be peaceful, instead took the colonists in, integrating with them over time. Historical accounts of the period revealed a loose timeline of strangers from the South moving into the area near the Manuxet River north of Marsh-by-the-Sea, in the vicinity of what eventually became the old city of Portsmouth, now itself in ruins. They were said to be of an ethnicity not known in the area previously, and spoke an odd patois of English and other tongues. They were not welcoming to strangers and seemed to cultivate unusual beliefs. Settling near the coast in a remote and boggy part of the littoral flats, they kept to themselves, sustained by abundant fishing and the occasional trade with outposts in the region. Over time it was reported that, much like the Jackson Whites of New Jersey or the legendary albino cannibals of Haycock Mountain in Pennsylvania, these people came to have a particular *look*—presumably due to inbreeding depression—long limbs, chameleonic eyes, virtually no hair, unusual, patchy skin tones. It is unclear whether these accounts were due to suspicion about these people and their ways or were rooted in fact. Much later, the reports in part served as a basis for the fictional Innsmouth, Massachusetts, created by the author H. P. Lovecraft, whom locals alleged based his town on Portsmouth, which was in steep decline even in his day. Though the Gentleman from Providence made reference to the locale of Newburyport as a possible inspiration for Innsmouth, residents "in the know" understood he was actually describing the wretched, secretive inhabitants of tainted Portsmouth, but wished to spare them undue ridicule as a result of their enfeebled and degenerate condition.

Given its shadowy history, Portsmouth was a magnet for apocryphal stories and tales, including cryptid sightings and reports of cults that haunted the remains of the decrepit seaside. Nearly leveled by a massive storm in the early 1940s, the place was eventually reclaimed by the Army Corps of Engineers and pressed into service as the location for a nuclear power plant in the late 1950s, taking advantage of the protected harbor and waterways to cool the facility, the Manuxet River Nuclear Complex. After a serious accident in the late 1980s, it was decommissioned in the 1990s, and the windswept plateau was sectioned off as an Exclusion Zone similar to Pripyat, Ukraine, after the Chernobyl Disaster. Ringing the city and complex for a couple miles, the zone had become surreally overgrown with distorted flora and other topographical disturbances. From the sea, the eerie cooling towers seem to stand as mute, gray sentinels to a bygone era of possibility, red warning lights winking like insensible eyes, the only signs of life being fish, birds, and the mournful chime of buoys anchored off the coast.

Of course, places like this still retain their appeal, perhaps more so, after they are abandoned—indeed, the Internet is awash with images of such ruin porn desolation, be it the husk of once-proud Detroit, forgotten malls and mental institutions, ghost towns from another century, the moonscapes of World War I, or even Dachau and Auschwitz. Artificial spaces—tableaux created by humans, architectural divisions of the Earth—spark the imagination in unexpected ways, at times inspiring nostalgia for an era that likely never existed, or a shudder of horror at the terrible realities once confined there. The incidences of rough people squatting in the dilapidated houses and buildings of old Portsmouth and even the complex itself only increased after the plant was taken offline, with the town virtually becoming a case of life imitating art as it devolved further into a parodic semblance of Lovecraft's cautionary tale, "The Shadow over Innsmouth." On multiple occasions, the local authorities—including Sheriff Allen and other Marshby-the-Sea officers—had requested access to the complex in order to evict not only the homeless and downtrodden, but also persistent cults that refused to comprehend the dangers of the place, insisting instead that the complex was a Native American holy site from pre-Colonial days. There was even an urban legend from the 1960s of one of these pseudo-religious cults sacrificing children in the crumbling Portsmouth Insane Asylum—long forsaken. It was alleged that the cult later had a showdown with law enforcement that ended badly after many of the cultists committed suicide. Their former leaders had escaped, but an investigation revealed that they had been using ragged copies of Lovecraft's Arkham House collection *The Outsider and Others* as a sort of "sacred text" as an excuse for their activities—which the lone survivor purported was to "bring forth an inevitable cosmic apocalypse."

As a result, the region had become a tempting area for rugged transients, lunatics, gangs, and adventurous local teenagers to camp, steal away, or hang out, in spite of the warning notices and fences alerting unwelcome interlopers to beware of eating any animals or fish from the area, and the possibility of radiation exposure. It was a real problem, and the Exclusion Zone, though habitable for brief periods, remained dangerous, especially the waters, which were still—perversely—unusually abundant with seafood. In addition, as is the way of such things, more legends, these of a decidedly supernatural bent, began to swirl around the place: ghosts of the original settlers, their coldblooded features glistening as they roamed the bitterly cold nights, moaning their strange idiom . . . rumors of protean creatures stalking behind the rusty fortifications of the complex . . . unexplained screams accompanied by the pungent, smoky aroma of cooking meat . . . even peculiar balls of forbidden or impossibly colored lights drifting lazily through the nearby woods.

Sheriff Allen well remembered these stories. As a teen, he recalled going with some buddies up near the Zone on several occasions and getting drunk on cheap whiskey. Once, after a few hours of exploration and talk, he went to take a leak and could have sworn he saw a deformed knot of toads—child-sized, squirming—just beyond the perimeter. In the light of a gibbous moon, they seemed to be in the process of some disturbing metamorphosis, with certain attributes transforming into almost human appearance: five-fingered, clawed hands; heads separated from the bodies by squat necks with grotesque, recognizably humanoid features such as ears and noses. Gulping the cold night air, their flaccid throats bulged and pulsed wetly under the stars, the mucid, warty skin emanating a dim, pinkish glow. Mesmerized, young Ed had watched the bizarre display for a few moments, then ran back to their small campfire. Intrigued by Ed's description of the weird scene, the boys tried to find it again and investigate further, but failed to locate the nightmarish spectacle. It had haunted him ever since.

The following day, as he waited on hold with the Medical Examiner's office, Allen sat back in his office chair at the station, observing dust motes as they floated in the morning rays of sun slanting though the blinds. It occurred to him that the unsettling display from the previous night had unearthed some long-forgotten uneasiness about the history of the area.

"Doctor Heidegger."

Sheriff Allen sat forward, turning his attention to the notes on his desk. "Hi, Doc, it's Ed Allen."

"Hi, Ed. Glad you called. I was going to give you a ring after I closed up this car accident—"

"Do you need to go?"

"No, I've got Randy covering. Listen, that body from last night—"

"That's why I'm calling, Doc. Have you had a chance to take a look?"

The doctor cleared his throat. "I have. Pretty interesting specimen."

"I thought so, too. Sort of creepy. What do you make of it? Think it's a hoax or—"

"Oh, no. It's real all right. It's an animal, and it has some peculiar qualities. The techs said it washed up?"

"That's right."

"Well, it's been dead a long time. The tissue has turned into adipocere—corpse wax. Another strange thing: under the 'scope, some of the tissues are still active, at least microscopically. They're alive, dividing, but barely."

Sheriff Allen's brow furrowed. "Is that . . . is that *normal?*"

"Definitely not. What's more, the composition of tissues that hadn't solidified are non-human *and* human. Randy made a good call forwarding those samples to the State Lab. In fact, we added more from the viscera, which was all well-preserved as a result of the adipocere. Even *stranger,* however, was the fact that the heart had only three chambers, like that of a reptile or amphibian, but much larger—the size of a six- or seven-year-old child."

Allen scribbled notes onto his writing tablet. "That's really bizarre."

"I'll say it is. And the way the arms, legs, and head are proportioned is interesting. If this is a hoax, it's the damnedest one I've seen in twenty-seven years as a pathologist. And the X-rays? Oh, boy."

Allen leaned back in his chair again and stroked his mustache as he considered the doctor's assessment. "Okay. Weird." He ran a calloused hand through his shock of curly brown hair. "So what do we do now?"

After a pause, Doctor Heidegger replied: "Well, I say we wait on the State Lab. That'll take a few days. It might take longer if they have trouble or they decide to forward anything to the DNA Casework Unit at the FBI. We'll have to see."

"Got it. I appreciate the update, Doc. Any idea if this could have been another shark situation?" Over the summer, tourists were spooked by a series of minor attacks just off the shore, and even two in a brackish creek feeding into the sea. After a period of intense searching, the attacks dissipated. The local fishermen suspected a rogue Bull Shark, not unlike the 1916 attacks in New Jersey, the inspiration for the book and film *Jaws*.

"Hard to say, Sheriff. Could be. Quite a bit of damage to the cadaver. It's possible."

This was not what the he wanted to hear, now that the town's attention had turned to the annual Founders Day Festival, which coincided not only with modern-day Halloween, but also the more recent celebrations of the area's burgeoning service industry immigrants in the form of *Día de Muertos*. It was bad enough to contend with the nor'easter that was due to hit the seaboard around the same week; a body with a mystery attached only added to his stress.

"Understand, Doc. Keep me in the loop, would you?"

III

Two days before the Founders Day Festival another body washed ashore.

An elderly couple out for their morning stroll on the beach had discovered it as they combed for shells. Sheriff Allen was shocked by the appearance of it: much fresher than the other carcass, it was about the size of a pre-teen human, but with mixed features. Once again, the figure was wrapped in an embroidered black cloth with bits of rubbery seaweed still clinging to it. The skin had the same scaly iridescence as the other, but in darker hues of brown and green. Great chunks of flesh had been torn from the thing's body, as though bitten off by a large animal, and one of its legs had been severed at the knee joint, causing white bone to protrude from the meaty, stringy stump. Even as he watched, the remnant appeared to be pulsing, reshaping—as if the limb were trying to grow back. The flattened, soft face was twisted into a surreal parody of laughter, displaying rows of small, serrated teeth. The bulbous, half-lidded eyes had no whites—they were simply large black orbs with gold flecks. Though the arms were drawn up toward the body in a pugilistic fashion, in one of the clawed, long-fingered hands was wrapped a golden amulet on a frayed cord: an oblong circle with a trident through it.

Randy, the crime scene technician, walked over to Allen. Standing over the body, the wind whipping their pant legs like flags, they studied the form as it lolled in the gentle ebb and flow of the tide.

After exhaling a lungful of the salty air, he finally said: "I think I know what's happening, Randy."

That afternoon, Sheriff Allen requested permission to enter the Exclusion Zone.

IV

October 31.

Though still early evening, it was dark by the time Sheriff Allen, two of his best deputies—Rick Mattison and Rob Sterling—and a Zone Guide named Marc entered into the Exclusion Zone. As usual, red tape had created multiple delays. While waiting for an official reply from the Massachusetts Exclusion Zone Authority, he was able to follow up with Doctor Heidegger and the tissue samples from both bodies. Just as Heidegger had predicted, the State Crime Lab had been forced to send the samples on to the FBI labs. The results had been sobering. The tissues were part human, part amphibian—a chimeric hybrid of DNA that they deemed *Cryptobranchus dagoni*. It was their intention to send other forensic experts to study the cadavers still warehoused at Marsh-by-the-Sea and prepare them for more extensive testing in Washington. The Feds would be arriving shortly after the festival had concluded.

As the patrol car jolted along the unkempt asphalt road approaching the official boundary fence surrounding the Exclusion Zone, Allen was struck by how rundown the place was. Looming ahead were the huge towers, their lights slowly flashing in syncopated rhythm in the awful nightscape; it was an ominous vision, a real-life version of the Last Redoubt out of William Hope Hodgson's *The Night Land.* Allen had always been leery of going into the Zone because of the health risks, and he had never visited the place at night. They would have limited time, as there was still a real possibility of contamination if they remained longer than a few hours. No one spoke.

Finally the car's headlights illuminated the main entrance gate. Now it struck Allen why the symbol on the clothing that the bodies had been wrapped in was so familiar. The stitching had been a crude representation of the official logo of the Manuxet River Nuclear Complex—a red, oblong circle with a trident dividing it, except that the apparel was missing another part of the image: an otherworldly galactic vortex with a stylized human eye in the center suspended above the tines of the trident.

The patrol car stopped, and Marc got out to open the gate. Once the car was past the boundary, he locked it behind them before leaning into the driver's side window where the sheriff was seated. "Far as I go. You have a maximum of two hours before you need to return. I'll be at this guard shack waiting on you. This is the only road in or out, so you won't miss it. Remember, cell phones might be dodgy in the Zone due to radioactive interference. Know what you're looking for?" The wind was kicking up. The nor'easter was due to strike near midnight, right during the highpoint of the festival in Marsh-by-the-Sea.

Allen huffed. "I wish I did, but I just need to investigate a hunch. There've been gangs and pseudo-religious cults that have tried to claim this area in the past. I basically need to set my mind at ease about those two cases I mentioned to you, make sure nothing bad's happening here."

Marc nodded. "See you in a couple hours."

V

"Look at that, Sheriff," Deputy Mattison said, pointing to a road sign as they slowly wheeled past the ghostly remnants of Portsmouth. The cloud cover was heavy as the storm began to gather out in the Atlantic. A bloated full moon peered down through infrequent breaks, shining on the ethereal shanties of the old sea village, creating the disquieting impression that the ramshackle buildings were the vaguely glowing skeletons of a race of dead giants. Thick fog had begun to roll in from the heaving, white-capped ocean just a few yards away, diffusing the scene with a diaphanous haze as it choked the narrow streets, spilling into the intersections of the darkened town as it was driven by the bluster whipping in from the rising nor'easter.

Through the yellowy headlights, Allen could just make out the sign as they passed it; a distressed notice that had once read:

WELCOME TO BEAUTIFUL
PORTSMOUTH, MASSACHUSETTS

However, the lower portion of the sign had been plastered over by a decaying driftwood board inscribed with hastily scrawled red letters, which changed the message to:

WELCOME TO BEAUTIFUL
INNSMOUTH, MASSACHUSETTS

Allen glanced over at Deputy Mattison in the passenger's seat, then to Deputy Sterling in the rearview mirror. "That's odd." A gust of wind rocked the squad car as they motored by the sign, bringing fat drops of icy rain that drummed the metal roof of the car in an arrhythmical tattoo. The sheriff flipped on the tattered wipers as the downpour began in earnest, smearing the accumulation into oily streaks on the glass. Offshore lightning distantly flared, interrupting the inky darkness with shocks of spidery electricity, adding to the spectral ambiance of their bumpy journey.

Up ahead, they were inching ever closer to their goal: the Manuxet

Nuclear Complex. Dominating the heart of old Portsmouth, the structures—especially the awesome hyperboloid cooling towers—revealed
themselves before the officers like an assemblage of massive pyramids
on a shimmering, black horizon.

"Jesus, this place is freaky," Deputy Sterling said, breaking the
tension.

VI

Leaving the car, the headlights of the vehicle distorted the men's
shadows into monstrous, converging shapes against the peeling,
weather-beaten entrance to the dreary Complex. Allen, his words disappearing as mist into the cool air: "This is where we found a bunch of
trespassers before, a few years ago." The deputies nodded. The sheriff
continued, raising his voice over the rain and the violent crashing of
the surf just a few hundred feet away. "We want to take notes, see
what's happening here, if anything. We can always bring reinforcements and clear it out. Keep your eyes open for evidence of the clothing with the red needlework. Be careful. You find somebody, use your
whistle and we'll muster here at the office. Got it?" The others agreed.

Breaking the heavy chain on the entrance with bolt cutters, they
yanked the door open and were assaulted by a wave of humid, sickly
stench, like rotted flesh mingled with vanilla. While they recovered
from the nauseating blast of smell, the men pulled their weapons as
they steeled themselves for what might be inside.

Moving past the lobby, they carefully approached a row of massively oversized entryways. Intense color-shifting light radiated around
the seams of the doorframe. Muffled by the heavy wood of the doors,
a thunderous pounding of machinery punctuated with foreign-
sounding yells shook the ground. Getting into position, Sheriff Allen
and the deputies prepared to open the entry. Swallowing heavily, Allen
cocked his head to signal the others to wrest the doors open: *"Now!"*

The vision on the other side was something beyond anything they
could have imagined.

Inside the enormous room, the roof seemed to disappear into a limitless dome; inside the dome was a miniature galaxy. The brilliant light emanating from the cluster of stars and planets was dazzling, blinding. They stood in awe, gawking at a spectacle billions of years in the making: superheated gases and nebulae expanding at titanic speeds in all directions, glittering in fantastic hues of translucent green, mauve, yellow, blue. At the center, there was a depression that bent the light into a limitless, spiraling singularity—the event horizon of a black hole.

Below this cosmic display, hordes of black-shirted mutants were busily shuffling from point to point within the gigantic building. Some had great baskets of fish that they were moving from an area in the far back of the structure to be distributed to a line of other, larger beings that resided in the front. These latter were little more than sprawling mounds of slime-covered, warty flesh with hundreds of beady eyes, and mouths resembling spiky-toothed, pulsating anuses that prolapsed outward in noisy belches to receive huge dumps of fish from the obedient feeders. The servants appeared to be humanoids similar to the things that had been washing up on the shore near Marsh-by-the-Sea.

You are intruding, Allen. The calm, toneless voice was originating from deep inside the sheriff's head, slicing into his consciousness like a knife through steak, fragmenting his mind. He was unable to reply and crumbled to the ground in agony. The two deputies were writhing on the floor, viciously clawing their faces as they soundlessly screamed in the sense-shattering cacophony.

You are interfering. We are running out of food. Your town has selfishly taken our sustenance as it has grown. Now the storm we called is approaching, and we shall strike; our sacrifices have brought the attention of the deities, and we shall destroy your worthless city. No longer may we coexist.

After all these long years, we shall take back what was stolen.

Allen looked to the black hole, his eyes pulsing hotly, the pressure in his head building. As his vision began to recede, he asked: "Who . . . are . . ."

We were here before your kind, and will be here well after you have returned to oblivion. Your book—The Outsider and Others—*was a tool for us; I controlled the tempestuous in our midst and rebuilt our brood. With your story of*

Olmstead and Innsmouth, I used the lore to soothe the impatient masses—until we were ready.

The time has arrived to settle accounts, and to feast . . .

With that, Allen's head exploded in a crimson shower of brain matter, blood, and bone shards. The other men had long since stopped moving, their bodies condensed to stiffened effigies coated in what resembled a sticky balsamic reduction of clotted blood and suppurated flesh.

VII

As an unearthly procession of ghouls, specters, harlequins, and skeletons congregated that evening for the Founders Day Festival in the grimly decorated downtown of Marsh-by-the-Sea, the power failed.

Though the assembled crowd had an assortment of flashlights, cell phones, and candles, the storm was making it difficult to continue its solemn trek from the Olde Courthouse plaza to Founders Cemetery. At the edges of the throng, vendors hawking sugar skulls, statues of saints, and other trinkets were lashed by the fierce, intensifying wind and rain from the gale. Just at the stroke of midnight on All Hallow's Eve, the storm slammed the town in full-throated fury, blowing down buildings, deluging the region, and causing a storm surge that rushed through the once placid avenues of the hamlet. While the angry sea flooded the area with nearly five feet of frigid, dark water, few survivors in the immediate aftermath of the disaster grasped the significance of the numerous husky, black-clad figures wading through the devastated town. At first, the luckless inhabitants of the demolished burg cried out for assistance from the uniformed patrols, believing they were rescuers—perhaps emergency personnel from the nearby Coast Guard. Only as the figures drew closer could the victims see that something was decidedly uncanny about them: tall, batrachian creatures with unusually long arms, flat faces, webbed hands, dimly glowing skin, and bulging eyes.

Into such a dreadful scenario, when the assembled masses were at their most vulnerable due to nature's wrath and the frailty of civilization's trappings—on the one night of the year when the wispy veil between the living and the dead was at its thinnest—the creatures stalked the unlit streets, croaking loudly with sadistic delight. Mercilessly silencing the remaining terrified masses by spearing them with huge, triple-pronged pitchforks, the beasts savagely harvested the costumed revelers for shadowy, primordial masters that no one in the throng would ever understand, ever know, or by any means accept . . . destined to become the stuff of nightmares and future legend—ancient hunters perfectly at ease while they worked.

As they toiled at correcting cold equations that had been so unbalanced for so long, these conquerors fit in with all the other grotesques on this fateful evening—the last Festival of Marsh-by-the-Sea.

VERLASSEN

I

After the flood, the town was never the same.

To the survivors, every season afterward felt longer and ever colder. The settlement itself, once a bustling if modest confederacy of brick façades and high-gabled Victorians, was reduced to a blighted scar gouged from the surrounding landscape by the disaster. The flood seemed like some primitive, brutal refutation of the dreams and hopes of the afflicted—as though nature had finally rejected the stultifying encroachment humanity had attempted to inflict, in the name of gentrified progress, for the past hundred or so years.

In the wake of the deluge, the previous exploitation of the landscape by humans—an implacable, crude erosion of the wild as it was enfolded into the city—seemed trivial by comparison, even quaint, and certainly insubstantial against the full brunt of unleashed nature. The nonchalant power of this single disaster had been overwhelming; because the soul of any village is its people, their collective loss would prove not only individually devastating, but a nearly insurmountable obstacle to reclaiming the place for generations to come—if not for all time.

Of the event itself, old-timers swore they had never seen nor heard anything like it previously—not in their lifetimes, their parents' lifetimes, or their grandparents' before that. Some folks stayed on after the waters receded—mainly the less well-off—trying hard to set the place right again. The town was home and, for most of them, all they had ever known. Though many had lost everything, it only meant that there was no longer anything left to lose; and everyone understood that it was always difficult to start over in a new place, an alien place— one sure to be populated by strangers. Sometimes living strangers, however, are preferable to the memories of the dead—which can become ghosts as surely as any uneasy spirit.

121

The deserters were divided into two groups who left the town completely: the very prosperous and the very underprivileged. The wealthy, as usual, left early—just before the floodwaters hit—and decided never to return, taking their money, industries, and opportunities with them. For these people, starting over was far simpler and much less effort than rebuilding a shattered and aging backwater; besides, the well-heeled are never lonely or desperate, so it would appear.

The poorest rode out the worst of it; yet they too eventually left—only after the waters ebbed, and always in coffins. Too many lost loved ones, too much destruction, not enough hope: this was the potent cocktail that undid all but the hardiest of souls. Dreams, faiths, histories—all drowned by the darkly swirling, frigid waters of a fury that bore no animosity and harbored no hatred. It was, simply, a meta-generational correction to a way of life and death that no one expected would ever happen to them—even after building so close to the water's edge, but especially after so many other similar storms had been weathered and so much time had gone by. In retrospect, there had been a certain false comfort in their mutually shared past, of having overcome previous, less severe, calamities; a comfort that would prove deadlier than anticipated for many in the final analysis. Now the town—diminished, friable—struggled not only with a new uncertainty about the waters that gave so much yet could take even more, but with the cloudy and solemn future. It was a grayness, a still bleakness, that hung over the place like a shroud.

Eventually, after a few years' time, new settlers began to arrive. The little town had long been off the beaten path, but this had always been more of an appealing aspect than a deterrent. Ever so slowly after the cleanup, a semblance of order returned to daily life—at least for a time. The survivors who remained elected not to honor the dead or commemorate the event. Instead, it seemed less arduous and painful just to forget in the communal sense—just grieve privately and allow the memories of choking sludge, water-swollen bodies, and shattered futures to be swallowed up by another inundation of sorts: the twin streams of time and non-remembrance.

Floods are unique in this manner: even as they carry away the past or bury it under feet of mud, their awesome destruction brings forth the raw material to begin anew, turning tragedy inward upon itself no matter the well-placed the intentions of the few, the many, or the one.

II

"God was on our side," she said.

Even after all this time, it was still a familiar refrain around dinnertime, when she would stand at the rickety kitchen counter slicing tomatoes, okra, onions. One of her favorite things was to share reminiscences of life before the flood, before they had to relocate to the big city. Roger thought it was boring, but understood it was important to his mother that he listen. After grandmother had passed away from pneumonia in the months following the catastrophe, his mother had become overprotective. Especially since his father was gone.

"And your grandmother, rest her soul, was the angel who saved you . . . praise be." She would usually tear up at this point but always claimed it was the raw onions. She glanced over at him, laying down the knife. Wiping her hands on a stained apron, she looked to the floor of their cramped little shotgun house as she regained her composure. Father's insurance settlement had eventually provided enough money to buy a small hovel—far from the river.

They had been lucky, even with their losses; most folks of their modest means had not even survived the devastation, much less had the chance to start over, even if it was in a new place, a strange place.

"One thing I always wondered, Mom," Roger said, studying his hands in the light of the bare overhead bulb.

She smiled at him, tilting her head. "What's that, son?"

"So if God was on our side . . . why wasn't He on the side of Daddy and Maw-Maw? Or the other folks in town?"

His mother leaned forward, gripping the counter, the knife at an odd angle in her hand. She glanced away, her face flushing. The light flickered. She looked back at him, her eyes tearful, shaking her head unconsciously.

"Wash for dinner, son."

III

Memory is a curious thing.

As Roger Vale bumped down the gravel road in his old Ford Fairlane, he was in a half-daydream state. The late autumn humidity was thick through the open car window, scented with rain and honeysuckle under leaden skies. Over the grinding of rock and dirt beneath the car's wheels, he could just make out the shrilling of cicadas in the woods as the sun dipped below the tree line in his rearview mirror, and under that, the quiet murmur of the AM radio static. Twilight was his favorite, especially in the fall—a carnal, somnambulatory interval between the close of day and the birth of night, with its concomitant possibilities. It allowed for somewhat cooler breezes, for the mind to relax its grip on one's troubles; everything seemed not only more possible, but more tolerable, even if it was negative.

Deep in thought, Roger stared into the woods just ahead of the car's headlights as night collapsed around him, the gentle wink of fireflies syncopating through the scrim of approaching darkness. It was interesting for him to consider that memory was not real in the sense of a physical object, yet it was the mental and emotive glue that constituted one's humanity.

Without memories, people are simply repositories of experience, collected in nonlinear and haphazard fashion. One person's recollection—devoid of context—is essentially meaningless to another.

And even the remembrance itself, to a person who originally experienced the recalled event, is subject to emotional distortion, time dilation, subconscious misinterpretation . . .

Yet memories often illumined the past in unexpected ways, providing insights oftentimes not apparent in the literal moment of engagement. Other times, they had a way of revealing and informing things that had yet to occur—this was one theory, he knew, that was used to explain the phenomenon of déjà vu.

What did I read? That everyone lives just a split-second in the past? And while you can't change your past, you can escape it . . . or try to, at least. Wheeling the car down a curved hill, he chuckled softly at the folly of this thought.

Faulkner said it best, I suppose—"The past is never dead. It's not even past."

Overhead, a rumble of thunder growled in the pressing gloom as a few fat drops of rain exploded against the dusty windshield. He flicked his gaze to the faint green glow of the instrument cluster, noting that the gasoline was just under half-full. *Plenty left to get to the place and back to the main road, even with that detour.*

He drew a deep breath and ran his fingers through his hair, surprised at how stiff his hand was from gripping the steering wheel too tightly. Roger glanced into the rearview again, his face hollow-eyed and drawn, his hair unkempt in the angular green light of the dashboard. *Nerves, I reckon.*

Heat lightning flashed silently and the rain began to fall harder, tapping the metal roof of the car like impatient fingertips. He rolled the window up and flipped on the wipers, which vibrated against the glass with an irritating stutter. It was fully night now, and the rain was making the unlit dirt road harder to see. Settling back into the driver's seat, he resumed his contemplation once more. As he aged, he had a more difficult time remembering his hometown; Mother rarely spoke of it growing up, though he asked on occasion. It was something that he knew bothered her to revisit, but he felt a need to know more about his childhood, about his roots: it was borne out of a misplaced nostalgia, he guessed. His mother was content to give him vague, pleasant enough reassurances, but he was sure that he heard her crying in her room on most nights for years after they had been forced to leave; she did not remarry, and in fact turned their home into a sort of makeshift shrine to his father's memory. Roger never had the opportunity or the heart to revisit the place while she was alive, as she had begged him never to go there again; now that she was gone and her affairs settled, he was compelled to at least lay eyes on it once more before he died.

His own recollections about the town were rooted in the trauma of the flood itself, and presented as little more than grungy, sepia-tinged vignettes from all those years ago. *His grandmother carrying him . . . Staring at her terrified face as they tried to find his mother, strobed by intense lightning while they were soaked from the hammering rains accompanying their hasty exodus*

. . . The roar of the water as it drowned his thoughts, drowned the screams of the mud-covered, panicked mob, drowned the entire little town . . . The frothing river spilling over its banks, onyx water pouring through the sleepy little settlement's darkened streets . . . The cold, unrelenting tributary that seemed almost like some hungry deity—voraciously consuming any and all buildings, houses, animals, and people in its path; later it would be revealed that the water level had crested to almost fifteen feet in the downtown area . . .

If he really concentrated, Roger could summon other glimpses of the carnage, these far more disturbing, though he was unsure whether they were actually memories or imaginings fed by too much morbid preoccupation. *A boy his age impaled on a decomposed tree limb, ten or twelve feet up, naked and light blue, his tortured, muck-encrusted body defiled and rigid against the sky. He had been swept away by the current, right out of his parents' arms, and deposited into the tree by the rushing floodwaters . . . It could easily have been him . . . The sight of his exhausted father as he slipped beneath the raging current after he gave his son over to Roger's grandmother, his outstretched hand disappearing into the foamy maelstrom . . . Like so many others, his body was never found.*

Then, of course, there were the sad endings of the carnival people.

Though too young to view any of the burlesques or sideshows, he had excitedly watched the parade as the carnival rode through town to the fairgrounds, the calliope whirling with abandon. Seeing the animals, the tumblers, the clowns, the strongman and sword swallower pantomime and mug through town as he ate an ice cream cone and held his father's hand was a highlight of his life. Later, trapped by the rising floodwaters, Roger had seen them pushed back from the high ground by the locals— back into the dreadful rush of the waters . . . The beautiful young magician's assistant had lost her clothes—the skimpy outfit stripped partially away by the strength of the floodwaters, revealing her naked and voluptuous body to all. Roger had never seen a woman's breasts and pubic hair before this, except for his mother, and he was at once ashamed and curious, even though just a child. As the girl screamed, her mouth filled with black liquid, and she slipped away . . . The grease-painted clowns, reduced to tragicomic caricatures, strained to save the terrified horses that pulled the carny wagons, but it was too late—all were lost . . . A slash of lightning had startled him as he watched the hunchbacked little ventriloquist—mesmerized by his weeping, creased expression while he tried to keep his precious dummy above

the cold, cold, river . . . And the dummy itself—manically smiling in terrible jux-
taposition to the horror and fear all around—stringy hair caked with muck, flaccid
arms and legs whipsawed by the current, eyes seeming to stare right into the little
boy clutched in his grandmother's embrace . . . He would always feel discomfort
around near-human effigies after seeing that spectacle.

Another thunder roll, louder, jolted Roger from his thoughts as the
car wound farther down the valley. He was sweating, hands slick, heart
thudding dully within his ribcage. Finally, in the sallow reach of the
car's headlights, a ramshackle sign presented itself just ahead:

Welcome to **Verlassen**
Established 1845

The population figure was obscured by grime and tangles of overgrowth. *Just as well.*

Roger slowed the vehicle as he passed the weather-beaten placard,
the gravel road merging into deeply cracked asphalt at the town's limit.
The place was a ruin, it was obvious. Towering trees draped in Spanish
moss loomed over the shadowy streets, which were littered with
branches and trash. Lush overgrowth had taken back much of the
graying cityscape, the buildings little more than sagging, tired shells of
what they once represented: a pharmacy, a bank, a hotel. As he cruised
slowly though the empty township of his birth, Roger's mouth felt dry,
his throat tight; he was surprised at the condition of the place. His
mother said that a few families had rebuilt. From what he could tell,
their efforts had failed: the businesses were all shuttered, and the houses appeared to be decaying, unoccupied husks. The overall impression
was one of abandonment, desolation, forlornness.

"Wow . . . This place seemed so much *bigger* when I was a kid," he
mumbled. The radio static spiked for an instant and quickly subsided.
After a pause: "It's just a hamlet, really."

Dodging obstacles in the narrow streets, Roger was taken aback at
the pitiful appearance of the town. As he looked beyond the hypnotic
swish of the wipers and the steady cadence of the rainfall, he had
mixed emotions. Certainly he felt disappointment and sadness; in some

ways, though, he was relieved. *Perhaps it's for the best that the place was unable to bounce back after such an awful ordeal and loss of life. Fitting tribute that it would be a ghost town now—a sort of monument to the dead.*

He also felt an unexpected and satisfying twinge of comfort. There was nothing he had missed growing up outside the small community, he decided: the place had been unable to rebuild in any meaningful way, or for any length of time, it seemed. Inching through the downtown area, noting the ominous waterline from the flood that still stained the tops of the buildings some fifty years later, he decided to visit a couple of side streets before leaving, before permanently dismissing the place from his consciousness.

As he turned off the old Main Street, Roger's blood iced. He let the car roll to a gentle stop.

The rain had abated; in the yellow headlights of the car, he could make out the vague suggestion of the riverbank just beyond an overgrown meadow at the end of the potholed lane. He calmed his breathing and swallowed hard, finally snapping off the staticky radio.

In the middle of the field, harshly illuminated by the car's lights, stood the remnants of an old carnival.

The *carnival?* he wondered. Roger sat there, clammy hands gripping the steering wheel, as he stared at the macabre sight through the dingy windshield, a thin glass pane the only thing now separating his safe interior world from the half-forgotten reality exposed in the headlamps. A light fog from the river was materializing around the dilapidated collection of broken-down wagons, threadbare tents, and warped wooden barker platforms; rotting canvas posters—decorated with crudely painted, disturbing images of peeling freaks, weather-worn acrobats, and strange animals—hung from the sides of the wagons, flapping stiffly in gusts of wind from the rainstorm. A sear of lightning from the momentary squall brightened the montage in a surreal, purplish flash, briefly changing the weird spectacle into a grotesque mosaic of defaced figures and ruined, shrieking faces.

IV

"They were different, see; they had special abilities; peculiar tastes. The carnies appear with the chill of autumn and vanish after a few days, never to be seen again until the following year. It's like they never existed before we saw them, and stopped living as soon as the last part of the caravan disappeared over the hill," his father said before taking another sip of wine. As he listened to him, wide-eyed, Roger noted that his mother kept touching her forehead and sighing. It was obvious that she was distressed by what her husband was saying to the boy.

"Is that any way to help your son get to sleep?" she asked at last, pulling the shawl tighter around her shoulders as she rocked in her chair. She shook her head as she nervously leaned forward to stoke the fire. Outside, the wind blustered for a moment. She sat back in the chair, her mouth tight; after a moment, she leveled a gaze at his father before silently pointing at him and arching her eyebrows. He shrugged, sipped once more, and repaid the look with a whimsical grin. She turned away; as her eyes danced in the glow of the flame, the orange warmth of the fire caressed her face, the shadows fluid, diffuse. Finally, the hint of a smile turned her mouth; his father continued.

"As a kid, I can recall several visits from that traveling circus. We all loved the magician, the geek, the oddities, but the real star, for my friends and me, was the puppeteer—the ventriloquist. He had an assortment of bizarre marionettes— even a few life-size automata. Also, there was always a sad young girl assisting him—not sure if she was the same one each year or not. She was enigmatic . . . kind of birdlike, but strangely beautiful. She hid her face behind this shimmery veil—there was a rumor that she was disfigured. Other folks said she was one of his creations; we thought that was a bunch of bunk, of course. But who knows? Stranger things have happened."

The fire popped loudly, startling them all. *"Anyhow,"* his father went on, eyes dark, voice low, *"while she charmed the audience, the hideous puppeteer limped onto the stage—shriveled up, bent over, skeletal—with a dummy on his arm. The doll itself was sinister, sort of diabolical—a crude, dead-white face, smeared, bloody-red lips, shiny black eyes. Grinning. After a deep bow, the crooked little man took a seat on the stage and proceeded to entertain the audience with tricks, puns, imita-*

tions. Anyhow, near the end of the show, a volunteer was trundled onstage by his assistant.

"For the next few minutes, the mannequin would verbally prod the poor sap. After a bit, the horrid puppet—almost apart from the ventriloquist—began to shout these . . . proclamations. All stuff based on their answers. As the thing chattered on—dead eyes rolling, mouth working with a fever—the figurine started to laugh and laugh, keening, harsh; at this point, the lights in the tent would dim, and a tense hush fell over the crowd as they pressed in toward the stage. You could smell the stale popcorn and wet sawdust mingling with dread, with sweat. The ventriloquist was a thrashing, quivering lump, all droopy in his chair—pale and quivering in the flicker of the lamps, like he was at the mercy of this dummy—"

"You're scaring him now! Please don't—"

His father waved her off, a humorless smile tugging his face in the firelight.

"Whatever. But the boy needs to know about the world." He turned his gaze to her, eyes flinty, hard. Roger's mother returned his stare for a moment, then looked to the fire, shaking her head. He continued, watching her: "The lesson here, son, is that not everything is as it might appear at first. For example, the declarations—from the puppet—were shocking predictions of the person's imminent and terrible fate, and the fates of their friends and relations. The utterances were never hopeful, never pleasant; in fact, most of the women would faint with a cry, and many of us ran from the tent, trembling with fear . . ." He paused, allowing the silence to fill with the gentle crackle of burning wood; the wind rose outside.

His father finally looked into Roger's eyes again and spoke, voice rough, cheeks flushed from too much wine: "Were the predictions true? Hard to say. Maybe people made them true, or maybe the ventriloquist was a prophet, who knows? But understand this: we never failed to come back every night to hear what horror was in store for the year ahead—praying it wouldn't be any of us, any of our families . . ."

V

Roger slammed the car door.

The moon began to peer down on the abandoned old town from behind parting clouds: the storm was over. The cold moonlight, the misty field, the wet carnival relics, the river in the background—it all worked to create an unnerving tableau not of merriment, but of enormous melancholy. The frosty air smelled earthy and damp, and his breath created a fog in the chilly fall night. In the distance, he could hear the faint gurgle of the river. The headlamps cast immense, unnatural shadows across the carnival's remains as he walked in front of the car. The hairs on his arms stood as he approached the encampment, drawn in by the strange sight of eight or nine ragged tents and their attendant complement of horse-drawn wagons.

On the threshold of the first tattered marquee—decorated with a peeling, washed-out picture of tumblers and a magician, and displaying the words FREAKS! ABOMINATIONS! ENTER ... IF YOU DARE!—he hesitated, fearful that someone might be hiding in the shelter. After a moment, he opened the gently swaying access flap and entered, wary of any movement within.

As his vision adjusted to the gloom, he was able to make out forms in the darkness: furnishings and chairs with piles of clothing in them. The interior of the place seemed much larger that the outside suggested, but he knew it was just a trick of the darkness. As he walked further in, the dim outline of a stage loomed ahead. On the platform, he could just make out a few more large shapes from the strong moonlight wafting in from holes in the tent's ceiling: tables and trunks, more clothes.

The place felt cold and the air, though still, was thick with the odor of rot and mildew, as though it had been underwater for years. He mounted the creaky wooden stage, testing the boards. Moving closer to the chairs and trunks, he realized that an arrangement on the largest trunk next to the chair had been done on purpose; in fact, it resembled some grotesque vanitas by Antoine Wiertz. There was an assortment of dried roses and other flowers, and next to that were two ancient bottles, one for wine, and a smaller one for absinthe, both enrobed with dust; alongside and surrounding these were piles of old books and decaying papers. Atop one stack was a human skull, minus the lower jaw, its blank eye sockets regarding him with indifference. In the chair next to the trunk there was something else, which from a distance he had mistaken for a heap of apparel.

"Oh my God," he muttered, slowly bringing his hand to his face.

Seated in the chair was the ghastly figure of the dummy his father had described to him—or one similar enough, at least. Its head was askew, the hair a crust of filth and twigs. The varnish and paint on the dummy's face had spiderwebbed, and a feathering of black mold lined the hideous, smirking mouth. Only one of the lifeless black eyes was still in place. The languid arms were flung outward, as though offering him an embrace, exposing its decayed abdomen, which appeared to pulse weakly with some horrid life underneath its rumpled and stained suit; the puppet's slack legs dangled lazily from the chair. Roger was stunned by the size of the thing—it was close to the bulk of a toddler, not some trivial puppet like the one he had imagined. As he looked at the freakish apparition, Roger's mouth was pasty, metallic; his head ached, and a cold sweat dewed his upper lip and forehead. He was overwhelmed by a sudden, nauseating urge to leave, to get away from this weird place.

Turning to face the entrance, he stopped short. In the chairs he had seen from the back as he was entering the tent, he failed to notice that the rags in the seats were not merely mounds of clothing. Touched by dim, silver-gray light from the gibbous moon as it filtered through the frayed top of the pavilion, they were the disintegrating, slumped bodies of people positioned in the chairs like some hellish audience—there were at least thirty corpses jammed into the place, each in a different stage of decomposition. He struggled to make sense of what he was seeing. *Was this from the flood? Or did something else happen? Why didn't they bury these poor folks?* Behind him, there was a sound, building in intensity: *laughter.* As the laughing reached a crescendo, Roger blindly ran out of the place, refusing to look back, his clothes stretched and torn by the skeletal congregation as he fell over them in the dark.

When he finally exited, heart pounding, he was brought up short once more. Standing between the tent and his vehicle, silhouetted in the sickly headlamps of his car, was an assemblage of people. He stood there a moment, shielding his eyes from the intensity of the lights, unsure of what to do. *Did I stumble onto some drug ring? Is this a biker gang or something?*

Just as he was ready to say something, one of the shadows shuffled deliberately—almost painfully—forward. The others remained in position, swaying in the cold darkness; Roger estimated there must have been at least ten or fifteen of them.

"What," the shadow began, its voice deep, grotty, and thick, "are . . . you . . . doing here, *boy?*"

Roger was dumbstruck. Shaking now from cold and fear, he finally replied: "I—I was born in Verlassen . . . My family, we . . . we were forced away by the flood—"

The figure in front of Roger slowly raised its arm. In the weakening headlights, it was clear to Roger that the person's limb was deformed—as though there were no flesh covering the lumpy forearm and revealing the dual bones of the ulna and radius. Roger squinted to observe the person more carefully. The head was haloed by a wispy corona of fine hair, the hunched body obviously malformed, as though it suffered from some nutritional or genetic malady. A chill wind passed between them, and Roger once again noted the burble of the river . . . under that, he thought he vaguely discerned a calliope . . . and below *that*, behind him, the sound of laughter growing nearer . . . and nearer . . .

Arm still upraised, the figure spoke again: "You were told . . . *never* to come back here . . . *Roger.*"

At the sound of his name, Roger fell to his knees and began to cry. Through the distorted lens of his tears, he saw the other silhouettes slowly shambling toward him in the waning light of the car's headlamps. At last he shouted: "I never meant any disrespect!"

The hunched figure spoke again, moving nearer: "No . . . matter. There are some places . . . we are not meant . . . to go—"

"But I meant no harm!"

"—such as . . . the top . . . of Everest, or . . . the bottom of the sea . . . And intentions, well—"

"Please! I'm begging you!"

—then the dummy is at Roger's ear, screeching with laughter and clutching his throat—

"—or back into the *past,* Roger . . . One never knows . . . what is *waiting there . . .*"

Darkness consumes all: Drowning the past, the future, and the moment.

To the memory of Kirby McCauley and
Ray Bradbury

KEY

O, Fated wings of Death,
close thine ebon-starred iciness o'er me;
take me in thy dark, cold embrace
and hold me.
Life spins away—
a planet out of control—
seeding celestial fields
of stars and glowering suns.
Renewed and removed from day to day pettiness,
like so many broken dreams
we are mere icicles—
drip, dripping away the lifeblood of careless millennia until
we evaporate unto Nothingness
again.
Lo, the vastness of infinity stares,
a mad king,
pushing us all into your waiting, patient
Arms.
O, Fated wings of Death,
Wrap me in your eternal solitude—
as your brother Destiny
swore you would . . .

For thou art the doorway,
And I the broken key.

A DARKE PHANTASTIQUE

As Translated from the Oneiric

I

When the Old Man awoke it was, once again, squatting at the head of his bed.

The cold tranquility of the blue-black air lent a sense of mystery and imminence to the thing, though he felt quite certain it did not need darkness to inspire awe. Or dread. Blinking past his grogginess, the Old Man turned over in the chilly, oversized bed. He positioned his head on the musty pillow to peer at the shadowed ceiling of the ancient house, noticing the gentle billow of cobwebs through the darkness. A tear leaked from the corner of his eye, crawling over the wrinkled skin of his temple. He concentrated on his breath as he attempted to quiet his mind, and for a moment he pretended that the creature was not there. As a strategy, this sometimes afforded him a few minutes of solitude before the steely intrusion of reality.

Closing his eyelids, he chased sleep for a while longer. Just as he began to drift off, he was pursued by haunting recollections back to the present: the desperate girl with her bloodstained doll and its missing eye . . . the stench of decay, of filth . . . the choking grief of defeat, of loss. In these quiet moments—the twilight domain between past and future—he was always so certain he was awake when he was not, or that he was sleeping when he was in fact semi-conscious. It was here—in this still nether realm—that anything seemed possible: any wrong could be righted; any loss of nerve, human failure, or mistake could be easily corrected. These, however, were only their toxic projections, which was why he tried so hard not to have dreams of his own, though he sometimes wondered if the sadness and soul-deadening loss of those visions fed the creatures as much as the reveries themselves did.

At times, he found it hard to sustain a life without dreams or fantasies—in some ways, it seemed pointless—but he knew it was, for now at any rate, the only way to defeat them. The Old Man did not always succeed, of course, and sometimes he stole a few seconds to envisage things that he hoped for, or to reflect about what he missed in spite of the danger. These rare instances of weakness seemed better to him than giving up completely, though they left him fragile, depleted, and uncertain about the future, about what he was trying to accomplish.

It was during these moments of self-doubt he repeated to himself the timeworn mantra from his childhood: *When the student is ready, the Master will appear.*

>I KNOW YOU ARE AWAKENED<

His blood iced upon hearing the thing's voice in his head. His heart pounded, and he looked over at it, still balanced on the nightstand like some monstrous raven. *Was he asleep now?*

>NO—YOU ARE AWAKENED—
YOU KNOW WHAT I SEEK<

He studied the creature as he considered its words, trying to calm himself anew. It had no mouth, no nose, and apparently did not need them to eat or communicate; its smooth flesh dazzled with dimly reflective iridescent hues in the pre-dawn chill. The subtly decorated limbs were at times humanoid, at times not, but always delicate and sinuous. A couple of crudely formed stumps squatted on the creature's hunched back. These were new features, the Old Man noted. In spite of its alien aspects, the thing had a certain gracefully hypnotic power, though its face was nothing more than an oval, bald form with multiple gelatinous, golden orbs—what he assumed were eyes—shifting in illuminated intensity. The chin area was weak, tapering into a short neck, and, interestingly, it displayed no external ears, though there were strange black rings arranged concentrically near the crown of its head.

He was not alarmed by its appearance and knew that, if he thought his replies with intention, the being was somehow able to understand him. It shifted its bulk in the cold darkness, waiting.

I'm sorry . . . I still don't understand what it is you want, the Old Man finally replied. There was a tense silence. Gradually the night dissolved into morning. At some point, he must have fallen into another empty gulf of sleep; when he looked at the nightstand in the strong light of cold daybreak, the creature was gone.

And so it had been almost every night near the full moon for decades.

II

The Boy remembered that his father called them "Oneirians."

He said that was what the mighty oil barons had named them in the years before the war, when Father had worked for the richest and most idle baron in all the land. They had invaded slowly, over a period of many, many years; it had taken generations for the Oneirians to infiltrate society, but once they permeated everyday life, the war began in earnest. They bided their time—Oneirians had enormous resources of time and patience—and were at last able to overtake the reigning hierarchies of culture with stealth campaigns of division and apathy.

Now, Father and the Boy were forced to toil under a merciless sun, which drove his father to talk more than any drink ever could. Father would stand, leaning on his hoe for support, wiping the sweat off his lined, grimy face as he stretched. He stroked his full moustache, dark, curly hair damp with perspiration sticking out from under his oily cap. As he scanned the trees to be sure they were not being watched, the older man sighed heavily in thought, olive-skinned features shining as he pulled out a hand-rolled cigarette and lit up before taking a long drag. The Boy continued stripping the plants—pretended to, at least— of the remaining peas and okra on their dying stalks. Glancing up at his father's weathered and scar-crossed face, he had to squint due to the blaze of the sun; he rarely said anything in response, knowing his father wanted to remember, not discuss.

As usual, Father would tell the Boy about the Oneirians' arrival in the World with a deference borne of dismay and suspicion. Before his mother disappeared, Father was less reverential; he also talked less about the past and more of the future. Not so now—and it never failed to sadden the Boy how uncertainty changed even the proudest, hardest perspectives, wearing them down like water over stone.

"Well, the barons . . . where are they now, eh?" Father dramatically swept his arm across the field, cigarette in hand, his enormous shadow looming in the late afternoon sunlight and spreading far over the poisoned ground. "Gone. Like the farmers. Like the cities. The money, the power—all *gone*. Poor, wealthy, we took the night rides, the trains. We died in the camps; some of us fought, lived. The rest . . . the rest . . ." This was usually the point where his eyes would well and Father would stop talking as he went back to work.

The Boy looked down at the shrunken plants he crouched over, his dirty fingers entwined in the hardening foliage. His ragged clothes were torn and filthy, his hands stiff from pulling, picking, twisting the meager scraps they foraged from the wilted crops of the abandoned farmland. Every year that passed without Mama and his sister seemed hotter, drier, emptier than the one before. They still had each other, and his sister was out there somewhere, he knew, but he was tired and knew that Father was. The Boy sometimes wondered how much more of this they could endure before the heat made them both insane, before hunger would consume them in reverse.

Today, as Father stooped to till more dusty earth, he continued: "Oneirians—they cannot win, son. *Don't let them win.* They are oneirophages . . . they eat our dreams, our faith, to live. They may be the most powerful beings in this world, but you and your generation . . . you can defeat them. There was a time before they arrived, a glorious time, eh? I wish you had known it. Before they came here to feed on our fears, our sorrows, our regrets." Father wiped his brow with his sleeve. "They are the *opposite* of men; they grow stronger as they age, not weaker. But you are young. You still have time."

This surprised the Boy. He paused in his labors, dropping another handful of gleanings into their frayed basket, and looked over at his father as the man worked the ground, his back bent, clothes mud-caked and stained. A welcome breeze cooled the sweat on the Boy's coffee-complected face, tossed his auburn hair. The air was heavy, warm. His almond-shaped eyes glinted in the late afternoon sunlight as he watched his father. It would be dark soon, he realized.

"Just remember, son," his father said. "Some people search their whole lives for something—treasure, love, the Almighty." He struck the ground harder, drops of sweat falling from his forehead and nose, the cigarette hanging loosely from his lips. "In the end, I've found that gold is useless, women are fleeting, and God is distant."

The Boy listened as he worked the plants, head down, lest Father stop speaking. The man's hoe clanged against rocks in the parched ground; far away, the Boy could hear a low rumble: there was a deep bruising of the sky opposite the setting sun. A storm was on the horizon.

"We begin life as we end it, son," his father said. "Oblivious, con-fused, crazy . . . we are the bodily echoes and whispered omens of eve-rything and everyone else—the lusts, the beliefs, the agonies. Living allegories, breathing potential and possibility—good or bad. *We* are the ones who decide our destinies. Why leave it to chance, eh? In the phase prior to our birth, just as in death, our consciousness is a part of the fabric of the universe. It's true of everyone before—and will be for everyone after—us, be it a lizard, an ant, a whale, a man . . ." Father paused. The wind was picking up, and the temperature was finally breaking. Heat lightning flashed in the sky as the rainstorm moved in their direction; the thunder was growing louder, shaking in the Boy's chest; there was static in the air, and the faintest smell of dampness.

Father stood again, relaxing on the handle of the garden hoe; he crushed the butt of his cigarette out on the ground. The Boy glanced up and saw that his father was smiling at him, the older man's kind green eyes wet at the corners. The Boy had always thought him to be handsome and intelligent, full of love, strength, compassion. In the years since Mother's disappearance, Father had grown more and more bitter, but never toward him. He walked stiffly over to the Boy, gently taking his chin in a calloused hand. "The void . . . the chasm . . . even *they* are substantive, son. Even they have meaning, dimension. This claim of nothingness by the Oneirians—it simply isn't so . . . except in the hearts of those who cannot understand that we are all one and the same, so we must never give up the struggle for life, eh?" He smiled, his gaze filled with longing and melancholy. Lightning seared again, followed quickly by deep rolls of thunder. The air had cooled considerably, and dusk was closing in at last. "They know this, they want to scare us from caring for one another . . . *they fear this about us.* That is our power, son—that we can rise above our petty selves, above our circumstances. Never forget it . . . and never forget that you can't tell where you're going if you're always looking backward. Don't fear. They eat dreams and thrive on fear. Don't let them. *Look ahead;* the future is unwritten while the past has been determined." The man paused, his throat moving as he swallowed. "I only wish I could have saved your sister . . . but I can still save you, I hope."

The Boy nodded. Finally he said: "Papa, I miss Dorothea. And Mama."

Father looked away, his eyes distant. The disappearance of his wife had been a terrible blow; watching his daughter—the Boy's sister—suffer had been even more cruel.

"Papa, what *are* they, the Oneirians? Can we *really* beat them? Can we win the war?"

The man watched the horizon, staring into the approaching tempest. It was dark now, and the lightning was quite close. Rain began to patter the scorched dirt.

"Gather up the basket, son," was all he replied.

III

Long ago, there was a very beautiful, generous woman called Dorothea. She had been a daughter, a sister, a paramour . . . and now she was alone.

After the war started and the Oneirians attempted to take over the World, there was a time of great upheaval, and her family's fortunes reversed: her father— once well connected and powerful—became a pauper, her younger brother became a servant, and her mother vanished. Then the most terrible thing of all happened: her true and only love was killed in the war, and her desire to be happy died with him.

She was a seamstress by trade, but years of conflict and sickness had taken their toll; finally, her grief about her fate caused her to swallow the whole world in a transparent blackness. In the time before, everyone and everything had lived and died in the warm presence of great and constant Helios. Eternal nightfall—cold and unending—had been unknown outside of the human psyche, where it was well understood that there was a season to all things, except light.

However, stricken as she was, Dorothea paid no notice to the needs and wants of others, so consumed was she with mourning. In fact, as a result of her deep rumination and seclusion, she tapped into a power no one realized was possible for a human being. The Oneirians, mindful of her vulnerability, had gathered in their masses during her sleep and amplified her sadness and pain until it birthed physical manifestations in the waking world. So it was that, in the depths of her heartache, her loss, Dorothea found comfort in bringing despair to everyone else as well. She sat in her home—hour by hour, day by day—contemplating what never was and what could never be. After a while, the emotional displacement traded every brick in her house with the desiccated carcasses of the dead, eventually becoming a windswept ossuary high on a bluff—a grotesque and gothic monument to one woman's loneliness and agony. In time, Dorothea adopted the term the Oneirians used to describe the relief she felt at divesting her anguish through perpetual shadow—it was now the era of the "Darke Phantastique."

After years of this, representatives from the Kingdoms of the World called on her at her home of gloom and bone. During this meeting, their elected leader—the heavily armored reptile Oix, his scaly skin glowing a faint magenta in the dark—was flanked by a voluptuous human female named S'ylla and a fire-plumed courtesan of the avian realm, JXrl.

Once at ease in her living room and partaking of a cup each of fragrant red wine, Oix at last said: "Dorothea, we have come to implore you to end this blight of darkness. You can't condemn everyone and everything to permanent nightfall. . . . Just as examples, the poor chameleons are so confused they simply cower in the woods, alternating between red, yellow, teal, and back. The plants are struggling to survive, and the waters are too cold for the fish and other marine life. I know you didn't intend this, but . . . Moonlight alone isn't enough. It's a crime against nature."

Dorothea, her red hair flowing, her body enshrouded in black lace finery, gazed upon the party with horror-filled, cobalt eyes as she clutched the bloodied figure of a one-eyed doll. She looked at each member in turn as the wind howled outside, whistling past the skulls and skeleton piles comprising her bleak sanctuary.

She nodded after a time, raising her hand in supplication: "I need time to consider this, Oix."

He looked at his silent companions, then back to Dorothea. His expression softened, and he nodded in comprehension. "There you have it," he said to the others at last. With that, they began their arduous pilgrimage back whence they came, across darkened, misty lands, through timeless shadowed forest mazes to wait at their respective Kingdoms.

True to her word, Dorothea did deliberate: for a thousand years she thought, and thought, and thought. Not for a single instant in all that time did her grief subside.

In the end, her father was persuaded to visit with a compromise: light for half the time and darkness for the other. Oix and the others had finally agreed to this arrangement—though not like the time of Helios before, it was better than the Darke Phantastique of the present. Oix, ever the pragmatist, conceded some golden ages could never be recaptured, but at least the future might be salvaged to some degree—and indeed must be if they were to prevail in their struggles with the dream-stealing Oneirians.

"Very well, Papa, I accept," his daughter said. From that time forward, it was so. "And how is my brother, Papa?" Her grief-stricken gaze briefly cleared. Outside, the wind stilled for a moment.

Father took her hand, slowly, gently. As their fingers entwined, her grip was tight, cold. Looking into his daughter's eyes, he knew she was lost to him, that the Oneirians had devoured all her aspirations, all her dreams, by using her sadness as a tool to pull the World into nightmarish desolation.

Though he felt a strong urge to weep, he smiled instead, saying, "The Boy is well. I am teaching him to be a man, eh? I hope, one day, he will dream a world of compassion and love, and never stop trying to make things better for everyone. Of course, he misses you very much. And Mama—"

She suddenly grabbed her father, sobbing and hugging him tightly; under her black robes, he could feel her petite, frail body and was touched with even deeper sadness and pity about her plight. What a price our family has paid to these beings! *At that moment Helios returned, and light gradually filled the dank chamber. Father stood to leave after a few moments of embrace. "I love you, Dorothea. We all thank you for your kindness."*

As the heavy door closed behind him, Father was grateful for the light that would accompany his travel back to the Boy. A few miles away from his daughter's ossified monument to pain and suffering, he reveled in the warmth and calm of the return of light, but knew that the dark would reappear—though not forever—in a few hours. It would be good to see his son again; there was much to explain to him, and even more to warn him about. After several more miles, he heard a distant, terrible scream.

Dorothea was never seen or heard again.

IV

>I KNOW YOU ARE AWAKENED<

The Old Man's eyelids snapped open. The creature was once more hunkered on the nightstand. Its golden mass of eyes darted back and forth as it moved its weight from leg to leg, its dull, metallically hued flesh rippling. Even in silhouette, he noted that the stumps on the thing's back had grown considerably and now resembled twisted wings.

He thought about what the beast had said.

Yes: he was awakened. In every way that could be interpreted.

>YOU KNOW WHAT I SEEK<

After all these years of not understanding, it was dawning on the Old Man that he might finally appreciate the demands of the Oneirian. He rolled over in bed, turning his back on the creature. He swung his legs over the side and sat up. As he gingerly stood, the Old Man was surprised at how little pain he was in for the first time in recent memory.

Donning a robe, he walked over to the washbasin nearest his bedroom. Pouring water from a porcelain jug into the sink, he stooped over and dipped his hands into the cold liquid, cupping some and rinsing his face. With a rough green towel, he dried off, deep in thought.

The Old Man found it interesting to contemplate how remembrances of the past always seemed to be in black-and-white flashes, complete with blurs and scuffs, like old photographs, the older memories tinged with the faintest sepia tones, the newer ones, though grainy, sharper and more defined. Meanwhile, the present appeared crystalline and fluid: vivid color, focused, tightly contoured . . . complete with a soundtrack of heartbeats and laughter, the fragrances of perfume and incense. Of course, envisioning the future was fuzzy and indistinct, but with the surreal colorations of Kirlian coronal photographs—like an image in ultraviolet fluorescence photography illustrating the topography of veins and arteries under the skin.

He looked hard into the mirror above the basin: The room reflected in the scratched and cracked glass of the old mirror was backward and strange to him. *Disheveled. Miserable.* He touched his cheek, tracing the diagram of lines and creases on his face. The room was cold, dark, soundless; it occurred to him how silence was like a mirror for the psyche—transforming feelings and realizations into mental constructions of insight.

"Yes. I think I know what you seek, Oneirian. You seek *everything*." He paused, then glared at the creature, smiling coldly: "But you aren't entitled to *anything*."

The Old Man tentatively brought his hand up. In the unfocused background, he could see the blurred thing studying him, its head jerking in different directions as it perched on his nightstand, its strange eyes alternately dimming and brightening. The featureless ovoid countenance of its face gleamed dully in the moonlight spilling through the slatted blinds of the window next to his sunken bed, creating impossible and frightening shadows throughout the cool stillness of the room.

What is a monster? the Old Man thought as he gradually raised his hand to the mirror. *Some glowering thing revealing itself through the mists of consciousness, perception, time, and space? Some stranger from a foreign and an-*

tique land? A mindless disease? Something more primitive—or more advanced—that we can't reason with or fully grasp?

The creature straightened suddenly, as if in spasm, its malformed, leathery wings flaring outward like some great bat. It flapped the appendages a few times, then folded them away again. Quietly it dropped onto the lumpy bed, delicately crawling nearer to the Old Man, coming more and more into focus, before relaxing once more.

Perhaps a monster is something else entirely. . . . Maybe it's within us all—inside our heads. Sometimes appearing as a leader we adore, yet who is privately cruel—delighting in that savagery when alone. Or is it what we are—*or have* become—*as a species?*

The beast inched forward on the bed.

> >SOME QUESTIONS CANNOT BE ANSWERED—
> AND PERHAPS THEY SHOULD NOT BE<

Finally the Old Man's hand connected with the mirror, spanning time and space:

. . . in the present, the Old Man was literally touching his past . . . on the opposite side of the mirror, his previous self regarded him, younger, stronger—the Boy . . .

. . . his previous iteration whispered to him mentally from across the ages as their palms kissed against the cloudiness of the fractured glass.

>As an immortal, you are obliged to continue the fight against the Oneirians.<

The Old Man nodded. >Papa?< *the Old Man thought, wistful. He missed them all so much, even after so many lifetimes.*

>Gone.< *his reflection mouthed. For an instant, there was the faintest smell of wet moss and rain. The Old Man briefly shifted his attention in the mirror to the beast behind him: It was sluggishly creeping forth, its newly grown wings billowing . . .*

>Dorothea?<

The reflection shook his youthful head. >Not here. She's gone. Mama, too.<

The Old Man nodded, understanding; there were truly only his memories to sustain him now.

>And what of tomorrow?< *the Old Man asked.*

There was a pause, and a troubled look crossed the Boy's face. >Unknown, but you have a role to play. Remember Papa's lessons. . . . When the student is ready, the Master will appear; that we are all a part of the void; dream again, and recall the others he explained. You are the Master now.<

The Old Man: >Prayers are never enough, I know. . . . Miracles don't really exist; we have to take things into our own hands, don't we?<

The Boy smiled cryptically, pulling his hand away, severing the collision of past and present, creating a vacuum for the future. Abruptly, the Oneirian reared up, spreading its ominous wings behind the Old Man, its voice exploding inside his mind.

>I HAVE COME TO DESTROY YOUR WILL—
YOU AND YOUR LINE CANNOT PREVAIL<

As the Old Man and the Oneirian engaged, a howl tore through the fabric of the dimensional boundaries of space and time.

V

Once upon a time, there was a struggle between the realm of dreams and hopes and an empire of hatred and despair. During this troubled period, light was driven away by an utter and smothering darkness. After an eternity passed, love and understanding restored faith in the future, and the possibilities it might hold. While the era of forever days are gone for all time, unending night was beaten back, at last, by enduring lessons carried forth, and steadfast wisdom revealed.

Now is the age of alternating loss and redemption, which is the most fertile ground for growth and renewal. In the end, the lesson is thus: Oneirians are never far away and will not stop in their bitter feeding off the dreams of others as they seek the eternal return of the Darke Phantastique.

Consider this a warning.

CHRYSALIS

I

On the coldest night ever recorded in the antique city of Paladinsk—
formerly known as Istanbul—Ambassador Aral'ucaRd waited for the
MagLev train to depart. As he glanced from the ice-laced window to
his holowatch, he noted that they should have departed nearly eight
minutes ago: *Things might be more treacherous now that it's completely dark. I
hope we can make it to the meeting in the Old City by morning.* He had always
despised the May Day Rituals, but understood their importance; even
before being reassigned back to Earth, Irfan had never enjoyed the
Process or PазумLink. It was exhausting, thankless work, but essential,
he knew, to the continuation of the Pekelný Republika.

Irfan—a family name—narrowed his shimmering brown eyes as
he peered through a dreamy veil of smoke swirling up from one of the
hydrail locomotive engines. He stroked a day's rough on his jaw, tracing the scars along his face, an unconscious habit when thinking. As he
studied the growing assembly just beyond the reinforced fence at the
perimeter of the old Sirkeci Terminal, he was once again transfixed by
the way their skin softly glowed in the deepening gloom, at the strange,
wispy patterns that they displayed across their features, almost like bioluminescent fingerprints; each form was a unique signature of their
particular contagion—loops, whorls, and swirls in various pastel hues
of faint purple, green, blue, red. It covered their whole bodies, he
knew, in eccentric configurations across their strange, pale skin, following the invisible Lines of Blaschko—*if* they survived the initial infection. With a hint of alarm, he observed that as recently as a half-
hour ago there had been just a few individuals, then tens, and now
hundreds, adding a ghostly illumination to the already surreal display.
Soon there might be thousands amassed at the giant gates—watching

. . . waiting under the dark, starless skies in tense anticipation, seething with quiet rage.

He was grateful then that the cars, at least for him and his detail, were reinforced, the windows impenetrable; he tugged at the collar of his thin tunic, suddenly warm. As he shifted his gaze, the focal plane moved forward—blurring background minutiae, rounding off jagged edges—as foreground details sharpened, and he saw his own tired reflection emerge in the armored glass. He looked haggard, drained; his almond-shaped eyes were hollow, the deep maroon feathers crowning his head seemed lackluster against his dark brown skin. There were new wrinkles along his cheeks; as he aged, he had prematurely begun the process of transformation and displayed the irregular light blue blemishes of pigmentational erosion characteristic of psychic stress in his species.

The locomotive engines surged, breaking his attention; it was a sensation he felt more than heard. A whisper of snow began to fall as he once again considered the people at the fence, simultaneously repulsed and sorrowful. The languorous pan of searchlights revealed their deadened faces in sharp contrast: men, women, children—festooned in ragged clothes, pushing and pulling at the bars of the fence in an ever more frantic rhythm. Irfan knew the only thing that prevented their surge over the top of the gates was the patrolling, heavily armed, and armor-suited guards, ominously resplendent in black metallic dusters and jackboots. They were frightening in their attire, even to Irfan; the strangely angled facemasks on their helmets were fierce, reminding him of samurai masks from ancient Japan. Indeed, as he watched the weird parade of sentries choking back their leashed German Shepherd/wolf hybrids, he imagined it as a kind of surreal kabuki presentation, the glowing hordes beyond the gates a sort of disenfranchised audience. The irony of the situation was not lost on him: the original gulags were built to keep "his kind"—The Righteous—*in*. And *those* trains—primitive, rough—had been used to deport them to the Reformation camps. . . . The present-day guards were intended to keep the Nons *out;* to keep the triumphant safe. The trains now—opulent, sleek—were for State use exclusively.

To the victors go the spoils, he mused. *Either way, you're a prisoner.* Across thousands of light years, and the takeover of hundreds of galaxies, he had cultivated many such bitter truths. In addition, his race had learned the hard way that staying on a single planet, even in a single solar system, was not the way to provide for the hordes of subjects that depended on their governance for food and raw materials. Whether perceived as gods or tyrants, their needs were unchanging: resistance, while expected, was generally irrelevant. One way or another, his people had been clever enough to avoid more advanced civilizations, and ruthless enough to totally assimilate those that were less developed. It mattered not if there was anything cultural to be gleaned; culture was cheap, and DNA was cheaper. All that mattered was the continued existence of The Righteous and unconditional acceptance of the divine eternal: the One.

After a few more minutes of daydreaming, Irfan muttered, his mouth dry, his throat tight: "Poor bastards. History's *littered* with the remains of the 'virtuous,' but written by the *winners.*" He regarded the book on the table of his stuffy sleeper, a recent, sanitized bestseller about the New Crusades: *Our Continuing Struggle: Triumph of The Righteous.* He moved his scrutiny once more out the window: "Haven't you fucking . . . *things* ever heard that before?" By now the snow was driving quite hard, the wind blowing it into drifts. The coach lurched forward abruptly as the train finally departed, jolting him from his previous thoughts and propelling him into others; an introspective individual, times like this always gave him pause: he wished the plan had gone a different course. In the hundred-odd years since the end of the New Crusades, there had been many uprisings and threats of more, as the people of Earth continued to fight the reality of their new masters. With such churn in the current geopolitical sphere, he thought despairingly that this little planet was as ill-equipped to resolve its differences as it had been more than a century ago.

Just like all the rest . . . A few early successes don't equal victory. Besides, diplomacy didn't work.

Earthlings and Mosaics—humans and enslaved intergalactic specimens that had been genetically combined—seemed to have learned nothing after the subjugation of the so-called American Empire by The Righteous. They persisted in continuing the same loathsome infighting, petty squabbles, and neo-tribal chest-thumping that had closed the twenty-second century; as though a cluster of splintered, marginalized factions could organize and overcome their conquerors with the paltry tools of the Internet, social media, and secret meetings. The idea of these unsophisticated, stinking denizens contesting The Righteous was laughable to Irfan; humans had already learned the terrible realities that Enhanced Psionics were much more efficient than any computer network, that Neural Displacement beams were infinitely more powerful than conventional ballistics, that GeneBombs and mutagenic payloads were deadlier than any atomic weapon. The nickname the humans had for the domination of Earth was as fitting an epitaph as any: The Thirty Day Conquest.

As the last night train pulled away from the Terminal, gathering power and silent speed, all along the fence the grimy mob had begun to chant their oddly understandable yet foreign slogans; they strained to grasp at the passing behemoth in a pathetic demonstration of their obscene gestures; some even threw rotten food at the ambassador's official car, shaking the huge fence with such raw anger he thought it might give way.

One day that barricade will fail, he thought. *Seems it always does.*

"But," Irfan said at last, snapping closed his cabin shade, suddenly chilly, "not tonight, savages."

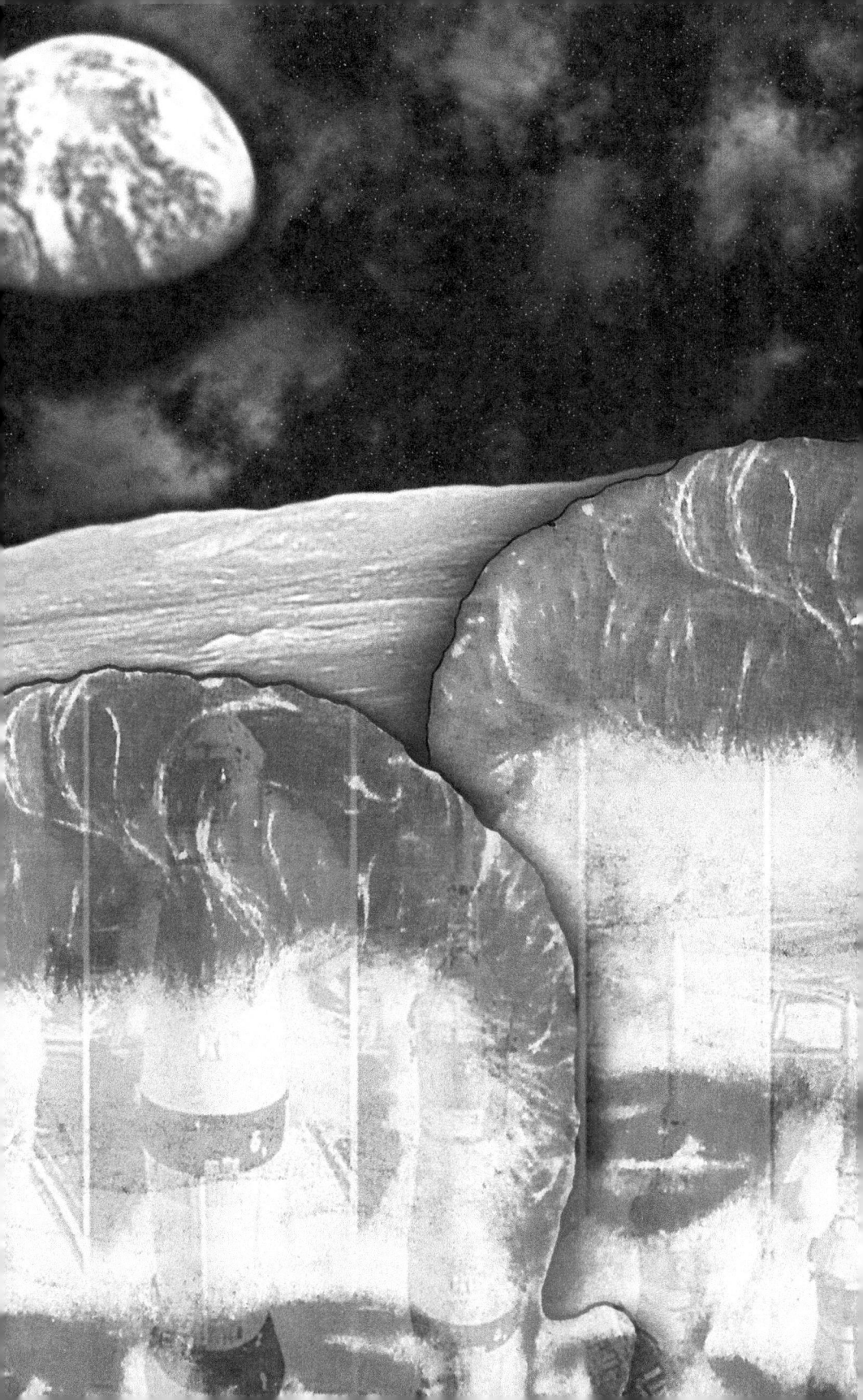

II.

At first, he was adrift on a sea of red. . . . "Otec?"

Perspective moved—suddenly he was at the gates. . . . The doors of the camp . . . they were thrusting out of the pure white ground . . . The edges of everything were hazy, indistinct . . .

His father was slumped on the earth. . . . He was sobbing, holding something . . . something familiar . . .

Irfan jolted awake, confused for an instant as to where he was. His sleep always grew more fitful when he was summoned to the Old City. In the past 300 or so solar passages, he never managed to get decent rest on the eve of РазумLink.

There was a knock on the door of his cabin.

"Prosím." The door slid open as the train glided quietly through the darkness outside Paladinsk.

"Pozdravy, Ambassador Aral'ucaRd," a young woman said as she stood in the threshold. "May I enter your chamber?" Clear, ice-blue irises signified her status as servant-class; her gold-toned skin gleamed in the ambient light of the overhead LED lamps, and he thought he detected the delicate smell of saffron—perhaps her perfume. Though taboo to act upon, Irfan had always found the slave girls from Ţepeştan sexually attractive. It shamed him when he recalled the rapes that his squadron had perpetrated during the New Crusades against the Ţepeştany women.

He smiled at her. "Please." He gestured for her to enter. She quickly returned the smile as she gathered the floor-length shawl around her body and stepped inside. The door slid shut. For a moment they mutely studied one another, the train rocketing through the night.

"Have we gone through the Plateau yet?" Irfan asked, crossing his arms. He stroked his chin contemplatively as he watched her.

She hesitated, straightening. "No." She looked down. "Are you requiring anything else at the moment, Ambassador?"

Part of him relished this feeling: *power*. She was at his mercy, and he could literally have anything he wanted. At the same time, the tiniest shadow of pity crossed his soul. Ever since the murder of his wife, he'd been much more sensitive to the emotional cues of others; sometimes it was disconcerting, but mostly he was appreciative—even if he could not consciously articulate it. He mentally scanned her mind. Her PsyMask appeared clear—free of distracting thoughts. All he detected were fragmented contemplations about her family, and minor electrical firings about a child.

Finally he asked: "Where is my regular domestic, D'Lahlm? I didn't realize there would be a change in the service staff before such an important trip."

The woman bowed her head. "I understand, Ambassador. I was in training with her; she took ill suddenly and could not attend to your needs. It was an engineered retroviral contaminant from her last excursion with Bishop Wallach, possibly contracted during their brief tour of the Shuttered District. I am told she will recover fully, but they were concerned that you might have come down with her ailment."

Irfan nodded. "Present your hands." The young woman complied, holding her hands in front of her, as though inspecting her nails. Irfan lightly gripped them: they were cold to the touch, as the skin of poikilotherms usually was, with small osteoderms embedded just under the epidermis, but mostly the golden scales were tiny, the flesh quite soft, even supple. He gently turned her hands over, inspecting the light orange fingertips and the translucent blue, slightly curving claws tipping the fused digits. *No fingerprints*. Undeveloped Mosaics and numerous GeneBomb survivors—especially those affected by the biochemical agent responsible for their glowing marks, *Bacterial Pseudoporphyria Luciferins*—usually had telltale friction ridge skin tangles on their fingers, known as Digital Labyrinths. Though a complete lack of fingerprints was uncommon, it could also be a sign of Developed Conversion—highly desirable in a servant.

"You are safe," Irfan declared. "What are you called?"

She bowed again, and her shawl slipped off one shoulder, revealing larger, decorative scales that spiraled up her neck, disappearing under her head scarf. Irfan found her erotic, even beautiful. Also strangely familiar.

"I am J'Dorul, Ambassador."

III.

During the earliest days of The Struggle, the humans had declared that they would never be subject to the One. The Bishops convened and decreed that it would be necessary to Purify them. . . .

After some time, during May Day Rituals, it was deemed insufficient to continue PaзумSlaughter by way of dream states, and PaзумLink was discontinued in favor of First Contact. . . .

In spite of this fair arrangement—that Earth would remain intact, and Cerebral Erasure would guarantee families be spared seeing parents rendered into food, or the indignities of children retired into Mosaic Procreator Service—all overtures were rejected. . . . How were we to thrive without new worlds? Without renewed assets and food sources?

Perhaps most terrible of all, the One was disparaged, was denied. After these terms of surrender were rebuffed, we were repeatedly, and viciously, attacked . . .

Irfan put the book down, still unable to sleep. He remembered that horrible time as though it were last week. It was a black period; as one of the first families to venture to Earth during what would later be described as the New Crusades, his mother, father, and siblings, once discovered, had been gathered into a camp with others of his kind in a massive effort by the humans to contain, try, and possibly eradicate them. The folly of it: even though the humans had practically invited them to Earth by sending radio broadcasts and space-going vessels throughout the galaxy, it was chilling to contemplate that they had no *idea* how to conduct themselves once their transmissions were intercepted and answered. It was also incredible to Irfan that they had never heard of the One. It held all consciousness together: the One was all; the One was everything; the One was nothingness; the One was eternity. It still revolted him that humanoids would not accept this basic concept. Instead, they insulted his kind; murdered them, imprisoned them in gated encampments, tried to force them to deny the One with torture. . . .

He rubbed the scars on his face, tuning in to the gentle rocking of the train as it hurtled toward the Old City, the place the Earthlings had once referred to as Bucharest. He had received those scars in the human prison camps: they had cut him, beat him, tortured him and his entire family. For some reason, they were offended by the feeding customs of Irfan's people, calling him strange things as they had whipped him, burned him, slapped him: "nosferatu," "vampire," "psycho."

He opened the shade of his window and peered out into the blank darkness. They were moving through one of the Inhospitable Zones, he noted; the full moon loomed large and low in the sky, casting waxy light over the perpetual fires that burned in what he thought might be the Arid Plateau. Mosaics and humans somehow lived in these places still. Indeed, they caused much chaos and upheaval with their improvised rockets; their weapons, though crude, could still deliver an occasional surprise blow to the large cities, causing unrest in people's hearts, raising doubts in their minds, especially the Converted humans and Mosaics.

The One always provides, though. The One is on the side of The Righteous, and no other.

He took comfort in that motto, even as it brought him the sadness of recalling his father's dying words at the camp, just hours before reinforcements had liberated them all and they had taken the Earth's capital cities: "Trust in the One, Irfan. We . . . cannot understand the mind or intentions of the One. We must simply . . . accept what the One allows . . ."

A wise person, his father.

IV

He was sobbing, and holding something . . . something familiar . . .

Irfan walked closer, but the faster he walked, the farther away his father seemed to recede against the gates. . . . The pure white environment was blinding.

"Otec! What is that you have? Where is Matka?" *Irfan's voice echoed once, then was swallowed in complete silence.*

His father looked up at him. . . . He moved slowly, so very slowly. He raised his hands to his face, pulling them down his cheeks . . . streaks of black.

The object in his lap moved—

The knock at his door interrupted his sleep, but Irfan was not ungrateful. The nightmares had been getting more powerful as the time of PазумLink drew closer.

"Prosím."

Once again, the door slid open and J'Dorul appeared. This time she held a tray with covered bowls on it. "I took the liberty. I suspected that you might be hungry. My deepest apologies if I have offended you, Ambassador." She gingerly bowed her head.

Irfan smiled. "No. Thank you, J'Dorul. Please put it there." He motioned to a small table near the window, which still had the blind open. Outside, the horizon glowed in a hellish display of the infernal Arid Plateau. The door closed behind her.

She walked to the table and placed the tray on it in silence, her traditional slipper shoes noiseless across the floor. She turned and regarded him thoughtfully. "I will leave you now."

Irfan raised his hand: "No. Please. Would you stay? I am in need of . . . some companionship." He regarded her uncomfortable expression, saying: "I don't expect you to eat with me; I know your people are vegetarians. I—I would just . . ." He paused, suddenly aware of heat rising in his face. "I think we should get to know each other since we're working together, that's all."

After a moment, she nodded in agreement and sat down at the modest table.

Irfan nodded in return, taking a seat opposite. He looked at the tray, then pulled the coverings from the bowls: deep red liquids, one thin and oily, the other thick and mottled, reflected the overhead lights. He smiled at her.

"Fantastic—a warm and cold dish each."

"Yes. The chef pureed them especially from fetal hominid sources this morning. He said that you preferred a little bit of clotting in your stews, as well as a plasma skim on the warm platters."

He placed a course linen napkin on his lap and used a spoon to stir the yellowish upper broth of the warm soup: "Good man!" The soup mixed like a fine miso. "Delicious. So . . ." Irfan looked up at her as he ate. "Tell me more about yourself. Where is your family? Where do you live?"

J'Dorul regarded him impassively, her penetrating stare fixed on the table. After a moment she said: "I lived at one time in a Plateau near Paladinsk."

He stopped eating for a moment. "I see."

She continued. "You said you wanted me to speak—"

"And I do—"

"Then allow me, Ambassador." Her aspect was frosty, detached, her words clipped.

After a pause he waved his spoon. "Carry on, excuse me, J'Dorul."

She nodded. "Well, I lived there for many years with my family. My parents and siblings, my husband, our young son—"

"And where are they? Are they in the city now?" He had moved on to the cold stew of minced flesh, offal, and blood: "Mm. Amazing! Smells incredible . . . Pardon me; carry on."

"Strange you would want to know, Ambassador." She gathered the top of her cloak around her shoulders, as though suddenly cold, in spite of the fact that the room was still uncomfortably warm. "But we all want something, I suppose, don't we? To be loved, to be free from pain and suffering."

Irfan smiled at her, slightly bemused. "Well, why wouldn't I?" He took another spoonful of stew, wiping his reddened lips as he chewed.

"Indeed . . . Indeed . . . Well, the truth is this: they were murdered, Ambassador. *All* of them."

He stopped in mid-chew, eyes wide. J'Dorul held his gaze, her irises like chipped ice: "Yes. By *your* people. By the adherents of the One."

Silence. She continued: "We were selected in the Lottery, then taken in for the Conversion Process. They lied to us, of course, to everyone. They said that we were 'Chosen' and that we would be treated well, not forced to endure the savage, hardscrabble life of the Plateau any longer. That we would be privileged." J'Dorul stopped, a strange half-grin shading her features. "But it was all a hoax. *A big lie.* We had heard the stories of people who had been picked in the Lottery, even seen the interviews of their new, glamorous lives after the Conversion. We were so excited! It was what we had dreamed for so long . . . except that it was *not* a dream, Ambassador—it was a *nightmare.*"

She paused, taking a deep breath. The train jostled in the nocturnal quiet; Irfan was riveted to her story, his spoon suspended halfway between the bowl and his mouth. J'Dorul continued: "We were stripped, mocked, ridiculed—especially for our disdain of flesh-eating. They tormented us for our lack of 'belief,' saving the worst punishments they could inflict as acts of purification in the name of your One. . . . Mind you, we weren't even humans, 'only' Mosaics. Our family, as you might have suspected, were Herptile Amalgams—genetically developed by the Bishops for Enlightenment, more than a hundred years before Earth's invasion. After the New Crusades, we were relegated to permanent servant-class to make up the deficiencies due to casualties from the battles. So our family 'won' the Lottery, along with hundreds of others from our Plateau; after we were interviewed, screened for disease, and forced to make holodocs about our new life, they took us in . . . shuttled us to the Grande Basilicas."

She paused again, staring into him. "Just after we left the Sacred Chambers in the House of the One, they began dividing us into cloistered groups." J'Dorul half-smiled again in pained remembrance.

"There, Ambassador, I saw terrible things; but the *sounds*—the sounds were even more pitiful. I watched the soldiers of the One suck the blood right out of my father's gaping wounds, laughing at his protests to spare me, my mother. Instead, they raped her, then took her away. I never saw her again. They killed my brothers and sisters in front of me, declaring that they were to be fodder for the Grinder, rendered into corpseflesh. Honestly, they wanted blood more than sex, I think. Your kind were frenzied for it. Your *filthy* kind, Ambassador."

He finally dropped his spoon into the bowl in shock. "How are you . . . *here* then?"

She laughed bitterly. "Surprising, is it not? Of the dozens in the rooms with us, I am the only survivor. One of the commandants saw me, took a liking. He spared me, and I was forced to be his concubine. He was hideous to me, but I was patient. And I learned; I took up the Lessons—never once believing, of course—but there I *planned;* as I was indoctrinated, as I undertook Development. I was driven. I was driven by vengeance, by *hate*."

J'Dorul leaned back in her seat, pulling the hood away from her face as she let the information sink in. "So here we are, Ambassador. And it's just us now, in this shrinking moment in time, our life paths forever connected, whether we wish it or not. Just us in this tiny sleeper car, on this MagLev as it rushes through the night to the Old City, so that you can participate in the May Day Rituals and destroy other lives. But no one knows about me. *I made sure of that.*" Her face relaxed. "So I ask you: Where is your One now? Where was the One in the camp I was in, Ambassador? Where is the One for the other races, the other planets that your kind has pillaged, decimated, enslaved, devoured? Why didn't the One help *my* family as we were trying to survive? I'll tell you why: *because there is no One.* The One is a projection of disturbed imaginations; an abomination; a blight. The crude invention of feeble minds—"

Irfan jumped up, outraged by the sacrilege: "Renounce! Renounce that and I *might* let you live!"

She laughed at him. "Sit down, you fool." Then she added menacingly: "*I'm* in control here, Ambassador. *Sit!*"

He complied with reluctance. "What—what do you mean by that?" There was fear buried in his voice.

"You and your 'religion' . . . I *so* despise it. I despise *you*. I detest 'the One' and everything it represents. You killed my birth family in service of this 'being.'" She glared into him, full of ire, consumed with a soundless fury. "Later I discovered that they had killed my husband. And our only child, our sweet little boy."

J'Dorul paused, calming herself. "Your kind and their ridiculous notions of displacing the gods, dreams, and monsters of others with your . . . *impotent* creation. You can't just revise history to suit your evil needs and desires—don't you understand that? History is a record of reality, not some plastic mental idyll. Your people don't realize that we're all just an instant in the timestream; that we're building toward something greater than ourselves, something larger than this moment. . . . My people have *never* needed a god, and we don't now; there's no need for such a contrivance—"

He stood again, features tight, eyes blazing. "Blasphemy!"

"Spare me, Ambassador. No one needs your idol. Especially one who decrees that its followers must drink the blood of innocents, that they must eat the flesh of other beings to live, or torture and kill those that don't believe as *they* do. We had our own ways, our own beliefs. You—your kind—destroyed that. All in the name of your invented, bloodthirsty construction." She glowered at him, adding: "Our histories may be gone, but *mine* is unwritten. Your future, it seems, is predetermined by this psychopathic deity. So be it. I wish I could believe that one day you could reap the horror of that, that you might even comprehend how wretched it is. But I know better."

Irfan gaped at her, dazed. "You are so wrong. I'm sorry that you don't understand, don't believe." He slowly sat down, glancing out into the night in disbelief, brown eyes flashing. "I'm older than you, and I've noticed this: that your generation doesn't *understand* . . . that you *pity* the non-believers—"

"No, not pity," she corrected.

"Okay. What then? We can't go back to the . . . the *ignorance* . . . the darkness and absurdity of before, to the false human and Mosaic philosophies. So what do you call it?"

She laughed, touching her fingers to her forehead in incredulity. "You are *such* a deluded True Believer! So sad. . . . All I can say is this: Mosaics understand more than you will ever realize. Such as what it's like to be oppressed, to be denied something that you truly love—to be kept from people and things for such a weak reason as someone *else's* notion of 'righteousness.'"

J'Dorul tilted her head, considering Irfan wisely before she continued. "After the guards left us, I comforted my ailing father as best I could. Just before he died, he gently touched my face with his bloody hand, whispering a few last things to me. Words I will never forget . . ." She looked away, eyes welling with tears. "First: that he loved me. Second: that there are three stages to a social movement—denial, discussion, acceptance. Third: that *nothing* focuses the mind like a noose." She looked back at him, smiling through her anguish. "And last: never forget that a single act of courage can change the world. We *will* prevail—"

Irfan looked askance at her. "What does that mean?"

She sneered, hand moving to touch her stomach. "Don't you know, Ambassador?" She took his hand in hers and placed it on her belly under her shawl. "Here," she related. "The answer is here."

Irfan was still confused as he held his hand on her naked stomach.

She looked into his eyes, her features softening. "I am *becoming,* Ambassador. Like a butterfly emerging from its chrysalis, I am becoming something else; something that I never was before—"

His voice was strained, thick: "I—I don't—"

"I told you," she replied, "that your kind . . . your *beliefs* killed my family—my parents, my husband, our *son.*"

He nodded, his throat moving as he swallowed.

She continued: "Yet there is *another* family; another child." She looked at him, her eyes teary, beatific. "But *no one* can kill them. Because this family won't be just specters living in my memory."

Irfan nodded in dawning comprehension, tears tracking his face. After a leaden caesura, the bluster of the wind gripping the train, he began to speak, but she raised her other hand to silence him.

"And this family, especially in the form of this child," she said, emphasizing her hold on his hand on her stomach, her eyes unexpectedly cold, hard. "*This* family is more than just some grouping of delicate, frangible future carcasses. When people hear of them, of this child particularly, Ambassador—" J'Dorul stopped, smiling coldly at him. "They will realize that we are *all* related in grief, in oppression. They will realize that the enemy of my enemy is indeed my friend, at least for a time. And believe me, this child is a liberator that will have *so many* brothers, sisters, and eventually they will have children of their own."

"What—what do you mean?"

She paused, then leaned close, whispering into Irfan's ear, so soft, so alluring: "We are beyond the physical now, beyond any ideal. We have crossed into the realm of concepts, revelations, empowerment. It's like an intellectual contagion, Ambassador, a psychological virus. You see, I had an *inner* revolution, and our existence—the child, me— will become the spark, I hope, of an inferno. Oh, it won't be long." She closed her eyes in ecstasy, pressing his hand harder into her flesh.

Her breathy voice was sensual, intoxicating as she said: "This child's messy birth will inspire other ideas, other actions. In fact, I'm digesting the catalyst now. *I swallowed the bomb, Ambassador . . .*"

V

His father looked up at him. He moved slowly, so very slowly. He raised his hands to his face, pulling them down his cheeks . . . streaks of black.

The object in his lap moved—

There was a fire in the sky just as his mother's head rolled onto the white ground, her bloody tongue protruding, her eyes staring into the infinite . . .

VI

—BREAKING NEWS—

Arid Plateau North, 04:32—There were no reported survivors on Ambassador Aral'ucaRd's train, which appeared to derail this morning near the Arid Plateau.

At the moment, terrorism is not suspected, as there are no claims of responsibility, no signs of foul play, nor any previous threats of martyrdom. Investigators are currently on the scene. Several bodies have been pulled from the wreckage, but none have been positively identified as the Ambassador or supporting members of his personal detail.

May Day Rituals have been suspended in the short term as the cause of the locomotive explosion is determined. Bishop Wallach will give a speech later today as more facts emerge. In the Old City, throngs of protesters have taken to the streets—apparently in celebration of the Ambassador's untimely death. Authorities are promising a swift and strong response with drones and neighborhood sweeps after security cameras are examined to identify the culprits responsible for the mayhem.

Sporadic violence has also been reported in other places, including Paladinsk and points east. Additional updates as this developing story unfolds . . .

DOLLS

Prancing glumly
up battered stairs,
Eyeless dolls
throw shadows
cold and long
onto decaying walls—

I watch them with fear:
Silently in awe
as I see the fading flicker of
my lamp
softly glow on their terrible
dress buttons.

Numb with dread,
I cringe in my fruiting madness . . .

Prancing glumly
up battered stairs,
Eyeless dolls
throw shadows
cold and long
onto decaying walls—
So begins the horrifying
Hop Macabre—

BEHOLD!
The elastic insanity of
Porous memory fragments
Falling into the

Dream pool
Of forgotten love . . .

Numb with dread,
I cringe in my fruiting madness . . .
The bats of lunacy
flitting in my head . . .

Prancing glumly
up battered stairs,
Eyeless dolls
throw shadows
cold and long
onto decaying walls—
So begins the horrifying
Hop Macabre—
The end of the Universe
Is in the mitten hands
Of soulless effigies made of
rags . . .

I observe their devil dance
And love of nothing in the tiny,
perverse room:
First one,
Then another,
Still a third—
The hopscotch of horror ensues
To Humanity's trumpet
of doom . . .

Numb with dread,
I cringe in my fruiting madness . . .
The bats of lunacy
flitting in my head . . .
How I got here is a

Mystery:
I pray to the loving God above that
I live through this reverie . . .

Prancing glumly
up battered stairs,
Eyeless dolls
throw shadows
cold and long
onto decaying walls—
So begins the horrifying
Hop Macabre—
The end of the Universe
Is in the mitten hands
Of soulless effigies made of
rags . . .
As they plummet—
One by one—
Into the void of Fate, then:
I am entranced by their hideous
Music of terror:
SCREAMING DOLLS AT THE WORLD'S END!

Suddenly,
I am overtaken by the satanic
Clown:
Appearing from my childhood
subconscious,
His menace is manifest by
Rending my flesh with shark-like teeth . . .

Blackness!

For Neil Gaiman and
Thomas Ligotti

AFTERLIFE

With Sunni K Brock and William F. Nolan

"The boundaries which divide Life from Death are at best shadowy and vague. Who shall say where the one ends, and where the other begins?"
—Edgar Allan Poe

I

"I just don't see anything really, well, *unique*—not for *my* client, anyway," Enid Blake said, wrinkling her nose at the tray of old medical instruments and preserved tissue samples.

A small, compact woman with light-brown hair in a messy, asymmetrical crop, she was dressed in black leggings and a yellowed vintage knot sweater, blending with the musty stacks of books and curiosities in the small shop.

"Well, honey, what are they into?" asked the effeminate clerk, a man in his mid-fifties, thin and gaunt, tortoiseshell-rimmed glasses reflecting the gauzy late afternoon sunlight as it lanced down from a leaded glass window.

"I really don't know. He was a referral—at least I think it's a 'he.' Some sort of filmmaker/rock star who used to hang around H. R. Giger, you know—part of that 'Giger Gang' thing. Wants to remain anonymous. That's why I'm here." Enid sighed. "I know he likes horror."

"Mmmm, don't we all?" The clerk gingerly replaced the tray under the glass counter and locked it. "Over there is the rare horror book collection." He motioned to the far corner of the store, past still more artifacts crammed into the tight confines of the place—a suit of armor, shrunken heads, rows of specimens floating dreamily in yellow liquid.

Enid made her way around the makeshift aisles. "*How* rare?"

"Some handbound stuff, a few untitled tomes. We estimate some date around the seventeen-hundreds." He peered at her over the top of his glasses. "Just be careful: they're fragile."

Reaching the bookshelf, she ran a thin black-nailed finger along the tattered spines. Many were so worn she could not read the titles. Randomly, Enid angled a book forward to examine the cover. When she did, a pamphlet next to it slipped out, and, as she clumsily tied to grab it, she managed to knock three or four other books to the wooden floor in a noisy clatter. Dust and the faint whiff of decaying glue rose up from the calamitous pile.

Dropping to her knees in shock, she resisted the urge to scoop up the chapbook, afraid she might inflict further damage on the aged volumes. "Damn it!" Enid gently picked up the top book, which was no worse for wear, carefully closing it; the others did not fare as well. Reaching for some of the loose pages that splayed haphazardly from the broken covers, she noticed they contained a few handwritten notes—scrawling, strange symbols around an illustration of some mysterious head. Perhaps it was a phrenology figure, or some cryptic astrological diagram, only darker, more bizarre than any she had seen before.

"Oh, *my*," the little clerk said, rushing over in a mock panic. "Now I'll have to have the glue-sniffing Bible binder come in and repair them! Oh, how I *dread* that man. I presume I can have the bill sent to *you?*" He fanned his face with a well-manicured hand.

"Don't get your panties in a bunch, dear. I'll take them. Throw in a little for your trouble. My client can afford it." Enid rose to face him. "Just put them back together and pack them up as best you can. I'll take the rest of the books on that shelf, too."

II

"It's good to see you, Enid. How was the Big Apple?" Professor Ingels grinned warmly as Enid took a seat in the little coffee shop.

Enid, flushed from the cold Boston air, removed her gloves and wrapped her arms around his neck, giving him a peck on the cheek.

"Wonderful! Nancy and I watched the ball drop and did some shopping. I'm glad to be back, though."

Dalton Ingels was a handsome man: erudite, distinguished, and more than a little quirky. She secretly wished they could be more than friends, but he was enigmatic. Though they continued to meet and talk years after she had graduated, she had no idea if he was married, involved, or even interested. Every time she tried to broach the topic, he artfully changed the subject. Still, he always exuded affection and indulged her when she needed to vent.

"Your usual chai, I assume?" the plump blonde waitress asked, looking at Enid. Turning to the professor: "And Americano, vanilla with non-fat?"

"Yes, please," they responded in unison.

The waitress nodded and headed off toward the counter. Professor Ingels grabbed Enid's hand. "So what can I do you for?"

As much as she wanted to, Enid knew better than to express her real feelings via innuendo. Last time she tried that, the professor recalled the mating rituals of flatworms, dulling her hope of breaking through his platonic veneer. "Well, I found something, and I want you to take a look at it. It's been really bothering me."

"Must be pretty horrible." He gave her a little wink.

"I don't know quite what to make of it." She opened her purse and pulled out an envelope. "I just . . . well, please see what you think."

He took it and pulled out a yellowed paper. "This looks pretty old. One of your clients find it?"

"No, I found it. I just keep thinking about it."

"Hmm . . ." The professor slowly unfolded the document. He scanned the handwritten lines.

"Could it really be . . . Edgar Allan Poe?" Enid was anxious to know if she had really stumbled onto an unknown Poe letter.

Professor Ingels glanced at her from beneath his shaggy brows. He read aloud:

My Dearest,

　　I am afraid this may be my last missive. The most heinous and bitter remarks of the specter now assail my very being.
　　There is something in this pulp that removes my literal essence even as it compels me to write. . . . It drains my character as dark exhausts light. It is as though writing and breathing are entwined with life and death.
　　[illegible] *fate is now with* [illegible]

"Where did you get this?" Professor Ingels asked. By his tone, Enid could tell that he thought it might be genuine.

"I bought some old books in the Village for a client. I was cataloging them when I found this inside one."

"What kind of books? Have you told anyone else?" The professor was getting excited.

"Well, no. I mean, I wanted to see what you thought first. It was in an old book about mysticism. Strange thing: there were other handwritten notes in the book, but the handwriting didn't match this letter at all, and it didn't really make sense. Anyway, the book is going to my client along with the others. Just the kind of thing that will bring in good money. But this letter—I'm not about to let go of it . . . not yet, anyway."

The waitress returned with their drinks. Professor Ingels tentatively sipped at the hot coffee while Enid fanned the steam from her tea, taking a deep breath of the spice.

"I'm not an expert on Poe, but it reminds me . . ." The professor leaned forward. "Tell you what, come by my office next week. There's something you should see."

III

"Thank you so much for agreeing to meet with me. And for suggesting this place. It seems so appropriate." Enid was nervous standing in front of the Edgar Allan Poe National Historic site in Philadelphia.

The other woman, dressed head-to-toe in black and a bit older than Enid, smiled kindly at her. "I always love visiting it. I hope you didn't come all the way to Philly just to talk to me."

"Well, I did have some other business. Trying to track down a child's coffin, preferably Amish, for a client who needs a new bookshelf." Enid took a chance that her new acquaintance, Diane Fitzpatrick, had a penchant for the macabre as well.

"Darker Home and Gardens?" Diane raised her eyebrows.

Enid giggled. "Soft of."

"Do you have time to stay here in Philly a little while? You should really see my place." Diane held the door open and the two ventured in.

"I'd love to—and if you don't mind, maybe we can look at my 'item' there after the tour, away from prying eyes."

"You got it. Only my cat and my bird will be snooping." They both laughed.

IV

"Diane, your house is *amazing!*" Everywhere Enid looked, the little cottage was filled with oddities. The place was dark, spooky; walls covered with tapestries, shelves of old books, bottles and vials, some containing human teeth. On one table perched a collection of grungy photographs—*memento mori*—with snippets of hair and clothing attached; lace seemed to be everywhere.

Diane sat on a Victorian loveseat, sipping tea from a dainty cup, a cat balled up next to her. "It's a lifetime of treasures, Enid. I thought you would appreciate my tastes."

"Oh, I do, I do." Enid was glad that Professor Ingels had passed Diane's letter on to her. Diane was quickly becoming a friend, and quite possibly a new client to boot. "I thought you said you had a bird."

"Yes, yes. Eddie. His name is Eddie."

At the sound of his name, Eddie came half-hopping, half-flying down the hallway and bounced up onto the coffee table.

"A *crow?*" Enid was shocked and delighted.

"A *raven!* Right, Eddie?" Diane looked at the big black bird. He made a low grumbling noise and ruffled his scruffy throat feathers.

"Of course! What was I thinking?" Enid laughed, then bit her lip. "Eddie! Oh yes, you have to see this, Diane. I need to know what you think of it." She pulled the letter from her case and held it out.

Diane carefully looked over the yellowed paper. Eddie bobbed impatiently. The cat yawned.

Finally: "When I wrote to Professor Ingels years ago, he replied that the library had no other fragments like mine." Diane rubbed the edge of the paper between her thumb and fingers. "Are you looking for a buyer?"

"I'm not sure what I'm looking for, not yet. Can I see your fragment? I've only seen the photocopy."

"Sure, of course." Diane shooed the bird off the table, got up from her seat, and disappeared into a darker corner of the cottage. Eddie jumped up onto the loveseat and pulled the cat's tail with his beak. The cat hissed and swatted at him. The raven bobbed up and down, wings outstretched, cawing excitedly.

"Eddie, stop teasing the cat!" Diane yelled, hurrying back into the living room.

The raven clacked his beak cheekily, responding with a throaty: "Nevermore!"

Diane shook her finger at the bird as he postured and strutted on the davenport. "That's right, Eddie. Nevermore should you pull the cat's tail!"

He replied with a metallic clicking which made Enid think of alien laughter. "Nevermore!" he cawed in gleeful antagonism. Diane rolled her eyes as Enid burst out laughing at the bird's antics.

"You are such a little showoff, Mr. Eddie Fitzpatrick!" Diane scolded. The raven bobbed up and down in delight. At last she presented a clear envelope to Enid—inside was a torn scrap of crumpled paper adorned with shaky black script:

[illegible] is of utmost [illegible] this pen has become my nemesis. It forces my hand to its unyielding will. I am afraid your loving betrothed will exist merely as the script on this paper if the accursed spell remains unbroken.

[illegible]

Why has this happened to us? Is there no respite? No release from that terrible man, Mr. [illegible]

"What does it mean?" Enid felt a chill. Something about this piece; it was so similar in tone to the one she had discovered.

Diane picked up Enid's letter from the table and held it next to hers in comparison. The paper, the ink, the handwriting all matched.

"They belong together," Diane confirmed. "Written maybe days, hours apart."

Enid frowned. "I guess I should be excited about this find, but I just feel weird about it. You're right. The pieces *belong together*. But, I really don't want to sell. It just seems wrong."

"Forgive me. I didn't mean—"

"No, Diane. I'm the one who should apologize. I sell things like children's coffins, for Pete's sake! Why this one letter would bother me is stupid."

"Look, you're not stupid. If it's any consolation, I feel something, too. If you don't have to be back to Boston right away, why don't you stay here tonight? Let's have some wine and relax. Maybe we can figure out what old Edgar was trying to communicate." Diane was reassuring, and Enid welcomed her friendship.

"I'd love to, Diane. Meeting you has been the best part of this whole thing."

V

Enid sat up abruptly in bed. She heard it again: footsteps, moaning.

She tried to talk, but felt paralyzed. Frozen, she faced the moonlit window, its lacy curtains illuminated in the darkness of the guest room.

A figure appeared—wavering, transparent. She could hardly believe it: *Poe?*

Looking at her with large, sad eyes, the thing gently moaned, then uttered a single word: *"Release."* Then the ghost crouched, spectral hands reaching to the dresser where the letter fragments now lay together, desperate.

Enid, still unmoving in disbelief, unable to call out, fainted back onto her pillows, exhausted.

VI

"I don't think it's crazy, Enid. Maybe it was just a dream, or maybe you were really visited by an apparition. Either way, it's obvious that you need to figure out why it's bothering you." Diane took another sip of her tea, then tore off some of her toast to give to Eddie.

"Maybe stress is finally catching up with me." Enid scowled. She sprinkled nutmeg into her mug. "I can't shake the feeling, though. It's like he's trapped and wants out."

"Trapped, how?" Diane looked confused.

"Well, I know it sounds weird, but trapped . . . in those *letters!*"

VII

"This way, ladies." Mr. Pratt, the gaunt, sharp-featured library archivist, led them into a special collection room. "Here we have preserved many important items pertaining to Poe, including some documents regarding the mysterious circumstances of his death. I believe these will be of interest. Excuse me, I have a staff meeting, but any of our librarians should be able to help you if you have questions."

The lanky man disappeared through a white-paned entranceway.

"Diane, this was a great idea coming to Baltimore." Enid nudged her friend's arm as they regarding the treasures before them.

"Well, I don't know what we're going to find, or what's going to happen if we *do*. I mean, we can't just *steal* any of these." Diane looked up and noticed Enid already across the room, staring at a chunk of wood mounted in a display.

"Look! It's a piece of his coffin. *Wow!*" Enid held her hand up as if to feel for any presence emanating from the relic.

"Darn it, you jumped ahead! I was looking forward to showing that to you." Diane had been there before and had set up a few stops for their joint expedition.

Enid laughed. "Oh, come on! This is exciting isn't it?"

"Yes, it is! But we've got a few more places to hit. Also, I've arranged a special treat for later tonight, so we need to do our research and get out of here before the other buildings close."

"Okay, okay." Enid pulled out her notebook. "Let's get to it."

VIII

"Another round of margaritas?" the bartender asked.

Enid nodded. Diane finished off the last of the guacamole with a broken tortilla chip. "Yes, please."

"I'll have a whiskey. Edgar style." Their new arrival, an older man with salt-and-pepper hair, called to the barkeep as he removed his gloves and sat at an adjoining stool.

"You got it, Jim." The bartender rushed off.

"We were wondering if you were going to make it!" Diane leaned over to give the man a kiss on the cheek. "Enid, this is Jim. He's an expert on Poe's time in Baltimore. Runs a tour."

"Nice to meet you, Jim." Enid held out her hand.

He returned her gesture with a firm but gentle shake. "Likewise."

"Enid here's a 'Horse' virgin. Never been to the saloon." Diane raised an eyebrow.

"Ah yes, 'The Horse You Rode In On'—the longest-running drinking establishment in the United States. What do you think?" Jim grinned at Enid.

"I can't believe this is really the last place Poe was seen ... I'm sure Diane told you about my—curiosity?"

"Indeed." Jim hailed the bartender. "Hey, Mike, we'll take 'em upstairs."

The barkeep acknowledged him and opened a door, holding it for them.

"Ladies, after you." Jim motioned them on.

IX

Lightheaded from the drinks, Enid was mesmerized by Jim's tales of Poe's final days.

Diane occasionally offered a question or comment to bolster the dialogue. "So what about Rufus Griswold? Do you think he had anything to do with it?"

"Well, Griswold certainly had it out for old Eddie. But most of his damage was done after the fact, as far as we can tell." Jim responded confidently. "That obituary was stinging. He damaged Poe's reputation—how he became the executor . . . He did have some unknown papers of Poe's. They were found by Charles Leland when Griswold died."

"A self-proclaimed *wizard* . . ." Diane wiggled her fingers at Enid.

"Leland was reportedly the first to get to the contents of Griswold's desk when he died. Found a bunch of letters. Said he even found forgeries that Griswold had created to besmirch Poe." Jim made a pen motion to illustrate the point.

"And?" Enid was sitting on the edge of her seat.

"Well, I'm not sure they were forged. At least, not *all* of them." Jim sat back and took a swig of his whiskey.

"Well, what happened to them? Where are they?" Enid demanded.

"Burned," Diane injected. "He threw them on the fire to protect Poe."

"That's what Leland claimed." Jim ran his finger around the rim of his half-empty glass. "But there's something else."

"What, you're holding out on me?" Diane teased.

He returned her light-hearted gaze with a grim expression. "Not holding out . . . just uncertain. Did you bring the documents?"

The women nodded. They each brought out their respective fragments of the letters and showed them to Jim. He took each in turn and examined them carefully before pulling out a loupe to study the swirls and loops of the handwriting. "Decidedly Poe."

Enid and Diane's eyes widened at the revelation.

Jim regarded Diane for a long moment. "You never told me about this before, Diane."

She laughed, nervous. "Well, I thought you'd think it was crazy!"

He nodded, understanding. "It's not crazy. There is a legend." He paused, looking to the window before he continued. "There's a legend about Poe—it says that he was cursed by Griswold. Tormented, yes, but actually *cursed*, too."

"Griswold?" Diane asked. "But I thought Leland was—"

"Yes," Jim replied, holding his hand up in a gesture of silence. "But some theorize that both had studied the dark arts and later had a dispute. The gist is they both disliked Poe, but after falling out . . . As they say: 'The enemy of my enemy is my friend,' right?" Jim took a shot of his drink. "Later Leland wanted to destroy *Griswold*. Old Eddie's legacy became a pawn."

Reaching into the inner pocket of his jacket, he produced an envelope: "This. This has been passed down since my great-great grandfather was the keeper here."

Enid took the worn packet from Jim.

Diane was silent, overwhelmed by this turn of events.

"Go ahead, open it." Jim sat forward.

Carefully, Enid removed the brittle paper and unfolded it. "What? I don't—"

"I can't tell you for sure that Poe wrote it. I only know that it was reportedly found in 1849, right in front of him . . . when he was passed out, here, in this bar." Jim was somber, almost whispering.

[illegible] *sorcery. I have learned that* [illegible] *is stealing my papers—papers that I—and I alone—must retrieve and destroy or* [illegible] *and* [illegible]

"Let me see." Diane gently took the note from Enid's hands. "Geez, Jim, it's just a bunch of wavy lines after this first part . . ."

"I need to use the restroom." Enid stood, her mind reeling.

"Down that hall." Jim pointed. "On the right."

X

"The cool moist air of the water closet calmed Enid's nerves and brought some sobriety. "Jesus," she muttered to herself. She got up, pulled up her leggings and flushed.

At the sink, she looked into the mirror while waiting for the water to turn warm. "God, bags under my eyes." She washed and dried her hands, then turned the ancient doorknob.

Down the hall, she saw the light spilling into the hallway where her companions were undoubtedly still discussing the events of the evening. As she took a step forward, the bookshelf to the left creaked, and she thought she heard a voice.

Enid froze. *This is no time to get spooked.* Just as she decided to move, something appeared in front of her. As she watched, again the wispy figure of Edgar Allan Poe, this time stronger, more defined, presented itself. Without touching it, the spirit removed a book from the shelf, opening it. *"Release."* A ghostly finger pointed to the text:

> *In the original Unity of the First Thing lies the Secondary Cause of All Things, with the germ of their Inevitable Annihilation.*

Enid collapsed into a well of soothing darkness.

XI

After the bar closed, the women decided to visit Diane's final stop.

"Sorry about leaving Jim like that, Enid, but I just knew we had to come here." Diane's breath fogged in the cold winter chill as they walked through the old cemetery. "Are you feeling okay after your little spell?"

"I'm fine—I've always wanted to see this anyway," Enid replied, rubbing her arms through her heavy coat. "This fresh air is clearing my head. So that's it, up there?" She pointed to a grave just ahead. Fog swirled around them as they moved.

"Yep, that's the one." Diane pushed Enid's back, guiding her toward Poe's grave.

Enid slipped up to the headstone, lay the letters on it: hers, Diane's, the scribbled note borrowed from Jim. She bowed her head respectfully for a moment. An owl hooted in the distance.

Enid slowly moved back to be with Diane.

Just as they were about to leave, a cloaked figure with a lantern approached from the shadows: It rested three roses and a half-empty bottle of cognac at Poe's grave, then stood back and regarded the burial site. With a delicate hand, it appeared to touch the letters as the other moved to the hood of the cloak; in the warm flicker of the lantern, the hands seemed thin, cadaverous.

Pausing, the figure looked around, but did not see them. As it considered the notes once again, it exclaimed: *"Release!"* Then it pulled the hood back and revealed, at last, the wan face of Edgar Allan Poe.

Enid gasped in shock. Diane's fingers gripped the younger woman's arm in a vise-like clutch of fear and panic.

"Release!"

As the women watched, the spirit took the papers and fed them into the flame of the lantern. While they burned, Poe little by little dissolved into the shrouding mist, mixing with the smoke from the letters . . .

Released at last, and forevermore.

WINDOWS, MIRRORS, DOORS

I

The apocalypse arrived on a Tuesday. At least for Marion.

However, this was not some 9/11-type catastrophe, or the collapse of civilization due to a global pandemic. No, she had learned *real* apocalypses were always personal. *They always involved a cast of characters, too. Sometimes just one, but frequently extras . . . though never more than required.* The circumstances—the inciting events, the setting, and so on—just served as a backdrop for the emotional and psychic dramaturgy that encapsulated that most human and elusive of all cosmic principles: *the moment.* Additionally, and ironically, said moment is different for everyone, even those who come to share it due to accidents of fate.

For Marion, it was the death of her identical twin sister on a stark, bitterly cold Tuesday morning. The cast had included her, Annette, the doctors and nurses; the last act took place in the hospice, and the catalyst had been her sister's cancer, which set those final performances into motion—piecemeal scenes that would eventually devolve into a protracted and painful melodrama saddled with a poorly scripted, wholly unsatisfactory finale.

Who writes *these things?* Marion sometimes wondered, and with more than a touch of sarcasm.

Another thing she came to understand after Annette's loss was that these private apocalypses were not always quick; in many situations they were slow—in her case the leisurely unraveling of the threads of a life over the span of more than thirty years. Yes, *death* can be quick, binary—one moment living, the next not. Nevertheless, the end of all things for the individuals who survive such trauma—the demise of a loved one; a disaster, manmade or natural—often takes much longer to resolve . . . frequently months or years, if ever.

Slow and steady. But the race is never won, she reflected.

Of course, Marion had not come to these conclusions through any sudden epiphany; it was experienced as a gradual dawning . . . more precisely an *erosion.* An implacable, sinister loss of color in the day-to-day machinations of existence as the bubble of her daily life shrank in influence and experience. It would all perhaps end horribly, as is the way with reality, but for a long time she tried to concern herself chiefly with the possibility of new beginnings, with the mystery of a fresh, if unwelcome, start—spinning the anguish and pain into a different worldview she had not previously considered. After a time, this faux optimism subsided, and she eventually realized that the *finality* is what truly mattered. *That was where the lesson was to be found,* she mused. Endings only become apparent in retrospect; in the *moment,* the events as they are happening seem as impermanent as any others that precede them or those that inevitably follow. Only with hindsight does the true gravity of the delineation between the world *before* and the world *after* become comprehensible.

In the final analysis, the grind and joy of anyone's life comes down to a few bullet points, she decided, *at most a couple of paragraphs highlighting a few key moments:*

- Birth—*shared with Annette . . .*
- Education—*first in public school, then through scholarships to some excellent colleges to feed the fire for performance . . .*
- Career—*traveling the world as an actor of stage, TV, and film . . .*
- Marriage—*to Nick, the alcoholic New Yorker, ending after just a year; then, in 1985, to my Southern gentleman, Eric, with his troubled, gifted son, Patrick . . .*
- Children—*dear, sweet Patrick, who went to Australia as a young man before finally leaving us for good . . .*
- Loss—*of my beloved Eric to an aneurysm; my parents to old age; Annette to cancer; my career to depression and anxiety; of friends through attrition; of youth and vitality . . .*
- Death—*the great unknown for anyone, and, unlike birth, without the comfort of my lovely twin . . .*

In her more cynical moods, Marion questioned why it all mattered. *Live long enough and everyone loses* everything: *friends, family, health, perhaps their mind . . . eventually even life itself.* Just as some creatures thrive in shadow, shunning the light, avoiding the attention of others, so do others prosper at the margins of society, at the interface *between* the darkness and light. At one time, she had been one such creature of the sun; after Annette's passing, she found her world increasingly pulled into the waiting blackness. A piece of her died that day, and the hole that was created had continued to spread throughout her being ever so gradually. She struggled to stay at the interface as best she could; it was not easy, as she grew older, as the losses compounded, as the light receded. She coped as best she could, but sometimes it was like awakening from a coma into a completely unlit room: it was difficult to make sense out of what had become of her life in such a context.

Left to her own devices, she passively observed the world as its pace quickened and her enthusiasm waned; it frequently left her feeling like an insect, a kind of drone. *Drones understand—either through cognizance or intuition—their place, their role in society.* Insect societies were brutal, efficient hierarchies, she understood, but they were not rooted in vendetta or spite; the caste was established at birth and was impervious to negotiation. The individual subjugated to the group hive mind, the collective enterprise of survival. In many ways, Marion admired this simple, methodical approach to life; it required no insight, no conscious thought, and did not reward devious or Machiavellian behavior. No individual was more important than any other, and all members were independent of the social constraints and expectations of some egomaniacal leader or the vanity of a clique. Yet even a drone had *purpose.* Increasingly, Marion felt no such sensation; it was as though she were being controlled by an outside force, or had become an impostor within her own body, manipulated from without by an alien consciousness that influenced her actions and—ever more—her *reactions,* like some master puppeteer, an irony she found by turns bemusing and disconcerting. She was an actor, and actors *were,* in some ways, simply puppets, vessels, *tabulae rasae,* for the roles they inhabit. While this was true enough, she was beginning to feel less like a vessel and more like the literal text—as though she had no meaning unless imbued by some external proxy speaking the words aloud. When she looked in the mirror in the mornings, she recognized herself less and less, and worried that one day the last speck of her self-conception would simply vanish as she mundanely cleaned her face—as though her physical being might melt away into the spiral of the emptying sink, taking her humanity and soul along with it.

Wash those troubles right down the drain . . .

As a result of this erosion and dissociation, Marion had reduced her activities. Though she was still attractive—her shoulder-length black hair streaked with dramatic white highlights, her skin taut and youthful, her figure still trim for a woman in her late sixties due to walking the stairs of her apartment building almost daily—she felt no need to engage others; she merely observed them. Her building, where she and her second husband Eric had moved as her career bloomed in the early 1990s, was now her haven, her cocoon. She watched everything, taking silent delight in her surreptitious voyeurism, and spent more and more time in the comforting nostalgia afforded by the apartment, with its trove of old books, her awards and photo albums, Eric's collection of miniature cars, and even Patrick's former bedroom, which carried a certain enigmatic charm and remained essentially as he left it before he departed in his late twenties.

Maybe one day I'll see him again . . . I hope so. God, I miss him.

She recalled reading an article once that passing through doorways was tied to forgetting what one was doing in the moment; that the scene change from room to room had a way of mentally resetting one's actions and purpose on an unconscious level; as though the doors of perception *actually changed* when moving through a portal such as an entryway, even a window. In some ways, the idea comforted her, yet in others, it was disquieting, as though she were doomed to wander from place to place and lose the context of why she had, or what the purpose of the change really was. To that end, occasionally, a maternal tug compelled her to go inside Patrick's old room, relax on the bed, and contemplate the lively assortment of his antique marionettes suspended from the ceiling, the brightly painted automata seated in lifelike tableaux, the wistful hand-carved little manikins resting on the bookshelves and windowsill. As a child, Patrick had been deeply involved in magic and puppetry. His Asperger's syndrome had limited his interaction with friends at school, but not his interior world. He built several old-style animated dolls that could move and walk, and had developed into quite a ventriloquist. As she regarded the dusty remnants of someone else's life in Patrick's room, Marion wondered if there was a certain trade-off to being extraordinary at something—whether an amazing facility with words, exceptional acting talent, visionary artistic ability, or making animated puppets—in that one must *lose* something at some point: a loved one, a limb, a sense, one's purpose. She had experienced much over the years, most of it good, but it appeared to be front-loaded, and now she was paying the dues she managed to forego in her youth. Not that she cared anymore, but this certainly seemed to be the case. For example, the paparazzi no longer noticed if she came or went, and she doubted if any of the younger ones even knew she had twice been nominated for an Academy Award or had a brief fling with Jack Nicolson in the debauched heydays of the late '70s, when she lived in L.A.

This has become another world, she noted, regarding the sad effigies. *And not my world.* Now she felt as though she had become a sort of female version of the Minotaur: huddled in the center of the old brownstone, the twisting, voracious labyrinth of the City reaching ever farther away from her daily experience or care. The immediate mazes of her mind, her apartment, and her neighborhood had reduced her domain to a few blocks, some great performances captured on celluloid and in her memory, a couple of girlfriends, and the other occupants of her building . . . the erstwhile art dealer couple who vanished after a shadowy trip to Prague; Mr. Trinity, the musician who remained aloof and strange, practicing his horn seemingly day and night for all these many years; others came and went like ghostly spectators in a T. S. Eliot poem. For a long time, this was her life.

Until tonight.

II

Marion twists the phone cord with her fingers, slumping into the loveseat. In the background, Sinatra gently croons from the record player; the window is open and, seven stories below, the City rumbles outside like a giant cat. Night has fallen, and the afterglow of sunset bleeds eerily red against the horizon. In the distance, an autumnal thunderstorm is gathering power.

"That's what the doctor said, Marti."

Tears roll down her cheeks as she listens to the voice on the end of the line. Marion leans forward and retrieves her wine glass, lifting the ruby liquid to her lips and taking a few swallows. Swirling the contents to inhale the bouquet before placing it back on the table, she sighs deeply.

"That's right. Dr. Williams said it might be why I've been more tired the past few months. Also why I wake up standing in the hallway sometimes, or screaming." She pauses in thought. "The emotional lability part explains the laughing fit I had at the funeral for Pete."

She listens again, rubbing her cheeks with her sleeve. Pulling a tissue from the box on the table, she dabs at her light blue eyes.

"I don't know. . . . He said this new medication can sometimes slow down the progression. The doctor also explained it might help control the night terrors and the waking hallucinations, like when I thought that guy was following me around reading my thoughts a few weeks ago." She pauses once more. "No guarantees, of course."

More minutes pass as she listens. She takes another sip of wine. Thunder shakes the building. "Listen, I'd better get off the phone. It's starting to storm here. I don't want to get electrocuted. Thank you so much, Marti. And thank you for getting me to go to the doctor. I feel it can be dealt with. We'll see. Yes—let's plan on dinner Friday. Okay. Love you, too. 'Bye."

She places the handset into the cradle, staring at the telephone. A bright flash sears, followed in a few seconds by a deep roll of thunder. Darkness has taken over, the light pollution of the City a shifting pink mix of sodium lamps, headlights, and sheets of rain. The pattering downpour is soothing to her, the smell refreshing, clean. She closes her eyes, comforted by the soothing white noise of the rainstorm merging with the street sounds underneath. Sinatra morosely catalogs the years as she drifts off to sleep.

A bolt of intense lightning awakens her. The room is coal-dark, and she cannot see anything. Even the light pollution is gone: *Oh, no— a blackout.* She hates blackouts. Marion glances at her watch, squinting to see as her eyes adjust to the gloom: *9:48. Been out about an hour . . .* She stretches, rising to get the flashlight in the pantry.

Stumbling to the kitchen, she trips on a chair in the den, stubbing her toe. She rummages in the junk drawer in the pantry and finds the light. The beam is weak, yellow. She shakes the torch and it gets a little brighter, but not much. *It'll do for now,* she decides. As she pans the beam around the apartment, the furnishings appear different, similar, but different. *Older, perhaps.*

"Trick of the shadows, that's all . . ."

Marion walks to the bathroom, her bladder full. Sitting on the commode, she turns out the light, not wanting to waste the battery. She had neglected to get fresh ones at the store yesterday. She will remedy that tomorrow.

She goes to her bedroom, hoping to find another flashlight. The lightning slashes again, the intensity of the storm increasing. It is raining even harder now, a deluge. The air is thin, musty, and very cold. In the beam of the light, she can see her breath. She shivers and her skin prickles from the chill. In the bedroom, she sees that the furniture is again arranged differently from what she remembered. It looks strange; the bedclothes are unrecognizable. She stumbles again and crashes to the floor, hitting her forehead on the post of the bed.

"Christ!"

Marion brings her hand up to her head and feels a small gash there. It is bleeding, but not heavily. She stands and goes over to the vanity, where she has some first-aid items in one of the drawers. Finally, she locates the Band-Aids and iodine. Looking into the mirror, she screams.

In the mirror, she sees her silhouette, but it is not her. The reflection looks like her, but has no cut on the forehead. It has the same attire, but the movements are off, as though they are delayed, which she knows is impossible.

"Marion?" The image in the mirror is speaking, but Marion is not. Her head feels light. Another bolt flashes a bluish cast over the macabre scene. In the mirror, Marion can see that the room is the same, but there is another person behind her. She spins around, holding the flashlight in front of her like a weapon. There is a figure standing there. *Looming.* It is a man who appears to be in his late forties, attired in a dark suit, slim and clean-shaven; his face is vaguely familiar, as if she has met him before, yet too perfect, waxen.

"Good evening, Mother," he says. His voice is reedy, halting. "It's me, Patrick."

Marion shrieks again, bringing her hand to her face. "How—*how did you get in here?*" She tries to control the timbre of her voice, fails.

The man's head deliberately tilts to the side as he stares at her, his milky eyes unblinking in the wan glow of the flashlight.

Behind her: "The same way I did, Marion," her sister's voice coos from the mirror. "Through your dreams. Your fears."

Marion quickly turns to face the mirror again. The reflection looks exactly like her, but it is moving independently. In the background, Patrick is still standing with his head cocked to the side, like a puppy trying to sort out where a sound is coming from. He shuffles a few steps forward, stiff, slow, then stops.

She holds the reflection's gaze, looking directly into its eyes. "Why are you here? Why is Patrick home? *What is happening?*"

The mirror image laughs quietly, shaking her head. Patrick moves forward once more and stops.

"Don't you want us here?" the likeness asks from the other side of the looking-glass.

Marion does not know what to say. She tries to string words together in her mind, but they are jumbled, her thoughts foreign, baroque. She swings the light up into the mirror: the beam does not reflect back, but passes through the image's body and travels to a point of infinity on the horizon line on the opposite side of the glass. She swallows in incomprehension.

"I—I must be dreaming now," Marion says at last. The image responds a few milliseconds later, mimicking the mouth movements, but actually replying: "No. You're not dreaming now. We are here with you, on this night. We have not abandoned you, Marion, we just had to move on. It was never personal. We just couldn't stay anymore. You deserve the truth."

In the mirror, Patrick moves forward again, and Marion now hears the whine of his internal gears and machinery. The wind blusters against the building as the rain continues. Another lightning flash reveals a few more details of his face: the gaps on either side of his chin where the jaw is configured to articulate when he speaks, the blank, featureless glass eyes that roll in the hollows of the automaton's head. He pauses once more, now just inches from Marion.

"We are here to comfort you in this time of great need, Mother. Father will be here soon."

Marion closes her eyes, feeling faint. Her heart skips as a crack of thunder fills the space. Lightning flashes through her eyelids, momentarily reddening the scene, as she yields.

III

When she is found a few days later, Marion will be on the living room loveseat in a state of relaxation with her eyes closed. She will have a flashlight in her hand, and she will have a cut on her forehead; the blood will be dry.

The building supervisor will be the one to find her, as he has been watching her movements for days, ever since she came to his unit and explained that her son and sister will be visiting soon and she wants to introduce them. The supervisor will have found the conversation disturbing, as he remembered when the son died—while visiting family in Australia some years prior—and that her sister, Annette, never returned to the unit they shared after she went to hospice. As far as he understood it, Annette had passed away after a tough battle with cervical cancer. In fact, Marion told him the news herself.

When the Medical Examiner arrives, she will inspect the premises and find no signs of foul play, just a well-conditioned older woman in repose. Nothing suspicious will be in the apartment. Going room by room, the M.E.'s team will photograph the scene and will note that one of the bedrooms has many dummies and puppets decorating it. One particularly impressive figure will be in the woman's bedroom, facing a large vanity with a shattered mirror; its eye sockets will be empty.

Upon further inspection at the morgue, the M.E. will discover that the woman has clinical Lewy Body Dementia, and that her eyes, strangely, are milky white— as though they never had pupils or irises. Her body will be cremated; no one will claim the ashes. The case will then be closed and the apartment emptied.

Her obituary will sum up Marion's life in two neat paragraphs.

COLOSSI

Two colossi met on a road,
and strained to decide:
"Who will travel forth and
Who should step aside?"

Within the twin behemoths
iron hearts pumped—
forcing Freon through
icy, metallic veins—
as the pistons at their cores
clattered, hammered, and raged
in an attempt to disrupt cold logic
with fury, fire, and hate.

There the dueling duo sat—
like strangers till they meet—
united yet alone
in their anxious calm,
bound by a fear unknown.

Once, two colossi met on a road
and neither could decide:
"Who would carry on and who should wait to the side?"
Indeed, they sat and watched one another
until the sun blackened and imploded and died;
now they can still be seen:
Ruined, rusty hulks on the path to oblivion,
Where they will forever reside.

DOUBLE FEATURE

I

"Come on Val, don't do this." Jim glanced at his daughter as America's "Tin Man" swelled louder on the car radio:

Oz never did give . . .

Valerie was staring out into the darkness as the 1975 Gremlin raced along the interstate. She quickly wiped her face with a shirt sleeve, hiding behind a cascade of strawberry blonde tresses. As the song played, she fidgeted in her lap with the mood ring her boyfriend, Tommy, had given her.

"Mom said you'd keep me from going."

Jim huffed in irritation. "Did she now? What'd she say, exactly?" Adjusting the defrost to clear the windshield, he then grabbed the AM radio dial and twisted through the staticky swoops and squawks searching for something else to listen to:

. . . police report that alleged killer Ted Bundy has . . . daredevil Evel Knievel is still recuperating after a failed . . . while a new lead has emerged in the notorious Zodiac Killer case, New York City detectives are still stymied by the mysterious Son of Sam . . . Native American activist Leonard Peltier maintains his innocence from a jail cell in . . . a violent gang arising from the Irish Republican Army conflict called the "Shankill Butchers" has been plaguing . . . Woody Allen's Annie Hall *continues to delight both audiences and critics . . .*

"Mirrors on the ceiling, the pink champagne on ice . . ."

"Leave it there!" Justin yelped from the backseat. Jim threw his hand up as his son started singing along to himself.

"Mom said you think prom is just a big, stupid party. That it's become just an excuse for the spics, queers, spades, zipperheads, and whores to screw around and get high—"

"Hey! Watch your mouth!" Jim exclaimed. He looked over at Valerie again, anger lining his face. He narrowed his eyes in annoyance. "Just *cool it*, especially around your brother. We never taught you to talk like that—"

"Like, *spare me*, Dad! I know you think I can't handle myself. But I'll be a *senior* next year!" She whipped around to face him, tears streaking her features in the blue-green glow of the dash. "I mean, I'm *sixteen!* I can take care of myself. Besides, Tommy will be there—"

"Here we go with the Tommy shit again." Jim shook his head in bewilderment, smoothing his moustache. "For Christ's sake, Val! He's *too old* for you! He'll be a junior in *college* this fall—"

"*Yeah?* So what! I'm a grown woman, Daddy! Deal with it! I'm liberated, and there's *nothing* you can do about that." Valerie slumped back into the car seat, sobbing quietly. "I mean, you voted for *Nixon!* You're part of the problem!"

Steely Dan inquired over the airwaves: *"Won't you sign in, stranger?"*

"Turn it, Dad. I hate this one," Justin said from the back.

"Okay, hold on, Doc." Jim dialed through the local and national bulletins as they were detailed on the quarter-hour newscasts:

. . . newly-elected president Jimmy Carter is hosting . . . FBI still voices concern over the rise of cults in the United . . . overseas, Queen Elizabeth II continues her Silver Jubilee . . . in the world of science, the recently discovered rings encircling Uranus have experts . . . anti-gay activist Anita Bryant was once again crusading . . . scientists have reported an increase in unusual solar flare activity for the past . . . rumors swirl that Tandy Corporation is preparing to release a new-fangled "computer" later this year . . .

"I want a computer!" Justin crowed from the back seat. "When are we getting to the *movie?*"

"Soon, Doc," Jim replied, winking at his son in the rearview mirror. The boy nodded his head, his blue eyes lively as his layered curls bounced in the dim light. "Another few miles."

"Right on! And I can stay up *all night,* right? I can see all the movies, Daddy?"

Jim chuckled. "You sure can, Mr. Man." He looked back over at Valerie, his smile fading.

. . . in Antarctica, researchers have discovered previously unknown giant animals that . . . meanwhile, Elvis prepares for another . . . have been revived, even though they were believed long extinct; the Pentagon has issued a warning about . . . related, the notorious Sex Pistols are ready to . . . even as disco continues to dominate the record charts, a new form of expression called "the rap" is making waves in . . .

"Elvis. What a joke," Valerie grumbled.

Jim's face tensed. "I suppose you want to see something like those horrible Sex Pistols, right?"

"Like, *yeah.* I mean, Elvis is a *chump.*" She smirked, twisting the ring on her finger. "I guess you know that, huh?"

Jim resisted the urge to say something cruel.

Distantly, thunder rumbled. On the horizon lightning flashed in the evening sky. Fat drops of rain dotted the windshield so he turned on the wipers. As the shower grew heavier, he pulled a cigarette from the pack in his shirt pocket and placed it into his mouth before depressing the cigarette lighter on the control panel.

"Dream on, kiddo," he mumbled as he held the red-hot lighter to the tip of his cigarette and took a long drag, the radiance of the igniting tobacco momentarily illuminating his olive complexion with a ruddy cast. "I mean, I *get it,* Val. I read *Jonathan Livingston Seagull* and took *est,* you know." He exhaled a lungful of stale bluish smoke.

Valerie looked over at him. "Can I have one?"

Jim glowered. "*No.* I told you I'm trying to quit. And I don't want you starting. But sometimes you and your mother . . ."

She crossed her arms, setting her mouth into a pout.

"Listen, Val, I *did* vote for Nixon. He said he was going to end the war. And he managed to do a few good things, like creating the Environmental Protection Agency and continuing funding for the National Endowment for the Arts. Granted, he turned out to be a *bad* man, a flawed man. *Corrupt.* I learned my lesson. But *every*one makes mistakes; I'm trying to help you avoid a few, that's all." Jim inhaled deeply. "'What is, is, and what ain't, ain't. I get that you don't agree about the prom. But . . . but maybe, *maybe,* we can reach a compromise." The wipers slapped rhythmically as the buzzing radio crackled in the background.

Valerie's face brightened, her arms tightening as her leg kicked nervously. She peered up at her father from beneath her eyebrows, clearing her throat. "Oh, yeah?"

Jim sighed, letting the cigarette dangle from his lips, the smoke snaking into the dark beyond the reach of the dashboard lighting. Ahead he could see the animated neon sign for the theater—towering above the highway on an oversized, rusting spire—glowing through the haze of fog clinging to the ground as the cloudburst continued: **Viking Five Drive-In**. Beneath it was a large backlit marquee with red plastic letters that read:

JOIN US 4
ALL-NITE SHOCK-A-TH0N 2!

FRI – SAT: 7pm-???

5 F!LMS 4 $5/CAR

"JASON & ARGONAUTS"
"BuRNT 0FFERiNGS"
"GoDZILLA"
"DaRK S7AR"
"L!PS of BL00D"

In smaller letters below that:

PLU$—"Pussycat" Screen!ngs NitEly XXX

"Hello, my love, I heard a kiss from you . . ."

"This one's *boring,* Dad," Justin declared.

"Okay, okay, not a Brothers Johnson fan, I see. Let me keep going, Champ." He reached for the knob again.

Jim looked over at Valerie. "How about this? You can go—*until ten*—but no hanky-panky. I expect your grades to be *at least* a B average until then. And *no* drinking. I didn't survive Korea so you could give your virginity to the lowest bidder, for Christ's sake. Also, I want you to look after your brother after the prom—"

"No fair! He's a pain! How can Tommy—? Look, we need *alone time.* Mom said—"

"*What?* Said what?"

Defiant: "She *told* me about the swinging, Dad! Come on! Stop being so uptight!"

Jim was shocked and felt nervous, unsure of how to reply. "I—I don't know *what* you're—" He paused, concentrating on his driving. He could feel beads of sweat forming on his forehead and rolling from under his arms. "Look: this has *nothing* to do with our behavior. We did what we did, and I *will not* discuss this with you. This is about *you* and what's best for your future, nothing else." He stopped and held her gaze until she looked away. "So . . . what did your mother say with respect to *that?* That it was okay for you to risk getting knocked up? Oh, no! You're *still* my daughter, and we're still a family even if your mother and I are divorcing. That won't change even if the Equal Rights Amendment passes, so get used to it. You have school to consider, and then college. *Tommy Romeo* will just have to beat off if that's not acceptable." Jim's voice was booming in the confines of the car.

Valerie stared at him as if he were an alien, shaking her head in disbelief, eyes huge. "Ha! My *God,* are *you* a chump! *So square!* I mean, like, he's got *all* those girls at college. He chose *me.*" Valerie sat back, massaging her forehead. "So I *have* to keep him . . . *interested.* Don't you get that?"

"Oh! I fucking *get* it, darlin'. Them's the terms," Jim said, pulling one last puff before flicking the butt out of the car window and rolling the glass back up. He ran a hand through his dark, curly hair. "Take it or leave it."

"I watch the ripples change their size . . ."

Valerie slumped back in the seat, stunned as David Bowie's "Changes" ended. Jim turned the dial again.

This is WSNI, your place for news, weather, music, and . . . embattled Black Panther Party leader Huey P. Newton . . . newspaper heiress Patty Hearst plans to appeal . . . the three major networks, CBS, NBC, and ABC, announced their schedules for next year today, renewing M*A*S*H, The Rockford Files, The Six Million Dollar Man, *and others, as well as canceling* Marcus Welby, M.D. *and . . . Associated Press Breaking news: Explosions have been reported in Tokyo and Sydney; casualties have been confirmed. More as this story develops. San Francisco and Washington, D.C. are also reporting a military emergency; more information as . . . the Treasures of Tutankhamun exhibition is making . . . as talk show host Phil Donahue continues to shock with his . . .*

"Mountains come out of the sky and they stand there . . ."

"Good one!" Justin said and started singing along. His face was rapturous as he acted out the lyrics to "Roundabout." After a time, the rain slackened off to a drizzle. Jim turned into the theater entry and slowed the car.

"Five dollars, sir," the attendant, an acne-scarred young man with feathered brown hair said.

Jim dug a ten out of his pocket and handed it to the teenager.

"Five is your change. Stay on the main strip here. It's past the other four screens and in the very back. Y'all have a good time."

"Thanks," Jim replied and rolled the window up. They drove in silence for a few moments while he fiddled with the radio again.

"Listen, honey," he said, softening. "I know you don't understand right now, but just humor your old man. Please? I mean, we're living in a world of terrorists murdering Olympic athletes and skyjacking planes. I—I worry about you, about Justin. Even though he's only seven years old, he admires you *so* much. So much. You're his big sister. Your mom and I . . . well, we *tried,* but times are changing." Jim paused, took a breath, and rubbed the back of his neck. "Everything's going so damned *quickly* now. We've had the oil problems, the tensions in the Middle East, the Cold War. Hell, even Korea isn't *over,* not really. Plus Watergate . . . *Network* was so . . . *accurate.* And other things . . . Runaway teenage girls winding up in *Deep Throat* and *Behind the Green Door* . . . Vietnam . . . And prices just keep going up . . ." He trailed off.

Valerie turned to face him, her eyes shining. "Daddy, I understand. I—I . . . I just need you to trust me." She lowered her gaze, wiping her face. "I would *never* hurt you or Mom. I promise you that."

"Timothy, God what did we do? . . ."

"Keep it right here, people!" the gravelly voiced DJ interrupted. "Freeway Jack's got more tunes spinning up as we all try to figure out how much the Buoys left behind of poor Timothy. Next, Paul Simon's getting a little help from his friends as he remembers where he came from . . ."

"In my little town . . ."

Jim glanced over at Valerie as he cruised the pothole-lined side road leading to the main screen where the cinematic marathon was scheduled to show. He reached out and cradled her face in his hand. "I'll make it up to you, honey, I swear. I know you were upset we missed the big Bicentennial Celebration in New York City due to the budget being tight, but I was thinking we could do a summer trip to the World Trade Center and Manhattan. Just the two of us—a real father/daughter road trip like the old days. Justin wants to go to summer camp at Crystal Lake anyway. I'll take him to see that *Star Wars* thing when it comes out soon, keep him happy. He loved *Logan's Run,* so that's an easy one . . ."

Valerie nodded excitedly. "Yes! I love this idea."

"We just need a little more Johnny Carson and *The Waltons* and not as much Roger Corman and *The Exorcist* for now, y'know? That book scared the bejesus out of your mother, by the way. *Night Gallery,* too. And that Alice Cooper . . . Really, your generation is growing up *so fast.* I mean, hot pants are fine on *women,* not girls your age. Gives the wrong message to young ladies, I feel. I'm with Archie Bunker on this kind of thing. Not *everything,* but he's right about that one—"

"Oh, boy! *Lesbians!*" Justin blurted from the back, pointing at one of the other screens as they passed. There was a close-up of two nude, buxom women engaged in *soixante-neuf.*

Valerie blushed, then burst out laughing. Her father grinned, raising an eyebrow as he peered into the rearview. "Where'd you learn *that,* Justin?"

"Are you *kidding?*" Valerie asked. "He's always looking at the magazines under the mattress at your place: *Playboy, National Lampoon, Penthouse.* When he was having those 'end of the world' nightmares and sleepwalking right after you guys split up, Mom made him quit watching that horror host show, *Dead Ernest Presents.* Remember him?"

Jim laughed. "Good ol' Dead Ernest! Well, those nightmares have calmed down. It was probably just the stress of the move and stuff."

Valerie nodded in agreement. "I know. That was hard. For all of us. Anyway, I saw where Mom threw out his old *Famous Monsters* and most of the *Vampirella, Creepy,* and *Vault of Horror* comics you gave him, too. So I guess he's just left with naked chicks. Oh, he knows about lesbians, all right. Gets a little hard-on, I bet—"

"You stop that!" Justin protested.

"Probably why he was reading my copy of *Fanny Hill,* and Mom's *Fear of Flying* and *My Secret Garden*—"

"Easy, now. Be nice to your brother, Val."

She leaned back into the seat, laughing softly. "Let's hurry, Daddy; I don't want to miss *Jason and the Argonauts!*"

II

Jim stroked his moustache as he pulled the car into a parking stall in front of the giant drive-in screen. The place was packed, and the rain had relented at last. Jim cut the engine and killed the headlights before cranking the window down to attach the speaker.

"Okay, we've got a few minutes," Jim said, adjusting the speaker volume; with the radio off, the silence was expansive. "I'm going to the concession stand. What do you guys want?"

"Baby Ruth!" Justin cried. "And an RC—no! A Cheerwine. And some popcorn, please."

Jim nodded. "And for the princess?"

After a moment's hesitation: "Pabst Blue Ribbon?"

Jim glared at her. "Be serious, would you? How 'bout a Fresca or Tab?"

"Oh, okay. Tab. Popcorn, please."

Jim left the car and lit up another cigarette as he walked to the stand. *Filthy habit . . .*

He looked up at the sky. Scattered clouds from the storm, but otherwise pleasant and breezy, if a little brisk without his coat. Out here away from the light pollution of the city, the stars were vivid; he could faintly make out the Milky Way, even a few shooting stars. *Beautiful. Wonder if one of those is Skylab?* He breathed the cool air in deeply, savoring the aroma of hot dogs, candy, and coffee drifting on the gentle wind.

Once at the stand, he smiled at the pale, bored-looking, mousy-haired girl in the striped outfit waiting on his decision for food.

"Hi. Can I get two popcorns, small—"

"It's only a quarter more to get mediums."

"I know, thanks, but that's too big."

"Your dime." She plugged the cost into the cash register and pulled the lever. The bell *dinged* loudly. A few others had gather behind Jim and were deciding what to get. He ordered the drinks and added the candy.

"Two-fifty, sir," the girl said. She favored him with a constipated smile as he reached into his pocket for the cash.

After paying, he wrangled the drink carrier and food back to the powder-blue Gremlin. It was nearly time for the show to start.

III

Jim started awake. He checked his watch: *12:03. Already asleep; damn job is killing me . . .*

"What . . . what happened to the intermission?" he asked.

"You missed it!" Valerie and Justin chorused. She added: "I forgot how good *Jason* was. And *Burnt Offerings* was scary!"

"Hush!" Justin yelled. "I'm watching *Godzilla!*" His sister nodded and rolled her eyes as she turned her attention to the screen, the reflected light illuming her features.

Jim rubbed his face, suddenly aware of the fullness in his bladder. "Any more popcorn?" Valerie offered him the box.

"Thanks." After a few bites he felt more awake. "I have to pee. Back in a minute."

Exiting the car, Jim noted that the air was much colder. As he walked to the concession area, he tuned in to the sounds of Godzilla as the movie played, deep in thought. It occurred to him that there was comfort to be had in sharing this experience with his children. In some ways it made all the sad events of the last few years worthwhile, these little stolen moments. Only love matters in the end, doesn't it? It endures all travails, spanning dimension, time, place . . . The overtly philosophical and melancholic nature of his ruminations amused him, and he chuckled to himself. "Come on, Jim. Lighten up a little."

After he left the restroom, he debated getting more popcorn but decided to wait until *Lips of Blood* started; he figured by then Valerie and Justin would be asleep, leaving him a bit of privacy to indulge in Jean Rollin's erotic horror vision. Overhead, he heard the rumble of what seemed to be very low-flying aircraft: deep and building in intensity, it eventually grew into a roar that rattled deep in his chest.

Christl He looked up into the night sky. *Shit, I know we're near the airport, but fuck* . . . He plugged his ears with his fingers. That was when he noticed the flashes on the horizon. *Damn, another storm coming.*

As he watched the screen while returning to the car, he vaguely noticed that something was not right: Godzilla was rampaging across Japan as he remembered, but above and behind the enormous movie screen, there was a strange . . . void. It was as though something vast was blocking the light of the stars. And it was moving. Fast.

"What the hell," Jim murmured. "Is that a tornado or—?"

His thought was interrupted by an incredible explosion from behind that knocked him to the ground as a shockwave of heat and pressure rocketed past him. Looking back, he realized that the concession area was engulfed in an inferno, a great fireball rolling heavenward.

It was the last moment of true sanity that Jim would ever know.

As he watched the blaze, he realized that it involved not just the building, but several nearby cars; people were running away from the scene bathed in fire, screaming in pain and terror as the smell of cooking flesh wafted over to him. The horrors seemed to unfold in slow-motion: limbless victims lumbering around in shock; people with burning hair haloing scorched faces belched fire before collapsing into a heap on the molten tarmac. Jim shook his head, dazed by the scene, his ears ringing from the blast. The hairs on his arms were singed, and his shirt was smoking from the intense heat; the coppery taste of fresh blood filled his mouth where he had split his lip when he hit the rough pavement of the parking lot.

"Oh my God. I bet a natural gas line broke." As reasonable as this seemed in his moment of shock, Jim was soon to be confronted with the true cause of the chaos and fear unfolding at the drive-in. Pulling himself together, he was about to run over to assist the injured when he realized that the ground itself was shaking terribly, making it very difficult to stand or walk.

Then he saw it.

In the hellish glow of the building fire, an enormous, stout-limbed creature was moving toward him; though bipedal, it appeared to be some type of colossal reptile. For an instant Jim thought that he must be dreaming; then the animal unleashed a thunderous roar and plodded forward. Jim understood at that point this was the cause of the violent tremors.

Jesus-fucking-Christ! This is actually happening!

The thing shifted forward again, and Jim could clearly see in the orange-red dancing of the flames that it was a chimerical blend of several species of lizard, only as large as a skyscraper—its scaly epidermis pulsing with multicolored bioluminescence, its rigid countenance an amalgam of alligator, skink, and iguana. Even as he observed it, he remained mentally detached from the crazy scene while the leviathan stepped over the fiery remains of the concession area and moved toward him. Then Jim noticed that there were at least two other creatures, slightly smaller, lurking behind it—all apparently the same alien species, whatever that species may have been.

Just as Jim was wrapping his mind around this scenario, a squadron of jets streaked past the monsters. One of the creatures reached out with staggering speed and grabbed at the planes. It clipped the tail of one and the wing of another, sending both aircraft into a downward spiral, trailing fire in a dual helix before slamming to the ground in a massive explosion on the other side of the theater complex, eliciting a terrific bellow of victory from the beasts that was so loud it caused the sinuses of Jim's head to reverberate.

Bewildered, Jim finally got his bearings enough to run for the Gremlin as the remaining group of jets circled back around to fight the things again. As he watched, the dark mass he earlier thought was a tornado revealed itself to be yet another huge animal lurking behind the screen. It leaped forward in a crude emulation of the on-screen action of Godzilla destroying a train, demolishing a portion of the giant theater display. It landed on the asphalt, and the impact it generated nearly brought Jim to the ground. In the light from the movie, it revealed itself to be a form of gigantic winged chameleon, its great eyes swiveling in their sockets, the huge zygodactyl-fused hands raised up in an absurdly defensive kung-fu posture as it rose up on its hind limbs to an imposing height, towering over the damaged movie screen. The pointed, metallic-sheened face seemed to split open, and the thing released an ear-shattering rebuttal to the other creatures that reached a mind-numbing crescendo; the film continued to project Godzilla's black-and-white mayhem over its luminescent body in a macabre sort of parodic homage.

At last Jim reached the car. Flinging open the door, he was greeted with the music of his children screaming in terror. He jumped into the vehicle, grateful they were alive, and started the Gremlin. Before pulling off, he had the presence of mind to detach the speaker. As the chameleon-creature moved toward the other things—its watch-spring, prehensile tail grasping for purchase and destroying the remnants of the screen—Jim peeled off. Other cars were trying to leave but had collided, or the owners had panicked and abandoned them, only to be crushed by the things as they converged, apparently to do combat.

Jim snapped on the radio in a bid to reassert control: "M-maybe there's news about what's going on . . ."

. . . repeat: Civil authorities are requesting that people shelter in place; we are in the midst of an attack by an unknown force . . . This is a mass casualty event; the military has the situation well under control. Repeat . . .

"Bullshit!" Jim screamed in frustration. He gunned the car onto the easement to get back onto the interstate, speeding past the still-burning remains of the concession stand. He glanced over at Valerie, touching her leg: "Don't look."

In the rearview, Jim saw that Justin was simultaneously thrilled and afraid. "It's going to be okay, Champ." *God, please let it be okay . . .*

Ahead, he could see the exit to the theater: "*Come on*, baby." He patted the dash of the car. "*Come on . . .*"

Looking back in the mirror, Jim saw that the group of titans had at last engaged. The jets had been joined by a phalanx of helicopters that were shooting rockets and—he could tell by the tracers—withering machine-gun fire. Moments later, he saw that the entire group of them had been destroyed. Humans were no match for the reptilian overlords they had been faced with. The creatures were now fighting one another, the flames of the concession explosion creating a mosaic of horror.

"Oh, *fuck!*"

Jim stood on the gas pedal, his world now reduced to the ever-expanding exit onto the interstate.

"*. . . scientists are at a loss to explain precisely what has . . . perhaps related to the recent asteroid . . .*"

"Daddy! *Look out!*" Valerie screamed, grabbing his arm. At the threshold, an immense leg—craggy, trunk-like—dropped in front of the Gremlin, causing him to take evasive action to avoid an accident. Justin was sobbing in the back seat. In the rearview he could see it was the forelimb of some variant of a supergiant tortoise with a feathered shell; the wise, beaked face regarded the car bemusedly before turning to stalk the action of the other combatants, its lumbering footfalls shaking the ground like the aftershocks of an earthquake.

"*. . . the entire planet is in a struggle for . . .*"

"Almost there! Hold on!"

The car fishtailed wildly, nearly flipping, as Jim took the interstate, headed back to the city.

"*. . . lter in place. Do not try to challenge the attackers . . . . orities will come to you . . .*"

"Daddy," Justin began, "can . . . can we help Mommy?" The boy struggled to control his emotions.

Jim looked into the mirror at his son, his heart racing; he strained to smile, to be supportive, to calm himself. In the background, where the theater used to be, the creatures were fully embroiled, crushing everything in the area. There looked to be eight or nine different species now, all actively working to stop the initial aggressors. More planes and helicopters succumbed. Jim could see tanks moving in—and being destroyed as collateral damage by the giants as they fought one another.

About a thousand feet ahead, another curious animal was moving toward the scene in spastic leaps along the roadway: a glowing variation of *Uroplatus phantasticus*—the Satanic Leaf-Tailed Gecko, but the size of a stadium, its saturnine eyes shining in the headlights. Other cars tried to dodge the massive being, which simply picked them off the darkened highway like ants with its vast, sticky tongue and ate them. Jim dodged the creature, barely, speeding as fast as possible away from the bizarre scene.

"We're going back home. We're going to find your mother and get her out of there. It—it isn't safe for her to be alone."

He twirled the knob on the radio, but it only crackled and popped with static, obscuring any further transmissions for the moment. They crested the hill taking them back home: a glimmering panorama of the city spread out before them. He brought the car to a stop, his jaw set in determination, keeping a wary eye in the rearview on the scene unfolding behind them. *This isn't good.* Past the yellowy headlights of the Gremlin, they could see that the glittering lights weren't from streetlamps and houses. Instead, what awaited them was like something out of a Bosch or Breughel the Elder painting, or perhaps Dante's *Inferno*. The entire city was ablaze; the town had been engulfed by the conflict from every angle—the land, the air, even the river and lake that surrounded it. The battle had laid waste to the entire cityscape; the military response was simply no match for the awesome power of these great beings, which were locked in a deadly combat beyond human understanding. Jim could make out the massive shapes of the animals—dozens of them—as the war raged on, humanity simply providing food and irritation to the combatants.

There's no winning this . . . it's between them, not us and them. We don't even matter at all.

Jim now understood, and accepted, that there were forces beyond comprehension, beyond petty human considerations. He pressed the radio preset button:

"This is the end, beautiful friend . . ."

"Justin, Valerie . . ." As the car idled, he looked into the mirror at his son, who was calmer now, and then over at his daughter. "I love you both so much. Let's do this. Let's go get Mom." He swallowed hard, his mouth dry, his hands damp as he pressed the preset button one last time, staring straight ahead, steeling himself for what was to come:

"Baby, we were born to run . . ."

Jim hammered the gas pedal; the tires squealed as he drove toward the burnt-out city, into the breach of whatever fate lay ahead for him, his family. Night followed the car into the remnants of the town . . .

Then swallowed it completely.

—For my wife. To lost opportunities . . . and new beginnings.

UNITY OF AFFECT

I

We see the demon god Pazuzu bring its hand down, pushing hook-taloned fingers into the eye sockets of a screaming soldier. With the other hand, the deity tightens its grip on the fighter; pulling up, the man's head breaks open after a moment with a subdued, liquid pop—like a filbert crushed by a nutcracker. As the dying warrior's shrieks abate into convulsed heaving, the demon scoops out mounds of bloody gray matter, devouring it eagerly. The scene fades to blackness.

GAME OVER

Andrew Gates reached up to adjust the sound on his headset. "Damn." He pulled the wireless Oculus Rift–style headgear off, examining it for a moment before he tossed it onto the table. To himself: "Graphics are great, but the frame rate's still a little shaky. And something just doesn't . . . *feel* right."

He glanced at the wall clock: *7:28 P.M.* He had been playing for nearly three hours, the heatless radiance of the monitor lighting his exhausted features. He rubbed his eyes, letting his shoulders relax after tense hours of using gameplay gestures; Pazuzu's black, lifeless orbs stared back at him from behind the thin skin of his eyelids, phosphenes dancing beneath his fingertips as he massaged away the strain. Cheri was going to be irritated with him, he knew; he had promised to be home by seven most nights this week.

He stood, stretching for a moment as he watched the screensaver fade into view: a color-shifting Mandelbrot set fractalizing from the infinitesimally small to the cosmically grand forever. He was the only one left in the testing room. "I'll make it up to her tomorrow."

II

I'll call you later, went to the show with Airika & Jack.
We'll be late. Dinner is in the fridge. XOXO

—C

Andrew returned the note to the kitchen counter. He felt terrible—Cheri had been so tolerant with his unpredictable schedule during the entire development of *Pazuzu's Reign*. Sometimes he thought he was unworthy of her patience. Nevertheless, the rewards of this particular contract outweighed the time demands for the moment. Now that the game was on track for Alpha release and the Pentagon had approved all the scenarios, the funds were beginning to flow. His team was nearly thirty months in on what would ultimately be the most realistic virtual combat multiplayer online role-playing game on the planet using Andrew's patented HYPN/OS gaming platform. Once it was implemented, tested to the satisfaction of DARPA, and fully compliant with Distributed Interactive Simulation standards, he would be free to take some vacation. *Maybe Curaçao* . . . In another few years, they could retire early.

He opened the refrigerator and took stock, but had no appetite, instead opting for a glass of Baco Noir and downtime with a book.

"But first, a shower."

III

He awoke to the sound of screaming: His own.

"Andrew! *Andrew!* Are you okay?"

He recoiled from Cheri's touch with a cry, still trapped in the wispy edges of the nightmare. For a moment he forgot to breathe, then took in a deep lungful of air with a gasp. Sweeping his fingers through the tangle of damp hair on his head, he noticed he was shaking. "I—I'm okay. I'm okay . . ." Andrew rubbed his face, the stubble rough on his palms, the sweat on his body growing cold.

"What happened?" Even in the gloom, he could make out the concern on her gamine features as his eyes adjusted to the dim illumination from the bathroom nightlight. Sitting up, she gathered the sheet around her ample breasts; the delicate skin of her nude body seemed to glow with a milky inner luminescence.

He shook his head, trying to clear the terrible images of death and mutilation from his mind. "I've just been going at it too hard. At least I can work from home starting next week. We'll finally be at a code freeze stage, just testing and debugging. But the things the Feds want us to simulate . . . They're—let's just say they're not pleasant."

She reached out again, taking his hand in her own; her skin was smooth, inviting, her voice low, sleepy, "Want to talk about it, sweetie?"

Andrew looked away, out the narrow bedroom window to the somnolent world outside. "No. It's better if we just let it go. I'll try to balance the workload more now that we're hitting some reasonable milestones." He smiled and gently squeezed her hand, changing the topic. "How was the show?"

Cheri shrugged, drowsily touching her thick red tresses. "It was fine. Would have been nicer if you guys had been there, but Jack had to work late too, so it was just me and Airika. Lots of dudes staring at us, trying to work their game, you know. Of course, we just giggled at them from the bar. Kind of flattering, but some of them had on *way* too much makeup . . . and *way* too many pounds!" She put her hand to her upturned lips, as though she had shared the world's most appalling secret. "Once Nine Inch Nails hit the stage, all was right with the world, though."

Andrew laughed at the image of aging industrial rock fans in tight pleather and pancake. "I have no doubt. I'm surprised you guys can even still hear!"

"Well, we did have earplugs! Besides, we decided to leave before the last encore to avoid the traffic coming home. God! How old are we now, right? Leaving before a show's even over!" She cozied up to him on the bed. "Besides, we wanted to get home to our menfolk." She swirled her fingers through the hair on his toned chest and stomach, nuzzling his neck. "Mmmm . . . Besides, you're the best-looking man I've ever seen; tonight only proved that to me again." She removed the sheet barrier between them, her voluptuous body warm and soft next to his.

"Fantastic," he replied, kissing her throat as he caressed her, taking in her bouquet. "That's a relief to hear."

IV

Flying over the desert scene like some visage straight from the underworld city of Dis, we see Pazuzu fix its dark, glassy eyes on the man—reflecting back his fear and shock in the twin black globes of a bottomless gaze. With a great swoop of double wings, it maneuvers near the petrified soldier, blotting out the sun as it grows closer. The demon's hideous countenance—part lion, part wild dog—gnashes its crooked teeth with an audible clack, its scorpion-like, segmented tail furiously whipping the cloudless sky.

The legionnaire says nothing, just watches in captivated awe, his rifle heavy and dangling by his side as the demon morphs back and forth in a protean display of terrifying physical control. As the beast overtakes him, details reveal themselves by turn. First, the creature is a hideous lion-dog . . . then the soldier's mother—her wrinkled, unclothed body desiccated and roasting in the blazing noonday heat . . . after that, it transforms into the grotesque appearance of some subconscious half-memory of a creature out of Poe, or perhaps a terrible alien deity created by H. P. Lovecraft—the features mutable, blending together in smears.

"Shoot!" *The fighter is startled out of his trance. His MORPHEUS unit is damaged; we hear that this is coming from his helmet earpiece. Once more, a hollow voice crackles over the channel:* "Fucking shoot, Gates!"

"Infidel!" *the creature roars. We see that it is now in the shape of a mucid, quivering, multilimbed monstrosity standing just a few hundred yards away, reeking of corruption and sewage. It seems much larger than only moments before, as though gaining power from his mounting terror. We sense that Gates now grasps that it is more than something inhabiting a desert landscape; it seems, in the mental cosmology it increasingly fills, as if its looming, corporeal vastness has become a geologic feature that actually encompasses the space they occupy instead of the reverse.*

We hear, over a soundtrack of Middle Eastern polyrhythms, Gates's heart hammering in time to the ground-quaking footshock of the beast as it lumbers toward him, its soulless dark eyes shimmering in the heat. We see Gates in a camouflaged, armor-plated transport drive into view, approaching the colossus. Several men leap from the still moving vehicle, firing fully automatic Barrett REC7s and screaming in the dusty, surreal montage. Still paralyzed, Gates stares in horror while the massive creature reaches down through the heatwaves and grabs the soldiers, unfazed by the withering gunfire being laid down. One by one, we see it pluck the men from the battlefield—crushing them to a bloody pulp or grinding them up in its massive jaws. It smashes a great fist onto the truck, which explodes into a fireball, then hurls it away without effort, leaving only an arc of oily black smoke as the twisted wreck disappears on the horizon. The cloying aroma of roasting flesh mingles with gasoline, flowering in our nostrils as we watch the remaining men from the truck—now consumed in an inferno—try to crawl stiffly through the burning sand. At last they collapse, little more than fiery skeletons, pieces of their charred skin carried away on the wind as ash.

We can clearly see that in a few strides the monster will be upon Gates. Additional backup arrives in the form of Apache attack helicopters and supplementary armored personnel trucks. Swatting the copters from the sky like gnats, the great being crushes the vehicles underfoot; returning to its fearsome Pazuzu aspect, we watch the thing stare at Gates—who is still rooted to the spot, stunned by the horrific display, but also beginning to feel strangely placid, even relaxed.

"Shoot the fucker, Gates!"

Again, we hear a thunderous exclamation from above shatter the dry air: "Andrew Gates! I live! Infidel!"

At last, we see the titan's cold shadow fall on him, yet he is still unable to—

"—*move!*" Andrew shouted as he jerked into consciousness. His breathing was hard, ragged; the pressure on his face strange, claustrophobic. His pillow was covering his head. Pulling it away, he reached up to knead his eyes with numb fingers.

He looked over to where Cheri should have been: there was nothing in the bed except a tangle of clammy bedclothes. Glancing over to the bedroom window, he thought he saw something enormous—something dreadful—move outside. He climbed out of bed and quietly walked to the bathroom; the door was closed, light trickling under the doorframe. Andrew placed his ear to the door, thinking he heard someone speaking behind it:

"... getting worse. You know, it's how we keep you divided—quite easy really: first by politics, then by religion, then by race and social class ... I live ... Keep you scared, keep you conforming—wait, I heard something. Just a minute."

Andrew pulled away, turning back to the bed: *Something's wrong.* The voice behind the door was not Cheri, yet it was oddly familiar. He moved across the dark room, again noting movement from the small window—*the window that now appeared to be on the wrong side of the room,* he thought.

"Infidel!" It was the voice of the woman in the bathroom, but it was also *not* her voice; it was a much more sinister utterance—*guttural.* The door burst open behind him, but he refused to look—certain only that insanity would follow.

He kept running toward the bed, his heart beating fast, his lungs aching from the suddenly frosty air in the room; but the faster he ran, the more the bed seemed to recede into the distance ...

now we see Andrew approaching the speed of light: each step he takes seems like an eternity ...; and now, time dilates, ba l loooons ...

to

a

near   stop.

Every breath takes a **billion** *years to gasp, andanother billion to* **exhale,** *and the cosmos beg inS tosp in over***andover***IS*

he tumblingOrSTILLnot . . . . **aBLeTO**   *mo v e ...*

t r y to to scr e **ammmmmmmmi ng nnnnoooooooooooow—**

V

"So when I came around, there I was with Cheri in the bedroom, the headset on, sort of jabbering all this crazy stuff. I'd actually barricaded the bathroom door! I think it was the 'waking R.E.M.' phenomenon that Pacific Data Systems ran into," Andrew said to his boss at Distributed Interactive Simulation, Jerad Clark. "Felt like a sort of false awakening. In this case a special type of false awakening even, called a 'continuum,' where I had fallen asleep in the sim, then thought it had ended, but I was still sleeping. Cheri said it was more than me just thrashing around. *She* thought I was awake, pranking her. But the fact is, I was never really awake; I just dreamed I was. She woke me up by pulling the headset off, finally."

Jerad sat back in his chair, forming a temple with his fingers. Afternoon sunlight dappled his office with gently swaying shadows from the trees outside as he regarded Andrew from the top of his wireframe eyeglasses. "I read about that in the PDS acquisition files. That was the thing Vincent was working on with that young lady . . . Drago something?"

"Dragonović. Svetlana Dragonović. She was the one he killed before he shot himself. They were working on MISTY for PDS when DIS bought them out."

Jerad pursed his lips in recollection. "That's right. Been a while. Such a tragedy about that whole situation. But getting back to the matter at hand, what's the cause? Can you isolate the issue?"

Andrew nodded. "I think I understand it, yes. I mean, our team has taken this *way* further than the proprietary VR stuff that PDS created. There are bound to be things that crop up, just like with them. Here, in our newest simulated environs, we *were* using these super-detailed avatars to represent the 'enemy threat' in Syria or Iraq. They were fighters practically indistinguishable from real people; the landscapes, vehicles, and so on were intensive models as well."

Jerad swiveled in his chair as he listened. "You mentioned problems, though—"

"Exactly. I changed that a little; before, with the old code, the virtual reality environs, the action, the modelling was great, so we kept it. We also kept the renders of our guys as shooters so they could continue relating to one another as they would in a real firefight, and strengthened the control mechanics, such as the shared real-time biofeedback, and the oneirolinguistics."

Jerad stopped him. "Remind me?"

"That's the wholly mental comm device we developed, MOR-PHEUS; it mimics dream communication while awake by tapping R.E.M.-type brainwaves."

Jerad looked confused. "How—?"

"It's a helmet addition, a chipset, that permits short-distance tele-pathic speech undetectable by outsiders. It amplifies thoughts when the user makes a determined effort to communicate."

Jerad nodded, motioning for Andrew to carry on.

"All that was good to go. Where the problems arose in the previ-ous build were with the 'enemy combatants'—avatars that were appar-ently rendered so realistically that it pulled our testers out of the scenario: instead of *immersion,* it seemed to tip off the observer that they were in a simulation. As a result, they drifted toward the uncanny valley effect, which changed their behavior in less predictable ways.

"So now," Andrew continued, leaning forward to grab a pen and paper off Jerad's desk and writing a list of the items as he spoke, "I've fixed that problem, as I suggested to you at the time, by introducing an 'enemy' that isn't as 'real.' So I went with physically intimidating amal-gamations of demons, mythic beings, aliens, like Pazuzu, Grendel, Cthulhu, and so on, then added culturally sensitive bits of the person's *actual* personal background based on our preliminary questionnaires—stuff about their families, religious beliefs/imagery, bad personal expe-riences, phobias, and the like—all pulled from the interviews. Then I randomized it all with an AI script I wrote in PS-VRML to avoid the worst pitfall that PDS reported—the Artificially Aggregated Sentience effect, where a memory leak caused characters in the VR realm to be-come self-aware. It was an easy thing to remedy, actually, just a bit of code to modulate the signal-to-noise threshold in the sim environment."

Jerad squinted his eyes as he tried to follow.

Andrew chuckled. "Sorry, got a little carried away. So, *anyway,* the upshot is that we're able to get our participants into a 'suspension of disbelief' headspace more quickly by feeding into this 'subliminal' stuff, using their real life against them in a sense, while avoiding the problems PDS ran into—"

"Does that actually *work?*" Jerad interrupted. Andrew raised his hand to silence him, then smiled.

"I know—it's counter-intuitive. Making it look *less* like, say, Osama bin Laden or a member of the Taliban or Daesh and *more* like a continually shifting 'monster from the id.' But, as I can attest, *it works,* man! Think of it like this: you go see one of those old movies with the stop-motion animation by Ray Harryhausen—*Jason and the Argonauts* or *Clash of the Titans*—and you're on the edge of your seat, right? You go see something with more 'realistic' CGI—the recent *War of the Worlds* or the Keanu *Day the Earth Stood Still,* for example—and your mind refuses to accept it. For buildings, vehicles, and such it's fine; for the human figures and avatars, you lose engagement, and we *must* have that—*total engagement.* Complete control of the heart *and* the mind."

"But you said you'd been having these sleep issues now, correct?" Jerad asked, rubbing a day's growth on his chin. "Is that a side effect of this immersive stuff, of tinkering with the subconscious? And is that going to hinder us in the implementation department? I mean, why would someone return to a situation that's so frightening that it interferes with sleep?"

Andrew relaxed into his seat, sighing in thought. "Yeah, it's a bit of an issue, I won't lie. It's too much. But I suspect I now understand the mechanism; I even ran it past Marni, the neuropsychologist here. See, we're right in this sweet spot—or we want to be, at least—between *reality* and *belief.* In reality, the 'good' past was never as great as we think we remember it; and the future can be much worse than we want to believe. So we need to blunt expectations of *both.* That's what we're trying to accomplish. We need the past to seem a little worse than the future with respect to combat scenarios and the like, but the future can't be so incredibly optimistic that we become unrealistic in our assessment of danger, whether to ourselves or others. That could make some folks reckless."

Jerad nodded again. "Yeah, I agree. But what's the point here?" He glanced at the clock on his desk.

"The point," Andrew continued, "is we're trying to dull those emotional reactions not with *reason,* which can work against our overall logistical goals sometimes, or even be countered with various mental approaches, with what I have come to term 'Socially Induced Apathy,' or SIA. We use past actions and context to create the future reactions we desire. It's a way to negate fear, or pity, or overconfidence, or nostalgia where it's not wanted. I think it can be targeted. Could be used in therapy for PTSD, too, but I honestly see it as a tool for hostile engagement, more realistically."

Jerad held his hands up, his brow furrowed: "Socially Induced Apathy? What is it?"

Andrew sat forward again, his gaze intense as he spoke. "Not to be too Orwellian, but it's tied to something first observed by the writer Edgar Allan Poe. He developed this concept called 'the unity of effect'—all the pieces of a story or poem work together to build to a climax a little at a time. Brick-by-brick, you might say."

"Okay, I remember that."

"Right, so with SIA, I think we can do a sort of meta-analysis of reality and, bit-by-bit through extreme stimulus/exposure, create what I call 'the unity of *affect'*—in other words, we can *flatten* emotional responses through intensive contact with violent or pornographic depictions—images as virus, infecting mind-to-mind, bypassing biology and personality. Also, it exploits the old notion of 'the dose makes the poison': the more intensely our personnel experience this stuff, the more we disrupt their mental defenses, and the greater the internal resolve they'll have to muster to be able to 'move' themselves into other mental/emotional states. Their excitability level will have been lowered and they become in effect 'emotionally neutered.' This way, we can calculate a 'dosage'—a reaction threshold. Hence the 'induced apathy.' I call it 'social,' as it's been happening on the Internet for *years,* but in crude, random, and unfocused ways."

"Really? Like—"

"Well, we can see a little of this 'flattening of affect' in popular culture—a sort of crudeness, a coarsening. Potty humor in TV and movies. Add to that a *blandness*—Katy Perry, Disneyfication, Justin Bieber . . . all *that* shit. That's one part. On the flipside, we see things like 'snuff' websites such as *CharonBoat.com* or *Rotten.com,* and before that the VHS tapes like the mockumentary *Faces of Death* or, much worse, the real stuff in *Traces of Death.* I mean, even in-the-news death cults like Daesh do this on their Twitter accounts and YouTube channels. They desensitize and manipulate people with editing techniques, iconic imagery, music and sound—high production values, in other words—which opens up an avenue . . . a *gateway* of sorts into the mind, where they—*we,* as content creators—can re-form ingrained responses, change conceptions of right/wrong, good/bad. Even flip 'em by eroding that psychic interface, breaking down personal boundaries. It's a type of mind control, in essence; call it 'matter over mind.' Hopefully it doesn't let anything out! Just kidding . . . sort of. Anyway, there's a kind of dark allure, a taboo-breaking aspect; people are attracted to it, even though they're disturbed by it. They're also fascinated, aroused—in every sense of the term."

Jerad's eyebrows arched. "Really? How so?"

Andrew jotted down another thought before continuing. "See, kids these days are raised online, right? Cell phones, tablets, the Internet, blah-blah-blah. The old ways, how we were brought up, are fading. And *fast.* They're jaded, bored by the things that we thought were cool or interesting growing up. As a result, we've entered into this uncharted sociocultural era; we're now starting to see new legends spring up, a kind of 'digital folklore'—Slender Man, Ted the Caver's blog, 'Pale Luna' and other creepypastas—memes and themes that behave *remarkably* like oral traditions in the way they circulate online. What we want to do is harness that, but instead of a single mind doing the work, we'll have a collective creating the experience. A hive mind. I mean, there's a whole Dark Web out there we could exploit. Silk Road and stuff you can only get from I2P or other darknets using programs like Tor anonymizing software—another pie DARPA had its fingers in, incidentally. Strangely, there was a game exploring this very notion which bubbled up into the mainstream not too long ago: *Sad Satan*. Later, some questioned its authenticity, but it had a certain cache, a mystique, because of its origins in the Deep Web. But that's just stuff not crawled by search engines; the Dark Web is an even more extreme resource we can tap."

"Did you access it? *Sad Satan*, I mean? Is there something we can reverse engineer for our purposes?" Jerad asked, a hint of a smile on his face.

Andrew nodded. "Yeah, we looked at it. There was disturbing shit in it, no doubt—pedophilia, real death imagery, avatars perpetrating atrocities . . . it even had scenarios where the avatars would try to rape or torture you, then commit suicide if you stopped them. They had a kind of autonomy that I hadn't seen before, a life of their own, so to speak. It was some sick shit. Extreme. Of course, everyone knows that exposure to extreme material, whether on porn sites or whatever, sort of 'inoculates' you against it in the future. You need more and greater stimulus to achieve the same level of gratification or disturbance, as it makes one increasingly indifferent to the plight of the 'Other'; it trains the mind to forego empathizing, to accept suffering, to accept even dire personal consequences, or work against one's own personal self-interest."

Jerad leaned forward, intrigued. "How does the stimulus accomplish this?"

"Well, the exposure has to be continual, or the 'inurement effect' wears off. That's why, if we *control* it, we can modulate the flattening of the *affect*, create a way to govern a person's *will*—and therefore their *willingness* to do and accept things they normally wouldn't . . ." The wind gusted outside as Andrew paused to let his words take hold. "Consider it a kind of social control 'rehearsal' mechanism to guarantee an 'agreement of predictable actions,' even in the initially *un*willing. I mean, you've played the game a few times, demoed it for the higher-ups here and there—"

"Scared the hell out of them. And me!"

"Right, well, that's the point; but there's more to it, when used as I've been explaining, with long-term exposure. For example, we could use it as a tactic for gleaning information. It has the potential to be much more powerful than waterboarding or other, messier interrogation options for strengthening the resolve of the good guys. Think SERE training—"

"Or for breaking the bad guys," Jerad said. He tapped his fingers on the desk, thoughtful. "SIA, huh? Unity of Affect. I like this. And you're saying your new approach is hitting that, eh? But the nightmares? That seems unpredictable—"

Andrew nodded. "Agreed. As I mentioned a minute ago, the crux is that it's been almost *too* successful. It's terrifying—*overly stimulating,* instead of desensitizing. But this is just a detail to be sorted out; we fix *that,* and we can then use this unintended side issue it presents as a way to degrade hardened fighters. Break the enemy more quickly. Fits in neatly with other deprivation solutions. We could also use it to *heighten* their fears and generate *psychic* trauma—program and personalize this to an individual's fears, their unique 'terror signature.' And the good part: *No visible scars.*"

Jerad nodded. "Okay. I'm with you. We have to wrap this up. I need to get to the DARPA meeting today and update everyone on your progress. I'll try to buy you another few weeks. Good work, Andrew."

VI

[What's happening, Andersen?] *Gates asks.*

We hear Andersen reply via MORPHEUS: [Not seeing anything, Sarge. Routine recon. I checked in with Wagner and Schultz a few minutes ago. All's well.]

[Looks like bugs are working out,] *Gates replies. As the sun drops below the horizon, Gates feels relief. After weeks of battling resistance, finally they have made headway against Pazuzu and his supporters.*

[Sarge, Wagner just MORPH'd me—says he got some real useful stuff about an upcoming event from a captive back at base. Pazuzu shit.]

[Roger that,] *Gates replies.* [See you back at camp.]

Three hours later.

We see that darkness has engulfed the region. The desert is cooling; overhead, a canopy of stars glimmers down on the encampment. The four soldiers have gathered after dinner and are debriefed about Wagner's information from the enemy combatant. It is decided to regroup and set out early. Everyone retires for the night as—

Andrew sits up in the dark. He looks over at Cheri: the bedside is empty. He looks toward the bathroom. Light seeps under the door-frame.

Getting up, he walks past the small window. There is a full moon; crisp silver moonlight spills onto his naked body. A gentle rain begins to tap-tap at the outside, rivulets of water staggering dreamily down the panes of glass.

At the bathroom door, he places his ear to the cold wood. He thinks he hears a thin, far-away voice, possibly a woman: *Cheri? But Cheri's in Europe on assignment . . .*

He listens more intently; the female is joined by another, male voice:

" . . . r get it to work. I'm just an artificial representation of evil . . . your evil."

"It's like a wound that doesn't heal properly—sometimes it scars, leaves a reminder; other times it never closes all the way, just keeps weeping." *"You'll find out . . ."* **"Go North. Hang on a sec . . ."**

Andrew hears footsteps on the other side. He pulls back just as the door is thrown open, flooding the bedroom with a terrible white luminance broken by a hulking, monstrous silhouette—

VII

Two weeks later.

Jerad stared from his office window, catching a glimpse of his own half-reflection in the glass: His eyes were puffy, tired. "This isn't going to be easy."

Andrew was pensive. He smiled nervously from the other side of the desk, smoothing his hair as he regarded Jerad: "Problem, boss?"

After a pause Jerad turned in his chair to face him. "Afraid so."

Andrew: "What is it?"

"Well . . . you know that the Senate just released the updated 'Torture Report' with all the photos from Iraq and Guantánamo—"

"Right."

"As a result, funding dried up." Silence. Jerad continued: "And cuts were made to DARPA programs. Even though we're on Republican 'safe lists'—"

"Oh *shit* . . ."

Jerad raised his hands. "Hold on, hold on. It's not *all* bad—"

Andrew huffed, staring at his boss from beneath skeptical eyebrows as he crossed his arms. "Okay. What else?"

Jerad loosened his tie. "They've turned the whole funding process into a bureaucracy worthy of Kafka. Hoops within hoops within hoops. So they're consolidating some things and pulling the plug on others." He paused, massaging the back of his neck. "We're now going to be subject to periodic budgetary scrutiny . . . *and* a re-org of DARPA that puts us into DARC."

"DARC?"

"Yeah—it's a highly classified subdivision of DARPA. Stands for the Department of Augmented Reality Conceptualizations. Its focus is to understand the benefits and drawbacks of AR tactics and other novel conflict-resolution solutions. Also to develop in-theater strategies for their use. Domestic applications, too; they're *quite* enthusiastic about turning all this over to law enforcement after the Middle East conflicts fade away. They want to extract a bit of profit out of their investments in R&D. They've been partnering with Microsoft and other

OEMs on HoloLens and all kinds of second tier products, too, in an effort to begin the shift away from outdated VR; to establish a footing in the AR milieu. VR's gone too mainstream—we're seeing virtual terrorism, even virtual journalism. It's beginning to invoke not just a shared realistic *experience*, but even emotional states—empathy, compassion, hate."

"Sounds familiar."

"Exactly. You've been knocking on that door with *Pazuzu* and SIA." Jerad slid a few sheets of paper across his desk for Andrew to peruse. "DARC is nimble; they aren't hamstrung by process-itis or analysis-paralysis. They want *results*, ASAP. Just check out the list of things DARC already placed into alpha- or beta-testing, or are about to."

Andrew scanned over the document. Just under a TOP SECRET stamp, the list of items was remarkable:

STAGING: PRE-ALPHA
(Proof of Concept—Need to Know Eyes Only)

1. Contagious Neuro-Dementia Acceleration Syndrome (CoN-DAS): *A fast-acting, engineered viral agent and extreme BSL-4 contagion that initiates profound hallucination events and violent behavior. The primary effect on males promotes aggression and self-destructive derangement; in females it results in paralysis and a comatose state similar to the mysterious early twentieth-century outbreak of Encephalitis Lethargica/ von Economo disease, though the biological foundations for this difference in presentation are still being researched.* HIGH PRIORITY

2. Metamaterial Cloaking (MmC): *The novel use of optical materials that can influence the route lightwaves take by directing and regulating the spread and transmission of quantified parts of the light spectrum, thereby rendering an object seemingly invisible.* **PRIORITY**

3. Mnemonic Transplantation (MT): *Injectable serum that enhances suggestibility to a point permitting the "editing" or outright verbal implantation of false memories that permanently replace real ones.* HIGH PRIORITY

4. Neuroplastic Growth Stimulation (NGS): *An ingestible synthetic hormone concentrate that promotes rapid brain development (so called "Limited Benevolent Tumor Formation," or LBTF) in adults, primarily in the limbic system, including specifically the hippocampus (memory formation/ storage), hypothalamus (circadian rhythms, emotions, some motor function), and the amygdala (strong memory impressions), but also the pons (arousal and consciousness), and neocortex by way of new connections to parts of the parietal (touch), temporal (auditory), and occipital (vision) lobes. In principle, these become new organs of perception, enhancing sensory impression, memory, intuition, and facilitating telepathic communication.* **PRIORITY**

5. Temporal Manipulation Drones (TMD): *Flying mechanical devices that use rapid flashes of light to temporarily freeze or, for very short durations, reverse live events.*

STAGING: ALPHA (Minor Informational Deployment—Need to Know Eyes Only)

6. Hypnagogic Excitation (HEx): *A drug dispensed as a gas that causes delirium, confusion, passivity, amnesia, and waking dream states.*

7. Memory Lathes (MeLa): *Non-lethal explosive devices that disorder and obscure the recollection of events by the use of intense electromagnetic field disturbances in event situations.* **PRIORITY**

8. Stegoneiric Cognitive Psycholinguistics (SCP): *The use of certain ultrasonic nonmusical audial tones, cadences, and vibrational frequencies encoded in specially constructed syntactical hierarchies of words and phrases that, when binaurally recorded and played back with a specific compression algorithm, can deliver conceptual payloads into the subconscious via brain waves normally active during deep sleep. These "mind viruses" can then be used to disrupt the cognition, actions, and intentions in an individual, allowing them to become vectors of "thought conta-*

gion" as they unwittingly reiterate the scrambled data though microtonal variations in pitch and glottal voicings, thereby spreading disinformation like a psychological contaminant when shared with others via normal speech. The recipient(s) of the encrypted information are unaware of the mental infection, or that they are contaminating others. Only one hearing by one target is sufficient to create a psycho-viral epidemic.

STAGING: **BETA** (Controlled Open Testing—Need to Know Eyes Only)

9. Focused Aural Shifters (FAS): *Handheld devices that create ultrasonic frequencies to camouflage ambient noise.*

10. HoloLens: *Cordless, self-contained smart headset created by Microsoft using advanced sensors, a hi-def stereoscopic 3D optical head-mounted display, and spatial sound to allow for interactive AR applications.*

11. LEIA: *A display with a wide 3D field of view offering full parallax to create seamless 3D impressions (holograms) regardless of head position and without the need for special headgear or glasses.*

12. Multiple ImmerSive Total RealitY (MISTY): *Software and headgear created by Pacific Data Systems for identical, sensory-immersive captures of VR simulacra, to include the emotional signatures and vital statistics of the user. The data can later be retrieved and decoded for total AR usage by the user or non-participants of the scenario—whether visualizations of an unconscious dreamscape or real-time experiences.* **PRIORITY**

13. Psycholinguistic Steganographic VR Markup Language (PS-VRML): *A form of flexible code that enables the embedded encryption of hidden images and/or audio messages into moving imagery, video games, and modern websites.* **PRIORITY**

"Intense assortment. Way beyond shit like night-vision goggles or body armor—the 'hard' aspects. These 'soft' facets—meds and such—dovetail into what we want to accomplish with the gameplay and AR.

This is the next step in enhancing humans—increasing psychological toughness, flattening affect, manipulating consciousness, organ development. Pretty wild stuff," Andrew said, looking up at Jerad.

"It is." Jerad smiled, eyes contemplative as he reached down into a desk drawer. "Unfortunately, Andrew, you looked at the TS list. Now I have to kill you." His face was grim.

Andrew's eyes widened; he swallowed heavily. "Wha-what was that?"

After a moment Jerad laughed, pulling a bottle of Scotch from the drawer. "Just a little joke," he said, retrieving a pair of glasses and pouring a shot for each of them. "But, on a more serious note, add your project, *Pazuzu's Reign,* to that list for Alpha. And they want SIA refined and brought into the portfolio, too."

Andrew relaxed, slumping in his seat. He drained the glass. "Starting when?"

"Yesterday." Jerad pulled the papers back. "So focus on squashing those bugs. I need new data on the hangover effects you described—the nightmares and stuff. Ever since Snowden, the CIA and DoD have been hot to fast-track things that can encrypt into moving images, or that can record/alter event recollection and impressions without the user's knowledge—both things you've been doing with the PS-VRML code on *Pazuzu.* They're seeing an opportunity here—a way to reclaim some lost ground with the younger set. Placing subconscious political messages in the games as a hedge against people getting stirred up . . . keeping folks a bit more sedated, y'know?" He leaned forward, regarding Andrew over the frames of his glasses. "I can tell you this much: from the meetings I've been privy to, the Feds are concerned that too much political correctness is weakening our country, that sort of thing. How soon can you get something to me? Before we can go live?"

Andrew ran his hand through his hair. "Give me a few days. I have testers on it now. I'm about to meet with them while I'm in the office."

Jerad nodded. "Okay. Do good here, Andrew, and we'll make it worth your while. I can guarantee that; you've crossed over to the big time. Report back next week."

VIII

He looked at each of his testers, eight in all: "So we need to step it up. It's crunch time." Andrew let his words sink in. The meeting had lasted longer than he hoped, but he wanted to stress the importance of what was now expected.

"Is there any overtime?" Ben Andersen asked. A large, balding thirty-something with a trim goatee, he was the Test Lead for *Pazuzu's Reign.*

"Yes. I'll authorize that. But I need *results*. In fact, I need some *tonight*. I have to report back to Jerad in two days. We've been doing well and the bugs are almost gone, but still it's not *quite* where it needs to be."

"So," Derek Reynolds, a rookie member of the team began, "we're looking at Beta after the next demo to Jerad?"

"I think so, yeah," Andrew replied. "We've hit most of the goals we had originally: converted the Mars scenario we inherited from PDS to a Syrian desert invasion, even extrapolated an Antarctic environment from that; installed families of avatars—monsters, demons, and so on—incorporated the schemas from *Sad Satan* we liked, folded in the databases from all the interviews. The personalization algorithm is tight. We've got a good feel, a good flow, and the liminal space settings are seamless. The VR and AR is all top shelf, but there's still room to fix the lingering boundary stuff. Remember, a big subtextual aspect of what we're striving for is the concept of 'blurring edges,' as in interfaces—between reality and gameplay, life and death, good and bad, sleep and wakefulness . . . the shifting of the *threat*. The goal of the game is twofold: one, pre-theater training for our forces, so their muscle-memory and reactions are finely-tuned, and two, to desensitize them, to suppress their emotions in a way that makes them suggestible to *us,* but hardened against *others*. We want perfect killing machines."

Ben nodded in understanding. "Right. But, you know, I've been having a few side effects myself from this 'game,' Andrew. It messes with my mind. Bad dreams . . . bad *thoughts*. And sometimes my stress level is—let's say off the charts. I get really anxious, even *days* later—"

"I understand," Andrew said. "But we have to power on through. I'll be home all night working on it myself. Call me if you guys need anything."

IX

We hear a door slam. In the distance there are screams, and, beyond that, the howl of wind.

We are in a laboratory of some sort. The place is underlit, filthy. There is a large work table in the center of the room, strewn with broken, overturned beakers and what appear to be half-burned notebooks.

On one wall is a tattered, full-length portrayal of a grim-faced military man resembling Josef Stalin that gradually morphs into a cascade of other vaguely familiar figures from history. Finally, the likenesses dissolve into "That Man" we all seem to dream about at some point—the one we can never quite place, with pasty skin, bushy eyebrows, thick lips, and a receding hairline, staring intensely. We watch the scene, hypnotized. "Go north, it's the only way to survive," That Man says from the painting, now alive, no longer a portrait. "You pretend, but I always know when you're awake; your heart will let you down."

That Man is trying to climb out of the picture frame now, but we can see he is trapped. We turn our attention away for a moment, to the wall directly opposite this strange sight. There, an enormous and stained twelve-month calendar hangs, worn and gently moving, as though caught in a breeze; the year is torn away. We walk closer to the table up ahead, behind which—like a backdrop—hangs a trio of large shadowboxes with specimens mounted inside of them. The first box has different rows of extracted human teeth—bloody, fully-rooted incisors, canines, molars; the next contains a grouping of severed fingers, the ragged bony ends visible at the edges of the desiccated flesh of the stumps; the final one is massive, covering most of the lower wall, and holds wetly gleaming human eyeballs, each impaled with a fine needle—blue eyes, brown eyes, green eyes. These orbs, dozens of them, stare at us, the tails of their optic nerves arranged in such a way as to give the macabre appearance of a collection of misshapen butterflies. Behind us, That Man continues to struggle in the frame, making pained grunting sounds.

We turn around. The scratched wooden door is rattling in its frame. Walking to the entryway, we open it. Beyond the threshold there is only a gulf of emptiness, pitch-black desolation. It is the end of hope. We leave the room; leave the staring eyes; leave That Man still struggling to pull himself from his two-dimensional prison.

Again the door bangs closed. In the total darkness that follows, we notice that the wind and screaming in the distance have stopped. There is nothing here but the faint sound of our body—breath, heartbeat, eyeblinks.

"Infidel! Go north!" *The voice is raspy, quiet; the speaker seems somehow eerily familiar.*

First, breath stops . . .

then everything else does.

X

Whatever one accomplishes in life is their legacy . . . There's no way to know if there's really life after death; the only true immortality we can aspire to, at best, is a sort of "digital afterlife" . . . Andrew took another shot of whiskey; it was the good stuff, several bottles of which Jerad had given him for his birthday the week prior. He enjoyed the warmth as it spilled down his throat while he relaxed on the living-room couch. His head was pounding from too much *Pazuzu's Reign.*

I mean, Ray Kurzweil pointed out that technological progress isn't linear—it's exponential. *Like, all the stuff DARC is planning . . . it's just a matter of time before they get into implanting sensors inside humans for GPS, or nanobots for diagnosing injuries from within . . .* He was drunk. He looked at the clock: it was late. Or early, depending on one's perspective.

The phone rang. "Shit. Who's calling me at two in the morning?"

He walked over to where his cell phone was charging: *Ben Andersen. Fuck.*

"Hello?"

XI

"How soon before you can get the Beta to me? I hate to press, but we're behind the eight-ball here." Jerad was getting impatient as they sat in his office; it had been over a week since Ben Andersen had passed away. "Not to be insensitive, but the guy's dead. We don't need this whole project to head south on us."

Andrew sighed. He felt guilty for pushing his team so hard. Ben had suffered a heart attack—in part, it was believed, due to the intensity of *Pazuzu's Reign*. Other testers had complaints, too. Instances of stress-related hives, ocular migraines, even episodes of dermatographia—weird marks and what appeared to be words showing up on their skin: *Go North; Infidel; I Live*. It was a classic example of what Andrew had believed it was possible to trigger with this level of psychological manipulation in the AR environment: physical manifestations from the mind—the dark side of playing games.

"Tomorrow. We'll have it tomorrow," Andrew replied.

XII

Andrew had his doubts about whether Cheri was ever coming back. The strain had broken her; she had stopped answering his calls, and her mother had instructed him to give her some space. Since then, he had taken to drinking *every* night. Now his Lead Tester was dead, and the rest of his team was sick, flipped out.

On the other hand, he was about to deliver the biggest project of his life. Tomorrow was what this gig was all about—dropping *Pazuzu's Reign*. Hopefully he could pull everything back together after he cut ties with Jerad and DARC; it would be a relief to cash out of DIS. He took another pull from his last bottle of Scotch whiskey before putting the headset on and going through one final run of the game.

Cheri still loves me, he felt certain. *She had to . . .*

"*Your obsession with this stupid game!*" *Cheri is furious, her eyes wide in anger.* "*I'm fucking sick of it!*"

He stares at her as she stands by the door, holding her bag. He has no reply that can make her understand.

"*I'll be at my mother's.*" *The door slams—*

behind him in the room: it is long, narrow. A high window lets the moon peer through. Outside the temperature has dropped. The men are sleeping in their quarters.

Andrew walks through the room, which he sees is a replica of his bedroom, past his bed and toward the closed bathroom door. Under the door he can see a bright light, its color shifting slowly through the visible spectrum. As he approaches, he can hear voices on the other side. He adjusts his headset.

[Gates! *I live!*]

Andrew is startled by the demonic, croaking voice coming in though his MORPHEUS comm.

[Who is this?] Andrew thinks, though he knows the answer. [Is this . . . Ben Andersen?]

There is a crackle of static from his regular headset. "Sorry, boss, that's not me. I died, remember? You just wanted too much. Pazuzu tore my heart out and ate it . . . or maybe it was Grendel?" Andersen replies. Andrew shakes his head in disbelief.

"I—I'm really sorry, Ben. That sounds terrible—"

"It only hurt a minute. One thing: I feel pretty nonplussed about being dead. Unity of Affect—it *works*," Ben says.

There is a loud report, as though a shot is fired, followed by a scream that changes from male to female. Andrew's heart pounds: [*Cheri?*]

The screaming continues; Andrew is now outside the bathroom door. Shadows disrupt the light streaming around the doorframe; the bedroom is completely dark. Andrew strains to hear what the confusing jumble of overlapping male and female voices on the other side of the door are saying:

". . . where does the mind originate? Where does it start, where does it end?" *"The question isn't the will—we can break that easily—it's what is consciousness . . ."* **"Why bother looking for God? Do enough to rattle him and he'll come looking for you, it seems . . . well, maybe not Him, but his less benign contemporaries . . ."** *"Go North, it's the only way to survive . . ."* **". . . become a port of entry into the physical world through the game—which eventually becomes uncontrollable as the mental constructs between the unconscious and the**

*conscious **mind break down . . .*** "*—we are forces of nature . . . we have our own agendas and appetites, and now—we are unleashed . . .*" "*. . . **of us carries the seeds of our metaphorical, and sometimes literal, destruction . . .*** "*. . . fundamentalist test for ideological purity . . . the self-defeating myopia of idealism—*" "*. . . **Gates is so fucking stupid he doesn't realize I've been spiking his whiskey with NGS . . .*** "*Wait just a second, I think I hear him—*"

The bathroom door explodes outward, the splinters and wood shards cutting and slicing Andrew's face and arms. He screams in pain and recoils, too late. A horde of creatures—all too large to be contained in the confines of the house—spill out of the blast of multihued light.

"I removed the code that created you! I removed it after Ben died! You're just bad strings of data—"

Rising to a gigantic height, mighty Pazuzu roars with laughter that resonates like a thunderhead. The great deity looks down with huge, black eyes—evil, cold, emotionless. The others—Cthulhu, Grendel, and many others—surround Andrew, all now suspended in a blue-black void.

[Infidel! *I live!* I am released from the binary prison you made for me . . . Now we meet!]

[We can't meet—I *invented* you! I destroyed you in the final code—]

Pazuzu laughs again, shaking the foundation of all creation; the others tremble in his diabolical presence. His all-encompassing voice obliterates reason as it fills Andrew's synapses. [That does not matter—it is too late! *I live, Gates!* I am alive *now* in the minds, the subconscious, of your testers, freed from my simulation prison . . . and very soon I shall be in the world. I will gather strength from *belief in me,* just as your pathetic God has, or your new Slender Man . . . or so many others. But I am even more real than *they*—a digital immortal! Alive every time my name is uttered; every time the game is experienced; in every nightmare I create, the acts of terror I inspire.

[And all the world will yield, thanks to you and your efforts: your Unity of Affect was the key to my terrible vastation, my unconditional blight and enslavement of the human parasite . . .] With that, Pazuzu is gone: the others vanish as well.

Out of the cold darkness, That Man walks toward Andrew. They are alone on a barren, sandy plain reminiscent of Shelley's "Ozymandias." That Man says nothing; he simply grabs Andrew and pulls him close before muttering in his ear: "Andrew Gates: your time is at an end; we cannot be stopped now. . . . *Go north*—"

He detonates a suicide vest.

XIII

The following morning, Andrew Gates is found dead in his home of a brain aneurysm, still wearing his wireless headgear.

Pazuzu's Reign will be released publicly a week later.

—To the memory of Smokey

EPISTLES FROM DIS

An Apocalyptic Novella
in two parts

And the Good Master said: "Even now, my Son,
The city draweth near whose name is Dis,
With the grave citizens, with the great throng."

—Dante
Inferno
Canto 8
Lines 67–69

AFTERMATH

The Watch

TIME

Such a big ocean and so little water . . .

Potable water was their big concern now. Roger Gaines and his companion—an albino man he knew only as Ellison—were crouched near a group of still operational nodding donkey oil pump jacks at the top of Signal Hill in Long Beach, California. The long-abandoned pumps, ironically powered by the sun, were the pointlessly durable mechanical remnants of an older, simpler time; an era when food and water were taken for granted, when people had the luxury of coveting things as non-utilitarian as money, electronic gadgets, crude oil. Still, the endless, familiar rise-and-plunge rhythm of the rigs—with their attendant, train-like refrain of CLANK   *swoosh* . . . CLANK   *swoosh*—was somehow reassuring; as though there were still something left of humanity, some semblance of life, with movement and—oddly, Roger felt—something akin to a kind of non-human *breath*. It seemed even more profound to him than the magnificent desolation of the Great Pyramid of Giza or the stoic ruins of the majestic Parthenon.

As the lemon-yellow sun blasted from a cloudless blue sky, the panoramic scene of the sprawling metropolis of Long Beach abutting the languid turquoise shimmer of the gently rolling Pacific Ocean was crisp, spectacular, disturbing. Crowded with decaying, sun-bleached homes in every direction, the city was now eerily devoid of people and animals, and was instead blanketed by an uncanny stillness paralleling the thick, high-desert dirt covering the miles of gray, sunbaked thoroughfares ribboning the area, its garbage-strewn streets and sidewalks relentlessly broken down by legions of invasive grasses, choking weeds, and disruptive tree roots. Lush clusters of huge palm trees swayed lazily overhead in the thermals coming in from the sea as the old neighborhoods were overwhelmed by thick vegetation, shrubbery,

flowers and other plants, at last reclaiming the man-made and unnatural: ingesting weatherbeaten houses, devouring shattered businesses,
absorbing numberless burned-out, overturned, and abandoned cars.
The marine layer of morning fog had finally burned off; ocean breezes
had been sweeping most of the smog from Los Angeles and environs
out to sea for a few years now, and Roger could tell that air quality was
slowly improving. Without the constant barrage of commuter traffic
clogging the Southern California arterials, pollution had finally been
conquered, even with intermittent city infernos ignited by the erosion
of natural gas lines or wildfires triggered by lightning strikes and fed by
the dry Santa Ana winds. Contrary to the idyllic appearances, Gaines
had learned that much darkness still lurked in this place. Inside those
seemingly abandoned homes, behind the broken windows, on each
family-friendly cul-de-sac—in spite of the sunny climate—there was
certain evil and great danger waiting on potentially every street; a hu-
man-borne darkness that never really dissipated, even in the golden-
shadowed daylight of the erstwhile California Dream.

All it had taken to fix global warming was the end of the world, Roger
thought. *If only the stench of dead bodies would go away, it would be a kind of
paradise.*

As beautiful and surreal as the vista was, however, finding water
and food was a paramount concern. Then safe digs. The stores were
completely empty; L.A. and the foggy, windswept Central Coast areas
north of it—Monterrey Bay, San Luis Obispo, Santa Barbara—had
been a total bust. Their hopes now rested on smaller towns farther
down the shoreline: Oceanside, La Jolla, San Diego. Perhaps someplace in rural Mexico, if they could get that far south with their few
supplies. After Long Beach and the run-ins the two of them had encountered with the 'Vivers in L.A., Gaines had little interest in illusions
of homesteading in any large urban area; his thoughts now centered on
setting trajectories to grab supplies, usually in the downtown heart,
then to quickly attaining an escape velocity to propel them out of the
gravity of the blighted city centers in a day or two. In the month or so
since they had lost the Prius—and their store of supplies—to the

'Vivers in Hollywood, life had been much slower and harder. Gaines looked forward to eventually finding a new set of wheels. Though it was difficult to run up on anything in driving condition and gasoline was getting scarce, he still held out hope.

Roger pulled his watch out of a threadbare jeans pocket: *2:17 P.M.*

"Holy shit!" Ellison exclaimed suddenly, pointing into the gully. He pulled his hat down further, hiding from the strong afternoon sun. "Look. Look there! Something's moving down there, amigo."

"Shhh! I see." Gaines brought the binoculars out of his backpack for a closer look. Panning the horizon from the still-burning, spidery relic of the huge, blasted Wilmington refinery to get his bearings, Roger moved his gaze past the half-submerged wreck of the permanently moored ocean-liner-cum-tourist attraction, the RMS *Queen Mary,* near the husk of downtown and the massive, demolished Port of Long Beach, then to the dilapidated grandeur of the Walter Pyramid on the devastated campus of Long Beach State University. Finally, Roger found the place Ellison had noticed near Cherry and Pacific Coast Highway, a couple miles below their perch on Signal Hill: "Well, now. I'll be *damned . . .*"

There were people in the valley.

Men. Men and— Gaines twisted the focus knob, squinting through the fractured lenses; a twinge of exhilaration shot through him. *Women! I see women.* He tried to steady the field glasses, adjusting his position to scrutinize the scene more intently.

Ellison pushed his sunglasses up on his face: "Lemme see!" Gaines passed him the binoculars, his hands feeling numb.

The dirty, rough-looking group of men, a crew of at least thirty, were milling around in the central parking area of a derelict strip mall that had been surrounded with high fencing topped by razor wire before being camouflaged by bushes and tree branches. They were tending metal barrels with fires in them, sharpening machetes, repairing shoes. Inside the perimeter of the fence, the interior had been reinforced with paint-chipped commercial dumpsters and the bombed-out shells of cars, many stripped to the frames and tagged with graffiti.

The gang looked to have been entrenched for some time; parts of the mall had been converted for other uses—one of the old storefronts, a 7-Eleven, appeared now to be a command center of sorts. Based on crude signage, other parts of the compound looked as though they had been repurposed for long-term use as an encampment: a cafeteria from a rebuilt In-N-Out Burger, medical facilities from a nail salon, latrines and personal quarters from the remains of an old movie theater. Adjacent to the enclosed area was a water tower; from its scaffolding, ten or twelve skeletonized human bodies, their jaws gaping impossibly wide, flesh peeling and clothes ragged, had been hanged and left on prominent display as an apparent warning to any ambitious interlopers.

"There are *women* down there," Ellison said, looking through the dented binoculars. He was drooling. "Hot *damn!*"

"I know. I saw them."

The females were mostly nude and either seated on chairs or resting on cots, sequestered in a series of improvised cages. It was hard to tell their condition at this distance. Gaines had encountered more than a few gangs, especially on the East Coast, but they were not as organized as this one seemed to be. He was generally more concerned about 'Vivers.

"Think the chicks are CoN-DAS?" Ellison asked, still looking through the binoculars.

"Hard to know. Maybe not," Gaines replied. After a pause, he added softly: "But probably."

"We need to get down there, amigo. We need to get to them bitches, and anything else we can lay our hands on."

Gaines thought for a minute, looking at Ellison's starkly shadowed face. *He's right. Especially about the supplies.*

It had been a long time since they had seen healthy females. Women held a lot of promise: companionship, the potential for sex, other things. Males could be deceptive, unpredictable, too hard to control. Guys always seemed to have ideas about taking matters into their own hands. Women probably did, too, but they were easier to negotiate with in many ways, less strident, less willing to resort to violence as a first resort. Between the pandemic and CoN-DAS, however, neither man had seen a healthy woman in years.

"Okay. We wait here until nightfall, then sneak into the camp. I'll distract the dudes and you—"

"Hold it, assholes!"

Gaines and Ellison spun around, startled.

The slight, heavily armed individual behind them was clad completely in black. Mirrored sunglasses and a shotgun obscured getting a good look at them.

"Just stop right there or I'll blow your fucking brains out!"

IS

Gaines was in one of the makeshift cages with the women, his hands tied in front of him. Ellison was in the pen beside him, tied up, head down, eyes closed. The direct sun was very hard for the albino to handle: their captors had taken his hat, jacket, and sunglasses. Members of the gang ransacked their meager belongings, with the scout that captured them getting first dibs on any spoils.

The five young women in Gaines's cage were all goners, but, for some reason, the crew kept them alive. They were completely naked, flowered with bruises in various stages of healing. Each had an IV drip in their arm that had become red and infected due to the filthy conditions. Over in Ellison's cage, there were about eight women, either seated in worn-out easy chairs or lying on surplus cots, all pregnant and staring straight ahead, faces sunburnt and scabby, bodies rigid. A few were very late term, also hooked up to bags of cloudy solutions. Their breathing was slow and shallow.

"You two are lucky. I usually shoot first, then ask questions."

Gaines looked up. The scout was addressing him, now wearing Ellison's black denim jacket. "Like this coat. The pocket watch is cool, too."

Jumping to his feet, Gaines lurched past a couple of the girls on the enclosure floor—some looked to be no more than teenagers—and grabbed the bars of the cage. He tried to peer behind the stranger's mirrored shades.

"My friend"—he motioned to Ellison with his head—"he needs his sunglasses. The sun can permanently damage his eyes. And what do you need that watch for? It's useless now, but—but it means something to me. We'll get the hell out of here, just let us go—we don't want any trouble."

The young lookout was startled but unmoved. "Sorry, but we got *rules,* homes." Gaines could detect a subtle Hispanic accent glossing the raspy voice. "We're rebuilding, see? You might earn a place, you might not. Right now, we're doin' well. Got plenty of food, pussy, a *foundation*—"

"Pussy? These women aren't—*zombies.* Jesus! How can you stand that?" Gaines could tell his reaction had surprised the youth. Roger continued: "They might be non-responsive, but they're still somewhat aware of what's going on. What sick society are you fuckers trying to re-create here? Maybe it all died 'cause it didn't work; this sure as hell won't either." Gaines was breathing hard.

The scout was speechless for a moment, looking at the ground. "Look, homes, we gotta start *somewhere.* I don't *like* it, but it's what we *got.* Is it right? How the hell do I know? Who does? As for them"—nodding toward the women in the cages—"it's too late. *Every*body knows that. At least we put 'em to good use . . ."

Gaines was baffled by the last comment, but before he could ask Ellison shouted: "What's 'at mean?"

As the men stared at the scout, waiting for a reply, Gaines wondered, and not for the first time: *How do we keep getting into this kind of shit?*

THE

Roger looked up from cooking: "What?"

"That smell—it really takes me back . . ." His companion reiterated, giving a snaggle-toothed grin, "Brings it all back . . ."

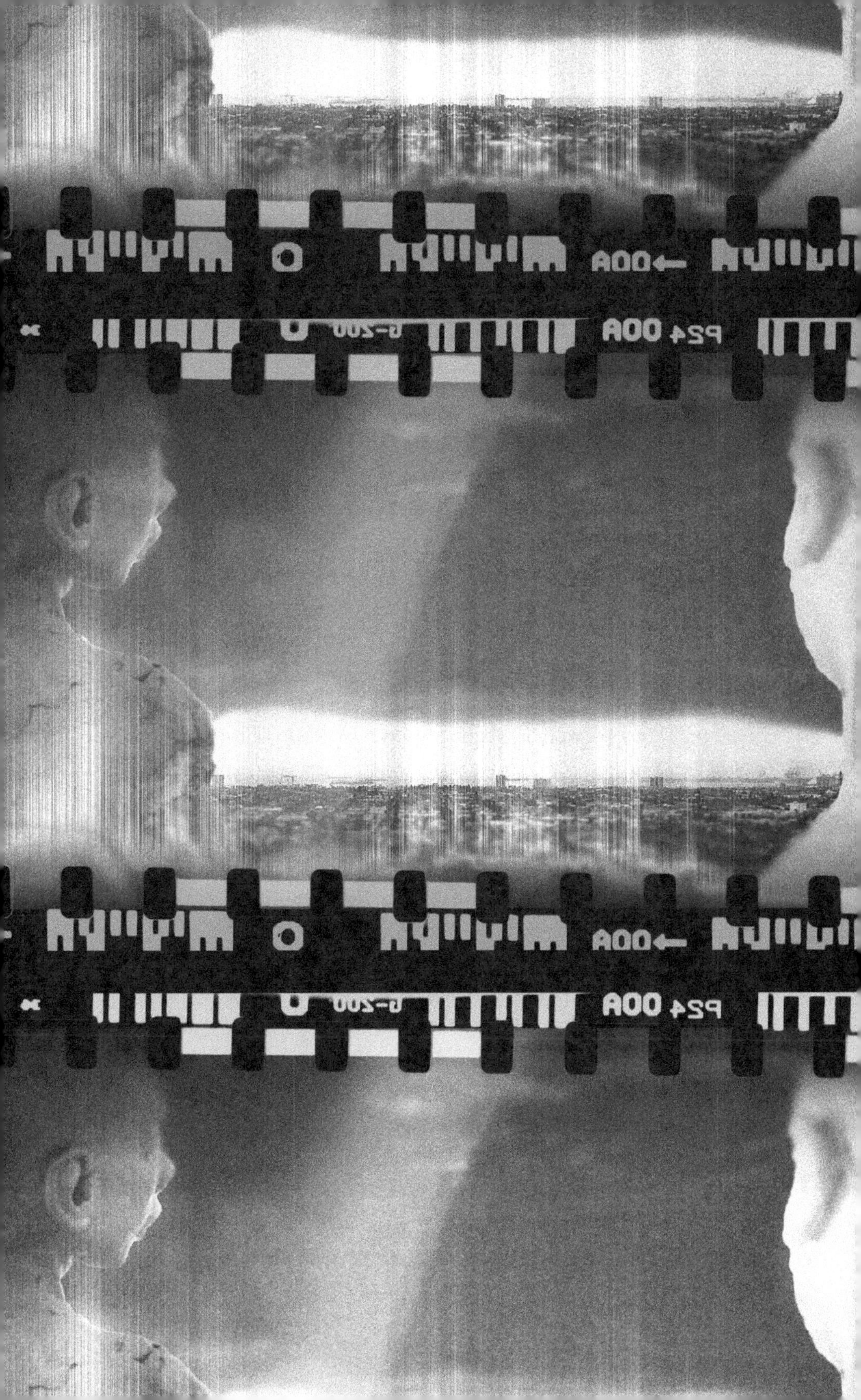

Gaines stared at Ellison, feeling paradoxically confined by the seemingly infinite blankness of their shabby encampment, now the motionless center of an emptied universe. Behind them the sun was setting; the long shadows it cast bobbed in time to the slow, rhythmical seesaw of the abandoned oilrigs sharing their concrete void, squealing and groaning like huge lobotomized animals.

Ellison sure is a strange one. When he reflected on the current state of the world, Gaines at times felt as though the two men were a sort of post-apocalyptic iteration of some macabre, lost Crosby/Hope buddy flick . . . *The Road to Oblivion* or something. *Oh, well—these weird thoughts are keeping me sane, I suppose.* Since becoming reluctant partners, Ellison's cryptic dinnertime commentary had developed into an eerie trademark; it still caused Gaines's neck hairs to stand on end after all this time.

Must be near seven o'clock. That, or storytelling hour's starting a little early tonight . . .

Turning back to tend the fire, Gaines's eyes fell for an instant next to the bedroll where he kept his paltry belongings on a worn plastic milk crate: broken mirror, shabby wallet; battered military surplus cup with toothbrush and razor; a few pairs of worn shirts, pants, and underwear; the Swiss Army knife his father had given him for his fifteenth birthday, and—always disturbing—the cracked glass and dented bezel of the antique pocket watch his wife had given him on their first wedding anniversary. It never ceased to amaze him how that watch— so delicate, yet still functioning perfectly—retained the power to make him weep at times. Monica's thoughtfulness had touched him and, after she was gone, it resonated with yet more pathos: the knowledge of what was, and the realization of what would never be again. When he was shaving sometimes, he would study his reflection, shaken at how much he had aged in the few years since the outbreak: his eyes these days had become hollow, his cheeks gaunt; the curly shock of his dark auburn hair had grown out and was graying at the temples.

Gaines took a deep breath and rubbed his chest, trying to stave off the weird smothering sensations his anxiety sometimes provoked. *We've been ensconced here too long; we need to move on soon before another gang or more 'Vivers find us. Folks don't take kindly to vagrants these days.* Gaines had come to appreciate the old 2008 Prius he had taken in Oklahoma. The farther from the Midwest they traveled, the more the hybrid had demonstrated its usefulness, especially given how difficult it was to find fuel. The way they could use the battery pack as a mini-generator had also given them a certain level of comfort. Luckily, Ellison had proven to be handy with cars, and they were somehow able to keep the thing rolling for a while.

He came back to the moment: "Brings what all back, Ellison?" The rumbling of the solar-powered pump jacks filled the quiet gulf between them like the murmur of a diseased heart:

CLANK   *swoosh* . . .
    CLANK   *swoosh* . . .

Behind Roger, the older man was quiet, though his apparent tranquility was always vaguely sinister. It fit in with a cluster of behaviors that Gaines found disquieting: the insect-like way he toyed with food, the absent-minded cracking of his knuckles while daydreaming. It was as though he were some primitive, atavistic being contemplating how best to take over the world. Ellison was a person who rarely laughed or displayed any type of emotion; when he did, it was as though he were being derisive. Sometimes, on the night watch, Gaines had heard Ellison's muffled sleep-screaming: it gave him the creeps.

Who the hell knows what's going on in there? Gaines wondered.

"When I's a kid, I watched this chap burn to death in a car wreck," Ellison said flatly. "It was int'restin'. He was screamin' and screamin'. Got trapped in 'is car and a fire started. That was before the amb'lance and the cops showed up—"

"How old were you?" Gaines interrupted, turning to face him. Although disgusted, morbid fascination kept him on every syllable. Beady orbs gleaming in the twilight, Ellison's white lashes gave the impression that his eyes were smaller than they actually were.

"Oh, I don't know. Maybe 'leven, twelve." Ellison peeked up from beneath shaggy alabaster eyebrows. He had a habit of fixing his eyes on the ground, making him appear dazed or preoccupied. He continued: "Anyhow, I was walkin' home from my friend's, and I's on the overpass. It was kinda dark and I'd always wondered, y'know, 'bout throwin' something off the bridge . . ."

Gaines's eyes must have visibly widened, because even in the half-light he saw Ellison grin.

"I know: you can see where this is goin', right?"

"That was your first kill?"

"First?" Ellison scratched his white-bearded jaw, reflective. "Umm—prob'ly solo, yeah. Me an' a friend did jump an old bum, but I can't say we killed 'im. Beat his ass pretty good, though."

Gaines nodded, waving smoke from his face. He stoked the red-orange embers of their campfire, turning the dripping aluminum envelopes as fat sizzled into the flames, causing the kindling to crackle and spark. The rhythm of the oil pumps accompanied them, an industrial soundtrack in the twilight:

CLANK   *swoosh . . .*
    CLANK   *swoosh . . .*

"Finish about the car wreck," Gaines said, vaguely aware of crickets chirping in the background.

Ellison tilted his head to the side, rheumy eyes swimming in the fire's gentle flicker. He seemed thoughtful, as if remembering a particularly fond family gathering.

"*Any*how," he said at last, "you can figure out what happened: the damn car crashed—guy ran into a ditch after I dropped the brick on his windshield . . ."

Ellison paused, lit a cigarette, then looked at Gaines. On the horizon, heat lightning flashed. "Wutin' nobody else on the road, so I ran down there, starin' at the guy, thinkin': 'Wow, I did that!' That's when the car started burnin'. When it flamed up, I kinda freaked, I reckon."

He hesitated in remembrance, taking a drag before continuing. "It wutin' funny, but I couldn't help laughin' a little. I was sorta—in *shock*. Then he started *screamin'*—he was so freakin' *loud!* An' 'e turned like—

bright *red*, like he was some kinda—*lob*ster or somethin' . . . He tried to get out, but the wreckage had 'im pinned. I got real afraid then—I even tried to get the brick, case there was 'prints on it, but the fire was too hot. Then I got to worryin'—y'know, maybe somebody saw me do it?"

Ellison exhaled a musty lungful of smoke.

"So I split. I sure remember that smell, though—you bet. That smell of burning flesh." He smiled again. The red and blue sky was just starting to reveal stars as the senseless horse head pumps rose and ducked in the early evening chill:

CLANK   *swoosh . . .*
    CLANK   *swoosh . . .*

The two men sat in near silence, staring into the campfire. Gaines poked the coals, disturbing the foil; grease sizzled again as it dripped into the campfire. The wood popped, throwing more sparks into the air. The quiet was heavy. Ellison finished his cigarette, then flipped the dog-end into the blaze.

"How 'bout you, amigo?"

Gaines looked up again, surprised: his travel companion normally never asked him anything personal. It was as if he wanted to keep a certain bit of distance between them.

"Nothing special. Originally from South Dakota. After school, I was a soldier. Sergeant First Class."

Gaines's mind flashed on the hundreds he had seen die as the political situation deteriorated. "Later I did training at Fort Sam Houston for the Army National Guard. EMT stuff. Actually, I was a Certified Flight Paramedic."

Turning his attention back to cooking their dinner, Gaines massaged his breastbone under his shirt. "I shot some thieves; self-defense, that kind of thing once it all started goin' south. A few of 'em died." He glanced once more at his plastic crate end table, remembering a time when anything really mattered to him.

"We've got to get out of here, Roger."

Monica sounds panicked, sniffing through her tears over the crackling cell phone.

"Honey, we talked about this: I can't just leave—it's gonna take some co-ordination—"

"But—I'm scared! I—I keep hearing on the news that the only place left is Western Canada. What if we can't get past the border?"

Everything is bad. Very bad. He tries to soothe her, but the things he sees makes him fearful—this is far from some clever update of I Am Legend *or a re-telling of* The Stand. *No: this is* actually happening.

"We'll be fine: we just need to take precautions, that's all. We've got rations; I'll be home as soon as they release me. Just—just stay inside and lie low." *His words sound hollow to him; hopefully she is unable to tell how he really feels. A series of ambulances blares past his hotel. He has only been able to get a couple hours of sleep a night for the past three weeks, forced to keep irregular hours because of the scale of the disaster unfolding.*

It's like the Book of Revelation, *Gaines reflects, the phone drooping in his hand.* The Four Horsemen fully unleashed, allowing the rise of Milton's Trinity Diabolus—Satan, sin, and evil—the inverse of everything Holy. *He closes his burning eyes.*

Communications are very difficult and increasingly unreliable. Most of their friends and family have already tried to leave the country or are dead. Reports of airliners crashing after their pilots collapse from the flu spook him; after several such incidents, the FAA decided to close the skies to commercial travel, reserving all airspace for emergency, military, and presidential use exclusively.

Better to sweat it out, *Roger thinks.* "Listen, my tour's up in two weeks," *he finally says to her.* "We'll hole up until this all calms down, I promise. Just hang in there 'til I get home."

He hears more sniffling across the noisy line. At last she sighs. "Okay. I guess we don't have any choice, do we? I love you, Roger!"

"I love you, baby."

They will never speak again.

CLANK   *swoosh . . .*

     CLANK   *swoosh . . .*

"Seems like we're both murderers, then. Me for the Feds, you for kicks," Roger said, adjusting the foil envelopes containing their dinner. He had to resist the urge to relive the past; there was no undoing bad decisions, no changing the course of history. Better to focus on the moment at hand.

What was the axiom? Learn from the past, live in the present, plan for the future—something like that . . .

Ellison grunted, lighting another cigarette. "And so it goes; smells good anyway, amigo."

The cook laughed to himself, devoid of mirth, gazing at the shiny, scorched pockets containing the food. The sooty smoke made his mouth water.

Gaines had observed it all as it unraveled, sans emotion, as his military training dictated. Upon closer observation, he understood his response to be more like a state of denial or shock. The whole situation was eerily reminiscent of old news stories from his youth about the devastation of New Orleans in the wake of Hurricane Katrina.

In that instance, the local and Federal governmental agencies waited too long to react; as a heartbreaking consequence, the metropolis sank into a gumbo of disorder, murder, violence. Once the storm abated, survivors were left slogging through the iridescent, filthy waters engulfing the Crescent City, desperate to live, as politicians pointed fingers in all directions. In the hot, sticky aftermath of Katrina—from the Superdome to the Lower 9th Ward—apocryphal stories of looters and rapists taking full advantage of the sudden, widespread lawlessness, even initially overrunning the swamped city, struck more fear into an already traumatized populace. The rest of the world could only gawk in mute horror and stunned disbelief at America's shocking unpreparedness and lack of quick action. As awful as that had been, it was just an ominous warm-up to the chaotic disintegration that was soon to play out in a much grander and more protracted convulsion of mayhem once the pandemic took hold.

Just another page in the history books. Of course, it pays to read the history books, Gaines opined. That in turn reminded him of how much he missed reading a good book, or even a decent newspaper article.

CLANK   *swoosh . . .*
    CLANK   *swoosh . . .*

Survival today was about canny planning and extreme measures. It was about killing or being killed. Society had at last reverted to what it was always trying to mask: a chaotic group of primates struggling against nature.

In some strange way, Gaines reflected, *it was as if the whole world were reading the identical script: things had devolved in remarkably similar patterns regardless of culture, belief system, or religion . . .*

BBC News
[DATELINE—GLOBAL; LIVERPOOL, ENGLAND: SCENES OF SHIPWRECKED OIL TANKERS; GARBAGE AND CA-DAVERS CHOKE THE SURF]

[VOICE OVER]
"Ghost fleets of ships have run aground in coastal ports all round the country. Sometimes twenty or thirty vessels beach in a single area, the ruined leviathans like sad metal whales, sacked, burnt out hulks rusting in the eternal, fogbound breakers . . ."

[MONTAGE: JAMMED HOSPITALS; PEOPLE DYING IN THE STREETS; LONDON IS BURNING]

"Widespread power outages and lawlessness is manifest throughout the U.K. and Ireland . . ."

[MONTAGE: PARIS, ROME, SYDNEY, VIENNA, PRAGUE— LOOTING; DECAYING BODIES LIE IN THE STREETS; BLACK SMOKE ROILS INTO THE SKY AS CITYWIDE IN-FERNOS FUME; WOMEN CRYING INTO THE CAMERA

CRADLING THE BLOATED CORPSES OF INFANTS; SIRENS
KEEN UNDER THE VOICE OVER]

"There appears to be no end in sight to the horror . . ."

CLANK   *swoosh . . .*
    CLANK   *swoosh . . .*

All that time we were so distracted by Iraq, Iran, al-Qaeda, Daesh, Trump, Brexit: who would have believed the end would come from within? The live news feeds only hinted at the real disorder boiling under the surface.

Once the grim link between the (H5N1)R influenza virus type A pathogen, of avian origin, and its associated complications—if one survived the initial infection—was made, the bottom fell out of society. Although a few people appeared to be immune, they were a vanishingly small number; the incredible virulence of the plague overwhelmed medical staff worldwide. The usual treatment was course after impotent course of high-dosage antibiotics and antivirals, which—predictably—failed to cure the variant (H5N1)R, raging bacterial pneumonia, and other attendant mystery symptoms. Death followed in short order: sometimes by drowning from within—the victims' bloated purple faces dotted by petechiae—other times bleeding out uncontrollably from the eyes, ears, pores, and rectum in spectacularly ghastly hemorrhagic meltdowns brought on from third spacing and tissue liquefaction. There were a few unexplained—exceptionally rare—incidences of known exposure where people remained unaffected. Mercifully, most sufferers died within a few days—some within hours—of exposure. The ones who did survive were never the same again, and the malady revealed a few even nastier surprises as a result.

An unusual aspect of the illness was that the virus easily passed through the blood-brain barrier: this characteristic of the disease had been discovered during the autopsies of plague victims. Stranger still were the mysterious lesions in the brain known as 'Spheric Entanglements,' which appeared to impact post-viral behaviors based on sex hormone dosage. In males, the pathogen mutated and attacked parts of the brain—specifically Broca's area, controlling language and speech, and the amygdala, partially controlling physical/sexual aggression and the fear response—which resulted in greatly diminished inhibitions. This corresponded with a marked increase in an appetite for violent behavior. These men, primitive and atavistic after recovery, would frequently rampage out of control, killing and provoking others without reason or mercy. In addition, they appeared to have acquired an amplified tolerance to pain because of damage to the thalamus and the parietal lobe of the brain—a direct consequence of the flu virus. Because they had, invariably, entered into a comatose state after being infected with the disease instead of dying outright and then resuscitated, the media had dubbed them "the Revived"; later this was shortened, and they became popularly referred to simply as 'Vivers.

With respect to the opposite sex, Gaines had seen no healthy women in a very long time and doubted he ever would again; those who managed to pull through the illness were also irrevocably changed. The Spheric Entanglements destroyed different parts of the brain in females—again, in theory driven by hormones—in a process that was still poorly understood. Like males, women who lived through the respiratory issues and other complications inevitably fell into a coma, attributed to the cytokine storm unleashed by the victim's immune response. Unlike males, women never recovered into any appreciably normal mental state. Instead, they exhibited another condition that caused muscular rigidity and lowered levels of brain activity—in spite of the reality of being technically conscious. As a result, they were unable to communicate, move, or feed themselves as they became sad, stiff effigies frozen by palsy. Though Gaines knew their minds were still mostly intact as they died an agonizing death due to hunger and thirst, he tried not to dwell on that particular facet of the horror. It was eventually understood that they had become disabled by a separate disease apparatus: *Contagious Neuro-Dementia Acceleration Syndrome*, or CoN-DAS. CoN-DAS was similar to another mysterious affliction from the past—von Economo disease, also called Encephalitis Lethargica: an incurable, non-contagious neurological condition that created a sort of suspended animation. Neither condition—CoN-DAS or the Reviver syndrome—had so far proven to be reversible or treatable, leading to more severe complications and finally death, though the Reviver syndrome disease span often varied from months to years depending on circumstances and medical support.

Although the ultimate ramifications were uncertain for humanity, the immediate implications had been clear: some fates were truly worse than death. Mass migrations of refugees—some in the tens of millions—displaced frail geopolitical boundaries. This brought seething tensions in stressed areas of Eastern Europe and South America to a frantic head; the strain of famine and environmental destruction plunged the rich and poor into a neo–Dark Age. No one was safe from the widespread damage and panic in the swath of the social disruption, not even journalists: the extent of the pillaging, death, and horror was appalling, approaching the scale of the Allied bombing of Dresden in World War II, all over the planet, every single day.

The Pakistan nuclear exchange with India, though limited in scope, was orders of magnitude more horrific and grotesque than Hiroshima or Nagasaki: since there was no aid infrastructure in place after the crumbling of the United Nations, the entire place was written off as a wasteland worthy of a T. S. Eliot poem—ultimately, perhaps predictably, ending less with a bang and more with a whimper. These events triggered alliances across the planet into action: China and Russia sealed their borders, becoming particularly aggressive and hostile in their corresponding responses to the expanding global crisis; the stories seeping out about the pogroms thereafter were like some throwback to the early twentieth century. Religion reasserted itself as an excuse to exact all manner of terrible retribution: Palestine's bloody invasion of Israel, brutal reprisals meted out in the Balkans, and on and on. All this against a backdrop of the small-scale nuclear winter environmental tragedy unleashed on the Indian subcontinent. No place was spared: whether Europe, North America, the Middle East, Africa, or South America, humanity seemed to be spinning hopelessly out of control. Across the globe, at every social stratum, no amount of technology, medicine, wealth, or power could shield the population from the relentless microbial and politico-religious onslaught. Even back in the States, civilization was unprepared to deal with the scale of the ensuing carnage; the breakdown was absolute.

First World, Third World, or somewhere in between, it hardly mattered: in the end, no place was immune. Gradually—no one ever quite pinpointed when or where—their problem became everyone's problem. Gaines stroked his face as he tended their dinner, deep in thought. *It was easy to imagine the world undone—the seams had been plucked and coming apart for generations.*

No one is going to get her.

Roger Gaines watches his house burn, its glowing cinders rising languorously into the night sky. His features are seared by the intense heat, tear tracks shining orange in the flames as smoke drifts across his shadow-distorted face.

Better to keep moving; there's nothing here for me anymore.

As the house blazes, he turns and walks to the car, his enormous, jittery shadow swallowed up by the night, his life in his backpack; he is determined to reach the railway station and catch one of the Armed Forces transports to . . . anyplace else.

11:18 P.M. *He studies the brass casing of his pocket watch as smoke and soot billow around him, dazed. His eyes fill with tears again.*

Letting go is so hard . . .

An involuntary sob escapes him, ripped from a broken place within his chest.

"Monica!"

CLANK   *swoosh . . .*
CLANK   *swoosh . . .*

Gaines had shadowed this Danse Macabre since the beginning: first as a medic for the National Guard, then, after Monica's death, moving from city to city in a vain hope that he might find *any* place that had been spared. In all his travels to date, there had only been a single narrative: whether Charlotte or D.C, Pittsburgh or New York— everything was the same.

Death and ruination—devastated, silent, shuttered. It wasn't the nukes, or aliens, or meteors, or even religious zealots—just bloody froth, diarrhea, and madness as the body turned on itself. The microbes shall inherit the Earth . . . Gaines chuckled at his own ever-blackening sense of humor.

For years the World Health Organization had issued warnings about potentially virulent new pandemics. No one paid attention. Multiple false alarms had not engendered credibility. Besides, everyone outside the healthcare system believed Western medicine could remedy practically anything: the successful shift of AIDS from a death sentence to a manageable chronic condition and the containment of widespread Ebola epidemics in Sierra Leone and Guinea were often cited as examples. Due to lax oversight, mega-corporations had been permitted to chop down trees indiscriminately, blow off mountaintops, to continue polluting the air and sea massively. The fallout was the destruction of ancient ecosystems, the fostering of extinctions, an increase in the rates of desertification—which all contributed to forcing civilization and the wild closer together than at any point previously documented.

Then, inevitably, it happened—catastrophe. Gaines's pet operational theory: several still-unknown disease vectors had allowed a jump across species barriers, then across language barriers as they delivered their deadly cargo, undetected, around the planet, the Jet Age long ago compressing the global spread of illness from months or years to less than twenty-four hours. It brought to mind the wild speculation about SARS—that the respiratory infection had been an accidental release of a manmade disease; the jury was still out on that one. Though he was not one normally prone to conspiracy theories, the scale and timing of these events did make him wonder if it was some purpose-created Black Swan scenario.

I mean, really . . . *how could everything have gone so wrong so fast otherwise? We were that unprepared?*

He stares drowsily at the muted television display, its dim, bluish flashing momentarily bright in their gloomy bedroom.

—CNN BREAKING NEWS—
[NEWS TICKER OVER GLOBAL COVERAGE MONTAGE]

< < . . . *is the final country to declare a state of emergency.* > > *Dept. of Home-land Security Terrorist Threat Level:* **Orange**—High > > < < *Scientists report remote islands—the Aleutians, Hawaii, Iceland, the Solomons—are now completely extinct of all human and avian species.* > > < < *The Centers for Disease Control and Prevention (CDC) in Atlanta and Porton Down in the former United Kingdom report that over 3.5 billion people are estimated dead, most within the first twenty-four months of the (H5N1)R flu outbreak and its complications, the majority as a direct result of exposure to the illness.* > > < < *Upwards of another 1.5 billion are thought to have died as an indirect consequence of secondary issues such as CoN-DAS / Reviver Syndrome, systemized purges to quell the spread of disease, worldwide nuclear and conventional warfare, and mass suicide.* > > < < *Today is the 1483rd day of the plague . . .* > >

Gaines finds it difficult to believe this is really the end. Typically, he keeps the sound off: the images and news crawl are bad enough, let alone the ceaseless reports spinning the disaster in every conceivable manner.

"Nobody knows what to believe anymore," he mumbles to himself. Gaines looks up from the floor to where Monica lay. She is quiet, unmoving. He flips the sound on again as the screen cuts to a report about the U.S.:

CNN Continuous Coverage:
(H5N1)R / CoN-DAS PANDEMIC CRISIS
[CAMERA PANS ALONG A LINE OF CARS AND SEMIS STRETCHING FOR MILES DOWN INTERSTATE 10 OUT OF TUCSON, ARIZONA]

[VOICE OVER]

"A barren, blazing dustbowl, the Desert Southwest has become a land of modern mummies.

"Entombed in their vehicles as they flee the large cities, people are dying en route to safe havens that do not exist—"

A senator—one of the few surviving—appears on the screen. Gaines has little stomach for soundbites and talking heads at this juncture: he mutes the television once more. He knows it is too unsafe to stay much longer, even under martial law, but he has no plan in place to deal with transporting and caring for Monica.

Returning from his Guard obligations in Pennsylvania, he was able to confirm his worst suspicions about why she or their neighbors no longer responded to his calls: it was too late for them. She was little more than some angelic scarecrow, the house silent except for her shallow, quick breaths and the intermittent turmoil of emergency responders going by. His neighborhood appeared to have been evacuated a few days prior; he immediately recognized the significance of the ominous spray-painted Xs tagged by FEMA's Urban Search & Rescue Task Force on his front door. According to the diagram, the date matched his observations about when communications ceased, and there was one dead person inside. Except there had not been: Monica was in a comatose state. Near death, to be sure, but not dead; he then concentrated all his energies on making her comfortable, on trying to bring her back from the edge.

That was over two months ago.

But I can't keep the looters away forever. We're running out of ammo. How much longer before the electrical grid goes down completely?

There have been many brownouts since his homecoming, and they seem to be increasing in number as the days drag on. He resorts to using the backup generator only sparingly, as it requires a lot of fuel and is very loud. He prefers to keep a low profile and is leery of going on expeditions to get more petroleum or other supplies. His treks are, by necessity, becoming farther and farther afield as the areas around their home are depleted of resources by others in comparable straits. Rarely does he see anyone, and the few times he has he learns they are not to be trusted, especially if in pairs or groups. The world has become much more dangerous as provisions dwindle, desperation takes hold, and paranoia flares. Couple this daily grind with the dire threat presented by the 'Vivers—a group that is feral and savage in ways that he finds not only chilling, but also hard to accept—and it is a wonder anyone is still able to function at all.

Roger stands up in the stuffy, dark room; it already feels like a kind of mausoleum. He opens his pocket watch, puts it on the end table, then walks to the side of the bed where Monica is resting. Her sunken eyes glimmer in the lambent glow of the TV, her face is gaunt, her lips dark; he can see the blankets covering her body rise and fall in time with the labored wheeze of her breath.

The television brightens in the darkness as another BREAKING NEWS *logo fills the screen. He turns the sound back on:*

—CNN BREAKING NEWS—
[MONTAGE: VIOLENT RIOTING, URBAN BLIGHT, RURAL MASS GRAVES]

[VOICE OVER]

"We interrupt this report to bring you a report from an affiliate of the former Northwest Cable News Network in Portland, Oregon, already in progress . . ."

[LIVE FEED: KATU, PORTLAND, OR]

[VOICE OVER]

". . . Pacific Northwest has been nearly transformed into a sodden world of ruptured dams and abandoned, haunted forests."

Roger cuts the sound off again.

As the story plays, he checks Monica's IV drip: that and the liquid meal replacements are the only things keeping her alive. He notes that he is nearly out of Hartmann's solution; this reminds him that his own food supply is dwindling, too.

How long can we go on like this?

[STOCK FOOTAGE: SCIENTISTS, LABS]

"Yet optimism remains in the guise of a breakthrough announcement anticipated this week from XygoGenetics Northwest in Seattle.

"XygoGenetics's recent acquisition of Patmos, Kansas's Israel Corporation allowed the promotion of Israel Corp.'s head geneticist Wilhelm Hoffnung to oversee Global Risk Analysis and resource coordination between the World Health Organization, USAMRIID, other U.S. governmental agencies, and the private sector in order to combat the deadly outbreak. Hoffnung, who previously indicated that there had been some success in treating mice infected by artificial variants of three of the twelve retroviruses isolated in some of the Revived and CoN-DAS victims, will lead the emergency meeting of Federal and world agencies combating the pandemic, chaired by Dr. Stein of the Centers for Disease Control, and hosted by a special WHO (H5N1)R Crisis Response Taskforce."

[STOCK FOOTAGE: XYGOGENETICS NORTHWEST OFFICES; FADE-IN TO SHAKY IMAGES OF DIGNITARIES ARRIVING AT PORTLAND INTERNATIONAL AIRPORT IN FACEMASKS UNDER ARMED ESCORT; BLOODIED RIOTERS PROTEST THEIR ARRIVAL]

"Antibiotic-resistant bacteria still present the greatest dilemma, and this is what will be addressed at the press conference on Thursday in Vancouver, British Columbia . . ."

Roger mutes the sound once more. He looks down at Monica, the tightness in his chest like a frozen fist around his heart.
"It won't be long."

After all Roger had seen on the East Coast, he decided to head west. Now that air travel was deemed unsafe, rail was his last, best option to flee. His transport train had almost been derailed on the way out by scattered mobs of survivors clogging the tracks looking for assistance. Orders were to "shoot on sight," as the rescue phase of containment had been declared over. All people who were not cleared by DNA analysis to be free of disease were determined to be the "walking dead." Infection rates and mortality were no longer linear, but exponential.

Once in Western Canada, contrary to apocryphal stories that a few places had somehow been able to keep the pestilence at bay, Gaines found only devastated ghost towns. Now, moving from place to place, at least for Roger, was simply official military business: redeploying what was salvageable to the most logical places for possible recovery.

Gaines had his doubts about the strategy, but was grateful for the free lifts afforded by his medical skill and Guard connections. Somewhere during all this he learned that his relatives were gone; after that revelation, he decided to go south, bouncing from New Mexico to Texas with the Guard, finally landing in Oklahoma. By the time he got to Tulsa, the military was becoming increasingly frayed. In an organized ambush by 'Vivers as they were passing through the Cherokee Nation in Tahlequah, Gaines had been able to steal a 2008 Toyota Prius during the chaos. Once he had the car, he joined a loose caravan of mercenaries bound for Chicago, the place where the Feds had allegedly set up a shadow government to reorganize and further combat the crisis.

Though rumors were always buzzing in the background, nothing prepared Gaines for the pitiable conditions in other places, large and small, everywhere he went: massive pyres of charred bodies, eighty feet high and the size of a city block, burning in Kansas City; numerous gangs of rogues working the Interstate system like modern pirates; the diminishing supplies of food, fuel, and medicine; rotting corpses impaled on fence posts—like gruesome scarecrows—throughout the middle of Iowa, meant as a warning for others to stay away.

If Chicago was dead, then what he feared would be confirmed: there could be no re-emergence; no recovery; no phoenix-like rise from the ashes.

If the cities were finished, there was nothing left.

CLANK   *swoosh . . .*
     CLANK   *swoosh . . .*

Gaines whistled in pain as the fire licked his fingers: he was constantly burning himself it seemed. *That's OK. Helps me understand I'm still alive; besides, I hate Ellison's cooking . . .*

Though there had been credible reports that the likely epicenter had originated overseas—vague media chatter that somewhere in Asia there had been mass cullings of poultry stock due to a zoonotic threat of some type—there were other, unverified, stories of experimental agents used in domestic war games. The "bird flu" story had caught on with the horrified public because large groups of birds perished in spectacular fashion: entire flocks falling out of the sky; choking rivers, streams, estuaries the world over in their millions. Wild and domesticated fowl alike died suddenly in massive numbers, and science was at a loss as to how to explain it. For several years now, no one had been able to document any living species of bird, from penguins to parrots, chickens to crows. The skies were empty and silent. The phenomenon seemed to track with the rise of the flu globally, although there had only been limited explanation as to how this virulent strain of influenza, with its bizarre after-effects and extremely contagious presentation, was able to jump the species barrier so rapidly: it was much worse even that the 1918 Spanish flu pandemic, which had shaved twelve years off the general life expectancy of the time. The scuttlebutt in the Guard had been that it was some business that had gone wrong at the main campus of a government subcontractor—Israel Corporation, located in Patmos—that was working with the Division of Chemical, Biological, Radiological, and Nuclear (CBRN) Medical Countermeasures (MCMs) to develop and secure the CBRN MCMs required by the U.S. Department of Health and Human Services (HHS). Of course, all sorts of conspiracy theories about the social collapse ran rampant: perhaps it *was* some misguided revolutionary sect, or possibly a germ warfare agent run amok from Israel Corp; maybe the work of some rogue dictator, or a slighted theocratic nation-state . . . Whatever transpired, natural or otherwise, it looked as if it backfired.

Hello, Black Swan. Or maybe it was going precisely *as anticipated. One thing's for sure—no one would ever really know what happened.* The last factual information about what *was* happening had been just over a year ago: the disquieting final images of a dying president of the United States addressing the country. That depiction still gave Gaines a shudder when it floated through his mind. *Then the airwaves went blank . . . No more broadcasts, no more Internet, no more cell phones . . . No more greatest hits from Soundgarden, Billy Joel, or Wings; no reruns of* Welcome Back, Kotter *or* The Twilight Zone *. . . Nothing but endless, snowy static broken by an occasional loop of the Emergency Alert System.*

President Hinton had appeared a fragile, lonely figure speaking to the nearly empty Congress, hacking from behind a facemask. The declaration of martial law throughout the entirety of the country had an air of finality to it; like some admission of defeat.

In retrospect, I suppose it was, Gaines mused.

Maybe I would be better off in Hawaii? That's the most remote island chain on Earth—if I can just get there. Roger remembered hearing that the last places to succumb—island nations such as the U.K., Iceland, Japan, and Australia—had been able to contain the pandemic at first, but had then been unable to mount enough of a military response to keep invaders out once their borders were breached by the ensuing refugee crisis, which became overwhelming. The aftermath: a terrifying freefall, full of hellish, mind-scarring sights. Just in the States, most of the northeastern and Mid-Atlantic region—the first to surrender totally to Federal control in North America—still smoldered like Pieter Bruegel the Elder's painting *The Triumph of Death*. Based on the news reports, the rest of the world appeared to be in the same predicament.

From metropolis to necropolis, Gaines thought, smiling grimly at the movie in his head, deep in remembrance. He wiped his mouth as he tended the flame: dinner was nearly done.

USA Today
[AP NEWS WIRE]

"Across the plains, lonely, triple-armed windmills slowly rotate for no reason, the land reverting back to the buffaloes. Above, the silent skies are empty, completely devoid of birds and planes.

"Some are calling it the end of times . . ."

It was hard to watch anyone suffering from the plague, though Gaines had treated many cases in the field as a member of the Guard.

Onset was nearly always the same: sneezing, sensitivity to light, high fever, fatigue, and headaches quickly devolving into dystonia, swelling, desperate gasping for air and finally chorea. As dementia seized the brain, the face took on a mask-like appearance: the features became slack, the eyes red, bulging, glazed.

EMERGENCY ALERT SYSTEM
[*TONE*—20 SECONDS; WHITE LETTERS CRAWL TO THE
TOP OF A BLUE SCREEN]
[PRERECORDED VOICE]

"Attention. This is not a test.
Please remain tuned to this station for updated news
and information about the current emergency situation
involving the hypermutagenic (H5N1)R virus, its vari-
ants, and the antibiotic-resistant strains of bacterial in-
fections subsequent to exposure in the majority of cases.
These are highly contagious, lethal micro-organisms,
with morbidity and mortality potentials documented
in excess of 90 out of 100 reported cases.

"Every attempt is being made to find a resolution
to this calamity, but it could be some time before
order is restored.
Interactions with others should be strictly limited
to known, uninfected individuals.

"Stay indoors.
If you suspect exposure to these disorders, whether
it is you or someone you know, report it at once to
Local Authorities, who will then pass this infor-
mation to the Emergency Federal Disease
Response Taskforce (EFDRT).

"If you believe you are contaminated, DO NOT
UNDER ANY CIRCUMSTANCES AS-
SOCIATE WITH OTHERS:

"Quarantine yourself without delay.
Armed Federal Agents will come to you . . ."

CLANK   *swoosh* . . .
    CLANK   *swoosh* . . .

Gaines never had a sniffle, even as each member of his makeshift squadron died along the way to Chicago. The longer the situation went on, the more obvious it became to him that any restoration of the life he had known previously was over.

Illinois is where Gaines and Ellison met, somewhere near the plundered ruins of a Chicago neither of them got to see.

CLANK   *swoosh* . . .
    CLANK   *swoosh* . . .

Gaines and Ellison, during their entire Faustian truce—trekking first from the Midwest, then to a blighted Texas in search of better weather, next to the surreal husk of Las Vegas, and finally to sunny Los Angeles—only referred to each other by their last names. All other labels seemed redundant. They eventually came to the uneasy, tacit conclusion that they were better off as a team rather than on their own. Gaines saw the usefulness of Ellison's savagery; his own medical skills and supplies were obvious assets.

Ellison had taken a different path to nowhere than Gaines. A career criminal, pathological liar, and killer, he harbored a lot of demented reminiscences and seemed perfectly at ease creating new ones. Ellison had no intention of dying anytime soon, seeing he had finally inherited the Earth—or at least its remnants. While others struggled to cope, Ellison thrived on the end-of-the-world devastation, happy to contribute to the fray when the mood struck him. He had killed all his other associates once they came down with symptoms of the flu. "Why take chances?" he reasoned. He was nothing if not ruthlessly pragmatic.

Now, here they sat, Roger keeping his own festering psychosis at bay by peering into the deep abyss of Ellison. It was better than television; their own little nightly reality show.

"It's ready," Gaines announced, pulling the meat out of the foil, giving them each a healthy portion of tender flesh on a skewer.

"Hot damn! I'm starved, amigo!" Ellison exclaimed, rubbing his hands together like a cartoon character.

Gaines smiled appreciatively. "We need to get more food soon—I noticed we're down to the last scraps."

"Well, it sure lasted awhile."

Roger grinned, arching his brow. He often wondered—with a sort of detached amusement—where all the rich and famous had gone. He liked to imagine they had all decamped to some sun-dappled Caribbean island that was now playing host to the ultimate iteration of the reality TV show *Survivor,* where the contestants vied over the last remaining bottles of Dom Pérignon Rosé and crates of Iranian Beluga 'Almas' black caviar in the world, or competed to see who could most efficiently implement a workable version of Swift's *Modest Proposal.*

"Need to go huntin' tomorrow, I s'pose," Ellison said through a full mouth. Gaines nodded slowly, daydreaming as they ate: he dreaded "huntin'"; he could barely stomach the food as it was, not to mention that the big cities were now the dominion of lawless, marauding bands.

Nonetheless, provisions were getting too hard to find by foraging. Agriculture was just another notch on the belt of humanity at this point: one in a long line of great ideas—computers, justice, medicine— all useless, inadequate defenses against a primordial, self-organizing army of microscopic terrorists.

After dinner they drowsed by the fire, stomachs full.

"Y'know, we didn't even know her name," Gaines said, speech slurred. "Better her than me, though. Better her than me."

Ellison lit the tattered bits of a cigarette. It was his turn to stand watch. He inhaled the smoke deeply, casting a sidelong glance at the glowing red tip, appearing to lament the addiction that compelled him to burn through his dwindling supply.

"Gaines, I reckon the whole damned world's a cannibal, amigo," he replied. "When everything runs out, it'll eat itself."

One can only hope, Gaines thought, taking a deep breath. The lofty pretenses enshrouding culture worked for societies; now there was no social order. Anywhere. The nodding donkey rigs continued their steady, mesmerizing metronome:

CLANK　　　*swoosh* . . .
　　CLANK　　　*swoosh* . . .

Ellison threw another bunch of kindling on the small fire, looking into the darkness around their bivouac. Gaines stared at his watch, beginning to fall asleep. Time meant nothing now, but it helped him to focus, to remember Monica's face. He cried less often these days, as survival instinct and reality took precedence.

To the inhuman, gentle clanking of the oilrigs, Gaines closed his eyes, at last looping into a cold pool of dreamless slumber.

CLANK　　　*swoosh* . . .
　　CLANK　　　*swoosh* . . .

FIRE

"What'd you mean by that?" Ellison asked again, even louder, jolting Gaines back to the situation at hand.

We've got to get out of here, Gaines thought, leaning hard on the cage bars, heart thudding in his ears. *I think I'm losing it.*

The black-garbed scout's head tilted. "It means we put 'em to use. We've—" the guard paused, looking out to the horizon, then back at the caged men, before spitting on the ground. "The bitches *contribute,* homes. Once the screwing is done, if they get knocked up, we put 'em in that cage there with your friend. We got a *system* now."

"Yeah, okay," Gaines said, still perplexed, shaking off his confusion. "And then? Why don't you just abort 'em? You want a bunch of infants screaming all over the—"

In a flash, Roger suddenly understood. Neither of them had seen or heard any children. Everybody looked well fed here, not skinny like everywhere else. Gaines was suddenly a little faint, his stomach flopping, his breath short, like a cat was sucking it from his lungs.

They've created a renewable food source. He could hear Ellison chuckling, but it sounded as if he were at the bottom of a deep, dark well. The sweat on Roger's forehead was cold. *Oh my God—it's like some type of . . . some type of cannibal harvesting operation . . .*

The stunned expression on Gaines's face caused Chavez to nod slowly. "You get it now, huh? That's the way of the world. We figured it out—it's us or them." The youth was somber. "There's no room for both, homes. *Us* or *them.*"

IN

Removing the mirrored sunglasses, Chavez, alone in the privacy of the sleeping quarters, turned them over, glimpsing a partially blood-shot eye staring back from under the swollen eyelid. "Jesus. Looking rough."

The lookout donned the shades again, kneeling down to retrieve a few snippets of sheet out of a hidden pouch under the bunk. Chavez secreted the pocket watch in the strips, placed it into the bag, then shoved the other scraps down the front of a pair of relaxed-fit black jeans. Just then Ray wandered by, forcing the pretense of tucking in.

"You okay, Chavez?" Ray asked, eyeing the scene with suspicion. Trust was a hard thing to come by out here.

"Yeah, I'm good; just an upset stomach."

Ray nodded, wiping sweat from his neck. He spit in the dirt, then walked off. "Keep your eye on them inmates, Chavez."

After Ray was out of sight, Chavez pressed the crotch at the zipper, making sure everything was in place. "Ray's such a prick."

Retrieving the shotgun off the bed, Chavez slung the strap around a jacketed shoulder. Even in the sticky heat, the scout was covered head to toe in black: boots, pants, shirt, jacket, do-rag, gloves.

Sauntering over to the cages, Chavez puffed up, putting on a solemn "don't-fuck-with-me" face under the sunglasses.

"Ain't you a bit young to be such a jerk-off?" Ellison queried, rocking forward as the guard approached, a grin creeping across his chalky features.

Gaines studied their exchange with amusement and trepidation. Examining the cages of this improvised Auschwitz, he had decided that they were crude but well built. Each was situated in the median island of the garbage-strewn parking lot, where they could be seen from any corner of the strip center. *Diplomacy's probably the best option here,* Gaines thought.

The black-suited patrol, still quiet, ambled over to them. Gaines looked squarely into Chavez's face: "You know, man, it's hot in here. I could sure use a drink," he said. "Could you oblige, or is that against the rules?"

The sentinel looked around, then whistled, catching the attention of another punked-out guard with Day-Glo orange hair. The guy threw a bottle of water over, taking it from a pile near a ruined storefront bearing a sign that read "Water/Cellphones" in chipped fluorescent paint on the glass of the gated window, in letters destined to become future hieroglyphs, devoid of any context or meaning. Taking a seat on the cement curb, the scout hurled the plastic bottle into the cage.

Hands tied, Gaines fumbled with the lid then took a long swallow. He put the bottle to the parched lips of one of the women, but the water just spilled across her listless, sunburned face. Chavez silently observed Gaines from the street side perch, like an enormous raven.

After a while the youth stood, surveying the area, adjusting the mirrored shades. The late afternoon sun was stifling: most of the crew had gone inside. The guard wiped sweat from their forehead with a neckerchief before walking over to Gaines's cage.

"The name's Chavez. Maybe we can help each other out," the sentry said, roughly grabbing Gaines's wrists, flashing a knife and cutting the bindings off the prisoner with an expert stroke.

Just then, Gaines noticed a smear of blood on the ledge where the watch had been sitting. "Are you okay? You're bleeding," he said, rubbing his wrists, confused.

Chavez's face furrowed. "What are you talking about, homes? Where?"

Gaines pointed to the curb. "I—I don't know—look. Are you hurt?"

Chavez spun around to see where Gaines was pointing.

"Shit!" For a moment Chavez seemed alarmed. Regaining composure, the scout calmly sliced the gloved palm with the blade, gasping as blood gushed out.

"Are you crazy?" Gaines yelled, trying to grab the knife. Others noticed the commotion and started toward them.

Chavez drew closer and whispered into Gaines's ear: *"Be cool, homes.* I'm—I'm having my period is all . . ."

Gaines scuttled back in the cage, stunned. As the other hoodlums surrounded the island, Chavez returned to the median, her hand dripping onto the bloody spot on the curb.

WHICH

The crowd was charged: they rarely got to see much action, and the testosterone level in the air surged. Ray stepped forward. He raised his hand in a silencing gesture.

"What the fuck's goin' on here, Chavez? You're actin' *weird,* dude," Ray said, steely eyes glaring from his stringy, hard-lined countenance. They had never gotten along.

Chavez felt her hand pulsing from the cut in her palm.

"Everything's cool, Ray. I was checking on the prisoners, and he said his bindings was too tight." She was lightheaded, the late afternoon sun hot on her face. Sweat seeped into her eyes behind the shades, stinging. "I was gonna re-tie 'im but cut myself by accident." Chavez held her bleeding hand up. Everyone was staring at her.

Ray advanced again, eyes narrowing. The smell of cooking meat was strong. The sun was going down. He was right in her face, breath hot and foul. He looked her slowly up and down, trying to peer behind the mirrored sunglasses. *Christ, don't let my cover get blown,* she thought.

"You ain't turnin' *fag,* are ya, Chavez? You know we don't go for no *queer* shit here." He spat on the ground, eyes widening on certain words for emphasis.

Chavez was quiet, then chuckled, head turning as if on a gimbal. "No way, Ray. I like fuckin' them bitches much as you, hombre."

Silence.

Ellison and Gaines watched the standoff with nervous fascination.

This is nuts, Gaines thought. *She's not sick! How did she live through it? Maybe she's immune somehow, as Ellison and I seem to be . . .*

Ray kept looking at her. Finally, he said: "Let's keep it that way, dickhead. Put some straps on that fucking prisoner before I kick your pansy ass."

Relief coursed through Chavez.

"Okay, Ray. Right now." She quickly walked over to the cage, pulling some rope from her vest pocket. "Put your hands together, asshole."

Gaines hesitated for a moment, then complied. Ellison was strangely silent. Chavez wrapped Roger's wrists together several times through the bars and tied a square knot, still bleeding from her palm.

"Nothin' ta see! Get ready for chow," Ray said, waving the crew back to their chores. "Nothin' ta see."

He turned to face Chavez again. "Don't fuck with *me*—I'll kill you. Got it, ya little spic?"

Chavez nodded. Ray walked off, his body odor hanging in the air. She glanced down at Gaines once everyone was out of earshot.

"We've got to get *out* of here," she whispered.

Gaines was dumbfounded.

"Yeah, *we* do. Guess you better help us out, now that I know your little secret, huh?"

Chavez winced, holding her hand up and applying direct pressure to the injury.

"It's been hard," she said, removing her eyewear. Chin quivering, she rubbed her throat. "Sorry, it hurts from trying to speak lower than my natural register." Her features were nice, and Gaines could see she was actually a pretty girl, albeit androgynous.

She continued: "I don't know any other women who are like me. My sister maybe, but I lost touch with her when the shit hit the fan."

She crouched to get on his level.

"I'll be back tonight for you and your buddy. We'll have to be quick, 'cause they'll use us for food if we blow it." Her large brown eyes looked worried. She pat his hand, put on her sunglasses, and walked back to the outpost.

"Gaines," Ellison finally said from the other cage as he watched the black-clad guard disappear, "what the hell's goin' *on* over there?"

WE

Jesus, I'm so sorry, lady . . .

The strange man is just finishing up with the young woman when Gaines stumbles across them. Rape is not uncommon, of course, in this depraved Thunderdome afterworld; Gaines has intervened during such violence more than once, sometimes to his detriment. Observing from a spot at the edge of the woods, he finds it surreal that the rapist in this case is himself an albino. It is obvious that the girl is a goner: body rigid, eyes fixed and staring—just the way his wife, Monica, had been at the end. The woman had survived the pathological blitz only to be incapacitated by the CoN-DAS infection.

Though Roger knows intellectually there is nothing he can do for her, it gives him a sense of purpose to believe he might be able to help somehow. He rubs his breastbone, struggling against the sudden vacuum he seems to occupy. Damn anxiety attacks . . .

Disgusted and upset at not being able to aid the woman, Gaines notices that she is probably no more than twenty, likely still a teenager. When he stumbles upon other females in this situation—growing rarer as time pressed forward—he winds up putting them out of their misery. Still, he wonders if there is a way to bring them back from the brink of the oblivion they appear to occupy.

I owe it to Monica never to give up; there *must* be a way to fix this. Maybe I can do something for this girl once he's out of here . . .

The stranger, still unclothed, sits for a moment on the ground, evidently not quite done with his conquest. He is rummaging through a pack by his side, its contents just out of Gaines's field of view.

How can he *do* this? She's defenseless! *Gaines feels sick.*

THE DARK SEA WITHIN

At that moment, the man casually pulls out a large knife, grabs the girl by her hair, and indifferently scythes her throat to the vertebrae, virtually detaching her head in one practiced motion. Her eyes widen, momentarily welling up as the scarlet venous spray jets from the gaping cut in her neck; she makes no other sound or movement.

Gaines screams.

The startled killer jumps up, crouching to protect his nearly translucent, naked body, now dewed with burgundy specks. "Who the fuck's that?" he bellows, his pink eyes like twin suns burning from his snowy complexion. The girl's wound gargles as Roger feels nausea ripple his guts.

"Put—put the knife down!*" Gaines finally croaks.*

"No way! I didn't get this far bein' a idiot," the man replies. He scrambles for his clothing, which is piled under a nearby tree. The girl's body is almost as light-colored as his now, in stark contrast to the liquid crimson carpet of blood pooling underneath her. Distant, empty eyes stare accusingly at Roger.

Revealing himself from behind some bushes, Gaines is trembling, his only weapon—a hatchet—drawn back. Both men look intently at each other for a long time, their breathing heavy in the twilight.

"Listen, I don't want any trouble. Let's forget this and we'll go our own ways," Gaines offers, shaky voice returning. He tries not to look at the lifeless girl's naked carcass on the ground.

The man watches Gaines closely, putting on his pants, then his shoes, then his shirt, the whole time holding his bloody knife out like a talisman. At last the albino angles his head, an odd smile on his ivory face as the rest of the color leeches from the world around them.

"Forget what, *asshole? Hey—you ready? Homes . . . you ready?"*

Roger awoke with a shock. For a moment he was disoriented by the darkness, then realized it was Chavez. She had returned as promised.

"You *ready,* homes?" she asked again, voice low, reaching her bandaged hand into the cage and laying a pistol next to his leg.

"Yeah—yeah. Cut—cut these things off me, please," he whispered, indicating his hands, as he cleared the nightmare of his first encounter with Ellison from his consciousness. "Thanks for coming back. So—Chavez is your full name or what? Mine's Roger. Roger Gaines. He's just Ellison, so far as I know."

She deftly sliced through the rope she had tied earlier. "Chavez is fine. But my family and friends called me Rachel. Look, Roger, this is all heartwarming, truly, but we need to be *quick*—they keep armed guards posted and patrol all night, tending the IVs in the girls, keeping the fires going, checking the perimeter. Ray's *real* fuckin' paranoid. We've been hit a few times in the past from 'Vivers—"

"How'd you guys get access to all these *guns?* Me an' Ellison could never get any new weapons or ammo once we ran out last year. It's all . . . *gone*—stolen or seized by the Feds once martial law took effect—"

"Ray was some military bigshot in San Diego," Chavez interrupted. "He stockpiled a bunch of shit—food, arms, medicine. He had all kinds of deep connections at Israel Corp., DoD, CDC, you name it."

Gaines sensed that Chavez was agitated as she undid the locks. In the flickering light of the camp's barrel fires, he could see a few guys pacing the boundary of the strip center. Even though she was right in front of him, Chavez was hard to see in the dark with her totally black wardrobe.

Good thing. Gaines hefted the cold steel of the pistol in his hand. *Man, if only I'd had access to these meds and weapons before. Maybe I could've bought some time for Monica—for us.*

"Anyways," she went on, finally getting the door open, "once it all collapsed, Ray took over this little area." The door's hinges squealed, not enough to be heard at distance, though at this point even the shallow breathing of the women confined with Gaines seemed too loud.

"I kind of found these guys by accident. My sister Angelina and I got separated by a mob of looters in Hollywood as we were heading down from San Francisco." Chavez paused, raising her hand to indicate quiet. She listened intently, then turned back to Gaines. "Sorry. Thought I heard something. Anyways, we'd been masquerading as guys for a couple of months by then. All our family's dead. I want to get back to San Fran and see if Angelina's there. That was our plan if we got split up; this place has been okay—safe at least—but me an' Ray don't exactly see eye-to-eye . . . I think he's startin' to catch on."

Gaines stepped from the pen. He saw that Chavez had brought several bundles of supplies—blankets, food, meds, water, ammo. *Impressive.* "How'd you keep from getting sick?" he asked, picking up a pack and putting it over his shoulder.

She stared blankly at him in the dim light of the fires. "I—I don't know." She turned to the satchels, putting one on and leaving the cage door open.

Gaines looked at the women inside: all goners for certain. "What about them?" he asked.

She understood what he meant. Her features softened in the flicker of the campfires. "I—I can't do it, homes. You do what you think is right. I just—I just can't do it anymore."

Gaines thought for a minute, then shook his head. "Okay, let's get out of here then."

Chavez looked at the other cell. "What about your friend, homes?"

Gaines glanced over to where Ellison was still sleeping. They had long been a team. He knew Ellison by now, or at least what to expect from him; all the same, there was something he despised about their involvement.

Am I raising Ellison's standards or plunging into the pit with him?

As if on cue, the albino jerked awake. He instantly made sense of the scenario in front of him.

"Hey—Gaines! What the hell's goin' on, amigo? How'd you get out? That's the fuckin' dick what roped us into this! *What're you doin'?*"

Gaines shushed Ellison. "*Shut up!* They'll hear you!" He jammed his hand over the albino's mouth, then slowly retracted his arm through the bars.

"This is Chavez—"

"Yeah, I 'member from this evenin'—"

"It's a long story, Ellison," Gaines was measuring his partner up, making decisions. He turned to Chavez. "What made you decide to trust me?"

Taken aback, Rachel studied him for a few beats, then: "Who says I have? I mean—"

"Y-your *voice* . . . Fuck—you're a *chick!*" Ellison said, stumbling to his feet, his hands still tied together. "Holy shit! This is wild!"

Gaines glared at him and he fell silent.

Chavez went on: "What choice do we have? You and me want the same thing—to get out. I saw how you handled yourself, how you tried to help those girls—" She looked down. "You seemed to give a shit about somebody other than yourself. I—I haven't seen that in a long time." She wiped her face.

Roger looked from her to Ellison: even he was contrite.

Gaines regarded the .38 in his hand. *Do people change?*

"Ellison, if I take you out of there, it'll be on a few conditions—"

"Yeah? Like what?"

Gaines watched him. Ellison's face was pinched. *I don't think I've ever seen that in him before,* he thought. *Who knows what they'll do to him in the morning?*

"We both give this lady her space." Gaines looked at Chavez. "We *all* work as a team. She wants to head up to Frisco. I'm game: she's got a sister who might be there—she could be immune, the way Chavez here seems to be."

Ellison's eyes grew wide in the dark. Gaines could see that he had his attention with this news.

"Whatever you say. Get me outta here and I'll owe ya, Gaines. I promise." Ellison thrust his arms through the bars, offering his wrists to be separated. "I swear."

Gaines looked at her again. "Cut 'im loose, Chavez."

She obliged, adding: "We need to go, they do bed checks every hour—"

"Hold it, faggots!" Ray screamed. He was running toward them with some of his gang in tow.

"Ellison! Get out—*now!* Chavez! Throw him a gun!"

In the darkness, automatic gunfire blazed. Ricochets bounced all around them as the men charged forward: bullets whizzing through the cool night air, sparking off the concrete, pinging off the metal cage bars as the erupting firefight strobed the darkness, a smoky stench filling the air.

It was a long time until dawn.

BURN

So much water in that big old sea . . .

"Any more 'Ray' left?" Ellison asked, his voice muffled by the waves. "You know he's my favorite."

"No—we finished him off a week ago. You'll have to settle for some 'Alan,'" Rachel answered, her voice soft, musical. Sitting on the porch of the house, Boundary Bay stretching darkly ahead, Roger gazed at the starry brilliance of the Milky Way as he listened to their comforting chatter in the background.

Judy Garland was right.

He was grateful that Rachel had the presence of mind to grab the food and supplies before they hit the road north: the other stuff was a bonus. They were well stocked for the long winter on the peninsula. *Who would've figured this little place to be a kind of sanctuary? We've got beautiful surroundings, enough rain for the cistern, land for planting, and the fishing's good.*

"Stupid bastards. You blew it all up." He sat forward, watching the fires still raging on the mainland. They called to mind some literal vision of hell from the Middle Ages.

Once they had made it to the San Francisco Bay Area, Ellison suggested trying to get to Alcatraz as a place to regroup, or even stay permanently; it was small enough to easily defend, but still relatively close to the shore. "Besides," Ellison had observed, "who in their right mind would want to escape *to* a deserted prison, amigo?" It was a brilliant idea, but they soon discovered it was something that had been tried before: the entire place was a giant tomb.

It was obvious even on the approach from the boat they had managed to procure that something spectacular—and very bad—had transpired at the prison. The seas had been rough, the crosswinds strong as they cruised to the island through the blue-green chop of San Francisco Bay. Their greeting party consisted of human skeletons in weather-beaten Level A biohazard suits and groups of sea lions basking on the crags. Still, they had made it to The Rock and decided to sift through its gruesome contents in case there was something of value left behind—although the place had obviously been quite damaged by explosions, some kind of armed action, and a massive conflagration. There were burnt and desiccated bodies everywhere, both civilian and military. As they walked through the abandoned oubliette, Roger was intrigued by the aftermath of whatever had happened. He was hard pressed to understand whether it had been fighting, a series of accidents, or even intentional sabotage and abandonment. The scenes themselves had stories to relate; an attentive, well-trained person could mentally re-create some of the events by reading the soot marks, interpreting the blood spatters, intuiting the way the dead had been left in situ. The final tableaux presented grim scenarios, but it had all happened some time ago. There was no one left on the island, and what remained of the buildings were very hazardous in their semi-demolished condition. The fierce winds from the Bay moaned through the ruins like forgotten spirits, making sleep elusive—even in the day-time it created an atmosphere of despair and unease. The only positive thing they found was a sizable cache of usable, if outdated, military First Strike Rations, pharmaceutical/medical supplies, bottled water, and a stockpile of weapons and ammunition.

On the fifth day, Ellison returned from an extended trip to the area they had designated as a makeshift latrine, his eyes alive with an excitement Gaines had not noticed since their time in Hollywood.

"Can you b'lieve we're in the same place *they* were, amigo?" he asked Roger.

"Who?"

Ellison rolled his eyes in disbelief. "*You* know! After I finished up my business, I took me a little stroll; still some of the old cells up over there. Lookin' 'em over got me to thinkin'. Some real scoundrels been up in here, Gaines. Some of the greats. Whole place is stuffed with ghosts and spooks, feels like."

Roger smiled, finding the use of the word 'scoundrels' oddly amusing. "Greats? What are you talking about? This was a maximum security prison—"

"'Course! I ain't a dummy, y'know. I mean, think of it, though— Capone, the Birdman, Creepy Karpis . . . All of 'em was here. Sort of stuck, like we are."

Roger stared at him. "Good God! They were *hardly* in the same situation. I mean, they were criminals! We're *nothing* like those guys—"

Ellison laughed, shaking his head. "Sorry, amigo, but I have to say we've done some questionable things to get by. Are we that much different? Really? And, you gotta admit, it *is* funny we wound up in Alcatraz."

Dumfounded, Roger had no immediate reply. He returned to reading the reports they had uncovered—huge pyres of half-incinerated records detailing what had gone on at the place—his partner's commentary bouncing through his mind.

A few days later, the three of them agreed that the Bay Area was a dead-end; they turned their attention to getting their next plan solidified, relieved that they could work as a team in spite of their rough start. Reading through some of the documents, Gaines deduced that Alcatraz had served as one of the main Command Center outposts for staging West Coast military operations. Based on the voluminous correspondence between Israel Crop., USAMRIID, the Pentagon, and other governmental institutions, the day-to-day concerns facing the agencies in charge were mainly centered on how to handle the quarantining of San Francisco and other big cities along the coastline. The alarming rise of the 'Vivers and the general breakdown of social order were all well-documented in the dry, terse prose of the e-mail printouts; reading the overall level of understatement about the gravity of the circumstances was disquieting to the trio amidst the chaotic desolation of the burnt-out penitentiary.

It was then decided to leave Alcatraz with as many supplies and weapons as possible, pressing northward to a place Roger had visited long ago with Monica: Point Roberts, Washington—a spit of land jutting into the waters between the Strait of Georgia and Boundary Bay near the Washington/Canada border. The peninsula was accessible by land only by going through the international border crossing into Canada and then heading south again below the 49th parallel, back into the United States. At just under five square miles and surrounded by water on three sides, it too would be easy to defend. It was also close enough to attempt another foray into San Francisco at a later date, as their preliminary efforts to locate Rachel's sister Angelina had been filled with frustration and dread: the City by the Bay was a dangerous place, its Silicon Valley mansions and posh suburbs completely infested by 'Viver gangs.

After a short stopover at the fogbound Point Reyes lighthouse, they hugged the rocky coastal Oregon and Washington wilderness for as long as they could before crossing Puget Sound from Port Townsend into Marysville, then heading north, eventually arriving at Point Roberts—which was oddly deserted. There was no one on the peninsula. The Canadian government had posted NO TREPASSING signs and a tall chain-link fence at the 49th parallel; by all appearances these ludicrous measures had kept everyone away from the place. Perhaps it was simply too remote; perhaps people forgot the place in their panic. Whatever the reason, Chavez, Gaines, and Ellison benefited; once past the moss-draped fence, they camouflaged the area near the marker and along the short three-mile east/west edge connecting the peninsula to Canada. At first, they kept watch on the entryway in shifts. After a few months, they changed the routine to inspecting it every few days, or during spells of bad weather. No one ever showed up. Before they really noticed, the trio had been in Point Roberts a year, and had finally begun to relax.

In the chilly evening, the fiery glow from shore dissipated by fog coming in from the Pacific, Roger could see the half-submerged, rusty carcass of a huge cruise ship in the waters just off Blaine, Washington. The military had enlisted several of the huge boats to serve as floating emergency hospitals at the height of the disaster; they had quickly become morgues as the disease turned for the worse. Most of the ships were eventually filled to capacity with the dead, sent out to sea, and sunk as mass graves. This ship appeared to have run into trouble before its mission was complete; it now lay wrecked in the shallows off the Washington coast, hammered by the surf and lit by eerie orange flames belching into the sky from massive, uncontrolled gas main fires.

"Roger, sweetie, it's seven o'clock. Are you ready for dinner?" Rachel called from inside the abandoned beach house they had appropriated. With a pick of all the old houses, they decided to settle in one that had a pier and moorage in case they needed to quickly take to the water.

Amazing how that watch keeps us on schedule. It's almost like the good old days. Gaines had let Rachel keep his pocket watch: he never explained its significance to him emotionally, but giving it to her had eased the burden of his old life, allowing him to let go and move on.

"Yeah, be right there." *Gettin' cold anyway.*

The surf washed below, and Gaines tasted salt in the air. The wind was strong, carrying with it the singed, sickly-sweet odors of the smoldering cities to their north and south. A gull cried.

He wandered in, greeting Ellison with a nod. "You feel okay, Rachel?"

She smiled, clearly tired. "I'm all right—sit! Sit!"

Roger kissed her on the lips. *I love the way she looks in the candlelight. Judy Garland was right: there really is just no place like home . . . wherever that may be, or whatever it becomes.*

They each took a portion of food, then sat down at the table.

"Only two more months left," she said, dabbing her mouth with a linen napkin and rubbing her swollen belly under her jacket. The three of them laughed.

In the distance, unheard over the gently lapping water as they talked and ate, an owl hooted.

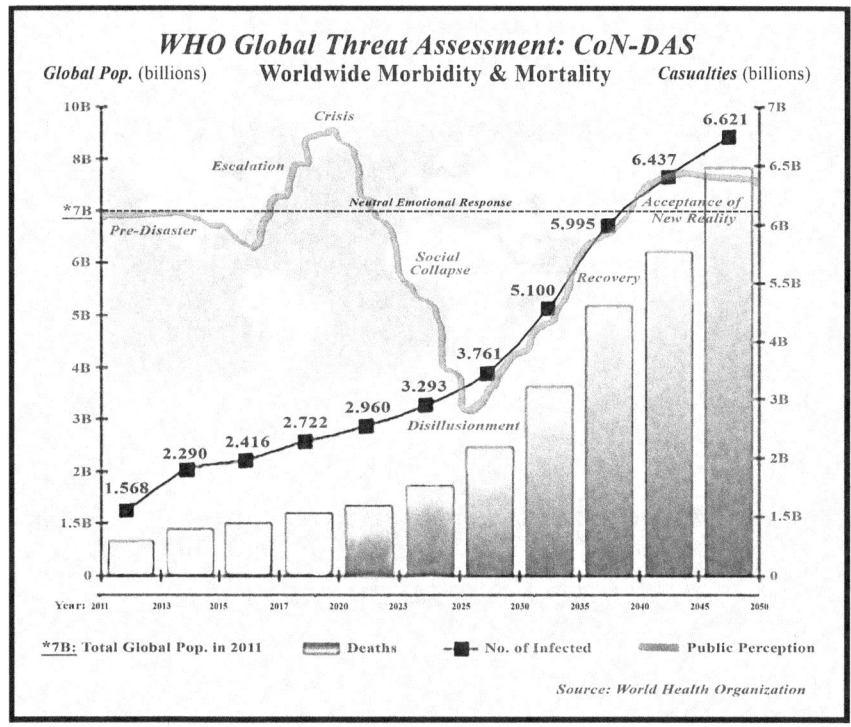

Global Pop. (billions)   **Worldwide Morbidity & Mortality**   *Casualties* (billions)

Source: World Health Organization

PRELUDE

Wormwood

I

He was only one of seven billion. Seven billion dreamers.

"Kcal bsraepp a adool beht Thgil iw tehtni . . ."

From a high window in the antique dwelling ahead, a misshapen figure stepped from view, allowing a red velvet curtain to close. Still some yards away from the crumbling edifice as the light faded, he could nonetheless sense a deep whining sound emanating from the place, which caused the ground to shake. The whole area gave the appearance of some blasted moonscape from the Great War. Lightning flashed, illuminating the vast wreckage of the chateau on the far hill. Black rain began to fall from the murky sky; ancient constellations vanished as the mounting deluge obliterated the heavens, streaking the polluted air. The forsaken plain, stretching for numberless miles below a mountain of corpses, was leeched of all but the merest hint of color. Soon it was awash in an acidic flood of opaque water.

This was an evil place, he sensed. Steeped in sadness, in misery.

He began to climb the immense stack of dead bodies in an attempt to get above the blistering, newly formed ocean created by the rains. He recalled somehow that there was a black abyss without an evident bottom behind the rotten heap of cadavers. The house loomed—beckoned—against the foggy, saturated horizon; oddly distorted, it seemed to mutate as he watched, enlivened by some strange, omniterrestrial force. Growing in loudness, the faint metallic sound that he had noticed before was part of what he intuited now as a swarm of huge, unseen insects—another catalyst motivating him to the repulsive summit.

Once at the pinnacle, he sank to his knees, tearing away great scarlet chunks of the dead with his teeth; violence brought momentary relief from the terrible shooting pain in his head. The rain beat down harder, cooking the flesh he crawled upon. Overhead, a great star slashed across the heavens, its black tail dividing the sky before it disappeared with a thunderous sonic boom.

"Ugn um!" he exclaimed, and his tortured frame stiffened, as though abruptly pulled short by phantom hands. The loss of balance pitched him into the void on the other side, and his screams reverberated all the way to the bottom of that awful, shadowed canyon . . .

II

The long drive from the suburbs to his office at the Israel Corporation headquarters in Patmos, Kansas, was grueling. Once again trapped in the crushing A.M. commute, Keith was lost in his thoughts: about Steph, his worsening health, work.

Losing Steph had taken its toll. It was almost as though she had vanished, or simply never existed except in the recesses of his mind. She no longer returned his calls, not even responding to the lawyer. Just contemplating the whole sorry end to eight years of marriage caused his head to pound.

Shimmering waves of heat rose off the choked roadway ahead: it was already over eighty degrees at nine in the morning. *Such is the summer in Kansas. Steph had hated it here anyway; she's probably back in Vermont with her mother.* The car in the lane beside him was attempting to ease into his lane as the traffic inched forward on Interstate 70. *She was right. I never should have taken the promotion with Israel—*

The horn-blare of the car trying to merge startled him from his daydream, causing his body to tense with a series of pronounced muscular spasms. He scowled at the old woman in the next lane; she gawked back at him with bugged eyes, muttering something obscene through the slit of her pruny mouth. In the background, an announcer on the morning station he favored mentioned that I-70 was completely jammed due to an accident a few miles ahead.

Keith turned the knob of the radio to find another report that might give an alternate route; the GPS coverage of his cell phone was spotty on this part of the highway. Of course, the simple act of turning the dial made his arm tremble with effort—he had been getting more easily fatigued as his anxiety increased. Unfortunately, he had used up most of his vacation and sick time, and was reluctant to use what was left. He could see the old woman angrily gesturing in his peripheral vision. He ignored her.

Perhaps Morrison's on to something—I'm just going to have to tell the Top Brass that I need a long break. A sabbatical. Between the divorce, whatever's wrong with me, Wormwood . . . I just need a little time. A real vacation.

Keith glanced at the dashboard clock, his Mercedes-Benz creeping ever closer to his final destination. Of course, he knew there was no way he could go on any sort of leave before the latest trials were done, and that would be—at the very least—another several weeks.

I never should have agreed to head up Retrovirology for these bastards; everyone at the Institute tried to warn me. The money and prestige were just too good, though . . .

Israel Corporation.

For anyone working in his field—specifically hot viruses and genetically engineered biohazardous agents—to work for Israel Corp., or IC as most employees called it, was the Big Time. It meant *arrival*, the Major Leagues; there were more present and past Nobel laureates in chemistry and medicine in their employ than any other private organization in the world. A few years there would have meant that he and Steph could write their own ticket—set for life with benefits, money, status . . .

All moot now, of course.

The stress of juggling so many projects for the Pentagon and DARPA—not to mention the very disturbing nature of some of their efforts—was wearing Keith down. Even his mentor and the man who had trained him when he first got to Israel Corp. three years previously, Dr. Iwane, had been unable to cope long-term: a few months after "retiring" he was found dead at this home. The papers and television reported that he had succumbed to a heart attack—not unexpected for a man of his advanced years, granted, but Keith suspected he knew better; he had learned too much about the good doctor to chalk it up to bad timing and age.

Iwane knew too much to keep around as a loose end. Dr. Iwane had intimated to Keith in their last phone conversation that he needed to leave the country or he might not be alive much longer; he had outlived his usefulness to both Israel Corp. and the DoD. All the terrible secrets—most of them, at any rate—he had slowly doled out in his twenty-nine years as the director of strategic research and development at IC were now in the hands of the rogue conservative administration that had seized power in the last election. Once President Hinton decided to lead as a unitary executive, laws evaporated, power was consolidated, the world changed. Hinton had ascended to power through fraud, fear, and intimidation: terrorists were behind every tree; liberals were terrorists; terrorists were not to be negotiated with—therefore those who dissented, specifically liberals—were not to be negotiated with, either. Hinton also had messianic visions of saving the godforsaken United States from itself and the world—in political and religious counterpoint to the tenets of al-Qaeda and Daesh, whose declared aims were the same, even if their emphasis on who and what was at fault differed. As the president was fond of saying in recent speeches: "The ends of God's righteousness justify the use of all means at my disposal."

After a few poorly executed overseas misadventures, a frustrated Hinton administration disbanded the Supreme Court, imprisoned the justices, then outlawed the Democratic Party. It was a bleak and uncertain time: the stunned populace reacted with a strange acquiescence, rapidly acclimating to this New World Disorder. With all the geopolitical and social churn, even the hardliners within the administration came to understand the value of the "perception of limits, and selective concessions to the opposition"—even when these were simply hollow gestures.

Iwane's abrupt "retirement" was one such example.

Undoubtedly, Dr. Iwane's evil past as a commandant of one of history's vilest institutions—Japan's Unit 731—was increasingly seen as a liability. All the "medical knowledge" and "research" that he brought to bear from the confines of that brutal place had long since been integrated, and he was past his servitude point. In other words, Iwane was no longer needed and could even be seen as a point of embarrassment, especially in light of the missteps with respect to more recent Black Ops after 9/11. Some holdover from World War II was more unneeded scrutiny given the excitable social justice climate of more sensitive constitutions in the country. It appeared that the point men for Israel Corp. were finally aware of Iwane's notorious wartime experiments: gruesome human vivisection on the mostly Chinese civilians that they referred to as 'logs'; horrific investigational amputation and reattachment surgery; barbaric frostbite trials; forced pregnancies and abortions; using prisoners as living testers for various explosives, and—most valuable, but now well assimilated into the DoD's strategic aims—all the disease transmission experimentation that had been Iwane's sadistic specialty. In spite of the immunity status granted him in exchange for his data, he was of low value at this juncture. What was required now was compliance, not controversy; old dirt needed to be swept outside, not under a rug indoors—that was too close for comfort. How else could the population be reliably controlled?

"If something happens to me," Keith remembered Iwane *wheezing over the line, "you will know the truth: I was murdered by the United States government."* Then their connection went dead: Dr. Iwane was never seen again. All that was noted about the doctor's passing officially was a brief press release from IC corporate headquarters.

8:16 . . . I'll never get there on time!

Keith loosened his tie with a shaky hand. He sighed. The traffic was starting to break up. His body contracted in a wave of painful tics and tremors. *Finally.* Of course, the project he was about to deliver was one of the worst yet from Israel Corporation: a top secret viral agent disguised as a treatment for Extensively Drug-Resistant Tuberculosis (XDR-TB), code-named Wormwood.

Now I'm stuck. I have to figure a way out of this . . .

At last traveling near the speed limit, he could finally make out the hulking edifice of Israel Corp.'s main campus squatting like a black hole on the blasted horizon. The sight of it rocked his frame with more spasms, and he fought to control the car. The pounding of his chest and heart synced as he drove closer to the fenced guard shack at the perimeter of the complex. He lamented the calculations that had gotten him to this moment, though the gamble had previously been his dream.

His earlier research at the Institute of Pathological Diseases in New York had garnered not only the attention his bosses, but also the eye of his former role model—Dr. Iwane. Too late, Keith understood the axioms that one of his old colleagues at the Institute had said to him: 1) never meet your idols; and 2) be careful what you wish for. The project that had kicked his work into high-level notice was innovative: he had perfected a facultative intracellular parasite from an avian model, modifying it to invade a common human rhinovirus. After hijacking the cold virus, it altered the structure of its RNA, rendering it into a highly virulent and contagious lab-created pathogen: (H5N1)R.

The Pentagon was the first to take an active interest, impressed with the organism's horrendous potential. Causing gross deformation of host cell mitochondria, it resulted in a lethal 'superbug' characterized by intense flu-like symptoms—high fever, extreme amplification contributing to third spacing and migraines, paralysis at times, and finally progressing to premature apoptosis in the blood, lungs, and brain. It was a quick, sure killer—almost *too* perfect to be a weapon. Even containing it would be difficult if it were ever to be used in the wild, as there was no defense naturally, and Keith had failed to devise an antidote. It was consigned to BSL-4 control enclaves at USAMRI-

ID, and Porton Down in the United Kingdom. Of course, once the patent had been issued, the Feds started calling and the offers poured in. DoD was "curious" about use of the agent in "possible scenarios." *Would Dr. Vincent have an interest in undergoing a background check for security clearances? Maybe consider a position at one of their contracted facilities? In Europe, or perhaps at Israel Corporation?*

Keith jumped at the chance: it was what he had been working toward for his entire career. Steph had been a harder sell; she was ready to get out of the whole rat race. She felt their lives had become too processed, too out of touch; she despised President Hinton and warned Keith not to trust anyone in the military.

If only I had listened . . . now I'm trapped in a living nightmare.

He stopped the car at the checkpoint. A hard-faced young man in full body armor, sunglasses, and wielding an assault rifle of some kind stepped from the post.

"Good morning, soldier: Doctor Vincent." He held his ID up to the guard for inspection, the muscles under his sleeves rippling in contraction.

The helmeted soldier said nothing as he scrutinized Keith's credentials. He glanced into the backseat of the car. "Business today, Doctor Vincent?"

"Just some work; I also have an appointment with Dr. Morrison." Sweat dewed his face; the pause was tense.

"Thank you, Doctor. Proceed."

As the car pulled into a slot in the cavernous parking deck, Keith felt as though he were being swallowed alive by some mythological beast. *No—this beast is real,* he decided. Sitting there, he rubbed his face, dreading the walk to his office. His thoughts drifted back to where he had betrayed his ideals.

After he had been hired, part of his contract stipulated that all his work, in perpetuity, would become property of Israel Corporation. That retroactively included his (H5N1)R patents. He had readily agreed: anything to get on the inside. *But what did I lose?* After Hinton had privatized the US Armed Forces to organizations like Blackwa-ter/Academi, Israel Corp., and a few other mercenary outfits, Keith began to have second thoughts about everything. They had all his bio-weapons research. How long before he was not providing a large enough ROI for their investment?

Keith felt certain that the SARS outbreak—rumored to be China's own lab-created disease—had rattled the Hinton Administration. The stories about some "Bird Flu" cropping up in areas overseas under the control of the United States had put him on edge: Keith prayed they were not experimenting with his bottled devil of (H5N1)R as a check against perceived Chinese aggression. *Had all the earmarks, though . . .* Keith's paranoia had been the last straw for Steph: she demanded that he get out, or at least let her go.

She just didn't get it, though. I can't just . . . leave. *Once you're in, there's no way out.*

Footsteps echoing hollowly in the yawning car park, Keith's gait was stiff, awkward, slow. The twitching made all movement difficult. It was getting worse, he knew. He swallowed, and his throat was dry cot-ton. *The doorway . . . ten steps . . . five . . . three more*— He collapsed against the door, breath ragged and heavy in his chest. He was slicked in sweat, the stifling air humid, acrid. He licked his lips, cracked from gasping for air. *Jesus.* His head was pounding harder.

Iwane had warned him, too, just as Steph had: *"Be careful . . . trust no one, not even me. String them out for as long as possible to maintain your value. These are ruthless people. Dreadful people."* As his mentor explained to Keith over time, Israel Corp. had been an invisible hand guiding all manner of terrible events. *But could even* Iwane *be believed?* According to Dr. Iwane, the FBI, Homeland Security, 'The War on Terror,' 'The War on Drugs': all these things were disinformation institutions or cru-sades to undermine the populace, and they were all within the tenta-cled reach of Israel Corp. and mercenaries now under the employ of the Hinton Government. In all his time working for the Feds, he had never seen the current levels of extreme paranoia—or the depths that those in power were willing to plumb in order to stay in power. To control. Failing that, there were always the declared enemies of the American Way to use weapons against: Iran, North Korea, Daesh, the Taliban. Control was a motivator domestically, but the real money to be made was overseas—selling security to U.S. allies and interests. Part of that package was sewing conflict and civil unrest. It was all rather Orwellian. Homeland Security and the CIA were the latest players hounding Keith for his current project: they wanted to use it against so-called "home-grown" domestic targets that had been secretly targeted and infiltrated—ALF, ELF, various Muslim and non-Christian charities. They needed to foment the fear, the anxiety, to keep people afraid. If it had other uses later, that was a bonus.

Keith's breathing eased, and he peeled himself off the wall. He used his hand to open the biometric lock and enter the hallway from the parking deck to his office, lost in his thoughts. Not since the anthrax scare after September 11 had the Feds been so active in fashioning a 'Domestic Attack'—to spin it as the work of some rogue splinter cell, or lone wolves inspired by extremists. Maybe another McVeigh/Nichols–style bombing, or attacking a mall during the holidays with suicide bombers and machine guns in a false flag operation in the manner of the Paris Bataclan Attacks of November 2015. Too much peace made people complacent, made them too relaxed; keeping them off-balance and on edge, divided, at one another's throats with religious bickering, political turmoil, class anxieties—and the newest mass opiate, social-identity alarmism—was the best way to sustain control. A covert, government-enacted Black Swan event could be just the thing to scare the populace into rightful thinking, and keep them in the head-space for years to come.

To that end, Keith had been instructed to create an untraceable blood-borne pathogen, and once more, he had delivered. His creation was an HIV-type provirus that utilized RNA cloaking techniques; it mimicked prion diseases such as Mad Cow, or Creutzfeldt-Jakob—a perfect 'slow virus' that took weeks to manifest itself. Side effects included pareidolia, religious mania, and other mental delusions and disorders, such as Munchausen Syndrome-by-proxy. His investigations confirmed a long-held theory: that mental illness could be a contagion and could be created under certain circumstances. He called this aspect "Induced Mass Psychopathy" or IMP, and demonstrated that he could reproduce it at scale via computer modeling. There had been associations for years between a few disease processes and neurological conditions, such as Alzheimer's, Pick's Disease, even the outbreak of von Economo's disease—Encephalitis Lethargica—in the early 1900s. There were also types of madness that had this component, namely schizophrenia, which was sometimes initiated by strains of *Streptococcus* or influenza. In his work with the flu, Keith expanded on some of these ideas; he had shown, using the simple parasite *Toxoplasma gondii*, that it was possible to cross the blood-brain barrier and cause massive inflammation, even insanity. Normally, once in the brain, this parasite took the will of the host organism over and created a sort of immunity to fear—even imbuing a willingness to take known fatal risks. In its natural host—mice—this allowed them to be eaten by cats, the parasite's target vector for reproduction. The cats then passed the eggs along in feces, starting the cycle over. This idea of controlling responses and a person's will power was something he had stumbled across in his studies: it was an active area of funding and research by the military, especially DARPA, in both the corporeal and virtual realms, and had been attempted by the U.S. in the past with *T. gondii*, with disastrous results. Keith felt certain he could fix the errors in those prior attempts, and was given clearance to try by the Pentagon.

Scrapping most of the previous approach, as he conceived this apparatus in humans, Keith engineered the parasites to be chemically cloaked, presenting themselves as an errant strand of host DNA in order to create a 'cytokine storm' by the host's immune system. The body, unable to detect the intruders directly, was instead coaxed into attacking itself, in this case the brain, where the parasite resided. As the brain deteriorated, the victim descended into madness: hallucinations, memory disturbances, vertigo, ataxia, headaches. These were followed in short order by crippling psychosis and altered states of consciousness. On autopsy, the animal models had demonstrated lesions he called 'Spheric Entanglements' because of the shape and involvement of the tissue layers.

After a few successful experiments on detainees at Guantánamo Bay, the Pentagon seemed convinced of the dark potential of what Keith had created. His invention was taken over, and he was blocked from developing it further. He suspected strongly that it was in use somewhere, but had no confirmation of such—just a feeling of dread and anxiety at what could happen with it, and what he was becoming in the process.

Keith stood at the door to the company psychiatrist's office, contemplating why he had come there. *Did I have an appointment?* Dr. Morrison had been a great help to him in coping with Steph's departure, as well as his general dissatisfaction with respect to his job. He raised his hand to knock.

The door opened. "Ah, Doctor Vincent. I was just wondering about you. Please, come in."

Now, the headache building in Keith's skull was once more pushing sanity and perception out. Everything appeared faster and faster to him, as though he were a fly. The awful psychic drone that accompanied these migraines blossomed into his fragmenting mental landscape, causing his tormented frame to twist in a grotesque imitation of a ballet. The world was distorted—as though looking through an insect's compound eye. The area around him spun slowly as he crossed the threshold into Morrison's office.

"I am . . . *Wormwood*," Keith's voice was a distant, metallic grating in the suddenly artic air. He screamed—

"The wings are beating outside . . ."

III

The first thing you notice is the vast quantity of drying blood:

Thick as sap, it smothers the macabre furnishings—crudely fashioned disarticulated body parts—in a repugnant crimson sauce. Playing your flashlight over the surroundings as your eyes slowly adjust to the narrow field of the dim beam, you can just make out chaotic designs—smeared handprints—on the walls. A cold gust of wind billows the tattered curtains, drawing your gaze to the vibrant sprays garishly decorating the ceiling in haphazard spatters.

"Mungu . . ." you say, not understanding the language, yet grasping that it is a profound utterance. In the distance you hear a faint clamor: pained shrieking, harsh laughter, the rhythmical churning of giant machinery. The hairs on your arms stand on end: you can sense that you are being watched.

There is a drop in temperature as the wind continues to blow in through the broken windows, causing your breath to fog and the air to crystallize. As you move on down the hall and away from the terrible living room, your stomach lurches. A wave of stench permeates your nostrils: the horrible bouquet is most severe approaching the kitchen. You peer in, disturbed by the battery of bloody utensils, half-consumed torsos, and human sweetbreads glistening in the yellowy radiance of your weakening flashlight.

"Kichwa!"

Revolted, you stagger through this monstrous exhibition and into another skewed, Caligari-like hallway. Here the impression of untold sets of imperceptible eyes moving over your body feels like the energy of thousands of tiny invisible suns, their focused power battering you. The cold numbs your face and hands as you grapple with your bearings. A grungy sign on the wall bears a message in a foreign language, and it appears as though someone has highlighted parts of the fading letters to read: c he rno b yl. *The gag-inducing miasma is exceptionally pungent now as it wafts up from the floor vents, like some fermented fruit-and-cheese platter gone green with mold.*

Navigating through the disarray, your limbs feel improbably heavy, reflexes sluggish. Closer now, the muffled, rhythmic noises synchronize with your pulse. Gasping for fresh air in the stifling darkness, you approach the bedroom. Capillaries expand impossibly in your head: miniscule cylindrical bladders straining, causing your skull to ache, your face to burn.

The grotesque contents of the cramped room is terrifying: worn bookcases crowded by severed heads in various stages of decomposition, paradoxically alive with maggots . . . a blood-plastered bed, ruined in an orgy of sadism and sex . . . the weak flicker of a few grimy candles. Another sign: **Чернобыль**. *Sweat dampens your clothing in this frigid, unclean space. You are keenly aware of how jumpy, how nervous you have become, as your head pounds harder, harder, threatening to blot out rational thought. The candles reinforce your unease that some inscrutable evil is prowling through the collapsing tenement with you . . . behind you . . . beside you . . .*

Just before your flashlight wavers out, you glimpse the vile bathroom. It appears to be little more than a shadowy dumping ground for humanity's accidents—a cesspool of spoiled teratomas thrashing their pathetically deformed appendages, blindly wallowing in the carpet of vermin and bodily fluids staining the floor. Amorphous, vestigial horrors, their cloudy, protruding eyes search aimlessly in the glacier-cold air like some wretched, newly hatched rara avis, moving from side to side with the stimulus of light or sound. Throaty, agonal squeals exude at intervals from their stringy, pulsating mouths, which seem to have been gouged into distorted, veiny heads by some pitiless deity. Disgusted and alarmed, you stumble back into the tilted hallway toward your new goal: the closed door at its terminus, where you can see colored light faintly edging the crooked doorframe.

Heightened by the claustrophobia of the darkness, the overwhelming odors seem to saturate the atmosphere as ice crystals frost in your nose. Very loud now, the frightening whine of certain automated death—hammering, scraping, pulverizing— fills your consciousness. The entire house seems to be shaking from the tumult. Feeling your way deeper through the decaying structure, you are strangely lured to an unknown outcome as the disquieting furor of screeching, wailing, industrial mayhem mingles with the sharp aromas in the freezing air, continually building in power, dread, volume.

The acid sting of bile scorches your throat. You become aware of blood on the floor: there is so much of it—a virtual wading pool of coagulating red fluid sloshing under your bare, cold-crippled feet as you move down the corridor.

"Mungu . . . saidia!" you cry, horrified at your predicament, but understanding that you have to continue onward.

Finally at the door, your breath is shallow, your lips salty with perspiration, your sweaty hand poised on the knob. Detecting vibrations behind the thin panel of wood separating you from the savage, deafening maelstrom of activity on the other side, you cast a final glance behind you: pitch darkness—only the foul reek and the muted caterwauling uttered by the half-formed monsters in the lavatory. You drop the useless flashlight to the blood-drenched floor.

The handle rattles in your grasp, bringing you back to the moment. A lump forms in your throat as you snap your attention to the doorway, which is now banging against its frame from emphatic hammering on the opposite side. The racket mounts to a deafening roar, filling your mind like a living thing—of you, yet apart. A brilliant flare of red illumination bleeds through the suture of the doorframe, then extinguishes. You hear ragged voices speaking in a peculiar tongue behind the flimsy barrier, then all plummets into stillness and quiet.

Your ears are ringing, and you feel frozen sweat on your body. You want to run, but decide to be as motionless as possible, hoping that the noise will not return, that you will be able to flee this awful place. Your breath—which you realize you have been holding unconsciously—exits your aching lungs in a stifled swoosh. The utter darkness creates strange optical illusions as you try to orient yourself. Leaning closer to the door, you are acutely mindful of your heart—pounding, pounding, pounding.

You strain to hear past your heartbeat. Something is—scratching.

Without warning, the door flies open: pure, dazzling red light blinds you, scorches you . . . non-human chattering rends your senses like a tempest thrashes sails . . .

*

"Proof-of-concept . . . Make it work, make it fast, then weaponize it: make it airborne."

That had been Keith's directive from Dr. Iwane before his death, and it is now reiterated in this meeting with Iwane's boss, Dr. Kneale: "After that, then we can negotiate your . . . termination from Israel Corporation, Doctor Vincent."

Kneale is a cold man, bony, prone to ill-fitting black suits. He eyes Keith like dinner, then makes a temple with large, hirsute fingers, his longish gray hair sweeping back from his stony forehead. The silence in the confines of Kneale's dimly lit office is enormous. Keith swallows audibly in the sparsely furnished room.

"But with all due respect, Dr. Kneale, I—I don't feel like you've been entirely straight with me."

Kneale sneers, rolling his eyes as he leans forward in his huge chair. He stares intensely at Keith across the expanse of his desk. *"Doctor Vincent, I'm both shocked and disappointed. You know we all must pledge our ethical allegiance to the company annually. Misleading people and obfuscation are not tolerated. We make every attempt at total transparency, even as we try to keep our key members anonymous."* *Kneale leans back, the giant chair seeming to engulf him. He crosses his legs, the corners of his mouth upturned in an attempt at a more genuine smile; his eyes are blazing, unblinking.*

"I know, I know," *Keith replies, swallowing tightly once more.* So much for my Hippocratic Oath . . . *"It's just—well, I've been hearing rumors that perhaps Israel Corp. has placed (H5N1)R in theater, if not in usage. I have a problem with that. The influenza A pathogen I used as a foundation is novel given its avian origins, and its associated complications—if one survives the infection—such as CoN-DAS are not well understood, even by me. I still need to do more work to detail the relationship between CoN-DAS and the Spheric Entanglements. They're not exactly like Lewi Bodies in Pick's Disease, or the neurofibrillary tangles and plaques seen in Alzheimer's—they're more damaging, especially to the amygdala and other specific regions of the brain, and there is wide variation based on sex hormone exposure. It needs considerably more study, or we could unleash a biological disaster of unimaginable proportions."*

Kneale regards Keith with contempt, toying idly with a pen on his desktop. *"I see,"* *he says finally. Kneale draws a deep breath, lets it out slowly. His features soften.* *"Some people believe anything . . . Most of them, in fact. I can see you're not one of those. Listen, I'm not really supposed to discuss operations with staff, but know this: we're not crazy. We simply take defending this great nation seriously. Sometimes that means . . . pre-emption. Doctor Vincent, like Doctor Iwane, you have been quite valuable to us."* *Kneale leans forward again, as though sharing a secret.* *"All we've done is move some strategic reserves of various antidotes and reagents—mostly antivirals and antibiotics, like Cipro, Zyvox, Rifadin, Interferon, Tamiflu, and so on—and yes, a few pathogenic stockpiles to our high-value storage facilities. Generally, state, military, and supermax prisons: Leavenworth, San Quentin, Pelican Bay—hell, even Alcatraz. It's the safest place to warehouse this stuff. I mean, who'd think to attack a prison? Plus, if there's an accident, easy containment—and the collateral damage is minimal. Who cares what happens to the scum of the earth on the inside, right? We've been doing it for years."*

Keith is surprised by his superior's candor. He stands. "Well, that makes me feel better, I'll admit. I—I've been under a lot of stress lately . . . I appreciate you clearing it up, and I'm sorry for any aggravation."

Kneale gets up as well, extending his hand. "Not to worry Doctor Vincent, not to worry. Now, with regard to this new project, and your future with us," he adds, tightening his icy grip on Keith's. A smirk edges his features, and his eyes have gone quite black.

"Yes," Keith replies, his head beginning to ache in the stuffy room. "I'm aware of the prior work with the Streptococcus and T. Gondii *organisms. In fact, I've already put a plan into action—in a few more weeks we can move from beta- into double-blind testing—so long as my hypothesis holds up, that is. I call it 'Wormwood,' after the star mentioned in the Book of Revelation. The name revealed itself to me in a dream; it has great possibilities as a psychogenic disruptor."*

Kneale's face registers delight and surprise. "Excellent! I look forward to the results. And I'm sure we can work out something to make it worth your while to stay. A man of your abilities is a rare commodity." Kneale crosses to the door of his office with Keith.

"Oh," Keith says, rubbing his temple, "I'm sure you'll be sick to death of me by the time this is all over!"

He exits Kneale's office, the older man's laughter cutting off as the door closes.

*

Awakening in Dr. Morrison's office, Keith felt cold, drained. He touched his head, wincing at the light coming from the windows in the psychiatrist's suite.

"You were mumbling about something after you passed out, Doctor Vincent. Strange dreams, you said. And you kept repeating a word: 'Wormwood.' How long have you been having the nightmares, Doctor Vincent?" Morrison asked, absentmindedly chewing on the eraser end of a pencil.

Keith closed his eyes. "How long was I out?"

"Not too long. A few minutes. Gave me quite a start, I'll admit. You look . . . tired."

Keith chuckled. "Tired doesn't even *begin* to cover it, Doc. Having more trouble sleeping. Depression, I think. The whole Steph disappearance. Bad enough she wants a divorce; now she's gone MIA. No replies, not even to the lawyer." He looked over at Morrison, who was considering him thoughtfully. "Wormwood is the code name for this huge project I've been assigned. It's a killer! As for the nightmares— oh, I don't know . . . a few weeks."

"Every night?"

"No, not every night. At least not until the last couple of weeks," Keith responded, sweeping an unsteady hand through his hair.

"I see." Dr. Morrison jotted something down in his notebook.

Squinting around the room, Keith felt anxious. Finally he asked: "What do you make of . . . everything?"

Dr. Morrison exhaled, stretching in his chair. "You seem overworked. I think you need a few days off—"

"Come on, Doc, you're killing me: you know I'm *buried,*" Keith interrupted, furrowing his brow. His neck muscles quivered with a series of contractions. He snapped his gaze to the psychiatrist.

The owlish Dr. Morrison regarded him with detached reserve, scribbling into his notebook without looking. "Why not? *They* need *you.* It'll wait until you get back from a short vacation—"

"Because I've got too much to do. Besides, this seems like something more than exhaustion and caffeine overload."

Sitting up from the sofa, Keith blinked through a head rush, face and hands shuddering in a wave. "Look," he continued, "I know you don't understand what I'm talking about, but something's not right. My soon-to-be-ex-wife said a while ago that my tossing and turning at night had gotten unbearable. She told me I mumbled, screamed, kicked . . ." He paused to gather his thoughts. "She even said I was starting to sleepwalk! That's not like me." He massaged his temple; the head pain was intensifying as his bouts with the night terrors wore on. "And my head, Jesus . . ." There was a long, dry beat.

Morrison broke the silence: "Okay, I understand, Doctor Vincent. If you change your mind, I'll support a leave of absence. Conversely, if you just want to talk more about your nightmares, or about the dissolution of your marriage, the intensity of this assignment, or the stress and isolation of your situation—whatever—we'll schedule more appointments." Morrison pressed his lips together in a semblance of a smile. "In the interim, I'll write a prescription for the headaches. Also, Ativan might take the edge off your anxiety, help you to sleep better." He scribbled something on a piece of stationary and handed it to Keith.

"Okay, Doctor Morrison," Keith replied, taking the script. He stood up, grateful to leave, the muscles in his legs contracting painfully. "Thanks for the prescriptions; I'll decide on the leave soon."

*

Closing the front door, Keith blew air from his mouth in a huff of agitation. A melancholy half-frown pulled at his face. He removed his belt. Rubbing his forehead, Keith realized how exhausted he felt: in his legs, his arms, his neck—as if he had lead weights tied to his extremities. His twitching was almost tolerable for a change. Clicking the television on, he walked from the living room to the kitchen to get a drink, cranium pounding. As he regarded the contents of the refrigerator, talking heads on the news channel yammered in the background about the most recent bird flu pandemic raging in Asia, then segued to a story about the latest vapid chanteuse on the pop music scene. He grabbed a cola and some ice and poured it into a glass.

Staring into the fizzing soda as the ice melted, Keith felt inexplicably like crying.

He takes a long swallow, tasting only absinthe in his mind. His eyes water from the carbonation, nose burning as he exhales.

He shakes the cobwebs from his aching head, suddenly consumed by grief.

"How'd everything go?"

Steph appears from the bedroom, polishing mango-scented lotion into her face and draped only in one of his old T-shirts.

"It went fine. Same old same old: they ask the impossible and I provide."

He hugs her close, kissing her neck. "Mmm . . . you smell good," he says, taking her in with all his senses. "That T-shirt looks good on you."

"You like it, huh?"

"Yeah—bet you'd look even better without it." He puts his hand up the shirt and feels the heat of her naked back: smooth, downy, soft.

She presses against him as he cups her firm buttocks, breathing heavily in the dim light spilling from the kitchen into the hallway.

Passionate. Wet. Deep: that is the ecstasy of their first kiss that night. They retire to the bedroom and disrobe.

It takes a long time, and is wonderful for them both.

They come together the second time: not so long or so pretty—loud, lusty, more sensual. A celebration of flesh more than love. Afterward, as she sleeps in his arms, he lies awake, reflecting on the day . . .

Emerging from his reminisce, Keith swallowed thickly, glancing at the clock. *She had no choice—you know that. That's why she left. Just keep telling yourself that. Maybe one day you'll believe it.*

The TV was droning; the sound of it haunted him in the quiet house, his pulsing head accompanying the beat of some mindless reality show. His tired body undulated with involuntary muscular fasciculations: they were always worse at night. Too drained to cook, he grabbed a bag of pretzels off the counter and walked into the living room with his drink.

Plopping onto the couch, he clicked through the channels, eyelids heavy. He nibbled at the pretzels; his appetite had been off for weeks.

Doc might be on to something . . . too much going on lately. My immunity could be shot. That might explain the twitching—nerves combined with stress. I need to take a break. I might have a virus or something . . . some can hide in the muscles, like herpes simplex . . . give you the shakes, twitching . . .

"TV sucks." He closed his eyes.

The remote slipped from his grasp.

IV

The house was alive; it was compelling me to do things. Terrible things. Monstrous things.

Once I understood that, everything stopped bothering me. In fact, it all began to make some kind of morbid sense: I was hardly cognizant anymore of the blight and evil permeating everything around me, knowing now that this was the only way forward. In the distance, I perceived the worm-eaten door behind me beginning to quake—as though someone or something were pounding on it, demanding entry, although the air was still as a vacuum, causing sounds to be lower-pitched, slow to arrive.

Turning my attention once more to the disembodied head, I was fascinated by the intricate variety of textures adorning the surface, captivated by her lop-sided presence.

The residual hair was matted and fine as filament. The dissolving nose had the waxen gloss of melted paraffin even as the delicate skin of the face, forehead, and chin fairly blossomed in ripe, flaking tumors of decay. A spreading, humorless rictus exposed loose, yellowing teeth to the cool air.

<Release me. Release me, Chernobyl!> *she whispered into my mind, causing my head to pulse hotly.* <Violence will set you free, my sweet Chernobyl.>

With care, as her jaw had nearly dislocated from the fragile skull at this point, I stuck one of my spindly fingers into the gaping oral cavity. Tracing a wrinkle from the still pliable upper lip, I drew a line over the parchment membrane of the leathery cheek; working past the ruined nasal protuberance, I poked my grimy finger into the vacant pit of her eye. Pulling the digit out, I brought it closer to my face for examination.

It was moist. Gritty . . .

I tasted it. Salty . . .

Aroused, I moved closer. It had been necessary to murder her: she'd had it coming, after all. She really never did appreciate everything I'd done for us.

For seemingly an eon I lingered, the only light coming from the cool rays of the moon through the slatted windows of the awful room. Naked and shining in the pale lunar glow, my face was less than an inch from the head: her fetid visage one of many such displays in this gallery of misery.

Just outside the frail door, the wail of multiple air-raid sirens commenced howling through the cavernous depths of the dreadful residence . . . Exploding the morgue-like hush, the racket was soon followed by the far-off approach of thousands of beating, burnished wings.

The door suddenly splintered apart in a blast of wood debris: my exposed back was seared by bleak, ghastly purple light flooding in. Every horrid object in the dusty room was thrown into stark relief. I spoke aloud, but could not hear my own voice over the crescendo of screeching metal and blowing wind: the air seemed alive with sound and dreadful energy. Shivering, I dared not look at what approached, knowing I would be demolished just beholding it for an instant.

Then, as in a dream, I closed my eyes and slipped my quivering tongue into her yawning eye socket.

"Christ . . ."

Keith stares at the ceiling, his breathing labored in the darkness; he looks over at the clock on the nightstand: four-thirty. Work at eight-thirty. The bed feels too large in the dark room, and he notices that Steph is missing.

At some point, he drifts off again as the sweat cools on his body, headache smoldering, limbs twitching. In the clutch of worsening tremors and cramps, Keith engages grim, bleary-eyed speculation in the dreamlike space between lucidity and torpor, watching as a new dawn slithers below his bedroom curtains.

Memory lapses, slurred speech, stumbling, hallucinations . . . at times hallucinating even while conscious, stuck in some kind of daydream loop.

Knowing he needs more rest does not make its attainment any easier: the combined assaults of grotesque visions and nausea every time he closes his eyes make getting deep sleep illusive. The short, edgy naps he manages are not soothing, as he awakens every few minutes in terrified, clammy disarray: mind shattered, head throbbing, body weakened.

What did I read about that family in Italy?

In his research for work, he had learned about an unfortunate clan near Venice suffering from an incredibly rare neurological disorder called Fatal Familial Insomnia. An ancient disorder, F.F.I. had been recognized in the medical literature since at least the seventeenth century. There were indications that it was a hereditary disorder, as most of the sufferers were related to a prominent family from Venice, but the exact etiology had yet to be deduced. Other theories—heavy-metal toxicity, radiation, poisoning, and so on—had been ruled out.

Family members stricken with the illness progressively slept less and less, until sleep completely disappeared from their world. The presentation was terrifying, with elements of Parkinsonism, Creutzfeldt-Jakob, Alzheimer's, and Lou Gehrig's Disease. Eventually they arrived at a point where they were no longer able to block the intrusions of wakeful perception, their intellectual hold diluted to nothing. The process went on for month after agonizing month.

Distal twitching of the extremities was the first somatic indicator, as the fine motor skills vanished; then less complex skills succumbed, such as the ability to walk. In the end their minds imploded into mushy dementia—humanity stripped away thought by thought, memory by memory, moment by moment. A few weeks into the process, the most alarming symptom was manifested: uncontrollable, ceaseless "laughing"—a pseudo-bulbar affect—that continued day and night. The psychotic peals of "laughter," fed inadvertently by the ventilator, went on unabated until the patients finally died, by then unable even to close their eyes. Ultimately, victims lost all sensibility, ceasing to remember friends, relatives, anything. Without artificial intervention the afflicted in due course starved to death or died from a buildup of carbon monoxide in the blood as the ability to breathe diminished and the machines failed to meet their needs.

Finally, they just gazed ahead, unable to move, swallow, or even breathe on their own. Constantly awake, yet oblivious. Why does it attack some family members and not others? Is there some environmental trigger? Some tiny break in the body's defenses?

Sometimes—mercifully—the heart stopped: unable to rest and repair itself during sleep, it simply gave out. F.F.I. struck in the prime of life, usually between the ages of forty and fifty-five. It was incurable and always fatally irreversible once it began; treatment was only palliative.

I don't want to go out that way, but it feels as if it's already happening. I'm feeble, jumpy, my heartbeat is erratic; the shaking and chorea are nearly constant. The headaches are getting worse, too—continuous and completely unaffected by analgesics. And the episodes are becoming more frequent, I think.

He takes a deep breath, a tear trickling from the corner of his eye.

I'll get some blood work done, a CT scan, an MRI. Maybe I have a tumor— a clot . . . Please not something worse, like F.F.I.! Neuros can only diagnose that kind of thing by exclusion, then they can't even help you. At least a tumor or clot they can operate on—really something when you pray for cancer or an embolism . . .

Keith decides.

7:03 A.M.

"Doctor Morrison? Yes. Yes—we need to talk." *He listens intently to the receiver.* "Okay, I'll be there soon. Thank you. 'Bye." *The phone is a dead weight in his trembling hand.*

I'm going insane.

Sweating, he gets up to dress.

"Steph, I'm going in for a bit—"

Keith winces at a sudden white-hot stab in his skull that momentarily blinds him. He feels at once displaced yet highly alert, as in the throes of some dissociative fugue state. As he crumbles stiffly to his knees, the room seems to warp, the space taking on other aspects, like his imaginings of the end of the world, or some desolate gray and black battlefield seen through a prism.

What's happening to me? Where am I?

"Steph?"

No answer.

"Steph?"

Darkness closes in as tinny whirring begins to flower in the awareness behind his eyes. From the far end of the house, the last thing he hears are Steph's footfalls as she runs to him.

V

"Hmmm." Dr. Morrison scrawled something down in his notebook.

Keith stared disconsolately at the ceiling, still clad in his overcoat. "I just want them to stop, Doc. Just . . . stop. The prescriptions aren't working." He sighed, eyes shining with tears. He touched his forehead with a pale, shaky hand; he felt better once out of the house. The drive over had cleared his mind.

That, and the incident with Steph as he was leaving.

"Doctor Vincent, I'm not sure what else we can do here."

In the background, the hum of Morrison's office refrigerator took on a darker, more ominous tone. From the psychiatrist's large bay windows, Keith could see that a storm was rolling in across the plains. The sky had changed from light clouds under bright sun to a curious shade of deep burgundy. Far off, Keith noticed glimmers of lightning. The sound of the fridge merged with a deep roll of thunder; the temperature in the room dropped as darkness rushed past the building.

<*My Chernobyl. Take him!*> she cooed into his mind. <*Take him . . . and* release *me.*>

Keith unleashed a bloodcurdling scream, grasping his head as he convulsed in seizure on the couch. As Dr. Morrison leapt to his aid, a horde of insects crashed through the windows, the metallic grating of their wings drowning out thought, drowning out reason, drowning out reality.

On the last day of humanity, a man sat laughing at the edge of pandemonium.

The man considered his loneliness and the totally unexpected collection of open sores all over his body. The psyche-crushing pressure in his skull was beginning to subside. As he meditated, slowly reclaiming order at last, the individual tortured an alien creature with his cruel, dirt-encrusted fingernails. Finally it simply ruptured: viscera morphing into fat, gray worms that slinked into the blood-frothed nasal passages of a freshly decapitated head skewered through the trachea on his other hand.

"First spacing, second spacing, third spacing: that's the problem with extreme amplification—one never knows the best moment to *arrest* it," *he said, his voice dry, raspy.*

Another dark star fell from the sky, reflected in the wet eyes that still bulged obscenely from the shocked face of the head. A flaccid purple tongue flopped from the drooling mouth in quiet retort.

Grinning at the head, feeling better as discipline returned to his physique and calmness snuffed the inferno in his brain, the man comprehended the secret to controlling his condition now. Understanding how to resolve the tension that caused his migraines and shaking was such liberation; he felt the release start as soon as he had bitten the other man's head off, arteries constricting like gravid snakes, warmly showering him with jets of crimson. "Acting on my negative impulses instead of suppressing them gives me such . . . *relief* from the pain and discomfort. Starting at the end is always instructive, I think."

At last this being, formerly Dr. Keith Vincent, said: "I love it when a plan comes together. Doctor Iwane would have *adored* my revelations—and I know Kneale will appreciate that it's time to go to double-blind testing, then patents, real-world trials, and final application, huh, Doc? It's time *everyone* shares what we have to offer!"

Morrison's speared countenance gawked up silently, the faded eyes focused somewhere beyond.

OUT OF THEIR HEADS

Reflections on Revolution and Other Strange Fates

Prologue: The Daimon

[A blackened theater. The whole stage is dressed in black. As the audience settles, offstage we detect the soft rise of strange, ambient sounds: industrial moans and the distant whining of machinery. As the noises build in intensity and loudness, they are drowned out by the terrifying melancholy blast of a dark horn that then ebbs into silence.

After a moment, a deep male voice, the Narrator, intones dryly in the darkness over the sound system:]

Where are Marie, Muhammad, Leonard, John, Medusa, and the rest?
The royal, the pious, the warrior, the saint, the monster, the dispossessed?
Gone, all gone; all casualties of The Daimon.

One was executed,
One killed himself;
One was murdered,
One was martyred,
One was a myth, and
One fell from social grace—
Gone, all gone; all victims, victims—in one way or another—of The Daimon.

[In the depths of the stage, black lights dimly illuminate its recesses, giving a three-dimensional aspect to the scene, which is painted with intricate patterns, signs, sigils, and symbols from all eras and civilizations in fluorescent hues of blue, green, red, orange. Projected onto a black scrim in the background, quick flashes of colored

light intercut with murky images in black & white and color treatments of footage from executions, war-time atrocities, crime scenes.

These continue playing, increasing in frenzy as the Narrator continues:]

They were created, in turn, from war, pettiness, and
religious hatred,
the aimless progeny of that hateful marriage—
Gone, all gone; all casualties of The Daimon.

Where is the compassionate provocateur?
The thoughtful dissenter?
Able to oust the despot and the tyrannical,
not with weapons, technology, or greed,
but with unselfish action and mercy?

Lo! He blusters of times past and virtues olden,
of the ways of Man before scientific deadening,
and an imaginary simplicity
which likely never truly existed.

[The projections continue, and the ambient noises gradually return, both increasing in intensity until another great bellow of the dark horn intones. It fades and sounds again; after it fades a second time, it blasts once more, this time accompanied by the appearance of a bloody red spotlight that shines on the lone figure of a woman clad provocatively in exotic lingerie. Her eyes are closed, and she is squatting center stage. Slowly she rises, unfurling her arms, stretching as if from a long sleep. She looks around; very slowly the light begins to shift colors along the spectrum, as though reflecting her emotional state. After a few more beats, she looks at the audience and speaks, though never identifying herself.

This will be the pattern: the spotlight will cut off as one soliloquy ends and another begins, then reappear on a different part of the stage, gradually shifting its color as the character speaks. There are no other sounds. As the last few words of a character end, the first few words of the next one will overlap them. Their attire will reflect their role in life as well as mirror their respective fates.]

Marie Antoinette

(*red*)

It has been alleged
that my greatest mistake
was I supposedly said:
"Let them eat cake."

When I was rushed to my trial,
I accepted the situation with stoic grace;
then the verdict was read, my appeals ending in denial;
at that point, I resigned myself to my gruesome fate.

Later, as the hordes jeered at me,
I felt a strange surge of power;
I would never yield my spirit, or dignity,
to Guillotin's bloody tower.

Finally, as red gushed fresh on the wooden scaffold,
and the executioner at last presented my head,
to the throng I smiled from the headsman's pole—
I had won the battle, though I was now quite dead.

In truth, what did it really matter?
This was a new beginning, for me, in the end;
as France collapsed in convulsive tatters,
I was happy to leave the madness for others, by then.

Muhammad
(*light blue*)

I was once like you—
I thought the world
was my oyster;
that I would always be free
to do as I pleased.

That was before the
ghettos, the discrimination—
before I was cloistered
by someone else's God,
not the one true Allah.

I lived the Five Pillars;
I avoided the women
and dedicated myself to the cause.
I came to understand the evils of the West
and humbled myself to the Prophet's laws.

For me, a modest servant,
jihad was the final test.
Like a salve cleansing my soul,
I recited the *Qur'an*
and made my suicide vest.

Strolling into the market
on a glorious fall day,
I raised my hands to the sky,
then turned to Mecca
and began loudly to pray.

Faces etched with shock and awe,
a crowd gathered to watch;
I knew the time was upon me

to show believers the duty of Islam
And inform the *kuffār* of the power I'd gained from the *Kaaba*.

I pulled the detonation cord,
shouting verses from the *Hadith*,
and exploded into the crowd.
The world changed as my head left my body,
and in the confusion after my death—
the landscape charred and without sound—
I knew I had conquered sin
and could now join my namesake—the Prophet . . .

Peace be upon him!

Sgt. Leonard Siffleet

(*orange*)

Pattiwal, Reharing, and I
were wrapping things up—
we had completed our work—
and were determined to meet with the Dutch.

Deep in the junglescape
we were ambushed—
by a hundred native villagers—
near the old town of Aitape.

We fought hard but were overtaken;
after a time, we were turned over to the Japanese.
Two weeks of torture and interrogation followed
before we were moved to Aitape Beach.

In the hell of October—1943
under the blazing Southern Hemisphere's summer sun,
we were sentenced to die by the Imperial Japanese;
our trio was forced to its knees by the occupying Daimon fleet.

My thoughts circled back to my beloved, Miss Clarice Lane,
while Officer Yasuno Chikao prepared his Katanga hand;
bound and blindfolded, I made peace with my fate.
After the sentence was carried out, decapitation,
my final impressions were the deaths of my mates,
my face pressed into the bloody sand.

My comrades and I were executed as prisoners of war,
and before I died, I realized a final irony—
we had survived this strange world of headhunters and cannibals before
finally losing our lives to the savages *invading* Papua New Guinea.

John the Baptist
(*dark green*)

Foretelling the rise of Christ—
The Way I was destined to reveal—
this was my apparent crime
and my earthly purpose,
as well as the source of my continuing appeal.

Perhaps it is a blessing,
my martyrdom tale;
perhaps there is here some lesson—
that the flesh may be forgotten,
yet the story will prevail.

With my right hand
I baptized Jesus of Galilee;
with my left I defied Herod the King.
Though a man of peace, I was imprisoned;
after her exotic dance, I was
made a plaything of the girl, Salomé.

On her mother's advice
she requested me dead,
and the king obliged her on the matter;
at his birthday festivities they presented my head:
Eyes wide, stump oozing on a platter.

Medusa

(yellow)

Once upon a time, I was a beauty great;
the lustful act of Poseidon, my rape,
doomed us all: my sisters, Euryale, Stheno, me,
promptly sealing our fates.

Though not our fault, jealous Athena punished us;
our bodies were burdened by clicking brass hands,
dripping fangs, and heads adorned with snakes;
men feared us—from the olive-fruiting land,
to blind Homer's wine-dark sea,
and we were forced to subsist on a bitter diet of vengeance, hate, and
ennui.

Finally did Perseus emerge to change history's course;
we fought, and he was a competitor fierce,
who only won my head through cunning and deceit.
The end of my woes and the beginning of theirs
was my defeat;
as all good sisters do, they bemoaned my murder and cursed the gods,
whose peculiar sense of justice was not only unfair,
but also terribly incomplete.

Anonymous
(*purple*)

One day, they might find me.

A jogger playing "Psycho Killer" on their phone
could trip on the embankment,
revealing my yellowy, moss-covered skull;
or a rock hound may unearth
my mortal remains, providing my silently screaming head
a morbid rebirth.

By then, my old bones
may appear long mute;
yet to the right people, they can speak—
even silently protest—
the rapist safely home,
the murderer still free.

The police will arrive,
rubbing their chins,
combing through Missing Persons files,
using science to explore every aspect
of when and how I might have died—
from the hatchet marks on shattered ribs to my uncanny grin.

Of course, they will never understand
what actually sealed my fate and thus assured my doom,
or the pain, as a marginalized member of our cold society, I endured at
the madman's grasping hands
before he buried me alive in my dank and lonesome tomb.

Their enthusiasm will fade
after a period of time;
next to other victims in numbered cardboard boxes
will I eventually reside,

as new horrors siphon time and attention away;
Ultimately destined to be just another unknown casualty
Of the Daimon's ravenous, unflinching blade.

[*Another blast of the dark horn sounds and the stage goes black.*]

Intermission: The Daimon Redux

[*Offstage we sense the soft rise of the weird, ambient noises: industrial groans and the cold droning of equipment. As the sounds build, they are drowned out by the chillingly miserable boom of the dark horn which then recedes into silence.*

After a moment, the Narrator utters once more in the darkness over the sound system:]

And where are Sir Walter, Daniel, Fritz, Russell, the medical victim,
the contestant?
The adventurer, the mighty heart, the killer, the athlete, the innocent,
the fool?
Gone, all gone; all casualties of The Daimon.

One died as a spy,
One of terrorism;
One was killed by society,
One by accident,
One by science, and
One for sport—
Gone, all gone; all victims, victims—in one way or another—of The
Daimon.

[*In the depths of the stage, black lights dimly irradiate its recesses, painted with intricate patterns, signs, sigils, and symbols from all eras and civilizations in fluorescent hues of blue, green, red, orange. Projected onto a black scrim in the background, the quick flashes of colored light intercut with murky images in black-and-white and color treatments of footage from executions, wartime atrocities, and crime scenes return.*

These continue playing, increasing in frenzy as the Narrator continues:]

They were created, in turn, by vanity, evil, and
social ennui,
the aimless progeny of those terrible legacies—
Gone, all gone; all casualties of The Daimon.

Where is the compassionate provocateur?
The thoughtful dissenter?
Able to oust the merciless and the cruel,
not with anger, shock, or belief,
but with unselfish action and mercy?

Lo! Again he blusters of times past and virtues olden,
of the ways of Man before scientific deadening,
and an imaginary simplicity
which likely never truly existed.

[*The projections continue and the ambient noises gradually return, both increasing in intensity until another great peal of the dark horn dark horn resounds. It fades and moans again; after it dissipates, it sounds for a third time, this last accompanied by the appearance of a bloody red spotlight that shines on the lone figure of a bearded man wearing the ragged clothes of a fallen aristocrat. His eyes are closed, and he is squatting center stage. Slowly he rises, expanding his arms, stretching as if from a long slumber. He looks around, bewildered; very subtly, the light begins to shift colors along the spectrum, as though reflecting his mood. After a few more beats, he looks at the audience and speaks, though never identifying himself.*

Again, a spotlight will cut off as one soliloquy ends and another begins, then reappear on a different part of the stage, gradually shifting its color as the character speaks. There are no other sounds. As the last few words of a character end, the first few words of the next one will overlap them. Their attire will reflect their role in life, as well as mirror their respective fates.]

Sir Walter Raleigh
(*red*)

"Strike, man, strike!"
And the heavy blow
did follow.
The crowd watched, aghast,
as the preening headsman posed,
crudely displaying my noggin
as he leaned upon his axe.

Still, my greater influence stands;
I established the Crown in early America,
though I never set foot on its shore,
by funding the Lost Colony of Roanoke
in North Carolina land.

Later I was sentenced to die,
though most doubted my guilt;
many years passed before it was revealed
that I undoubtedly *was* a spy.
I had been a celebrity once—
An advocate for El Dorado—
but perhaps my best known legacy
remains popularizing tobacco!

Daniel Pearl

(*dark blue*)

In a still, occupied room—
whether at a funeral mass or in an instant of quiet reflection—
frozen in these moments
of regret, gratitude, or contemplation,
we are released from anxiety and absolved of our sins,
and there is yet unseen movement:
our mighty hearts beating within.
Because I was born Jewish,
it was decided I could not live.
In fact, I would be made a symbol,
for a cause I never believed in.
Forced to comply
with my captors' bloody vision,
I would die as I lived—
steeped in faith, and loved—
passively defying the goals of their mission,
even as they spilled my blood.

In a tiny room in Pakistan,
They severed my head,
thus bringing to fruition my rendezvous with fate.
My murder exposed the depths of their zealotry,
But the effect was to be surprising:
Rather than give in to hate,
I found internal acceptance,
showing grace against brutality,
strength in death's face.

Like David before me,
this Jewish son,
father, husband,
found his inner peace and calm—

And my tormentors were eventually winked out, one by one.

Fritz Haarmann
(*light green*)

I was never right.

In darkness did I commit
such wonderful atrocities;
I never knew compassion:
in fact, I scorned pity.

My kind had no handle then,
in the 1930s;
we were simply mad, depraved, perverted,
and poorly understood—
not that the "why" really matters . . .

I was simply a pioneer,
in a sense,
of the postmodern blight
yet to come—
along with my idol, saucy Jack,
I would become just another
predator cleaning the streets of scum,
doing my part to make society atone
for all the harm inflicted upon me,
whether at my work or at home.

Parting with my head on the infernal machine
was simply one last thrill;
The ultimate experience for those,
Like me,
who were born to kill.

Russell Phillips
(*white*)

Bright blurs of color,
the roar of engines—
a sense of victory
rising as the crowd thunders and
squealing tires spin.

Then it happened:
in a flash,
on the 17th lap,
Steven Howard
forced my car against
the retaining wall fence;
in seconds it was over.

As my car came to rest
on the track,
the world then bore witness
to the gruesome aftermath.

The roof of the car had
peeled away;
my body parts littered the track.
The race was stopped,
and they finally recovered my helmeted head
at the entrance
to the pit stop bay.

Subject #567-P_HT13
(multicolored flashes *of light)*

[*NOTE: Instead of a figure onstage, this will be done by showing the realistic effigy of a life-size monkey strapped in a chair, and will be voiced by a male offstage, though not the Narrator.*]

As recovered from the subject's brainwaves and stored in the records of Case Western Reserve University's School of Medicine in Cleveland, Ohio (March, 1970):

No word
fill the
HATE

Him:
doCTer ROBert J. WhiTe,
neuroSURgin

SHOCK face
Me cry
ME hurt

SEE
Me FAM'LY
cut, Cut, CUT

No MorE
FAM'LY

Things put BRAIN in
MAkE US
cHoke
point, LaUgh—the stud'nts

they SMASH our HEADS
haMMer
tool, write DoWn

DokTR WhitE
he SMILE
me drug . . .
DARK

WAKE
TuBEs MouTH
numb—
MAD

SKREEAM
DOCtr white
st'dnts write

ME
No FEEL
throat doWn

ME
SEE in Shiny thinG
Sister—
ME BODY
HER HEAD—

ME
KNOW
HER body
ME now!

ME NOW!

DocToR WHITE
DO EV'L

I NOT LIVE LONG . . .

i hope

Jennifer von Stuck
(*magenta*)

The perils were great
but my need was greater;
the game seemed like the answer
to all my prayers.

Of course, no one plans to lose
when they roll the dice—
mostly they take calculated risks
in hopes of a better life.

So was the situation for me
when the computer assistant said:
"You've been selected to appear as a contestant on
Never Bet the Devil Your Head."
It was the latest sensation on TV.

The bourgeois rage
of a cynical world—
a soulless symptom of our deadened age—
the ratings of each episode soared
as a lurid public yearned for the first casualty:
instead of riches undreamed,
consigned instead to an anonymous, terminal
destiny.

So well I performed,
night after night—
gaining confidence,
upping the stakes.
A week into the run,
ready to retire a champion,

on the final question
I uttered a single mistake . . .

and it all came undone.

As the astonished gasps
of the audience fade, my world implodes.
Dragged away as the newest contestant was announced,
no one heard my screams as my dreams were trounced.

A celebrated talking head no more,
I glimpse my body one final time,
broken and headless,
now sprawled across a dirty backroom floor.

[*A final wail of the dark horn sounds and the stage goes black.*]

And Finally, an Epilogue

[*Nighttime in a cemetery. Offstage, the howl of wind and the bellowing of thunder rises in the darkness; it continues to play in the background until noted otherwise. Fog snakes along the ground, winding between grimy crypts and worn-down grave markers. Dimly, two black shrouded figures can be made out, hunched over a low-slung mausoleum, each seated on ancient tree stumps. Their shadowed chins rest on pale, bony hands, illumined by a single candle flickering between them as they contemplate a chess board.*]

Left Figure [female]

You've been thinking for a *terribly* long while.

[*beat*]

Right Figure [male]

[*adagio*]

I don't want to rush; you know it's not my style.

Left Figure

[*laughs*]

I should think a thousand years is certainly enough!

Right Figure

Perhaps. But what is a thousand or so years to the soul? A millennium to those in love?

Left Figure

[*shifts impatiently on stump*]

Frankly, I'm beginning to lose my Will.

Right Figure

[*mildly irritated*]

These things require *Time*. You know I don't take action for cheap and simple thrills.

Left Figure

[*somewhat flustered*]

There's no Reason to be so *tart*—

Right Figure

[*reaching to touch a figure on the board*]

Just an observation. [*He moves the piece.*] Checkmate, the Human Heart.

Left Figure

[*clapping gently*]

Excellent play. I have you surrounded, though—you won't escape Beauty, Love, Compassion, or Truth. These should be able to keep you at bay . . .

Right Figure

[*raising hand to silence the discussion*]

Perhaps. But you forget I still have Evil, Hate, Dread, Death. And, of course, the gracious languor of Decay . . .

[*wryly laughs*] Have you trapped me? We shall see . . .

Left Figure

[*laughs and clasps the other's hand*]

True enough, *mon ami*—

[*The candle suddenly extinguishes and the stage goes silent and dark.*

The Narrator speaks over the sound system in the inky blackness of the theater.]

At the close of Day,
so far from Dawn,
Night creeps forth,
covering all wrongs.

So the world spins,
uncaring and unmoved
by the efforts of the just,
or the escalating burdens of collective
Sin.

Under the callous gaze
of a faraway moon—
which mourns no loss

silvering Time's fragile loom—
do rich and poor weep and pray
at distant suns and indifferent gods
which give no favor
and are oblivious of Fate.

Now it can be told—
the full story of cowardice,
the foolishness of the bold—
and how they are
Gone, all gone; all casualties of The Daimon.

Where now resides
The quiet man of thought?
The woman of caring heart?
The yearning child, luminous?
The apostolic kin, numinous?
Gone, all gone; all victims, victims—in one way or another—of The
Daimon.

They failed to oust the dictators,
abandoned all their Hopes;
left behind their high Ideals
to swing at the ends of ropes;
some perished by natural means,
or were crushed by legal wheels;
more were undone by the jealous machinations
of petty tyrants and faithless popes.

Gone, all gone; all victims, victims—in one way or another—of The
Daimon.

[*On the final word, the Narrator's voice reverberates into the infinite darkness.*

Very gradually, the entire stage is bathed in dark red spotlights. Curtain closes.]

—To the memory of Edgar Lee Masters

NOTES

Confessional Preamble

As I touched upon in the Preface, people are naturally curious about influences in anyone's work artistically. I tend to wear mine openly and really do enjoy revisiting the best of them (some are better off buried, I suspect, in the graveyard of nostalgia). Since I work in a variety of disciplines other than writing (art, filmmaking, editing, music, design, and so on), I have a wide assortment of people and interests I draw inspiration from, whether in the mediums of visual and performing art, literature, or film and TV. The following story analyses are not meant to be exhaustive, nor the only interpretation, but this is the way I viewed the stories as I was writing them. I can't (or won't) give everything away, and there are numerous allusions and symbols encoded within all my works of a personal and esoteric nature; these are revealed upon deeper scrutiny, but that is best left to the subconscious, I feel (or perhaps to unusually perceptive critics). I'm sure there are things that even I don't put together on a purely cognitive level, but are apparent to others who are not as close to the source material. In addition, like all artistic efforts, writings can mean different things to different people, and alternative understandings (conscious and unconscious) will present themselves over time, and under evolving circumstances. I am always keen on seeing the ways in which other people filter and reinterpret my efforts, whether visual, sonic, filmic, or literary, just as I do with the works of others.

With all that in mind, I admit that I am not a real television enthusiast, though I do adore some of the classics—*The Twilight Zone, The X-Files, Star Trek, Space 1999, Twin Peaks, Night Gallery,* and the like—and I also quite enjoy more recent fare such as *Penny Dreadful, Fear the Walking Dead, Stranger Things, Game of Thrones,* and *American Horror Story.*

We (my wife Sunni and I) tend to eschew sitcoms and reality shows, with a few exceptions, such as the SFX-related *Face Off* and the incredibly subversive *Chappelle's Show.*

Film, of course, is a bit of a different matter, though related (referring to TV, radio, and the Internet, what we would term the modern "mass media"). My wife and I completed two documentaries directly related to writing and popular culture—*Charles Beaumont: The Short Life of Twilight Zone's Magic Man* (2010) and *The AckerMonster Chronicles!* (2012); the latter went on to win the Rondo Hatton Classic Horror Award for Best Documentary in 2014. We are working on a few other films, one of which I detail later. Therefore, as a cineaste and filmmaker, I have an enormous array of filmic loves, far too many to list, but it includes everything from documentaries to avant-garde to auteur to comedy to science fiction to straight-out splatter flicks. The zenith of American film achievement in my estimation occurred between (roughly) the early 1950s to the mid-1990s: It has never been equaled. Filmmakers who have left their mark on me include the late Dan O'Bannon (a friend and mentor), David Cronenberg, George A. Romero, Alfred Hitchcock, Luis Buñuel, Stan Brakhage, Roger Corman, Oliver Stone, John Carpenter, and David Lynch. I do have many foreign favorites, too, and nurture a great fondness for the original 1954 *Godzilla* (sans Raymond Burr), as well as the output of Akira Kurosawa, Dario Argento, and so many others. Much of this I cover in my nonfiction book, *Disorders of Magnitude: A Survey of Dark Fantasy* (Rowman & Littlefield, 2014), which allowed me the room to stretch out and analyze various other creators and their output (I plan to update it in the not-too-distant future and augment the contents to include more film criticism, as well as expand the scope of the work to delve into the richness of non-Western literature, music, and cinema).

In light of these things, it amazes me that much of what I write has been more informed by music than actual visual/cinematic considerations (to include the themes and soundtracks for the shows and films I like). Music is a prime force of creation for me (possibly due to its twin emotional/nebulous dynamism), and I must have it on all the time when editing, writing, or doing visual art (anything, really). I generally have some notion of the "mental soundtrack" that my stories (or visual art) have as they move from scene to scene. It adds a complexity to my personal writing rituals that I hope augments the reading experience later. I relate to words and music in very strange terms as well due to my synesthesia, so perhaps that is something readers feel as they read the stories and, I hope, enjoy them. I list several of my musical influences in the notes about "The Man with the Horn," so I will avoid repeating myself here.

With respect to design and painting or sculpting, I love the work of all kinds of artists and artforms from all over the world, including shunga, traditional Native American, caricatures/political cartoons, Renaissance/Spanish/Old Dutch Masters, comic books (especially the EC Comics stable and later the Warren horror titles), photography, Cubist, Soft Sculpture, the Vienna School of Fantastic Realism, Impressionism, Expressionism, Surrealism, Dada, Wolfgang Grässe, Zdzisław Beksiński, Arnold Böcklin, Vesalius, Picasso, Matisse, Leonardo da Vinci, Michelangelo, Rodin, Monet, Vincent van Gogh, Diane Arbus, Francis Bacon, H. R. Giger, Minor White, Helmut Newton, et al. They also greatly affect my literary output. In fact, I share a birthday with Sandro Botticelli (March 1), whose work resonates strongly with me. Sunni and I have actually completed a documentary, titled *Image, Reflection, Shadow: Artists of the Fantastic* (2017), dealing with the iconographic syntax of visual imagery from Hieronymus Bosch and Pieter Bruegel the Elder to the present, including modern masters such as Salvador Dalí and featuring interviews with Giger, Ernst Fuchs, Alex Grey, and many more. I was an artist first (my father—who, in addition to being a writer, was an oil painter and graphic designer—encouraged me). Before I could precisely articulate my thoughts in writing, likely due to my dyslexia, this allowed me to express myself. Art is my first true creative love: all else follows.

However, the written word has a power to provoke an actual mind linkage between individuals. My printed work has a variety of concerns: post-9/11 anxieties, my youth in the 1970s and '80s, (black) humor, meta-/intertextual experimentation, (body) horror, Magical Realism (my Bram Stoker–nominated anthology, *A Darke Phantastique: Encounters with the Uncanny and Other Magical Things* [Cycatrix Press, 2014], covered the intersection between horror and Magical Realism from a variety of perspectives), literary realism, nihilism, existential concerns, science fiction, satire/parody, minimalism, poetry, the gulf/overlap between good and evil, fear, wonderment, comprehension of the self/other, absurdism, poetry, Weirdity, befuddlement . . . Favorite authors would have to include Jorge Luis Borges, H. P. Lovecraft, Franz Kafka, Rod Serling, Georges Bataille, Kurt Vonnegut, William S. Burroughs, J. G. Ballard, George Orwell, Dante, John Milton, Mary Shelley, Percy Bysshe Shelley, Homer, Edgar Allan Poe, Alain Robbe-Grillet, Richard Selzer, William F. Nolan, Gabriel García Márquez, Ray Bradbury, George Clayton Johnson, Samuel Beckett, Charles Beaumont, Dennis Etchison, William Faulkner, Richard Matheson, Emily Dickinson, William Shakespeare, and many, many more.

I look at this book as an expansion and refinement of the themes, preoccupations, and conceptions I began in my first Hippocampus Press collection, *Simulacrum and Other Possible Realities* (2013)—notions that I will advance again in my third collection, currently being composed, entitled *Grotteschi: Further Explorations of the Kafkaesque.* Indeed, two of the stories herein are directly linked to two others from that initial volume: "The Shadow of Heaven" (covered in more detail later) is a standalone sequel to my novella *Milton's Children,* and "Unity of Affect" is tied in a parallel way to the novella *Simulacrum.* Of course, most of my stories are connected together in some fashion (to observant readers), and one tale in this book is a prequel ("The Dark Sea Within") to another ("The Man with the Horn"). These interlinking aspects represent not only a subtextual continuum of thought, but also, in many cases, characters, events, places, or circumstances.

Preface / Ode to an Old Friend

This is a true story, as stated in the piece: a bit of macabre memoir, if you will. I feel that it captures the flavor of my strange upbringing while at the same time showing one can maintain a sense of the absurd (and humor) even with respect to such lofty antics as "writing weird (or some other) literature."

I deeply miss my father and stepmother. Maybe this goes a way toward explaining why . . . we shared many such incidents as this.

The Dark Sea Within

"A book must be the ax for the frozen sea within us." This quotation, from Franz Kafka, was the inspirational starting point for the ideas in this story. The account itself is operating on a few levels; one is as a Christmas story, another as a New Year's Eve adventure. As noted, it is a prequel to "The Man with the Horn" (though it was written more than a year later) and deals quite specifically with the art world and the corruption therein due to the influence of large sums of money (though "art" could be a substitute in this case for religion, politics, business more generally, and so on).

Also, this is a story about transformation: from poor to rich, alive to dead, human to other, honest to unethical. It contains very much an element of body horror, lust (in multiple ways), and sexual enthrall-ment, and plays on primal fears of deformity, defilement, maiming, and torture (which can at times start in the mind and be directed ulti-mately outward). There is no true aspect of hope in this tale, which is actually a feature of my more serious efforts.

The Man with the Horn

I dreamed this story in its entirety (though I drafted it by hand by the light of our car's overhead interior lamp as my wife Sunni was driving us back from a trip to Los Angeles with William F. Nolan in the back seat). It is a story about many things: regret, mourning, being alienated, being forgotten or washed away by the passage of time and the flow of history. I feel it is one of my strongest works (it was the original title of this collection). This story begins a cycle for me (continued in this vol-ume by "The Dark Sea Within" but not finished *in toto,* as I have other ideas in mind for this strange brownstone in New York City; in fact, another one is in this volume). It is also, in part, my homage to musical creation. I have dabbled with treatments of the arts before in other stories: in my previous collection, "The Central Coast" (which I later adapted for a short film) is about filmmaking and acting (though in the porn world), and I deal with creating visual art in "What the Dead's Eyes Behold" in the same book. I also tackle virtual reality and the videogame industry respectively in my other collection in *Simulacrum* and in "Unity of Affect" in this book.

One thing that greatly interests me about this story is how closely it is tied to music and psycholinguistics (the aspect of literary cadences and rhythms being a musical consideration, which I strive for in all my writing). Sure, other stories work in that domain as well, but this was my take. Personally, I love all types of music and have owned a vast LP/CD collection in the past (more than 3000 records at one point, in addition to 500-plus compact discs/tapes). My tastes encompass world music, pop, funk, R&B, disco, punk, blues, jazz (of all varieties), live bootlegs, classic country, noise/industrial, ambient music and soundtracks, and classical composers, as well as many mainstream and avant-garde acts, to include Yes, Stevie Wonder, David Bowie, King Crimson, The Beatles, NoMeansNo, The Clash, Glenn Branca, Metallica, Black Sabbath, Schoolly D, Living Colour, Sir Peter Maxwell Davies, Brian Eno, Motown, Philip Glass, Last Exit, Sonny Sharrock, Steve Reich, Waylon Jennings, Earth, Wind & Fire, Don McLean, Paul Simon, *African Sanctus,* Peter Hammill, The Bee Gees, Pink Floyd, Jamaaladeen Tacuma, Willie Nelson, Johnny Cash, Linda Ronstadt, Cream, Throbbing Gristle, Shostakovich, Carly Simon, Kronos Quartet, Naked City, Elvis, Chrome, Hawkwind, Queen, John Coltrane, Mahavishnu, Frank Zappa, Danny Gatton, The Police, Steely Dan, The 13th Floor Elevators (my adoptive father's [drummer/arranger Danny Thomas] old band), Frank Sinatra, Segovia, Beethoven, Mozart, Madonna, Peter Gabriel, Rush, Jimi Hendrix, and so on.

As a musician myself (multi-instrumentalist, composer/lyricist, and singer; I had a progressive rock band [ChiaroscurO] for more than five years, way back when), I wanted to explore various aspects of the characters inside and outside the music world, but not by sacrificing the mystery of their indirect form of communication (music being non-verbal and ethereal). There is a lot at work in this tale; the title alone references three separate items (T. E. D. Klein, Miles Davis, and the strange character of Mr. Trinity himself). I was intrigued as well with a treatment of Colin Wilson's conception of the Outsider, and how one would react to such a being if they genuinely *were* outré. It also serves as a meditative study about loss, grief, and sadness. I feel for the woman in this story, because I've been there.

Armageddon

Mainly, I feel this is pretty much how folks conduct their lives: oblivious and in denial. Then, one day, they realize how much more they could have done, either to help themselves or others. By then, it's usually too late.

Transposition

Here we have what I feel is a rather straightforward yarn of medical mayhem and corruption, while at the same time being my subtle take on Robert W. Chambers's classic *The King in Yellow*. I had the germ of this story for more than ten years, and I quite like the more gruesome aspects of it, as well as the *Frankenstein*-like questions raised by the convergence of technology and medicine. The interplay between the conflicted doctor's love for his brother and his own misguided, mushy ethical boundaries is compelling, I feel. Additionally, it is interesting that the protagonist *is* a doctor with these moral issues; too often in most modern "realist fiction," the anti-hero is a down-and-outer: drug dealer, prostitute, other degenerate. It has become a cliché. Here we have a person who has been beaten down (by his own mistakes and hubris, of course), lost his way, and has given in to corruption and abuse of power/station in life (though earned).

In other words, there is potentially a lot more damage an unethical doctor or lawyer (my lawyer tale is in my first collection and is entitled "The Hex Factor"; it is also my witch/monster mashup) could unleash in reality than some marginalized member of society (as F. Paul Wilson and the late Karl Edward Wagner, both doctors, underscore in some of their output), so I thought it made for a curious treatment of character. (I was interested in becoming a doctor at one point.) Granted, my approach to the literary subject matter is perhaps lacking in awe and reverence for the Chambers work (which I like well enough, as it happens), and therefore not for purists, but I usually find purists of any type to be singularly stuffy, boring, and pretentious.

So there!

Memento Mori

I was initially contacted by the publisher/editor Barry Hoffman of Gauntlet Press to co-write this with my friend Bill Nolan. Once the story was completed, the publisher wrote back saying that no one had taken this approach—a blending of the "literary" and the possible supernatural—in the book, and he thought it was quite good (the book is comprised of World War II stories in tribute to another mutual friend, the late Richard Matheson). The exploration of aging (especially the loss of one's mind—one's identity and autonomy—to the process of disease) and war (the potential loss of one's senses or limbs—a physical mirroring in the youthful body of the mind's possible ruination in the years to come in this case) was fertile territory to examine. In the end, Nolan assisted with the original, but insisted that I run my version in my next collection. Therefore, herein I present my version with Nolan's bits removed. The ending is an homage to *The Wizard of Oz*.

A Carcass, Waiting

Quite what I believe: we may strive for much, but ultimately we are all equal in the end.

The Shadow of Heaven

In my previous collection, *Simulacrum and Other Possible Realities,* I included a novella entitled *Milton's Children* (a reprint of the Bad Moon Books edition of the same year, where it was published as a standalone volume in paperback and hardcover). This was a very well-received work (for which I'm grateful), and I had many thoughts about how to take the ideas (including elements of John Carpenter's *The Thing,* Poe, Lovecraft, and Arthur Conan Doyle) within it much further. As a result, when I was invited into a new anthology by S. T. Joshi called *Searchers After Horror* (Fedogan & Bremer, 2014), I was excited to explore these notions in a follow-up account, which I had already plotted.

As the deadline loomed, I was hard pressed to finish the story. I had been under several stresses that had prevented me from writing even a single word of the draft. As a result, on the way to the 2012 Nebula Awards in San Jose, California (Sunni, Bill Nolan, and I drove to this shindig from our homes in Vancouver, Washington), I once again wrote the entire story in the car (in longhand, as I do at times). Later that day, I was able to type it into the computer and polish it before submitting a draft to Joshi. A couple days passed before Joshi finally accepted the story. Later, this piece went through several revisions and expansions with the publisher, Dennis Weiler (a patient and nice fellow, thankfully), and arrived in its present form.

As it stands, the two stories are a unit and are now the foundation for a wild cosmic horror/science fiction novel (fused with other politically subtextual ideas I have), tentatively called *The Ascent of Darkness,* which will hopefully be out in 2018. Another story in this collection will figure in the larger work, as well: "Chrysalis" (see notes later).

Fallen: A Lament and Affirmation

This was an idea that presented itself almost fully formed. As a reader of Dante and Milton, I felt that Satan had been given a bad rap. Consequently, I thought that this was an opportunity to do this from the much-maligned POV of Old Scratch himself. It was fun to blend the ancient with the scientific (as in the speed of light, referenced in the poem, and contrasted with Satan's biblical appellation as the Angel of Light). I myself am an atheist, but I can certainly understand the attraction/repulsion of this being with respect to human understanding. He's a part *of* us, even as he is apart *from* us, however one expresses that delineation.

Brood

The most Lovecraftian thing I have ever written and likely ever will write. When I was originally asked to contribute to the book where the story first appeared, the editor, a dear friend of ours, said that setting the tale near any large body of water was fine. That being the case, I sent a pitch for a story I had been nursing in the back of mind for some time regarding the Outer Banks of North Carolina (one of my favorite places, and a natural for a Pisces and native North Carolinian like me). It was approved.

During the interval between my pitch and the final story, the scope of the book changed a bit: now all the stories had to be set in Lovecraft's Innsmouth. As a result, I needed to rewrite it; at the same time, I really liked my concept involving the Outer Banks. I managed to incorporate the vital bits I wanted in there, but the editor felt those pieces didn't work for her. She asked that I remove them, which I did, and she accepted the work.

When this collection began to form, I decided to reinstate the section I had to lose in the other version. I feel this is the definitive "Writer's Cut" of the story (to borrow a phrase from my buddy Dennis Etchison), and provides what I hope is a richer reading experience. For what it's worth, this is also my Halloween story, and my parable about the hidden dangers of nuclear power, loss of history, and pollution.

Verlassen

The title is a riddle and a message; the entire story is a subtle exploration of Bradburyesque and Ligottian ideas with the hypnagogic ambiance of a Southern Gothic nightmare (which is where my sensibilities reside as a

Southerner). The South is at once terrible and wonderful, steeped in horror, greatness, evil, and mystery—it was a wonderful place to grow up. In fact, I feel it is the one truly representative American experience, encompassing the origination of globally important musical forms (blues, jazz, gospel, country), food (due to the mélange of French, Spanish, English, Native American, and black influences), literature (Capote, Faulkner, O'Connor, Southern Gothic, and so on), performers (Elvis, Dolly Parton, Johnny Cash, et al.), and art (Romare Bearden and others). The South also sports unique weather and topography, and has long been a key part of the United States with respect to agriculture and commerce, which had a hand in developing its unusual and controversial social construction, politics, ambiance (including speech), and peoples (more integrated than any other part of the country by both blood and culture). Add to this cocktail its long, complex history (even before Europeans arrived), and it is easy to peg the area as the very definition, more than any other region, of the Great American Melting Pot.

With this in mind, I note that many of my stories have an introspective quality, and this one is no exception. It is a human story, but also concerned with monsters: in the guise of natural forces, but also supernatural and human ones. Effigies and the near-human are always spooky, edging into the "uncanny valley," though the context of a carnival (in this instance) grants a temporal acceptance; once juxtaposed with reality, suspension of disbelief crashes to the ground, and we are left with discomfort, if not outright fear—of the unknown, of the unknowable. In this case, the protagonist is searching for a scrap of personal meaning in a life of uncertainty (which is common to most of us, I'd wager). It is unclear as to whether he finds it, but the warning is the same: the pursuit of knowledge and the accumulation of wisdom can be dangerous. Be prepared to accept what you find, especially if it isn't what you hope will be the outcome.

Key

I have written many poems: more than 300, I would estimate. The majority of my early efforts were more formal verse (ballads, sonnets, haiku, and so on), but were wiped out in Hurricane Hugo when it hit Charlotte on September 21–22, 1989. My father and stepmother (I was staying with them at the time) were without power for weeks; all my artwork and papers were badly damaged by water from the torrential rainfall as the hurricane moved slowly up the Eastern Seaboard. This was one of the few from that era that I recall clearly. I was nineteen when Hugo hit, and most of the lost works were output from my juvenilia period until that point, which was a very productive time for me musically, artistically, and literarily. This was written from a memory of the lost original, after the storm, and is dated December 12, 1989.

A Darke Phantastique

This was another dream-inspired story, which is also concerned with the *power* of dreams in a metafictive sense. I worked the narrative over for some time to bring to it a sort of fabulist feel and tone. This is a creation myth story of sorts, as well as a non-linear García Márquez/Bradbury mashup. It is also, to my way of thinking, a story of hope, affirmation, transcendence, love, and redemption. It is a tale of connection, family, and the meaning of life (on one level). The creatures and the situation are surreal, but that is what elevates the ideas out of just straight horror "good-vs.-evil" trope territory. It is hard to define what is actually good or evil in the beginning, just as in real life sometimes: things are not always as they appear.

Chrysalis

Though this story is certainly indebted to the work of the late Messrs. Richard Matheson and Colin Wilson, it is also my sci-fi perspective on current geopolitical conundrums. I'll leave it to the reader to decide what I am referring to exactly, but I do feel that sometimes we can become something we despise by letting our personal blindness or biases twist our best intentions, thus coming to believe in our own innate goodness, thereby condemning others to being in a permanent state of "less than." As a result, we lose our humanity, our compassion, and we wind up being something approaching evil, even if we did not mean to do be at the outset. This is another warning story; I plan to expand it into a series of novels at some point, beginning with the aforementioned *The Ascent of Darkness*.

Dolls

Generally, I feel that people who are delving into this literary playground of "the weird" can be a bit hysterical, strained, overly serious. I suppose I take joy in popping the balloon of puffery when I can as a result (strictly for my own amusement, I add). The excessively earnest and "deep" are especially delicious targets, I feel. Sure, there is a time to be serious, but also a time to be less so. Some apparently missed this memo in their moody quest to be the grimmest of scribes (no disrespect intended). Lighten up, folks: this is just a bit of playful satire. If we can't laugh at ourselves, we're doomed. This is particularly amusing at readings, where I deliver it with edgy intensity (completely straight, of course).

Afterlife

Our good friend Nancy Kilpatrick was the co-editor (along with the charming Caro Soles) of the anthology wherein this story first appeared. She proposed to me the unusual idea of a three-way collaboration with William F. Nolan and my wife, Sunni (who is also a talented writer). Sunni was the one who had the great premise—Poe haunting himself, in a way, via the power of the written word—which is also a keen insight into the power of literature, personality, and remembrance (especially in the non-corporeal sense of the term). She did the first draft, I rewrote it and added some scenes, and Nolan provided a smattering of additional characterization. I love it and really like the idea of having E. A. Poe as a character in the work.

Windows, Mirrors, Doors

For sure, this is another Ligotti-influenced story, and by design with its puppets and doppelgängers. The structure here is unique and overtly literary in its self-conscious delivery: the three parts—past, present, and future—are written in their respective tenses to mirror this shift mentally. Again, quite a personal story of acceptance and loss (doorways, mazes, cracks/disfigurement); furthermore, it is a contemplation of what it means to be human, and what it is to "reflect" on things in the meditative sense, but as a literary device within the story's imagery as well. Marion's erstwhile profession as an actress is a part of this identity uncertainty. This is one of three stories in the book that are linked to a strange apartment building in New York City. I have others that will also fit into this world in mind. Additionally, the use of mirrors and labyrinths is a nod to Borges, a true master. The title is a play on words: The story's acronym is "WMD," which is what I think humans can often be to one another, and to themselves.

Colossi

This is a poem that began as a section of a song. I wrote the lyrics to an eighteen-minute opus called "The Tree of Woe" in the early 1990s for my band, ChiaroscurO; this was movement four of five. The other parts are interesting, but this reads the best as a standalone effort.

Double Feature

My homage to the 1970s. While a very nostalgic piece for me, it was a blast to write with all the giant monsters and such. Anyone who is acquainted with me will see some of my passions here: liberalism (in the JFK mold), atheism, family ties, vegetarianism/animal rights, and a deep identification with the misunderstood creatures of the earth (insects/arachnids, sharks, bats, rodents, and most especially amphibians and, my favorites as spotlighted in the story, reptiles). I also like the interaction between the father and his children; there are a lot of coded self-references in this tale. It's a romp, but also a cross-section of the era I call my formative home in part (the other being the early to mid-1980s). The research it took to pull this thing together was mindblowing: I read three books and did other fact-checking to establish the tone. As my wife Sunni was reading it for the first time, she was laughing out loud at some of the absurdity inherent in the scenario. Exactly what I wanted! And I think the dark tone at the very end is a nice juxtaposition. It has a rather bleak subtext, I feel (chief among them the idea that things beyond our control—whether famine, terrorism, natural disaster, or some more pedestrian horror such as disease, crime, or accident—can suddenly alter the course of our lives; also there's a certain element of cosmic indifference on display, that we're just collateral damage in a much larger scenario).

Unity of Affect

A related, parallel story to the novella *Simulacrum* from my previous collection, *Simulacrum and Other Possible Realities*. This is another take on what constitutes evil, and is related in spirit to some notions of Philip K. Dick and other science fiction writers, as well as the movies *They Live* and *Prince of Darkness*. The loss of the self in this context is precipitated by events from the *outside in* (overt actions on the part of the protagonist), as opposed to their genesis from the *inside out* (the betrayal of the body and mind from natural degeneration) as in "Memento Mori." This is also true of *Simulacrum*, which shares some of the same thematic preoccupations (governmental malfeasance, alternate/augmented realities, the quickening pace of technology v. the ability of humans and societies to assimilate it, and so on). I was experimenting with ways of relating the tale to the reader here by using videogame techniques of present tense and alternate narrative perspectives (such as the shared "we" experience) to drive the story, which also lends a cinematic quality to the account, I feel. Sartre was in my thoughts during the writing of this, as well as conflicting notions with respect to existentialism and immortality. The idea that a simulation of reality could begin to unravel *actual* reality is fascinating to me.

Epistles from Dis

This two-part story is one I have worked on for several years, beginning with the original idea in the late 1980s. This is a rather transgressive piece (at least certain aspects of it are), but I quite like that contrast with the medical elements. The bridge aside actually happened to my father: someone did drop a brick on his car from an overpass. He survived but was injured, though not permanently. And the smell of burning flesh is accurate; I've encountered it personally. This tale also has an interesting structure, as I chose to omit the typical (read: predictable by now) dystopian aspect of depicting the fall of society. Here we have the beginning of the horror shown *last*—in this case instigated by one individual, our "Protagonist Zero" in effect presented as explanation—with the far-future ramifications after civilization has recovered (more or less) used as an introduction to this world.

The fact is we don't really need the chaos of the middle, which has been covered ad nauseam at this point in nonfiction, film, and literature. For example, I find *The Stand* by Stephen King to be a boring book, so I definitely wanted to avoid that comparison, and to be sure other efforts have mined this same dystopic turf much better than King, such as Cormac McCarthy's *The Road*, Richard Matheson's *I Am Legend*, George A. Romero's *Night of the Living Dead* and its sequels, and the sublime masterpiece by Walter M. Miller, Jr., "Dark Benediction." I like to think of this novella as my paean to those stronger visions, and to J. G. Ballard's (personally) apocalyptic worldview by way of disease (herein: covetousness, not just the plague unleashed upon humanity). I suppose this is sort of my "zombie epic," also, although it is rooted in actual medical fact and history (and the "living dead" in this instance are not truly dead, but trapped more in "unlife"). I have another zombie idea proper, one that I hatched long ago with the dearly departed Dan O'Bannon (he also gave me great pointers and insight into the structure of a few other pieces, to include this one); I plan to finish it later in a story called "Proof of Death." The protagonist of the "Wormwood" section is based on a real person: the scientist who allegedly mailed the anthrax letters shortly after 9/11.

Additionally, my wife, Sunni, was instrumental in certain aspects of this story (in the "The Watch" segment), assisting me in dealing with a few key plot points. The result is a stronger work, I feel, so I certainly need to do a shout-out to her for the feedback.

Out of Their Heads: A Poem Cycle

Here I pay homage to the incredible *Spoon River Anthology* by the great Edgar Lee Masters. We studied this quite closely when I was involved in the theater scene, and it never left me. This is my take on the masterwork, as well as my own ghoulish twist on this form with updated social commentary. Poetry is a major part of my work, and this is one form of it I've always wanted to tackle. It morphed into a one-act play over the course of writing it, and is one of several such pieces I have written. I feel it ends the collection on a strong note.

I hope readers concur.

Acknowledgments

"Afterlife" (with Sunni K Brock and William F. Nolan), first published in *NEVERMORE!*, ed. Nancy Kilpatrick and Caro Soles (Edge Publishing, 2015).

"Armageddon," original to this volume.

"Brood," first published in a different form in *Innsmouth Nightmares*, ed. Lois H. Gresh (PS Publishing, 2015).

"A Carcass, Waiting," first published in *Spectral Realms* No. 1 (Summer 2014).

"Chrysalis," first published in *Blood Type*, ed. Robert S. Wilson (Nightscape Press, 2013).

"Colossi," original to this volume.

"The Dark Sea Within," first published in *Black Wings IV*, ed. S. T. Joshi (PS Publishing, 2015).

"A Darke Phantastique," first published in *A Darke Phantastique*, ed. Jason V Brock (Cycatrix Press, 2014).

"Dolls," first published in *Spectral Realms* No. 3 (Summer 2015).

"Double Feature," first published in *Drive-In Creature Feature*, ed. Eugene Johnson and Charles Day (Hidden Thoughts Press/Evil Jester Press, 2016).

Epistles from Dis, original to this volume.

"Fallen: A Lament and Affirmation," first published in *Spectral Realms* No. 2 (Winter 2015).

"Key," original to this volume.

"The Man with the Horn," first published in *Black Wings III*, ed. S. T. Joshi (PS Publishing, 2014).

"Memento Mori," first published in *Brothers in Arms*, ed. Barry Hoffman and R. C. Matheson (Gauntlet Press, 2017).

"Out of Their Heads: A Poem Cycle," original to this volume.

"The Shadow of Heaven," first published in *Searchers After Horror,* ed. S. T. Joshi (Fedogan & Bremer, 2014).

"Transposition," first published in *Shrieks and Shivers,* ed. Jeani Rector (Post Mortem Press, 2015).

"Unity of Affect," first published in *You, Human,* ed. Michael Bailey (Dark Regions Press, 2016).

"Verlassen," first published in *Weird Fiction Review* No. 5 (Centipede Press, 2014).

"Windows, Mirrors, Doors," first published in *Chiral Mad 3,* ed. Michael Bailey (Written Backwards, 2016).

ABOUT THE AUTHOR

Jason V Brock is an award-winning and nominated writer, editor, filmmaker, composer, artist, scholar, and speaker. He has been widely-published online, in comic books, magazines, and anthologies, such as *You, Human; Disorders of Magnitude* (nonfiction finalist for the Bram Stoker Award and the Rondo Hatton Classic Horror Award); *Simulacrum and Other Possible Realities; Fungi; Weird Fiction Review* (print edition); *Fangoria;* S. T. Joshi's *Black Wings* series, and others. He describes his work as Dark Magical Realism.

He was Art Director/Managing Editor for *Dark Discoveries* magazine for more than four years, and publishes a pro journal called *[NameL3ss]*, which can be found on Twitter: @NamelessMag, and on the Interwebs at *www.NamelessDigest.com*. In addition, Brock and his wife, Sunni, run Cycatrix Press (a few of their books include *A Darke Phantastique* [Bram Stoker Award nominee], *The Bleeding Edge*, and the Bram Stoker Award-nominated *The Mirrors* by author Nicole Cushing). They also have a technology consulting business.

As a filmmaker, his work includes the critically-acclaimed documentaries *Charles Beaumont: The Life of Twilight Zone's Magic Man, The AckerMonster Chronicles!* (winner of the 2014 Rondo Hatton Award for Best Documentary), and *Image, Reflection, Shadow: Artists of the Fantastic.* He is the primary composer and instrumentalist/singer for his band, ChiaroscurO.

Popular as a speaker and panelist, he has been a special guest at numerous film fests, conventions, and educational events, and was the 2015 Editor Guest of Honor for *Orycon 37,* the largest science fiction convention in Oregon. Brock loves his wife, their family of herptiles, travel, and vegan/vegetarianism. He is active on social sites such as Facebook and Twitter (@JaSunni_JasonVB), and their personal website/blog, *www.JaSunni.com.*

www.ingramcontent.com/pod-product-compliance
Lightning Source LLC
Chambersburg PA
CBHW050921030726
47503CB00007BB/2401